The Darkness Within

Lanie Windsor

To my Dad,

Thank you for always being there to listen and let me bounce ideas off you.

Contents

Also By 425

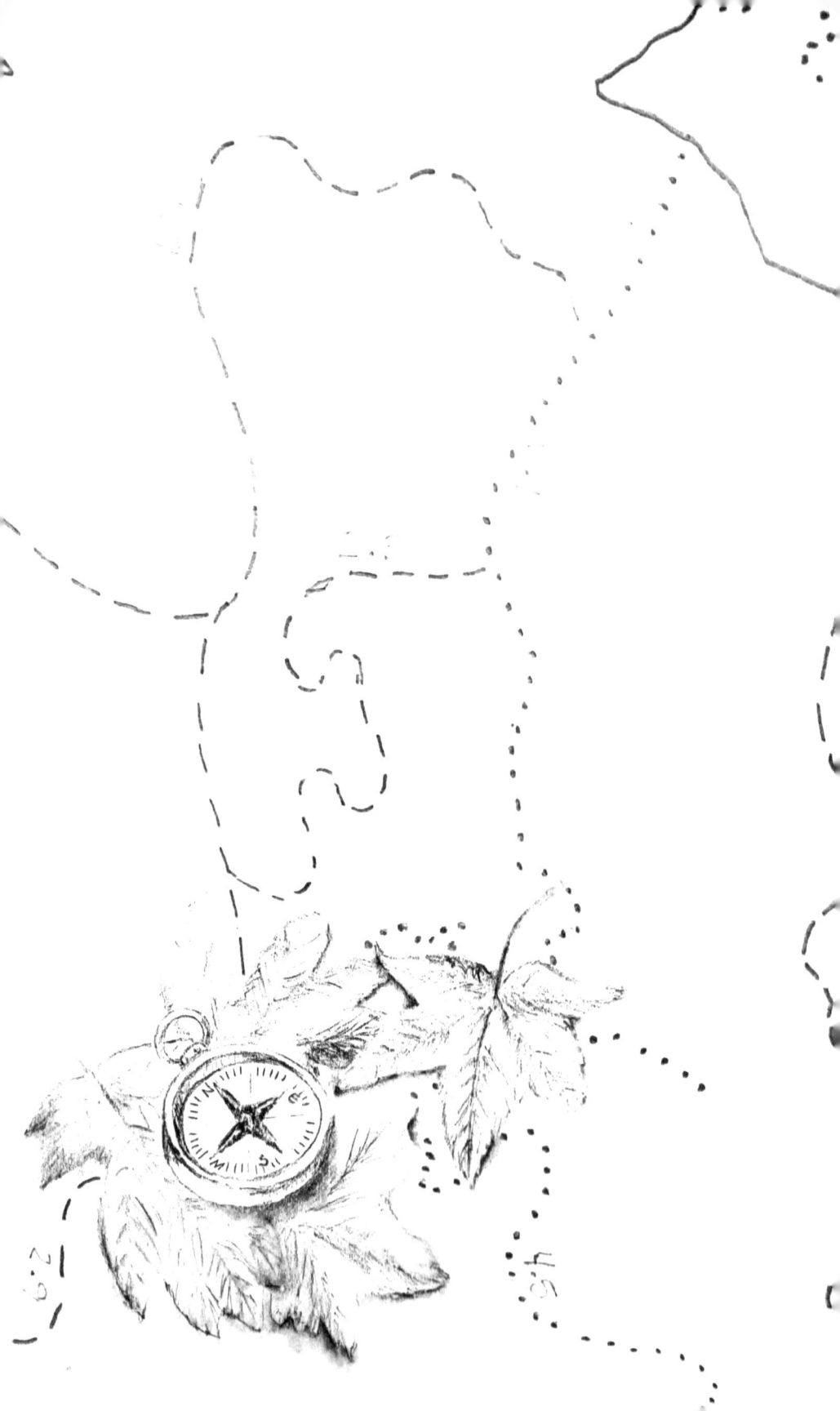

Chapter One

*T*he monster was going to get her.

Her lungs burned, and her legs ached like they might give out, but she couldn't stop. Not now. The air was thick and hot, sticking to her skin like a wet blanket.

Damp leaves covered the ground, muffling her footsteps. Birds still chirped in the trees, singing like nothing was wrong. Stupid birds.

She wanted to stop. Just for one second. But if she did, he'd catch her. And this time...she didn't think she'd get away again.

She wanted her mama. Tears blurred her vision, dripping down her face before she brushed them away.

"Sherri, oh sweet Sherri...where are you, baby?" His voice lilted in a taunting sing-song closer than before.

A cry caught in her throat as she fought to hold back her tears. Cold, piercing terror gripped her heart as she risked a glance over her shoulder. He was out there. Somewhere. Silently closing in.

The trees loomed over her, their gnarled branches clawing at her clothes, grasping as if trying to hold her back. The damp earth clung to her feet, mud squishing between her toes with each frantic step. Leaves clung to her skin, slick with sweat and dew.

Above, unseen creatures rustled the canopy—moving freely, untouched by fear. Freedom. A thing Sherri had never truly appreciated until now.

Fear of what he would do if he caught her fueled her desperate need to keep running. Her heart pounded against her ribs. She couldn't go back. Not to that horrible place.

She wanted to go home. She wanted her room, her bed—her mama.

Exhaustion pulled at her legs, each step weaker than the last. She stumbled over roots and jagged rocks jutting from the damp ground. Her legs trembled, threatening to collapse beneath her. With every stride, her strength dwindled. So did her hope.

Then, she fell.

Sherri hit the forest floor hard this time, too weak to break her fall. Dead leaves and dirt filled her mouth, the taste bitter with defeat.

Slowly, she pushed herself up, wiping the mud and tears from her face.

"Oh, Mama, where are you?" she whimpered, her heart squeezing in fear.

Her hands trembled as she struggled to stand. She couldn't stop.

"Just keep going. Just a little longer," she chanted, barely above a whisper. He couldn't catch her if she could keep going.

"Well, hello there, little one. I thought I had lost you." He stepped into view, moving with a calm and lethal stride. She felt his hands clamp down on her shoulders, the pressure causing her to wince.

Sherri choked on a sob. "No." How did he get in front of her? She had run so fast. His cold, dark eyes made her want to turn away. He was a bad man, just like Mama told her about. She hadn't listened; she had wanted the ice cream cone. It had been her favorite kind of ice cream, too. All she had to do was walk with him, and no one would know.

It hadn't been long before she started to feel tired and couldn't walk anymore. When she woke up, she was in that horrible place, tied to the wall and all alone, until he came back for her.

"It's time. I wanted to play a little longer, but you ran from me," he said, looking at her with emotionless, flat eyes. He shook his head calmly as if reprimanding a small child. With a sigh of resignation, he explained, "It's time to go home now."

Hope shimmered in her eyes. "I can go home now?"

"Of course you can. Come with me; I will take you there." With his hand outstretched, he waited for her to take it.

Sherri hesitated before stretching out to take it. Even though those same hands had hurt her, she wanted to believe him, just one more time. "Okay, I'm ready to go home now."

Fallen leaves danced in the restless autumn breeze as the trees stood as silent witnesses. In utter stillness, innocence lay broken. Her vacant eyes fixed on the sky, waiting for her mama to find her.

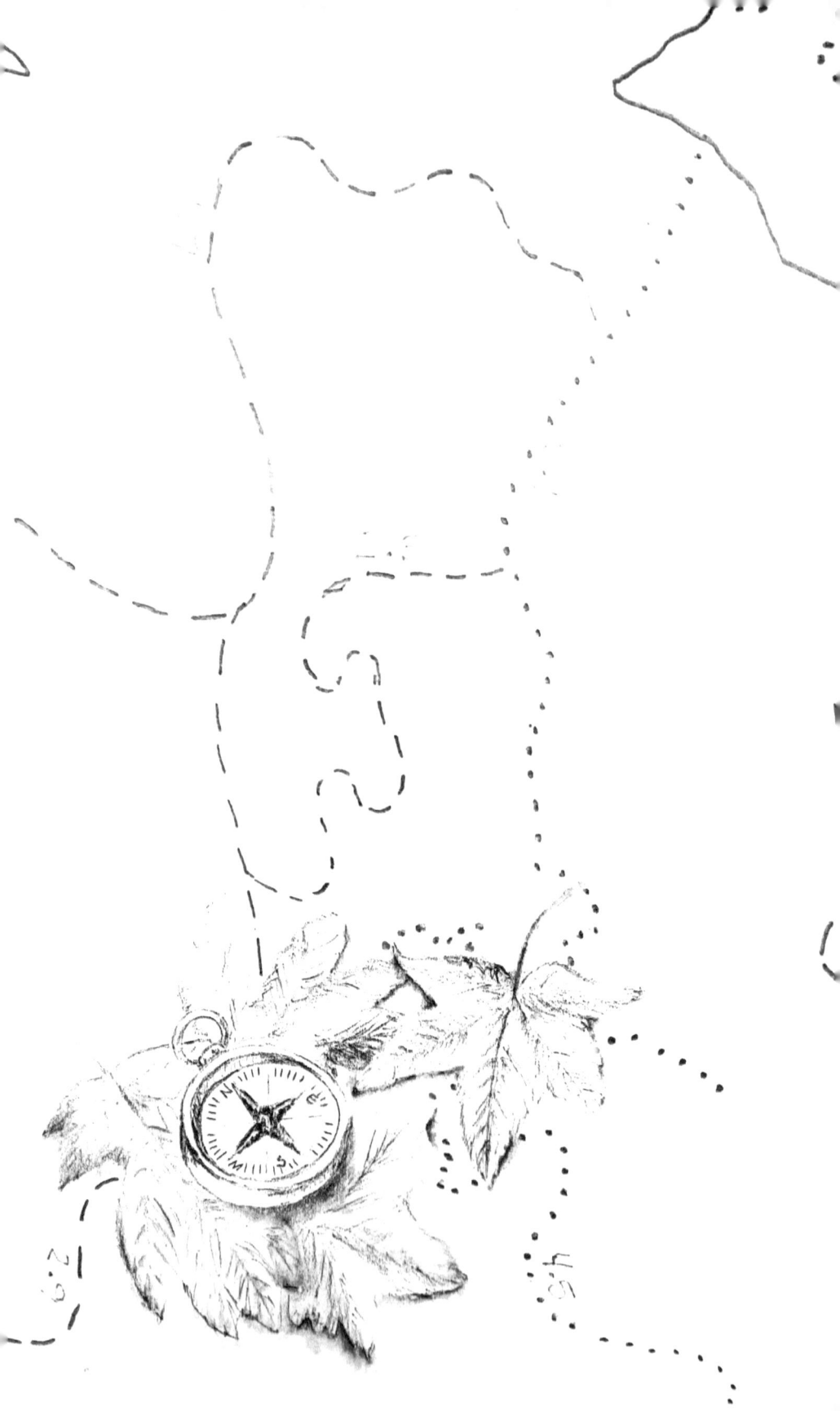

Chapter Two

He was late.

Kate Millard shifted. A slow, maddening itch crawled beneath her right shoulder blade. A cool breeze whispered from the west. She adjusted without thinking, her rifle an extension of her body. Wind speed, temperature—small details drilled into her until they became second nature. No longer cognitive thoughts but honed instincts.

Impatience flared, her pulse drumming. Jaw set, eyes sharp, she scanned the crowd below. Tourists milled about, oblivious. No one looked up. No one saw her, just the way she wanted it. It was the job. Invisibility.

With each ticking minute, unease twisted in her gut. Staying still too long invited attention—a dangerous risk in her line of work. She didn't like waiting, but at least the view wasn't bad.

In autumn, Paris transformed. A vibrant palette of red, orange, and yellow leaves draped the trees, their fallen counterparts painting the sidewalks in sunset hues. Above, a crisp blue sky stretched wide, wisps of white clouds drifting on the cooling winds of the season. The enticing aroma of freshly baked pastries wafted up from the streets below in a carousel of delicious scents swirling around her. Kate took a heady breath, toying with the idea of someday playing a tourist. Being free to wander and sample, indulging in normalcy.

A flicker of pink snapped Kate back to the job.

A child's arm shot up, the bright pink of her fleecy sweater catching Kate's eye. Perched on her father's shoulders, the girl grinned, dimples deep, cheeks rosy from the crisp air. With one slender arm wrapped securely around his neck, the other waved wildly. Her blonde ringlets bounced with every step, golden strands catching the sunlight like spun gold.

An odd ache of longing stirred, making Kate shift as if moving would ease the sudden emptiness in her chest. She clenched her jaw. Enough. This unexpected yearning had no place in her life—it was just a distraction from the job.

The job.

It's what she was. What she would always be. Nothing more. Nothing greater. Just the job.

Kate shoved the grim thoughts away. No time to dwell on life choices. Not when, at any minute, her ever-elusive target would show his face. Ignoring the incessant tug of something she refused to name, she refocused.

The crowd shifted, flowing like water around a stone. At its center stood a man—the rock in the current. Raul LeBarc. The one she'd been waiting for.

His presence commanded attention, though he was not particularly tall or large. Even from above, she saw the ripple effect—people shifting aside, unconsciously sensing the predator in their midst.

It didn't matter that his extravagant suit fit him to perfection; he couldn't conceal the monster beneath the expensive fabric.

She surveyed the entourage that surrounded him. Men like LeBarc understood their mortality and took extensive measures to ensure no harm befell them. Her eyes swept over the hulking men in suits, surrounding him in a safe cocoon of muscle.

Her mouth twitched. She adjusted her weapon, waiting for the perfect shot. He could have fifty men around him, which still wouldn't be enough to prevent what was coming.

For this particular narcissist with obsessive tendencies and no moral compass, time had run out. Raul LeBarc was a man who was willing and able to get whatever any terrorist, cartel, or bad guy wanted. Up until now, none of these qualities put him on her list. However, when he provided a terrorist group with a lethal toxin, the 'powers that be' decided he'd finally crossed the line. So, here she was.

While some may believe that the life of an assassin was thrilling, enigmatic, and perhaps even romantic, the reality was that it mainly consisted of meticulous planning and patient waiting. She executed most assignments flawlessly, leaving no trace of her presence. However, occasionally, a job would require the implementation of Plan B or even Plan C, yet she always managed to achieve her objective in the end.

She had chosen this life and had no regrets—well, mostly. She helped the world by eliminating bad people. Her bank account was healthy, and she had a lovely little house in the woods of Nebraska, where it was quiet and she could let her guard down.

Aside from her best friend Cara, no one in her tight little community knew about her actual profession. She learned long ago that people only see what they want to see. To the folks of Windsor Brooke, she was just a friendly boutique owner. The truth would make her a pariah.

"All right, time to get to work," Kate mumbled, adjusting her weapon as she searched for an opening. She had a narrow window between the two goons at his rear, and if anyone shifted even an inch, they would catch the bullet instead of LeBarc.

Despite the difficult shot, Kate still preferred to remain removed from the kill rather than getting up close and personal. The window she had been waiting for opened wide enough for her to feel confident. She gently tightened her grip on the trigger when her target turned abruptly, walking right in front of the family she had been watching earlier. "Well, shit," she grumbled. The little girl and her father obstructed her view, causing her to lose sight of the target.

Kate sat back on her heels. *Damn.* The shot was gone. No point in dwelling on it. Time for plan B. She efficiently disassembled her rifle. The pieces fit snugly in her camel pack, concealing them from prying eyes. She seamlessly slipped the bag onto her back, hardly noticing the weight while descending the stairs two at a time. She had only a ten-minute window to get to him before LeBarc would be off the streets and out of reach.

Kate set a casual jog pace. She slipped a simple gold ring with a small setting onto her left ring finger. Anyone who may notice would see only a wedding ring, not the tiny needle containing a lethal dose of toxin. The same poison he had sold only two months earlier.

Settling into her pace, she jogged up to her mark. She stumbled into one of the goons at just the right moment, knocking him off balance. Kate allowed herself to be pulled by gravity, effortlessly passing through his barricade, her arm outstretched. She smiled when her fingers connected with the exquisite texture of Italian fabric. Wrapping her hand around LeBarc's arm, her grip tightened before pushing away.

She murmured a shy apology in French, letting one of his goons help her. With a sweet smile, she jogged away, satisfaction curling at the corner of her lips. "Goodbye, Mr. LeBarc," Kate murmured. A scream shattered the courtyard. She didn't turn back. She never needed to.

Kate jolted awake to the shrill of her alarm. She groaned, swatting at the snooze button before flopping onto her back. Her sheets were a tangled mess, a testament to another restless night. Exhaustion clung to her, made worse by the two-hour airport delay and a flat tire on the way home. But it wasn't just a sleepless night; mornings, in general, irritated her—like a chigger bite festering under the skin.

Kate stretched, her gaze shifting to the golden streaks of morning light cutting across the ceiling. With a weary sigh, she settled against her pillow.

Windsor Brooke moved at a slower pace, but there were still obligations to meet. No point in delaying the inevitable. With a final groan, she dragged herself out of bed and to the bathroom. Like it or not, the day had begun.

Standing at her kitchen sink, Kate waited for her breakfast to pop out of the toaster. Her gaze shifted towards the window, where the breathtaking view held her captive. Numerous trees stood proudly, with their branches interwoven in a tangled web of bark and leaves. The lush green of the summer months had given way to the exuberant colorings of fall.

She studied her distorted reflection in the rippled windowpanes. Her image merged into the mysterious woodland beyond.

There was solace in this place, a quiet seclusion that had drawn her in when she chose to put down roots. She had built a life here—her boutique, her home, and the safety of solitude. It wasn't perfect, but it was hers.

The pop of the toaster broke her reverie. As she moved to grab her breakfast, her phone vibrated across the counter. She barely glanced at the screen before answering. "Hey, Cara, what's up?" she asked, absently sucking on her burned fingers.

"Oh Kate, things are terrible! I don't know what to do, what to think." Cara's voice hitched with another sob. "Can I come over? Can I come now? I really need your help." She begged, near hysteria.

Kate frowned at her toast, shoving the charred bread away. Her appetite gave way to the sudden tightening in her stomach. Cara was prone to dramatics, but this was different. There was real fear in her voice. "Of course. Come over."

Twenty minutes later, the kitchen door flew open, crashing against the wall. Cara rushed in, her face blotchy and streaked with tears. She barely made it to a chair before collapsing into it, clutching a crumpled tissue. "Oh, Kate, it's awful. What are we going to do?"

Kate scrunched her nose. Once she became part of Cara's family, her best friend's troubles inevitably became hers. After losing her parents at fifteen, Kate had been taken in by Cara's family, a kindness she could never fully repay.

But grief had left its mark. Even before tragedy struck, Kate had struggled to connect with others. Losing her family only deepened the divide. The emotions were too raw, too consuming—so she simply stopped feeling. It was easier that way. She learned to navigate life at a distance, keeping everyone at arm's length, never allowing anyone to get too close.

She sank into the chair, exhaling slowly. "What happened?"

Cara gulped in the air, struggling for control. "While you were in Paris, the little girl Chloe plays with disappeared. She was in her front yard after school and then—gone. No one saw anything. We searched everywhere, hung posters, and talked to the sheriff, but there was nothing. Then yesterday..." Her voice broke. "They found her body in the woods. She had been missing for three days, Kate. Three days. The police think she died early yesterday morning. Do you understand what that means? Someone had her for days. Someone did who-knows-what to her, and now she's dead. And they still don't know who did it."

Kate waited for Cara to speak, but she didn't. Instead, she cried into her tissue, her shoulders trembling with silent sobs.

Kate's eyes flicked to her phone. She barely resisted the urge to check the time. The tension in her muscles hadn't eased since she returned—finishing a job always left her on edge. She wasn't ready to be around people, her skin prickling with agitation.

Cara's voice dropped to a whisper, raw with desperation. "What if he tries to take Chloe? I can't—I won't survive it."

Kate tapped a nail against the table, gazing at her friend. "What do you want me to do?"

Cara met her eyes, her expression eerily steady. "I want you to find him. And I want you to kill him."

The room seemed to shrink around them. Kate sat back, stunned. Though Cara knew what she did for a living, they never spoke of it. It was an unspoken rule, one that kept them both safe. And yet, here Cara was, breaking it without hesitation.

Kate exhaled slowly. "Cara, this isn't what I do."

"What do you mean? Of course, this is what you do. You just did it in Paris."

"No," Kate corrected. "I don't track people down. I'm given a target and a dossier. I've never had to hunt someone before. I wouldn't even know where to start."

Cara straightened, steel replacing her earlier hysteria. "Then talk to the sheriff. Talk to Trish. Figure it out. I don't care who you talk to. Just find the person who did this, Kate."

Kate clenched her jaw. She didn't appreciate being backed into a corner, even by Cara.

"In all our years together, I've never asked you for anything," Cara pressed.

Kate arched a brow at the blatant manipulation but said nothing.

Cara sniffled. "I have always been there for you. Now it's your turn."

Kate studied her friend. She had a habit of asking for the impossible, and usually, Kate indulged her—mostly. But this? This wasn't a favor or some fleeting whim—Cara was asking Kate to risk everything. To step out of the shadows and into a world she had spent years avoiding. Sanctioned or not, the AOD (Administers of Death) wouldn't protect her. If she got caught, she was on her own. And she wasn't sure this was a gamble she was willing to take.

She let out a slow, irritated sigh. There was no turning back from this, not really. "I'll look into it," Kate conceded, though doubt pricked the back of her mind. "But I'm not promising anything. There's a chance we'll never find him."

"I know, I know, it's just, I don't know how to feel safe again. One of the things I have always loved about Windsor Brooke is how you know all your neighbors. You can leave your door unlocked and know nothing will happen to your home. I feel like it has all been taken away as if Windsor Brooke will never be the same." Cara buried her face in her hands, her body shaking with sobs.

Kate grimaced. Fate had stolen her choices, leaving nothing but the bitter taste of inevitability. Sometimes, life was no better than one gut-wrenching blow after another. Unfortunately, Cara had yet to experience this harsh reality.

She sighed the harsh sound of in. "I'll take care of it. I promise."

Cara nodded, a glimmer of hope replacing the fear in her eyes. "Thank you, Kate. You're the best friend anyone could ever have."

Kate wasn't so sure about that.

Chapter Three

*D*ammit, they found her. He couldn't believe it. A surge of fury seared through his gut, burning through his veins like acid. He watched with clenched fists as the deputies taped off the area, barricading him from her. He exhaled slowly, forcing his breath steady. Tearing through those deputies would serve no purpose. Not yet.

If everything had gone according to plan, Sherri would have been buried deeply underground by now, far away from the pigs that were dirtying his sacred spot. His fists coiled as he struggled to control his rising temper, knowing it would do no good to lose it now, especially with so many prying eyes.

There was no point in wallowing in things he had no control over. How was he to have known Sherri could weasel her way out of the room? He was always meticulous with his girls: no slipups, no surprises. But Sherri had outsmarted him, and that failure scraped raw.

He hadn't counted on Sherri being cunning enough to escape. Well, he had learned his lesson. The moment he found her missing, panic struck like a lightning bolt. True panic gnawed at his insides for the first time in years, seizing him in a way he hadn't felt in ages. A primal, gut-wrenching fear that his perfect game was crumbling. He knew, logically, that there was no one for miles. A child couldn't possibly make it that far alone. But still, he had to find her first. He wanted to howl at the injustice of it. Sherri was his. His toy. His fun. How dare they take her away from him!

Hidden amidst the thick foliage of the forest, he leaned against an old bur oak tree. The rough bark dug into his back. His cold eyes burned with hatred as he watched the EMTs lift Sherri's body. A red mist blurred his vision, his fists tightening at his side. Now was not the time for him to lose control.

There was nothing he could do to change it. What he needed was to find someone new. A new little treasure to add to his collection.

Sherri was gone. But this wasn't over. Not even close.

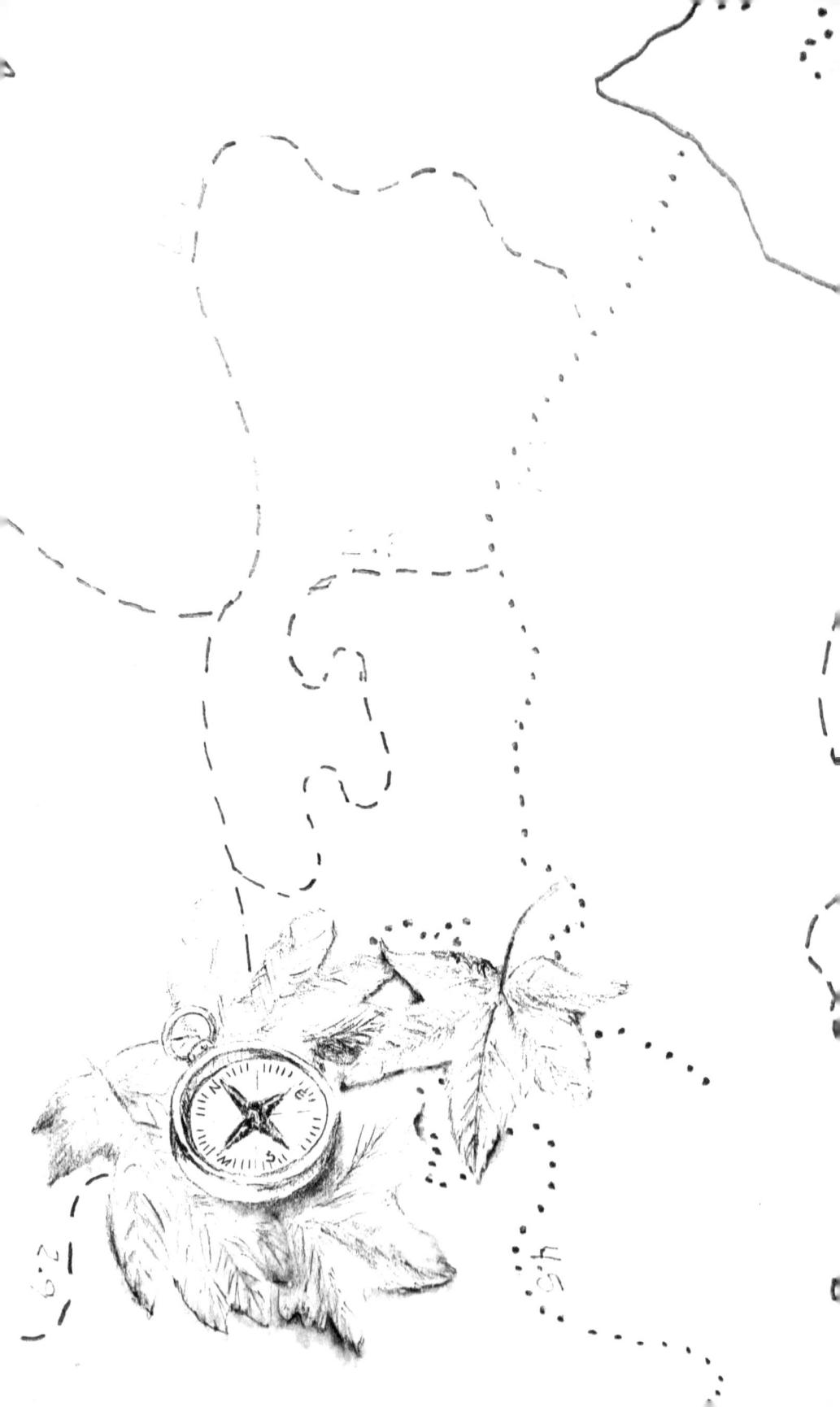

Chapter Four

"Hello there!" came a call from across the street.

Kate turned toward the sound and spotted a woman waving enthusiastically. She tensed. Lisbeth Rueland meant well, but conversations with her were exhausting and took more energy than Kate had to give, especially after just returning from a job. Suppressing a sigh, Kate made her way over.

"Back from..." Mrs. Rueland's brow furrowed. "Paris, was it?"

The older woman's weathered face crinkled at the corners of her eyes as she smiled and watched her granddaughter on the swings.

"Good morning, Mrs. Rueland. How are you today?" Kate paused beside the bench, lifting the corners of her mouth in what she hoped resembled a sincere smile.

"Wonderful. Have you noticed how much Sissy has grown?"

Kate turned in time to see Sissy launch herself off the swing, landing in the sand with a delighted shriek. She grinned. "I see she hasn't a lick of fear."

"Nor a lick of sense," Mrs. Rueland admitted, her mouth twitching with a suppressed smile. Then, her expression sobered. "It's a shame about what happened to Trish's little girl."

A tingle of awareness crept down Kate's spine. "I heard about it this morning."

"Oh, that's right—you weren't here when they found her body." Mrs. Rueland shook her head. "Terrible. Henry and I talked about it, and we both decided Sissy wasn't going anywhere without us. I mean, to think that poor girl wandered into the woods and got lost like that..."

Kate's eyes narrowed slightly. "Is that what you think happened?"

Mrs. Rueland leaned in, lowering her voice. "Isn't it?" Her gaze sharpened. "Do you know something? Did the sheriff tell you something different?"

Kate snorted. "Why would he?"

"Like you don't know." Mrs. Rueland gave her a knowing smirk.

Kate forced a chuckle, unwilling to fuel the town gossip. Sheriff Jacobs was harmless, but it was better to remain off everyone's radar.

"Did Sissy play with Sherri?" she asked, steering the conversation elsewhere.

Mrs. Rueland sighed, shaking her head. "Sherri is a couple of years older. I mean...was." She placed a hand over her heart, her voice trembling. "I don't think I'll ever get used to little Sherri being taken from us."

She reached out, her cool, frail fingers closing around Kate's hand.

Kate hesitated, uncertain how to respond to the unshed tears glistening in Mrs. Rueland's eyes.

Finally, she gave her hand a gentle squeeze. "No one will."

After a moment, Mrs. Rueland nodded, dabbing at the corner of her eye before turning her attention back to Sissy.

Kate stepped away, crossing the street. She waved to those she knew, the rhythm of small-town life settling around her like a familiar tune.

This was why she had chosen Windsor Brooke, its quiet charm, where neighbors smiled at each other, and the biggest scandal was a misplaced pie at the county fair. A far cry from the life she led before.

Windsor Brooke was small but self-sufficient: a diner, grocery store, hardware shop, bakery, and Kate's boutique kept the town running. She supported each business when in town, though the bakery saw most of her money.

No place on earth makes blueberry muffins like Sue's. And Kate would know, she'd searched.

Her boutique sat among the vibrant storefronts circling the town center, a mix of old brick and fresh paint that gave the place its postcard-worthy appeal. At first, it had been a convenient cover, a practical excuse for her frequent travels. Five years ago, she didn't care whether it succeeded or failed, only that it provided an alibi. But somewhere along the way, it had become more. She had built something real—a life, a routine, a place to return to.

Kate walked through the back entrance and found Bridgette and April working on the latest shipment that had arrived the day before. "Hello, ladies," Kate greeted. "How are things? Everything went okay with yesterday's shipments?"

Bridgette eyed the bakery bag and inhaled deeply, "Muffins?"

"Ooh, tell me you got blueberry," April said as she carelessly tossed a stylish teal jacquard pillow into an open box and hurried to the desk. She dug out her favorite and took a huge bite of the freshly baked muffin. Oblivious to the crumbs on her shirt, she went in for another. "You're trying to make me fat," she teased, mouth still full. "Good thing I have willpower, or I'd eat the whole bag."

Kate glanced around the storage room, pride settling warmly in her chest. The shop was thriving, giving her a cover and two trusted employees. And both were plugged into the town's gossip mill, something she hadn't fully appreciated until now.

Leaning onto the counter, Kate weighed the advantages of asking them directly about Sherri Price. But self-preservation made her hesitate. If anyone discovered what she truly did for a living, this idyllic life would collapse like a house of cards.

Kate lightly drummed her fingers on the counter, debating how to steer the conversation. Subtlety had never been her strong suit, and today was no exception. Finally, she said, "Cara just told me about the little girl they found yesterday."

Bridgette studied Kate for a moment. "It was awful. No one knew what to do or say. Ever since she went missing, the whole town feels... different. People aren't as open, as friendly as they used to be."

"I noticed the same thing," April agreed. "It's hard to smile and laugh when you know Sherri was somewhere lost and alone. She probably wandered into the woods and couldn't find her way home."

There was no mention of murder. Kate leaned back, considering. Maybe the idea of something so violent had everyone shying away, unwilling to let their minds go there. After her conversation with Cara, she had expected the town to be whispering theories, but instead, there was only quiet acceptance. Maybe Cara was overreacting. Maybe there was no murder at all. Her gaze flickered between Bridgette and April. Or perhaps no one wanted to believe it.

"Is that what the sheriff thinks happened? That she wandered away and got lost?" Kate prodded.

"I'm not sure what the police think, but it's what the town believes happened," Bridgette replied.

Kate leaned forward. "What about Sherri's mother? Does she believe Sherri wandered away and got lost in the woods?"

"No one knows what Trish thinks." A frown creased April's face, her voice sharper than usual. "She hasn't said a word since the night Sherri went missing—not even to her other children."

"Come on, April, you don't know what Trish is going through. You can't possibly know how you'd react if something happened to one of your kids," Bridgette said.

Kate was taken aback. She had never heard a single criticism from April before; she was always so kind and understanding. Kate's brows drew into a frown. "How well do you know Trish?"

April hesitated, looking down. She busied herself, brushing a few crumbs from her shirt as if needing a moment to gather her thoughts. "Pretty well. Our boys play together—they're in the same class at school. Bobby was at our house when Sherri went missing. We didn't even know anything had happened until the sheriff showed up at our door to take him home. You should have seen the look on his face. I think he blames himself. He believes she wouldn't have wandered off if he had been home watching her."

"How old is Bobby?" Kate inquired.

"The same age as Tyler, ten."

Nodding somberly, "That is a lot of responsibility for a ten-year-old to carry." Kate sympathized, "How did you know Trish hasn't spoken to anyone since Sherri disappeared?"

"Tyler told me," April said, frowning at the memory, "He rode his bike over to their house to check on Bobby and found him sitting on the curb out front. He told Tyler his mom hadn't spoken to him in days. Bobby thinks it's his fault they couldn't find Sherri."

Kate sat in silence, turning over what she'd learned. The town believed Sherri had simply wandered off. No one even considered a more sinister cause for her disappearance. Why would they? Windsor Brooke had always been a quiet town. The only villains people knew were on TV.

People seldom considered the more ominous side of life. Never realizing the dangers that lurked in the shadows. If Kate hoped to find the truth, she would have to go to the source.

"I think I'll take a walk over to the sheriff's office—see what he has to say," Kate said, grabbing her purse.

April and Bridgette exchanged a knowing look before snickering.

"You're probably the only one he'd reveal anything to," Bridgette teased. "The way that old grouch turns to putty whenever you're around is a sight to see." She laughed, clearly amused at Kate's expense.

Sheriff Don Jacobs had held the position for twelve years and hadn't spent that time sitting on his thumbs. He had plans, things that would leave his mark on Windsor Brooke. Not that the job was particularly demanding. In a town this small, being sheriff was an easy gig.

To say the position had fallen into his lap would be an understatement. The moment he returned from college, his predecessor made it clear he was next in line. With the retiring sheriff's endorsement and the town's unwavering loyalty, the election was a mere formality.

They had loved him since high school. Blonde, blue-eyed, and effortlessly charming, Don had always stood out. A natural leader—the golden boy. Quarterback, homecoming king, scholarship athlete. He never struggled for admiration.

Business never suited him. Numbers twisted on the page, and he had no interest in playing second fiddle. On the other hand, law enforcement gave him authority without extra schooling. And when the old sheriff retired, Don slid into place without so much as a challenger.

He had it good: no wife, no one telling him where to be or when. Just the job and his time, the way he liked it.

For twelve years, the job had been a breeze. A few DUIs, the occasional domestic call, nothing he couldn't handle. But when little Sherri Price went missing, his quiet world shook.

At first, he was sure she'd wandered off. They'd find her before dark, safe and scared but alive. But unease crept in as the sun dipped below the trees, and the search yielded nothing. By dawn, half the town combed the woods, covering as much ground as they could.

Still, having hundreds of acres of forest between them and the nearest town, it was impossible to cover all that terrain.

When his deputy found Sherri's body, dread settled heavily in his gut. She hadn't gotten there on her own. Someone had done this. Someone in his town. A real crime, a serious one, the first of his career. And he had no idea what to do.

He was more than willing to admit that he was out of his element with this case. He knew he would need help catching whoever had done this to Sherri. However, he was not thrilled to have some young hotshot from the FBI come into his town and be in his business, but there was no way around it. He didn't know what happened to Sherri and feared this was only the beginning.

The muffled noise from the squad room drew his attention. His deputies were preparing for the impending arrival of the FBI. He leaned back in his chair, raking a hand through his hair. Despite his advanced years, he still looked good. The few small wrinkles around his eyes and the corners of his mouth added character to his handsome face. The town still saw him as their golden boy.

Even though the years were slowly catching up to him, he had at least a decade to give to the job. And he'd be damned if this case ruined that.

He needed to solve this—fast. If that meant rubbing elbows with the FBI, then so be it.

"Ah, Sheriff?"

Sheriff Jacobs flicked his eyes up, giving his deputy a pointed look. "Yes, Shane, what is it?"

"Kate Millard wants to speak with you."

He shifted in his chair, masking his surprise. Kate Millard. Well, now.

"Go on and send her in," he said, straightening his shirt.

Kate. If he were ten years younger, he might have made a move. Hell, he still considered it from time to time. Women had never resisted his charms, not since he was a teenager. A slight smile twitched at the corners of his mouth. Despite the temptation, he knew his pass would be laughed off as friendly flirting. To his knowledge, Kate never dated. Never seemed interested in anyone. A shame. A woman like that should be interested in someone.

His thoughts evaporated as she entered the room, her stride confident, her smile just warm enough.

"Hello, Kate. What can I do for you today?" he asked, flashing his most crowd-pleasing smile that showed off every dollar he'd spent on whitening treatments.

Kate returned the smile and slipped into the chair opposite him. No small talk. Always straight to business.

"Hi, Sheriff. I wanted to ask you about Sherri."

The easy-going smile dropped from his face. His eyes became guarded.

"Now, Miss Kate, why would you want to talk about little Sherri Price?" His voice cooled. "If memory serves, you were out of town when she went missing; I don't suppose you have any information to share?"

"No." She shook her head. "I just heard what happened from Cara and wondered if what she said was true. Was Sherri murdered?"

The sheriff's fingers tapped once on the desk. "Now, Kate, I don't believe that's information you need." He leaned back, crossing his arms. "Sherri's death was a tragedy, but it is an ongoing investigation. I am not at liberty to discuss details."

Kate studied Sheriff Jacobs' unyielding expression. This was new. The sheriff usually folded under her charm. But this time? She might actually have to work for it.

She leaned in slightly, letting a note of admiration slip into her voice.

"Oh, Sheriff, I didn't mean to step on your toes."

He liked attention. He liked power. More than that, he liked being the one others turned to, the hero.

"I just knew if anyone knew what was going on, it would be you." Kate let her smile soften. "After all, a man like you would never let something slip past him, right?"

As expected, he preened. His shoulders rose. His chin lifted.

"Of course, I know everything going on in this town."

Kate bit back a smile.

She glanced toward the front office. "I noticed the commotion out there. Are they working on Sherri's case?"

"We'll have a guest coming tomorrow."

Her brows lifted. "Oh really? Guests are always good for the town. What will this guest be doing here?" She tilted her head, lowering her lashes just enough.

He exhaled, the weariness on his face betraying his true age. "It's the FBI. They think Sherri might be linked to several other cases."

Kate stilled.

Several cases. The words echoed, heavy with implication. But more startling was the hum of anticipation that followed. That familiar pulse of adrenaline stirred in her chest, unwelcome yet exhilarating. And yet, she was almost bemused to feel it now. She wasn't ready to dive in, but the scent of something bigger was already pulling her forward.

She pushed the urge aside, ignoring the tingling awareness of the hunt.

"Several cases?" She widened her eyes. "That doesn't sound good. Why wouldn't the FBI put out an alert? Do you think they are making something out of nothing?"

Then she did something rare. She reached out and lightly touched the back of his hand.

Jacobs blinked, stilling beneath her touch.

"From what I have heard, there are six cases." His voice was lower now as if unconsciously sharing a secret. "All the victims were about the same age. Blonde hair, blue eyes."

Kate feigned a gasp, letting her fingers drift away.

"That's awful." She leaned in, her eyes imploring. "How are you going to figure out who is behind this?"

His chest lifted slightly. "That's why the FBI is coming. We've never had something like this in Windsor Brooke before."

Kate gave a tight nod and turned for the door.

Outside, she stepped into the cool air and pulled out her phone.

Working for the government had its perks.

Connections, for one. The kind that answered on the first ring.

She scrolled through her contacts, stopping at Jill Burke.FBI.

Jill had a no-nonsense approach to her job. And the best part was that she never asked questions.

"Some FBI agent is heading to Windsor Brooke, Nebraska. Can you pull everything you have on their case and fax it over?"

A pause. Then—

"Same number?"

"Yep."

"You'll have it by the end of the day."

The line went dead.

Kate smirked to herself. That was Jill. No chit-chat. No questions. Just results.

If only she realized then just what she was getting herself into.

Chapter Five

The fax machine hummed as Kate stepped inside. Jill, as always, was as good as her word. The files of the six girls overflowed her tray—pages detailing their deaths, witness accounts, and forensic reports. As Kate sorted them into six piles, she realized she needed a proper workspace. Judging by the growing stack, the kitchen table wouldn't cut it.

A quick scan of her house revealed one option—the loft. Cozy but compact, it held a dove-gray couch, a small wooden end table, and a lamp. Overstuffed plaid pillows and a matching ottoman balanced comfort with style. The only full-size wall was perfect for a case board. In minutes, Kate cleared her few meager possessions, making space for the work ahead.

Kate pinned up the victim's photos in order of their disappearance. She grimaced at the grainy black-and-white copies—she'd need Jill to email color versions. Stepping back, she studied the wall. Death didn't rattle her anymore—she'd seen too much of it. The crime scene photos of Sherri's mutilated body should have stirred something. Horror. Disgust. Pity. Instead, Kate examined them with a cold, clinical eye.

One detail stood out: none of the bodies had been found. People clung to hope, but Kate knew better. She'd seen the dark underbelly of society, where dreams died and hope failed. If anything, she only wished the girls had found peace. Hope was useless. Reality was all anyone had.

Kate knew the FBI agent was due to arrive tomorrow—good news for the sheriff's Department, not so much for her. She could only do so much under the radar, and questioning anyone without it getting back to the agent would be tricky. If the FBI caught her sniffing around, she would be hauled in for questioning.

That was bad for business.

Technically, she worked for the government, but it was a fragile relationship. If she ever got caught or backed into a corner, she'd be on her own. She knew it. The powers that be knew it. And that was the deal.

So, she'd move fast and get as much legwork done as possible before the agent showed up. It was a risk, a gamble with her future, but she'd made her choice.

It was time to hunt.

On her way out, Kate looked back at the wall. Her stomach tightened. Six faces stared back.

The meadow was a patchwork of red, yellow, and orange, the fallen leaves scattered across damp earth and fading grass. A light breeze stirred the few still clinging to the trees. Police tape, long since loosened from its restraints, fluttered like a forgotten banner at half-mast.

Kate wasn't surprised that no one was guarding the site. Sheriff Jacobs probably never thought to station a deputy here until the FBI arrived.

She stepped into the center of the field, inhaling deeply, letting the space settle around her. With her eyes closed, she focused.

The sun warmed her skin, but the wind carried a sharp chill, raising goosebumps along her arms. Damp earth and decaying leaves thickened the air, their pungent scent made bearable only by the restless breeze. Branches groaned, leaves whispered, and birds called from above.

Slowly, she opened her eyes in increments, allowing a fraction of light in, then a bit more.

What had happened here?

Kate let the question take shape, playing out possibilities in her mind. She scanned the ground: no overturned dirt, no broken branches, no signs of a struggle.

Sherri was likely killed elsewhere and brought here. But why here? What was it about this place that appealed to the killer?

Kate brushed her hair back, only for the wind to toss it into her face again. In an agitated move, she shoved the piece behind her ear. Scowling at the ground, rustled leaves lifted and shifted, revealing the underbrush. A reflection of sunlight caught her eye.

She stepped carefully, dried leaves crunching underfoot, every sound magnified. Her eyes flicked toward the woods before easing down to the glinting object.

Squatting, she brushed the leaves aside, revealing a gold locket. Kate turned it over in her hand. Inside, a picture of a puppy. Engraved on the back: **MK**.

Kate snapped it shut and slipped it into her pocket.

She straightened in a slow and deliberate measure, scanning the tree line. The fine hairs on her neck quivered like an antenna tuning into danger. The forest had gone unnaturally still. No rustling leaves. No chirping birds. Even the wind seemed to hold its breath.

Someone was watching.

An electric thrill coursed through her, anticipation sharpening into something primal. This wasn't just a stalker in the shadows. This was a killer like her.

Where are you?

Her eyes swept the woods. Nothing. No movement, no shape out of place. But she felt them. She couldn't see them, but she knew they were there.

Her hand twitched. Her muscles coiled and ready to spring—but to where? She wanted to charge into the woods, headlong into whatever was waiting. The need to fight clawed for release. But what good would it do? Recklessness got people killed.

She grasped for restraint. Her body screamed for action, even as she forced her muscles to relax. Let them think she was oblivious. Let them feel safe.

Now she knew the killer was here, and she would find them.

When she did, she would do her job.

After all, they were nothing more than a mark.

"Bitch!" What was she doing here? What did she find?

Dammit. He already screwed up with Sherri. She wasn't supposed to die yet. She forced his hand and made him act ahead of schedule. And then, they took her.

He felt it every time he came back. The mistake. How could he have been so stupid? He left, thinking she'd be safe with the others, just until he got his supplies. Just until he could bury her deep, where no one would know but him.

She ruined everything. Ran from him. Forced his hand. Then the police stole her.

She was tainted now—handled, examined, contaminated. He didn't want her anymore. But it was incomplete, like a puzzle missing its final piece. He needed another.

This time, he had to be careful. Choose wisely. Not so close to his special place. If he gave them a reason to dig deeper, they'd find them.

And that could never happen.

They were his. Forever. No one would take them away.

He watched her slip into the trees, his breath hitching when she hesitated. For a second, he thought she knew he was watching her—her body still rigid—but then she seemed to relax, playing it off. Clever.

A thrill curled through him. He hadn't expected that.

Until now, he'd only taken little girls—small, fragile things, easy to control. Dolls he could break. But this woman...she was different. There was something familiar in her, something dangerous.

The predator in him recognized the predator in her.

He knew her and had seen her around town. She owned some shop on Main Street. Before now, she'd been nothing. Just another face.

Now, she was something else. A challenge.

Maybe even a new kind of thrill.

FBI agent Fox Anderson peered through the windshield of his rental car, his supervisor's parting words echoing in his head.

"Welcome to Nebraska. Check-in with the sheriff on Wednesday."

He hadn't even had time to cool his heels from the last case before the next one landed on his desk.

It came with the job—terrible hours, last-minute travel, unexpected cases—but he loved it. Nothing compared to the rush of putting a criminal in cuffs or bringing a victim home safe.

Unfortunately, women didn't share his enthusiasm for unpredictability. None had stuck around long enough to give him a real chance. Maybe one day, he'd have to make a change if he wanted a family. But not today.

Right now, there was a predator out there. A monster taking little girls. And Fox intended to find him.

Windsor Brooke's town center didn't offer much, but what it lacked in variety, it made up for in charm. Not that Fox had much use for small towns—nosy, well-meaning locals and limited amenities made things inconvenient. But none of that mattered. Not when there was a puzzle to solve.

Town Hall, a bakery, a salon, a pharmacy, a small market, an antique shop, and finally—the Sheriff's Office. A postcard-perfect town. The kind where parents watched their kids play in the park, shaded by towering trees that now blazed in reds, yellows, and oranges.

Under normal circumstances, Windsor Brooke was the kind of place where people felt safe. But not anymore. Fox wouldn't be surprised if, for the first time, residents were locking their doors at night.

It was a shame. He hoped to restore what had been lost, but he knew better. Catching a predator like this was never easy. And if HQ was right, it was only a matter of time before another girl went missing.

First impressions mattered, especially when a small-town department called in outside help. Resentment and, sometimes, even hostility were inevitable. He always tried to approach with an open and friendly demeanor. Not that it made much of a difference, but sometimes, people surprised him.

The serene outside atmosphere vanished the moment Fox opened the door. His appearance went unnoticed amidst the chaotic scene that greeted him. Men shoved furniture, carried files, and moved with a purpose only they seemed to understand.

He scanned the space—four brown metal desks clustered on one side while two doors occupied the opposite end. One bore the sheriff's name; the other, *Conference Room.*

Interesting. A town this small prioritizing a conference room? More likely, it doubled as an interrogation space. A smart move—people were less intimidated walking into a *conference room* than in an *interrogation room.* Guilt wasn't the first thing on their minds that way.

The only solitary desk, twice the size of the others, was in front of the sheriff's office door. It formed an L-shape and was cluttered with two monitors, a copy machine, and a fax. Despite the workload, the space was meticulously maintained, likely thanks to the woman seated behind it.

She looked as mean as a pit bull, and Fox hadn't seen her crack a smile since he walked in. She hadn't so much as glanced his way, too absorbed in her computer while answering the phone, which hadn't stopped ringing since he arrived. Fine by him.

Taking advantage of the rare opportunity to observe, Fox moved toward the center of the room, where two large folding tables had been set up as a workstation. Three bulletin boards fanned out in a half-circle at the end, covered in case details.

The first two held photos of the missing girls—images the FBI had sent over before his arrival. The last displayed crime scene photos from Sunday's discovery. The little girl whose body had brought him here.

She was the key. At least, that was the FBI's hope.

"Excuse me, can I help you?"

A voice pulled Fox back to the present. He turned to find a middle-aged deputy with an amiable smile and surprisingly kind eyes for a man in this line of work. Extending a hand, Fox returned his smile. "Agent Anderson, FBI. I'm here to see Sheriff Jacobs. Is he in?"

"Oh! Well, now, how are you?" The deputy grabbed his hand and shook it with enthusiasm. "Deputy Shane. We've been expecting you. Sure, I'm glad you're here. We're out of our depth with Sherri and all. Would hate to mess up this and let the bad guy slip through."

"Glad to help," Fox said. His gaze slid toward the bulletin boards. "Can you walk me through what you've got so far?"

"Sure, of course. Come on over." Shane gestured to the first board. "This here is what your office sent us. We don't have much to go on outside of the file. We didn't even know these other girls were missing." A frown flitted across his face. "Feels like we're playing catch-up in a game we didn't even know we were in."

Fox studied the deputy's expression. "I've gone through the FBI files. I'm more interested in anything you've uncovered locally."

Shane exhaled, rubbing the back of his neck. "Not much, to be honest. We were just about to figure out our next steps." His voice wavered slightly. "This kind of thing doesn't happen here. Worst crime I can remember was a bar fight—one guy needed stitches, and the other had a concussion. Now..." He shook his head. "What happens to our town after this? Will anyone feel safe again?"

Fox met his gaze. "Before we worry about what-ifs, let's focus on what we do know."

Shane nodded, taking a steadying breath. "Okay. Yeah, I can do that."

"Good. First, I need to speak with the sheriff. He in?"

"He sure is. I'll let him know you're here."

"Thanks, Deputy. I appreciate it."

As Shane disappeared into the office, Fox turned back to the boards. There was always something, a pattern. He just had to find it before another girl disappeared.

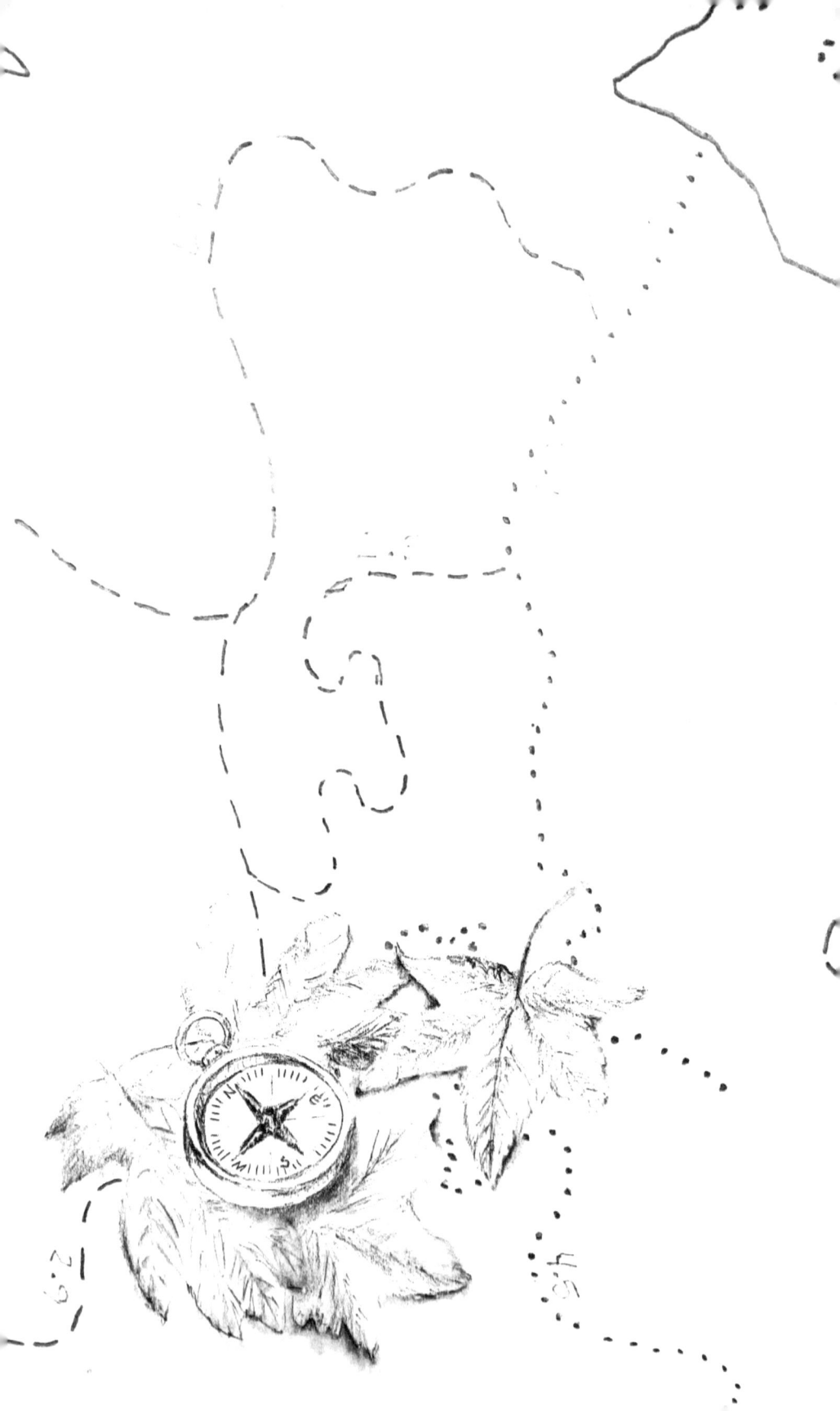

Chapter Six

Sheriff Jacobs watched the squad room through the two-way mirror from his desk. Few knew the mirror behind his assistant's desk was a window, giving him a discreet view whenever he wanted. That edge—seeing without being seen—had proven valuable more than once.

His gaze landed on the man who had just walked in. Broad shoulders, confident stride. Had to be the FBI agent. Jacobs had been around enough alpha males to recognize one, and this guy fits the bill.

Jacobs felt an old flicker of resentment. He used to be like that—fit, sharp, turning heads. Now? He was more creak than command.

Movement in the squad room snapped him back. Shane was heading for his office. Swearing under his breath, Jacobs jumped up and rehung the landscape over the mirror, settling into his chair just as the knock came.

"Sheriff, the FBI is here," Shane called, poking his head through the doorway.

"I'll be right out," Jacobs replied, quickly shuffling some papers on his desk for appearance's sake.

He shut his office door firmly behind him; leaving his space open to prying eyes wasn't an option. Stepping into the bullpen, he quickly read the mood before drawing the agent's attention.

"Agent Anderson, glad you could make it." He approached with a practiced smile and outstretched hand. "How was your trip? Find your way to the Windsor Brooke Motel, all right?"

Anderson's expression remained pleasant but unreadable. "Uneventful. And yes, the motel was easy to find."

He turned back to the board. "Sheriff, what are your plans moving forward?"

Jacobs hesitated, just a beat. "Well, I figured that's why you're here—to help guide us through the next steps."

"I can do that, Sheriff. But if I take the lead, I stay in the lead until the case is closed or I'm pulled off. Are you okay with that?"

Anderson's voice was calm, but the steel in his storm-blue eyes made it clear—this wasn't negotiable.

Jacobs looked away. It grated that he couldn't hold the young agent's gaze, but something about it made it difficult.

But he understood what Anderson was asking for. He gave a stiff nod.

"All right, I can live with that."

Relinquishing control didn't sit right with him. On the other hand, with the FBI taking the lead, any fallout would land squarely on Anderson's shoulders. If things went sideways, he could step in and play the hero. The idea lightened his mood considerably.

"Let me introduce you to the rest of the team." Jacobs gestured toward the woman at the front desk. "That's Sylvia—my administrative assistant and the gatekeeper around here."

Anderson glanced over to Sylvia, who still hadn't looked up.

"You've already met Deputy Shane. The rest of my deputies—Marcos, Johnson, and Riggs—are on patrol."

Fox nodded in acknowledgment. "Okay. With introductions out of the way, why don't you catch me up on what you have learned so far?"

He crossed to the first board, eyes scanning the photos.

"What can you tell me about Susie Miller?"

Deputy Shane answered, "Aside from the information already supplied by you guys, we have learned she was a bit of a mischief-maker."

A light chuckle filtered through the room. Fox waved the chatter down.

"Her mother told us she knew all the rules about strangers and staying in the yard. The minute someone asked for help or to play, she'd forget every one of them and be gone.

"When her mother first realized Susie was gone, she assumed her daughter had gone off with a friend and forgotten to ask permission. It was a town like this one—quiet, trusting. Folks didn't worry much about predators or anything bad happening."

Shane turned a page of his notebook, a scowl deepening the lines of his brow.

"After calling around and realizing no one had seen her, that's when the panic set in.

"We asked Susie's mom to walk us through her Friday and Saturday. Friday was routine: school, home, and then the family attended her brother's football game. It was a home game, so pretty much the whole town turned out.

"Afterward, her brother had a party at the house. A bunch of football players and high school kids showed up. Susie stayed downstairs for the first thirty minutes or so, and then her mom took her upstairs to watch a movie in the parents' bedroom.

"Saturday was quiet. Susie woke up, had breakfast, did some chores, and then went outside to play. Her mom noticed she was missing at eleven thirty-seven a.m. when she went out to call her in for lunch.

"Since the abduction, there's been zero communication—no notes, no calls, no ransom. Nothing from the kidnapper or kidnappers."

"All right, let's write her schedule down on the board and see what we see," Fox said, hoping a pattern would emerge. "Tell me about our second victim—Abby Davis."

Shane leaned onto his desk and reached for the file. "Abby was taken on a Friday night."

He flipped it open, eyes scanning the first page.

"Leading up to the abduction, everything was normal. Thursday—school, home, playtime, dinner, bed. Nothing out of the ordinary.

"Friday followed the same routine. School, home, played outside, had dinner, until she went to her friend's house for a sleepover—two doors down."

Fox nodded, his gaze down as he listened.

"Sometime after she got there, Abby realized she'd forgotten her favorite stuffed animal. She decided to run back home to grab it."

Shane's voice dropped. "She left her friend's house around eight thirty p.m. But she never made it."

Fox straightened, raising his gaze to meet Shane's. "No one saw anything?"

"The friend's mother—Susan Stone—called Abby's mom to check if she was back yet," Shane continued. "That's when they realized something was wrong. Abby's mom hadn't seen her. She had no idea Abby had even left the neighbor's house."

A bleakness had entered the young deputy's eyes as his grip tightened on the folder. Fox knew all too well the toll a case like this could take.

This was the kind of case that lingered. The kind that touched everyone involved and never really let go. The kind that left nightmares.

A steelier edge now marked Shane's voice.

"Both women ran outside...but there was no sign of her. She'd vanished somewhere in the space of just a few minutes."

"The house in between—didn't notice anything?" Fox asked.

"No. They were out of town at the time. Didn't get back until a week after Abby went missing."

Deputy Shane frowned, his gaze fixed on Abby's picture. "How did he know she would be out walking at night?"

Fox tapped a finger against the desk. "The timing—him being on that street just as Abby was between houses—it feels too convenient."

He picked up her file, flipping it open. "What else do we know about her? Her family? Is there anyone in their lives who could have been in on this?"

"Abby was the youngest of four—three older brothers, ages eleven, fifteen, and seventeen, at the time. She was eight when she was taken. Parents were married, no signs of trouble at home. Everything appeared normal."

Shane turned a few pages. "They had relatives scattered across the state, but no one raised any red flags. No one distanced themselves after her disappearance, either."

Fox tapped a pen against the folder. "Did the sheriff's department talk to everyone in both households?"

Shane glanced at his notes. "They took statements from both parents and Abby's friend. But as far as I can tell, no one spoke formally to the other children in either home."

Fox's frown deepened. "Okay, I want a deputy to contact both families to set up interviews for tomorrow. It's a few hours' drive—keep that in mind when planning."

"Have Deputy Johnson and Deputy Riggs handle the interviews," Sheriff Jacobs added. "They've got the best bedside manner. If the kids know anything, they'll talk to those two."

Fox nodded. "Good. Make it happen." He pulled the next file from the stack. "What do we know about Becky Larson?"

"Becky Larson was abducted from her front yard on a Saturday morning," Shane said, rising to tap a photo on the bulletin board—a modest house with a fenced-in yard. "She'd stayed home sick from school the day before but was feeling better by the weekend. Her mother let her play outside while she was hanging laundry."

He paused, then continued. "Her mom stepped inside for a few minutes to grab the next load of laundry. When she came back out, Becky was gone. She called the police right away."

Fox leaned forward. "Would Becky have wandered off on her own?"

"Doesn't sound like it," Shane said. "According to her mother, Becky was a shy kid. Didn't like talking to strangers. Had trouble making eye contact. She would've never left the yard voluntarily."

"How long was her mother inside?" Fox asked. "And was the door open or closed?"

Shane rechecked his notes. "She said ten minutes, tops. And the door was shut—she thinks that's why she didn't hear anything."

"Go ahead and add all this to the board," Fox said, pacing the squad room. "I don't want any details left out. You never know what small piece ends up being the one that breaks a case."

He turned back toward Shane. "Okay, how about Megan Sanders? What have we learned?"

Shane cleared his throat and glanced down at his notes.

"Megan was also taken on a Saturday," he began. "She's the only victim from a larger city. That sets her apart right away."

He flipped a page in his notebook.

"She went to her neighborhood park that morning to play with two of her friends. The girls' parents usually let them walk there alone and play for a while. They'd typically head home together before lunch."

Shane drove a hand through his hair. "But that day, the other two girls decided to leave early. Megan wanted to stay and play a little longer—at least, that's what her friends told the police."

Fox narrowed his eyes. "What time are we talking?"

"The local PD believes she was taken sometime between ten and ten-thirty a.m. A little after ten thirty, another family arrived at the park, and Megan was already gone."

Already, Fox could feel the weight of the case settling on his shoulders, heavy and relentless. His posture dipped slightly under the pressure. It was too soon after the last one. He hadn't had time to regroup, to breathe, to find even a moment of peace before diving back into the darkness.

His gaze drifted to the pictures on the board—small, frozen faces, their last known moments recited like an itinerary. Not that he blamed the deputy. This job had a way of draining the humanity out of you, turning tragedies into bullet points.

Shane's voice continued, flat and efficient, pulling Fox's attention back into the room.

"When she didn't come home by eleven like she was supposed to," Shane continued, "her mom went to look for her. After talking to Megan's friends, she realized someone had taken her daughter. That's when she called the police."

"What about the day before? Anything unusual happen?" Fox asked.

Shane shook his head. "No. A typical day. School, home, and then that evening, they watched her older sister cheer at a football game. After that, it was straight home and bed."

Fox rubbed the tension building at the base of his neck, his eyes scanning the board. He paused on the next name.

"This brings us to our fifth victim. What do we know about Emma Mathews?"

Shane adjusted the file in his hands. "Emma disappeared late Friday night. She's the only one taken from her bedroom. We're not sure why she's been grouped with the others. Not only was the location different, but she was also two years older than the other girls. The only real connection is physical appearance."

Fox ran a hand along his jaw, his gaze shifting from the file to the pictures on the board. They could've all been sisters.

Long blonde hair. Blue eyes. Petite frames. Fragile, like porcelain dolls.

Even Emma, who was ten at the time, looked no older than the rest.

"If this is the same guy," Fox said quietly, "he's got a type."

He glanced back at Shane. "What about Emma's friends? Did anyone talk to them? Anyone she was close with—maybe they noticed something?"

Shane looked through Emma's file. "No, I don't see any notes on interviews with her friends." He lifted his gaze, his head tilted. "What are you thinking? That her friends might know something her parents didn't?"

"Maybe," Fox said. "If someone had been watching Emma, she might've mentioned something to a friend. Kids don't always think to tell their parents the small stuff—but that small stuff could matter."

He pulled a chair over and dropped into it, the table in front of him cluttered with FBI files. "I want someone in Midstow, Iowa, in the next day or two. Talk to Emma's friends. Anyone close to her."

Sheriff Jacobs vehemently shook his head. "You are already sending Johnson and Riggs out tomorrow. If you send Marcos and Shane, I'll be down to nothing. I won't have anyone left to police the streets of this town."

Fox gave him a pointed look. "Sheriff, are you telling me you can't handle any issues that might come up for one day?" He raised an eyebrow, feigning surprise.

Shane choked on his coffee, quickly setting the cup down and turning his head to hide his grin. The sheriff scowled at the back of Shane's head.

"All right, I'll handle it," he muttered. Then, with a touch of snide sarcasm: "What will *you* be doing while my men are off interviewing potential witnesses?"

"I'll be going over the crime scene," Fox replied evenly. "And I want a list of everyone who was interviewed. I may want to reinterview some of them."

His phone rang. He glanced at the screen, then looked back at the sheriff. "I've got to take this. If you'll excuse me for a minute."

Fox stepped outside, savoring the fresh breeze that cleared some of the static from his mind. He answered the call, "This is Anderson."

"Agent Anderson," came the voice on the other end, "thought you'd want to know—yesterday, someone else pulled the five case files you're working on."

Fox tensed. That was unexpected. *Who else is looking into this case... and why?*

"Do you know who?"

"Yeah. It was Jill—a high-clearance tech."

Fox's brow furrowed. "Did you ask her why she needed the files?"

"Sure did. She told me it wasn't my business." A pause, then, more conspiratorially, "So I did a little digging. Turns out Jill sent the files to an email account. I traced the IP address—it took me through a maze, but eventually, I landed in Windsor Brooke. The address is tied to someone named Kate Millard."

Fox's pulse kicked up a notch. "Who's she?"

"From what I can tell, she owns a small shop in town—the Windsor Brooke Boutique. Travels a lot. Nothing jumped out on the surface—no red flags in her background. But I can dig deeper, see if I missed anything."

"No, not yet," Fox replied absently. His mind was already working the angles—why would an FBI tech be authorized to share sensitive case files with a small-town boutique owner?

"I'll see if I can set up a meeting with her. I'll let you know if I need anything else." He hung up and lingered by the steps, eyes scanning the Town Square. Directly across from the Sheriff's Office sat a quaint little shop—Windsor Brooke Boutique.

What would a shop owner need with the files of five missing girls?

And how did she even get clearance to access them in the first place?

It didn't sit right. Fox didn't think she had anything to do with the abductions—but that didn't mean he wasn't curious. People didn't just stumble onto high-level case files. If she had a reason, he wanted to hear it from her.

He turned back toward the building. *No time like the present to get answers.*

As the door clicked shut behind him, Fox looked to the sheriff.

"Sheriff, what can you tell me about Kate Millard?"

Sheriff Jacobs' head shot up, eyes wide, "Kate? Why are you asking about Kate? What does she have to do with any of this?"

"I just got word from HQ—Kate was given access to the files on the five missing girls yesterday."

Fox couldn't help the flicker of amusement as the sheriff's face drained of color. That reaction said more than words ever could.

"Do you know why she requested them?" Fox asked, watching closely. The sheriff's fingers tightened around his coffee cup, knuckles whitening.

"I'd like to meet with her. Can you arrange something for tomorrow morning?"

"Yes, I can call her now. I'll let you know what she says."

Turning away, Jacobs scowled and headed back to his office. His thoughts raced.

Why would Kate want those files? And did she ask for them before or after we talked yesterday?

As much as he liked Kate, he wasn't about to cover for her. He would help her if he could—but that was as far as he was willing to stick his neck out. Maybe if she told him the truth, he could help prep her for whatever questions Mr. FBI might ask her. If not...well, then she was on her own.

Closing his door, he immediately removed the canvas from his window. He wanted to keep a close eye on Agent Anderson. Not that he didn't trust him. Exactly. The whole situation just rubbed him the wrong way, and he wasn't about to let some outsider tear through his town unchecked.

He picked up the phone and dialed Kate's number. One ring. Two. Three. Voicemail.

Jacobs sighed. "Hey Kate, it's Jacobs. I need to talk to you about something...unexpected. Nothing bad, I just—call me back when you can."

Hanging up, he leaned back in his chair, eyes drifting toward Anderson, who was scanning case files and scribbled notes from his deputies. His gaze shifted to the bulletin board—Sherri's board. Crime scene photos were neatly arranged and labeled. Still, after all this time, Jacobs couldn't look at the photos of her body without feeling his stomach twist.

He forced his eyes away, back to Anderson.

What the hell has become of my town?

Chapter Seven

K ate studied the photos of the six victims now pinned to her wall. She had spent most of the day combing through the case files, her eyes blurring from the endless stream of notes and timelines. The details had started to melt together, a jumble of fragments that refused to form a whole. It felt like trying to complete a puzzle with pieces from different sets—nothing fit the way it should.

Emma's file drew her attention again. The fifth victim. The outlier.

Despite herself, Kate kept circling back to it. Sherri might have been the most recent victim and potentially the most revealing case, but something about Emma nagged at her. *It didn't fit.*

Maybe Emma wasn't taken by the same man. Perhaps she was a distraction—a red herring. But until Kate could rule that out, she wouldn't be able to move forward.

A shrill ring broke through her thoughts. Kate flinched, already scowling as she glanced at the phone. Probably Cara again, checking in.

The home phone line was archaic—cell phones had long since taken over. But Kate's number was only known to a select few. She kept the rest of the world at a distance, filtering messages through her life and preserving them in files.

She let it go to voicemail. Everything was too fresh in her mind—too close. She couldn't afford to lose the thread.

But then, a familiar voice drifted from the machine.

"Hi Kate, it's Sheriff Jacobs. Can you give me a call when you get this? I have a few questions for you. Thanks."

Kate's head snapped toward the speaker. Confusion creased her brow as the message replayed in her mind. She crossed the room and hit the button to hear it again. The sheriff's tone was calm, maybe even friendly—but something about it felt... off.

What questions could he possibly have for me?

Kate picked up the phone to call the sheriff back when it rang in her hand.

"Hello?" she answered, tentative.

"Well? What have you found out? Do you think Sherri was murdered? Does the sheriff have any leads? Tell me what is happening!"

Cara finally paused for breath, giving Kate a chance to speak.

"Hi, Cara. Yes, Sherri was murdered." Kate sighed, tucking the phone between her shoulder and ear. "The sheriff wants to keep it quiet for now, so please don't repeat that. And no, there aren't any solid leads yet. They've brought in someone from the FBI to help."

She hesitated, her stomach tightening. But delaying it wouldn't change the truth. "It looks like Sherri may be one of six possible victims—taken by the same perpetrator."

"What?!" Cara shrieked in her ear, just as Kate knew she would. She grimaced, holding the phone away slightly.

"How could the police know a serial killer is hunting young girls and not say anything? How are we supposed to protect our children if we don't even know they need protecting?"

Kate didn't say it aloud, but she believed children always needed protecting. It didn't take a warning or a headline to justify vigilance.

In her mind, the real danger came from the threats no one saw coming—unexpected evil that left the deepest scars.

"The FBI only recently put the pieces together," Kate said. "Sherri is the first real break in the case."

"I'm keeping her close from now on," Cara said, voice trembling. "I just—I need to know she's safe."

"Cara, I don't think this guy will go after Chloe," Kate said as calmly as possible, trying to help her friend latch onto some sense of control.

"Why not? Sherri and Chloe are the same age." Cara almost sounded offended that Chloe wasn't the object of this jerk's obsession.

Kate shook her head. Sometimes, Cara could be ridiculous.

"It's not just about age. He picks girls with blonde hair and blue eyes. Luckily, Chloe has brown hair."

"But she has blue eyes."

"Doesn't matter," Kate said firmly. "It's always blonde hair, blue eyes. No exceptions."

"Okay," Cara exhaled. "That makes me feel better." Then, with a sudden spark of curiosity, she added. "So...they called the FBI in?"

Of course. Kate rolled her eyes. Cara always loved a juicy update. At least now, she sounded more stable. It'd be a hell of a lot easier to track down a killer if she didn't have to manage Cara's nerves every step of the way.

"Yes. The agent should be at the sheriff's office by now."

"Huh. I wonder how *our* sheriff will like working with them. He's not exactly known for sharing the spotlight—especially if there's a chance to be the hero."

"True." Kate held back a sigh. She really hated chit-chat. Why did people feel the need to fill the silence with fluff? Why couldn't they just say what needed to be said and move on? And why was she the only one who seemed to feel this way?

Kate pinched her nose as the last shred of her patience slipped away. "Listen, Cara, I have to call the sheriff. Can we talk later?"

"Oh?" Cara purred. "Did *he* have something personal to ask you? Maybe he's finally worked up the nerve to ask you out?"

"Ha-ha, no." Kate did a mental eye-roll. "He just said he had a couple of questions. That's all."

Cara continued to snicker.

Kate didn't wait for more teasing. "Talk later." She hung up before Cara could say another word.

A tingle crept up her neck. She exhaled before dialing the sheriff's office.

Even though she had no reason to be on guard, something in Sheriff Jacobs's voice made her tense.

"Windsor Brooke Sheriff's Office, how can I help you?" a female voice sang out over the line.

"Hi Sylvia, this is Kate, returning the sheriff's call."

"Hold, please. I'll see if the sheriff has time to speak with you." Sylvia's tone turned clipped and cold.

Kate almost smiled. She didn't know what had caused Sylvia's obvious disdain—and didn't care enough to find out.

"Okay, thanks, Sylvia," Kate replied.

"Hi Kate, thanks for calling me back." The sheriff's warm baritone rolled into her ear—a pleasant sound, if not necessarily a pleasant man.

"Sure, Sheriff. What did you need to ask me?"

She heard him chuckle. "I guess that is enough small talk for you—let's get down to business. Mr. FBI showed up today," he led off without a preamble. "He asked why you would have access to the case files related to Sherri's murder."

Kate paused. She hadn't expected the field agent to be aware of her involvement so soon. Evidently, Jill hadn't covered her tracks as thoroughly as usual.

"I see...and what did you tell him?" she asked, cautious now.

"Well, I didn't tell him anything because, as of right now, I don't know anything. Care to fill me in? I can't help you if I don't know your involvement."

His tone held a warning, but Kate brushed it off. She was confident she could manage the FBI agent. He was just another man, no different from any other male she crossed paths with. Confidence and control were all she needed to manage the situation.

Kate smiled to herself, "I appreciate your concern, Sheriff, but I promise—there's no reason to worry. I can handle the FBI."

"All right, if that's how you want it," he huffed. "Mr. FBI wants to meet with you tomorrow morning. Can you be here by nine?"

"Yes, I can be there."

"We'll see you tomorrow." There was a pause, and then, just as she was about to hang up, the sheriff added, "And Kate? Bring your *A-game* tomorrow. This FBI guy's good."

With those parting words, the line went dead.

What did one wear when meeting the FBI?

Kate stood in front of her closet, skimming through hangers. A pantsuit felt too stiff, a skirt too formal, and jeans too casual—but comfort held a certain appeal. If she was going to have her ass chewed, at least she wouldn't be fidgeting. She settled on her softest pair of jeans, the ones that hugged her hips just right, and her favorite sweater—a deep green that brought out the color of her eyes.

Black calf-high boots completed the look. She gave herself a once-over in the full-length mirror. Comfy, casual, nothing to hide.

A glance at the clock made her curse under her breath. She was going to be late if she didn't hurry. Her pulse quickened as she raced downstairs, grabbed her purse, and headed out the door.

Kate hated being late. It left her feeling frazzled and off her game, and today, of all days, she needed to be sharp.

As she pulled away from her driveway, her gaze lingered in the rearview mirror. The clean lines of her prairie-style house sat nestled in a grove of trees.

Pride swelled warm and full in her chest. *Her* home. Her space. No one could take it from her.

The main road to town was lightly traveled, as usual. Cottonwoods lined the highway, showing off their vibrant fall colors. A cool, crisp breeze ruffled the leaves, letting shafts of sunlight dance through. Calmness and serenity surrounded her, and Kate treasured every minute of her drive.

She cleared her mind and shifted her thoughts to the upcoming meeting with Mr. FBI, as the sheriff liked to call him. Breathing was essential when it came to fooling someone into believing a lie. The slightest shift—an unsteady inhale, a flicker of nerves—could give you away, especially if the interrogator was any good.

Her biggest tell had always been the same. A blush. Seemingly innocent, completely damning. It had taken nearly her entire training program to learn how to control it.

She never thought she'd need that skill in Windsor Brooke.

He sat under a tree, watching the children play in the town's little park.

This one had a merry-go-round—his favorite.

There was nothing quite like the sight of it spinning, the girls clinging to the rails, their long blonde hair streaming behind them in the breeze. Joy lit up their faces. Pure. Untouched. Radiating innocence.

Round and round they went. Squeals of laughter.

They had no idea a predator sat just years away, close enough to pounce.

His breath slowed as anticipation stirred inside him, old instincts whispering promises.

A flutter of movement caught his eye. A sweet-faced girl ran past, chasing a butterfly.

He smiled. "Well now, hello, little darling. What's your name?"

She paused in her chase and smiled, "Chloe."

"Chloe." He repeated. Practically tasting the sound of it. "That's a very pretty name. Are you chasing the butterfly, Chloe?"

"Uh-huh." She nodded enthusiastically.

"I love butterflies," he said, his smile all warmth and charm. "So pure. So delicate. Just like you, I bet."

"Oh yes," Chloe said, her voice full of wonder. "They're prettier than flowers!"

The butterfly dipped low and landed on a blade of grass nearby. Vibrating with energy, Chloe hopped from foot to foot. "I gotta go—bye!"

He watched her sprint off again, her little feet pounding the grass, her laughter trailing behind her.

He let the anticipation grow. It was time.

Soon, his collection would have a new addition.

Chloe.

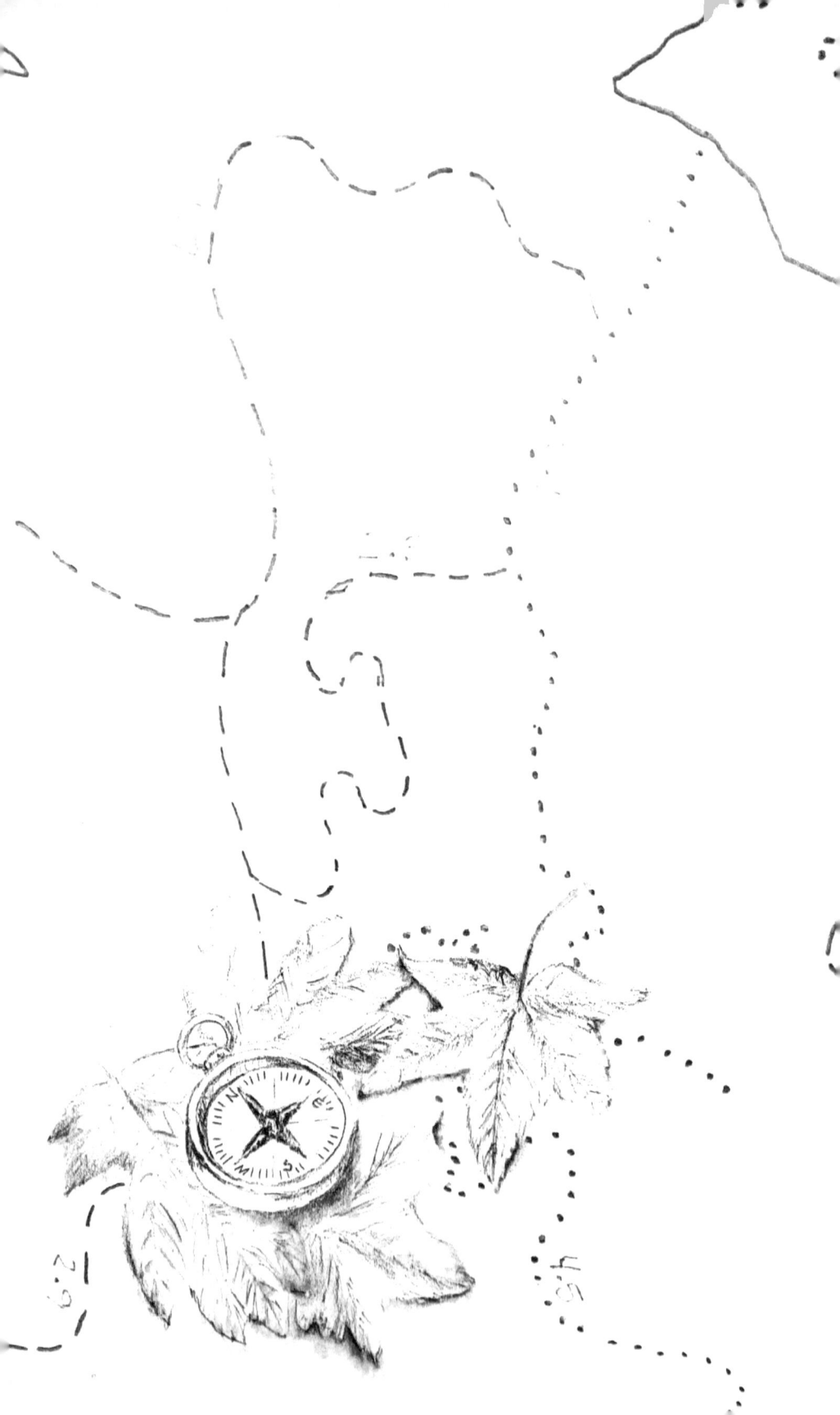

Chapter Eight

Fox arrived at the sheriff's office early, hoping to steal a few uninterrupted moments with the case files. There was something he hadn't seen—some thread that would eventually pull everything together.

He'd spent most of the night pacing his motel room, wearing down the threadbare carpet. Over and over, he ran through the facts, trying to catch the link that would connect the cases.

The office chair creaked under his weight as he leaned back. He rubbed his hands over his face and pressed his thumbs into his eyes. The frustration clawed at him. The beginning of any case felt like staring at a thousand-piece puzzle. The edges were easy enough, but the real work began at the center. Once a few pieces came together, the rest would follow—hopefully.

Loosening the tie at his neck, he unbuttoned the top two buttons of his shirt. He hated suits—too stiff, too restrictive. How the Bureau expected him to chase down suspects dressed like this was beyond him.

His fingers raked through his hair, and he frowned. It was getting too long. He'd planned to get a cut this weekend—until this case landed in his lap. Now, that plan would have to wait.

He sighed. Sometimes, this job was a pain in the ass.

Fox glanced at his watch; Kate Millard would show up any minute. He wasn't sure what to expect, but the sheriff's reaction left him intrigued and a little cautious.

"Hey Sylvia, is the conference room open for use this morning?"

She looked up briefly, her mouth set in a grim line. "Yes, it is," she muttered, already turning back to her screen as the phone rang again.

"Not one for small talk," he smirked, shaking his head. An unwelcoming receptionist seemed counterintuitive—but maybe that was just how things worked in Windsor Brooke.

The slight pause in the clicking of the keyboard was the only indication Sylvia gave that she heard him.

In the conference room, he pulled two chairs up to the table and set out a notepad, pen, and two glasses of water. He poked his head back out.

"Sylvia, could you show Kate Millard in when she arrives?" he said, knowing it would irritate her.

He selected the chair facing the door and sat down to wait.

Kate stepped into the sheriff's office at exactly nine. Her nose wrinkled at the familiar smell of old coffee and men. She glanced around. The room was empty except for Sylvia, who, of course, was at her usual station.

Kate sometimes wondered if the woman ever left the building. She never saw her around town or at the market.

"Hi, Sylvia. I am here to meet with someone from the FBI."

"In the conference room," Sylvia answered without looking up.

Kate turned toward the door just to the left of the desk. She paused, taking a deep breath. Then she wiped all expression from her face and stepped inside.

Kate's confident stride faltered when her eyes landed on the man at the head of the table.

Despite Sheriff Jacobs's warning, she hadn't thought much of it. She'd dealt with all kinds of men, especially the type who carried badges.

The FBI agents she'd worked with in the past were tense, strait-laced, and boring.

This man was something else entirely.

Even seated, he radiated virility. The room felt charged, as if vibrating with the power he exuded.

Her mind went blank, all thoughts drowned by the flood of her senses. Until two words floated to the surface: *Oh my.*

Heat rushed to her cheeks as she realized she'd been standing frozen in the doorway. She needed to move, make her body commit one way or another. With effort, she squared her shoulders and stepped inside, using the moment it took to shut the door to pull herself together.

Even prepared, the sight of him still made her stomach flutter. She couldn't put her finger on what about him left her so off-center.

Sure, he was tall, with his legs stretched out and ankles crossed, every inch of him radiating relaxed confidence.

The standard suit and tie did nothing to mute the raw masculinity he exuded so effortlessly.

Even his hair was tempting, just long enough to curl slightly over his collar, rich brown and thick, the kind of hair that begged fingers to get lost in.

None of this should've mattered.

She had a heart of stone, frozen over from years on the job. She was a cold, ruthless killer.

Not some flirty female who melts at the sight of an attractive man.

Kate frowned, ignoring the tango rhythm of her pulse. She lifted her gaze, intent on meeting his, but was waylaid by the roguish grin that tilted the corners of his mouth. Heat bloomed across her cheeks.

What was wrong with her? She was losing her ground and needed to get control back—fast.

She walked the rest of the way into the room. The only available chair was next to his, so close she had to be careful not to bump his leg beneath the table.

She was far too aware of him as a man to risk even a brief touch. The thought alone sent a different kind of warmth through her.

Kate held out her hand.

He rose from his seat in one fluid motion to take it, his grip firm, his gaze locked with hers, unwavering, intense.

His eyes were the color of the sea in a storm. Turbulent. Deep. Impossible to look away from.

"I'm Kate Millard. You wanted to meet with me," she said a little awkwardly.

"Yes. I'm Agent Fox Anderson."

He shook her hand, short, firm—but didn't let go. He shifted, bringing himself a little closer.

Kate instinctively took a step back, and her boot tangled in the chair. She glared at the smile tugging at the corner of his mouth.

"Thanks for coming down here this morning," he said casually, ignoring her effort to free her hand, "I wanted to talk with you about the case files you requested from Agent Burke."

Her head shot up, her eyes widening before she could hide her surprise.

It was becoming clear she wasn't going to have control of this conversation. Her mind scrambled for a new strategy.

Not trusting herself or her reaction to Agent Anderson, Kate decided that saying as little as possible was the safest route. Silence could be unnerving. Besides, no one liked single-word answers. With any luck, she'd rattle him just as much as he'd rattled her.

After a long pause, Kate arched a brow.

The urge to laugh caught Fox off guard. Watching the flurry of expressions flash across Kate Millard's face was more entertaining than squeezing a confession out of a hardened criminal.

He'd been studying her from the moment she walked through the door.

She was uncomfortable, he spotted that instantly and filed it away for later. But what intrigued him more was how hard she worked to hide it.

So far, she was failing miserably.

He had to fight the smile tugging at his lips. Her raw show of emotion was... refreshing.

At first, he'd given her the typical once-over—a man's instinctive scan of a physically attractive woman. And yes, the view was worth appreciating.

She moved with an effortless grace, her lithe body reflecting an intimate understanding of its capabilities.

Then there were her legs. Damn. Long, lean, wrapped in snug denim that sparked more than one idea.

But it wasn't just her looks that held his attention.

It was the blush.

That faint stain of color across her cheeks betrayed something deeper. Softening her sharp edges.

He couldn't help but wonder what thought had triggered it.

He should've said something and broken the awkward charge between them.

But he didn't. Couldn't. Not when she looked at him like that.

Part of him wanted to find out what would happen if he kept quiet. What would she do?

Fox had been about to invite her to sit when Kate crossed the room and offered her hand.

He took it, his much larger one closing around hers. Despite her delicate skin, he felt the strength beneath it, and he didn't let go for no reason other than wanting to maintain the contact. Even after the handshake should have ended, he held on, ignoring her polite tug to be released.

Instinctively, he stepped closer, inhaling the subtle, alluring scent clinging to her.

He felt like a stallion catching the scent of a mare in heat. The thought made something primal stir inside him.

Her startled step back, then stumbled into the chair, filled him with dark, masculine satisfaction.

At least he wasn't the only one affected.

Fox cleared his throat, forcing his thoughts back to the case. "Would you tell me why you requested those specific files?"

"I didn't," came her cool reply.

"You didn't what, Mrs. Millard?" he asked, confused.

"It's *Ms.*, not Mrs. I'm not married." Kate corrected him, keeping her expression carefully neutral.

Fox frowned, studying her.

"Oh. I see. My apologies. Is there a soon-to-be *Mr.* Millard in the picture?"

Why the hell had he asked that?

"No."

His jaw clenched at her clipped response.

"Would it be possible for you to give me a more detailed response to my questions?" he said, trying—and failing—to keep the frustration out of his voice.

"I suppose I could try," Kate said, a smile tugging at her lips.

"All right, let's try this again. Why did you ask for those specific files?"

She met his gaze, her eyes dancing with amusement before a slow smile spread across her face.

"I already told you—I didn't."

The smile that lit her face was both stunning and distracting, enough to make him lose his train of thought for half a second.

He'd thought she was attractive before, now that seemed like an understatement. That smile? It was devastating.

Scowling felt like the only appropriate response to a situation spiraling out of his control.

He tapped his fingers restlessly on the table.

"'I didn't.' isn't a detailed answer," he said through gritted teeth. "If you didn't request the files, why did Agent Burke give them to you?"

Kate tilted her head, her expression annoyingly amused. "I requested any files of cases possibly related to what happened to Sherri. I didn't ask for any specific file."

Fox wasn't amused. He gave her a hard look.

"Again—why?"

With a smile that seemed to mock him, Kate tilted her head. "Why what?"

Fox slammed his fist on the table.

"Dammit, this is not a game. A girl is dead, and five more are likely dead, too, victims of the same bastard. I need to know why you're looking at files related to this case. If you can't give me a straight answer, I'll assume you're involved. You'll be investigated as a suspect until I'm satisfied with your guilt or innocence. Now, give me a straight answer. What are you doing with those files?"

Kate sat still for a moment, her expression unreadable. Fox could practically see the wheels turning. She was calculating, he'd bet money on it. Either she'd tell him what he wanted to hear, or she'd try to bluff her way out again.

"Okay," she finally said, holding up a hand in mock surrender. "My friend Cara has a daughter Sherri's age. She heard what happened and worried that the same could happen to her little girl. I told her I'd ask the sheriff about it. When he said the FBI was coming in, I reached out to an acquaintance to see if other cases might be linked. She sent me the files. That's it."

Then, like she couldn't help herself, she arched one eyebrow and smirked, "Is that a detailed enough response for you?"

Fox glowered. Her answer wasn't what bothered him, it was the fact that she'd *won*. He'd lost control.

He was known for having a temper, and yeah, he'd had a couple of write-ups for losing it at a crime scene. But never in an interview. Never with a potential witness. He prided himself on charm, on reading people, making them feel safe enough to spill. But she wasn't spilling. She was dancing.

And worse—he was enjoying the dance.

He cleared his throat, trying to shake it off. "Why do you have an acquaintance in the FBI who's willing to send you classified files?" he asked, his tone sharper than intended. "I don't see how an antique shop owner has those kinds of connections."

"Boutique," she corrected, almost absently.

"What?" he asked, caught off guard.

"I own a *boutique*. Not an antique shop."

Fox narrowed his eyes. "What does that have to do with anything?"

There it was again, that cool, unbothered tone that made his blood pressure spike. He forced himself to take a breath before continuing. "How do you know someone in the FBI?"

"I'm sorry, I don't see how that concerns you or this case." She held his stare, calm and composed, like she dared him to push.

He almost laughed at the audacity. She really thought she could intimidate *him*.

Hell, maybe she could.

His mouth twitched with the threat of a smile, and before he could stop it, he let out a low chuckle. No one was more surprised than he.

How the hell did she get under his skin this fast?

"Fine," he said, raising his hands. "We'll let that go for now." He leaned forward slightly, still watching her closely. "You read through the files. Find anything interesting? Anything you want to share?"

"Nope, other than the victim type doesn't match my friend's daughter, which she was relieved to hear," Kate shrugged.

Fox nodded slowly. He didn't believe for a second that was the whole truth, but she wasn't going to give him more. Not yet.

"Okay. I guess we're done for now." He pulled a card from his wallet and held it out to her. "Call me if you think of anything." Holding her gaze, Fox emphasized, "And I mean anything."

As she reached for it, his fingers brushed hers, deliberately. The contact was brief, but it hit him like a jolt. Electric. Immediate.

Kate slipped the card into her purse without comment. Then, abruptly, she stood and gave him a quick nod.

"Goodbye, Agent Anderson," she said, her voice cool and composed again as she turned to leave.

Fox watched her walk out the door, a slow smile tugging at his lips.

Getting to know Kate Millard suddenly became a top priority.

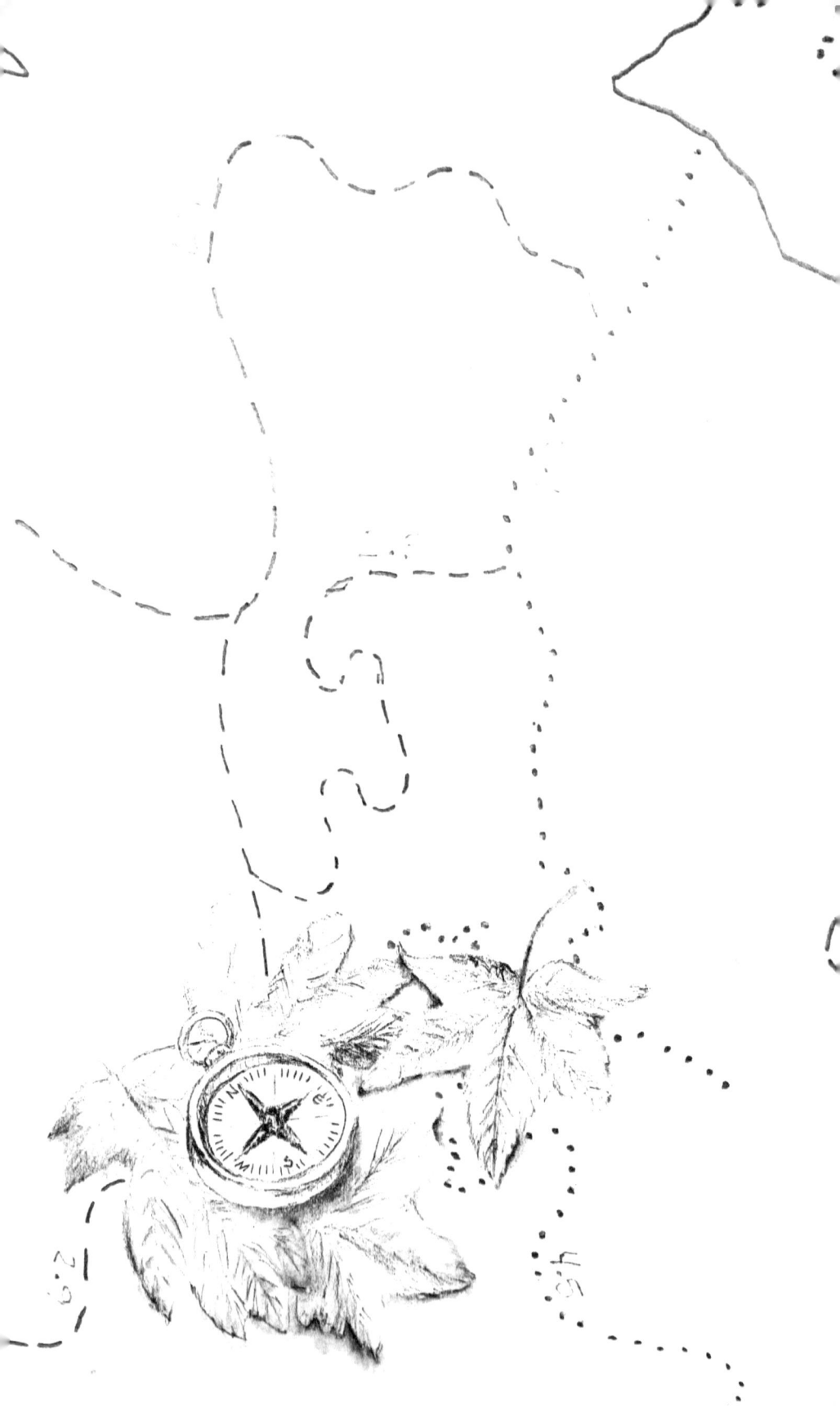

Chapter Nine

Deputy Johnson pulled up to the address listed in the file and glanced at Deputy Riggs. "You want to take the lead with questioning?"

Riggs sighed. Of course, he wanted her to. Just because she was a woman, her coworkers seemed to think that made her better suited for interviews. As if female intuition somehow gave her an edge they lacked.

She unbuckled her seatbelt and stepped out, stretching her legs. It was going to be a long day, she could feel it already. With a quiet groan, she squared her shoulders and started up the driveway.

The house was textbook suburbia: colonial revival, bright red door, manicured lawn. Except this one had something the others didn't, a thick, invisible shroud of heartache.

When she knocked, the door opened to reveal a woman whose face looked carved from grief.

Riggs steeled herself against the wave of sympathy that always tried to rise up in situations like this. Sympathy didn't help. Facts did.

"Hi, I'm Deputy Riggs," she said gently, gesturing to her partner. "This is Deputy Johnson. We spoke on the phone yesterday."

Mrs. Miller gave a wordless nod and stepped back to let them in.

She looked like every overextended stay-at-home mom Riggs had ever seen—messy bun, apron, no makeup—but there was a weight in her posture, a dullness in her eyes that made her seem older, beaten down.

"Thank you for letting us come and speak with you today," Riggs offered.

Mrs. Miller sat stiffly on the edge of the sofa, hands wringing in her lap. Her voice was flat. "Do you have any answers about what happened to my baby?"

"No," Riggs said, hating the word. "Not yet. We just have some follow-up questions."

She hated this part—keeping things vague, skirting the real reason they were here. She was a straight shooter by nature, but the job didn't always allow for that.

"Would you mind walking us through the day Susie disappeared?"

"If it'll help," Mrs. Miller whispered. "I honestly don't know what more I can tell you. We were inside most of the morning. Susie went outside to play around 10:30. I cleaned the house and got lunch ready. When I called her in... she was just gone."

She swallowed, bowing her head.

"I looked everywhere. Inside, outside. Then I started knocking on doors. Asking the neighbors..." She trailed off with a helpless shrug. "No one had seen her."

"Okay." Riggs nodded, checking her notepad. "How about the day before? Did you notice anyone new hanging around? Someone who wouldn't normally be in the neighborhood?"

Mrs. Miller shook her head. "No... we went to my son's football game. They played Windsor Brooke High School, so there were strangers in town. Visiting families and all. But I didn't see anyone paying extra attention to Susie."

Riggs' hand stilled. Windsor Brooke?

She flicked her eyes toward Johnson, who was already shaking his head—he hadn't seen that detail in the case file either.

"Just to clarify," Riggs said, keeping her tone even, "they played against Windsor Brooke?"

"Yes." Mrs. Miller gave her a confused look. "Is that important?"

"It might be," Riggs said. "Any idea why that wasn't included in the police report?"

"I don't know. Everyone goes to the games here. Maybe the sheriff didn't think it needed to be added—they probably assumed you knew who we played."

Riggs kept her face neutral, but inside, her pulse kicked up. *Windsor Brooke.* A new link. One that wasn't in the files. One the *FBI* hadn't clocked yet.

She didn't smile, couldn't. Not when a mother's grief was the price of her lead.

Moments like this were rare. Working in a boys' club meant constantly proving yourself, and she wasn't above admitting it—this felt good.

Standing, Riggs offered a soft smile. "That's all we need for now. Thank you for your time." She handed over a business card. "If you think of *anything* else—even something that doesn't seem important—please call."

Mrs. Miller took the card with shaking fingers. "Okay," she said, her voice trembling. "You'll let me know if you find anything, won't you?"

Riggs nodded. "We will."

Mrs. Miller stood in the doorway, watching the two deputies walk back to their car.

She had begun to give up hope of ever knowing what had happened to her sweet Susie.

Sometimes, the pain would sneak up, stealing her breath—doubling her over in helpless grief. Even though Susie had been taken two years ago, the loss still felt raw, like sandpaper scraping an open wound.

The memory lived fresh in her mind as if it had happened just yesterday.

She no longer hoped to see Susie again. She *knew* she was gone, forever out of reach.

That knowing had come like a wave about a week after the disappearance—sudden, unmistakable, hollowing. As though something inside her had died, too.

Since then, the urgency to find Susie had transformed into something quieter but no less consuming: the need to understand.

In two long, aching years, Mrs. Miller had never felt this stir of hope. But now... maybe these deputies would finally bring her the answers she needed.

Maybe then, she could find peace.

Maybe then, she could let Susie go.

Kate walked into her shop thirty minutes after meeting with Agent Anderson, armed with a white paper bag of donuts from the bakery—a peace offering for her continued absence. She hadn't been the most attentive boss since returning from Paris, and she knew it. Between her personal hunt for Sherri's killer and now dealing with the FBI interview, the store had been low on her priority list.

She only had an hour before heading out again—this time to Midstow, Iowa, where she hoped to learn more about Emma Mathews and whether she could be connected to Sherri. But first, she needed to smooth things over with Bridgette.

"Hi, Bridgette. How are things today?" Kate walked through the store, taking in the fresh displays. The new Paris merchandise—cool blues and soft grays—had already been beautifully staged. A deep navy vase sat next to a bright orange tray, and the contrast was stunning.

Kate smiled.

"Any trouble getting everything out on the floor?"

Bridgette, never one to miss a chance to shine, grinned. "Not at all. Took a little shifting, but I got it done. We've already sold half of what you brought back," she said proudly, her wink slow and smug.

Kate laughed. "You've outdone yourself."

Bridgette dipped into a mock bow. "Why, thank you. Kind of you to notice."

"Is April working today?" Kate asked.

"Yup. She's covering the afternoon shift. I'm coming back in too close."

Kate blinked. "I usually close. Why would you—"

Bridgette raised a brow. "Word around town is you're helping Cara with the Sherri thing. Add to the equation the FBI in town, and people are talking. Cara says you're obsessed with mysteries and that solving them is your hobby. Honestly? I never heard you mention it before, but she swears it's all you talk about on girls' nights."

Kate fidgeted with a glass paperweight, suddenly uneasy. Bridgette had a way of looking at her, like she was trying to see past the surface.

"Yeah, that's me," Kate muttered. "Mysteries. All the time." She cleared her throat. "I probably won't be around much for a while."

"We figured. April and I have already worked out a schedule. And for the record," Bridgette's expression hardened, "we hope you find the bastard—and castrate him."

Kate blinked. "Wow. I don't think I've ever heard you talk like that before."

"Yeah, well. No one's ever hurt someone I knew before. This town's hurting, Kate. We need it to stop."

"Thanks for covering," Kate said, the weight of Bridgette's words pressing heavier than she expected. Failure wasn't just a risk anymore—it wasn't an option. "I'll check in—and call if anything comes up."

Bridgette nodded, watching her carefully. "You be careful. I don't want you turning up as the next victim because you poked around in something you shouldn't have."

Kate forced a smile. "I'll be careful. Honestly, I probably won't find anything."

"Still," Bridgette said, her tone soft but serious, "be careful anyway."

Cara's life was pretty amazing—if she said so herself. She had a wonderful husband who was home every night by six and three great kids who did their homework with minimal prodding and stayed out of trouble.

Well, there was that one summer—four, maybe five years ago—when JT and his friend thought it would be funny to tie a string of lit firecrackers to a squirrel's tail. The poor little thing had run wild, terrified, before collapsing from what looked like a heart attack. JT had cried, swearing it was Tuck's idea. Cara wasn't sure. Tuck was a few years older, already in middle school. But JT had never lied to her before, and she wanted to believe he wasn't starting then.

She'd come outside just in time to see the squirrel lying still in the grass. The boys stood in a half-circle around the small body. JT and Bobby had tears streaming down their cheeks. Even without punishment, Cara could tell they'd learned a valuable lesson: life wasn't something to treat carelessly.

But Tuck stood apart from the group, staring at the ground with a blank, unreadable face. It was unsettling. He was always so full of expression—smiling, joking—but in that moment, there was nothing—just a strange emptiness that had stayed with her all these years.

Aside from that one incident, Windsor Brooke had been good for her family. They were happy, healthy, surrounded by friends, and doing well in school.

At least, they had been.

Now, everything had changed. Sherri was gone. A monster was out there, preying on little girls. Cara couldn't shake the dread that something terrible might happen again. She no longer let Chloe out of her sight, not even to play in the front yard.

According to Kate, Chloe didn't match the profile this maniac seemed to prefer, but Cara wasn't about to take any chances. Monsters didn't follow the rules.

"Mom? Mom, are you home?"

Cara spun around, startled to see Chloe stepping through the back door.

"Oh, honey!" she gasped, rushing to her. "What are you doing home? Why aren't you in school?" Her hands flew to Chloe's arms, checking her over. "Are you okay? How did you get here?" She glanced toward the door, half expecting her husband to follow in behind.

"I wasn't feeling good," Chloe said casually. "So I decided to walk home."

"You what?" Cara's voice pitched high in disbelief. She stood up so fast her chair crashed to the floor behind her. The sound reverberated from the wall. "You walked home alone? Chloe, you can't just leave school like that! Did you even tell your teacher?" Her words tumbled out in a panicked rush.

Right on cue, the phone rang.

One glance at the caller ID told her it was the school—they'd just realized Chloe was missing.

"Hello?" she answered sharply.

"May I speak to the parent of Chloe Norton?"

"This is she."

"Mrs. Norton, this is Windsor Brooke Elementary. I'm calling to inform you that your daughter did not return to class after lunch. Do you know if she's at home?"

"Yes, she just walked through the door," Cara said tightly. "May I ask how my daughter was able to leave the school without anyone noticing?"

"I... yes, I'm so sorry," the woman stammered. "During a small tussle on the playground, Chloe slipped through the gate while a delivery truck was unloading. We assure you it won't happen again. Would you like to bring her back to school?"

"No, I'll keep her with me today." Cara rubbed her forehead, trying to soothe the pounding behind her eyes. "We need to talk."

"Of course. Let us know if you need anything."

Cara hung up and turned to her daughter, taking a few deep breaths to calm the fire rising in her chest.

"Chloe," she said softly, kneeling to meet her at eye level. She took Chloe's small hands in hers, remembering how those same hands used to cling to her finger when she was a toddler. "What were you thinking?"

Tears stung her eyes. She couldn't delay this any longer. It was time. Chloe needed to know the truth.

She needed to know what had happened to her friend Sherri.

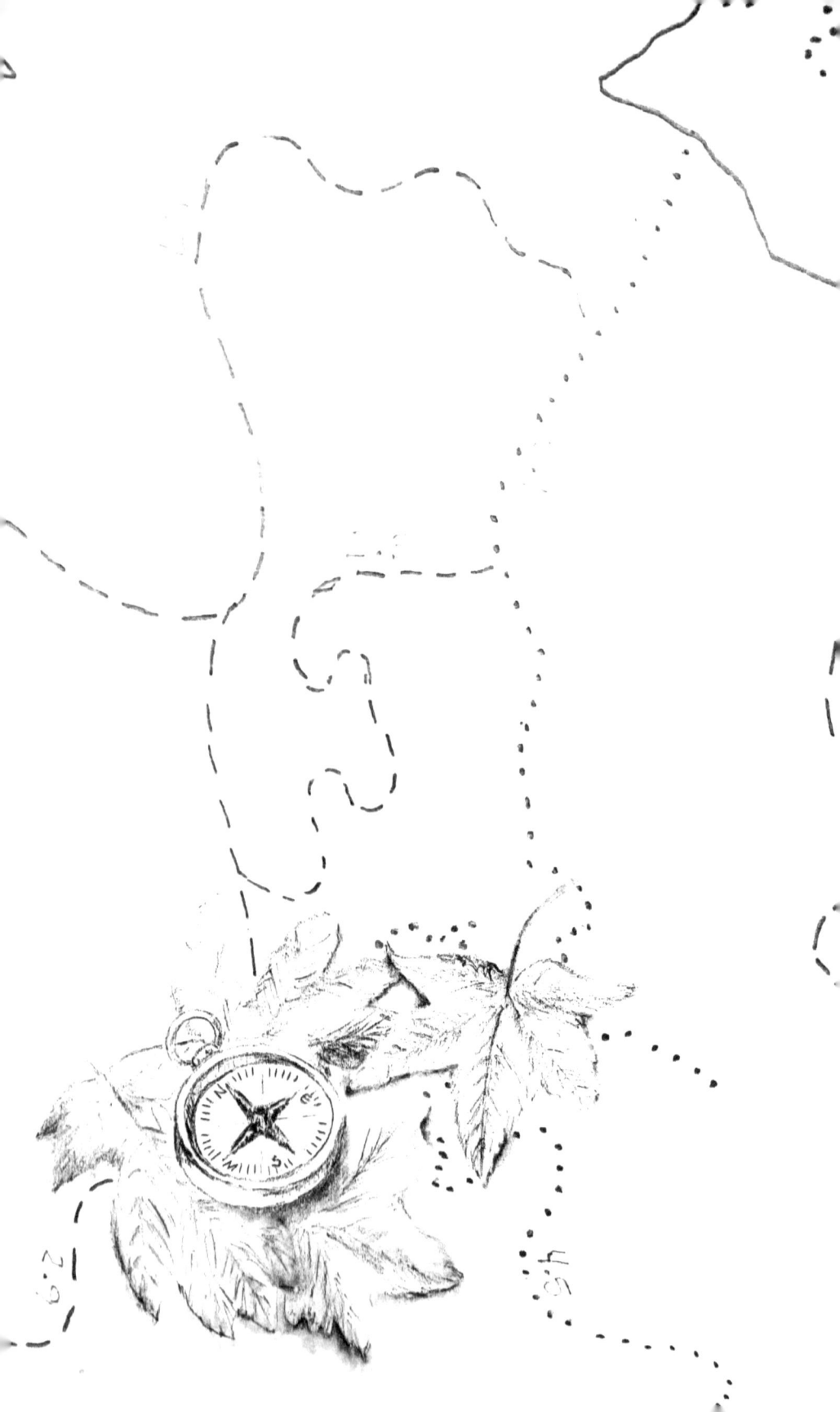

Chapter Ten

Kate pulled up in front of the Mathews' family home, a charming little cottage tucked into a sleepy neighborhood. It was quaint, with white paneled walls and gray stone facing. A massive shade tree dominated the front yard, and a neatly trimmed lawn was as green and lush as a golf course. A white picket fence wrapped around the yard like a ribbon on a gift. The decorative stone path leading from the street to the front door was an open invitation to come on in.

Kate took a breath and knocked on the door.

Insecurities scratched at the edges of her calm. She hated this part—talking to strangers. She much preferred to operate in the background. But sometimes, background wasn't an option.

The door yanked open, and a towering man glared down at her. He was built like a linebacker, his face buried beneath a thick, wild beard that gave him a distinctly mountain-man look.

"What do you want?" he barked.

Definitely not a fan of visitors.

Kate cleared her throat, trying to keep her voice steady. "I was hoping to speak with someone about Emma Mathews. My name is Kate Millard, and I live over in Windsor Brooke. We recently had a girl go missing, and I'm looking into possible connections between the two cases."

She grimaced. Total amateur hour. She knew better. Success depended on preparation.

The man's face flushed deep red, his eyes bulging. "The hell you say?" he thundered, stepping forward. One hand clenched the door like he was about to slam it in her face.

"I—I don't mean to upset you," Kate stammered, her voice soft but urgent. "But someone's out there, hurting our children. I'm trying to stop them. That's all."

After a long, tense pause, he stepped aside with a grunt. "Fine. You step outta line, and you're out on your ass. You hear me?"

"Got it," Kate said.

He turned without a word, leaving the door open as he walked toward the back of the house. Evidently, she was expected to follow.

Kate closed the door softly behind her. She quickened her step, hurrying to catch up. The house was as neat inside as it was outside. Someone had an eye for style, and Kate doubted it belonged to Mr. Personality.

Once they reached the living room, he stopped abruptly. Turning to face her, he said, "Wait here. I'll go get my wife," and left her.

Kate stood in the center of the room, taking in the thoughtful layout, the warm tones, the curated furniture, and the soft throws, which created a cozy seating area. All along the mantel were photos of a family who appeared happy together. Emma's face stood out the most, her smile bright and full of life. Poor girl. Why did they have to be taken so young?

Kate turned at the sound of footsteps and was staggered by the woman who entered the room. She looked nothing like the vibrant mother captured in the photos on the mantle. Gone was the bright-eyed woman laughing at the camera. In her place stood someone hollowed out; the light in her eye extinguished. Emma's disappearance had carved the life right out of her.

"Hi, I'm Kate Millard. Thank you for meeting me."

The woman simply nodded her head. She quietly walked over to the couch and sat down.

Watching Emma's mother was painful. Kate doubted she had anything left to give. Any hope of gaining insight from Emma's parents was slipping away.

"As I mentioned to your husband, a little girl went missing in my hometown, too. I'm looking into any other disappearances in the area with similar physical appearances."

A slight nod of her head was the only response Emma's mom gave Kate. Needing more, Kate walked over to stand directly in front of her, forcing her to lift her gaze.

"Aside from the open window in Emma's room, was anything else disturbed?"

"No." She whispered.

"Did Emma share a room with one of her siblings?"

"Yes. Emma's younger sister, Ashley, shares the room with her," her voice flat, stripped of emotion, as though she'd cried out every last feeling and was now just an apathetic shell.

Raw emotion always made Kate feel awkward and unsure of herself. She never knew what to say or do, but this was worse. The emptiness in the room was like a black hole, pulling the warmth out of everything around it. Kate felt cold, exposed, stripped bare by the weight of such heartache. It stirred something in her, memories she had buried deep after losing her own family.

Kate struggled to compose herself. Her voice sounded brittle when she finally asked, "Can I speak with Ashley for a few minutes?"

Emma's mother gave a small nod to Mr. Personality, who had been standing like a silent watchdog in the hallway. Without a word, he turned and walked out of the room, leaving Kate and Emma's mother in heavy, awkward silence.

A petite girl with a somber expression padded into the room. She cast a shy glance at Kate before walking over to stand beside her mother. Kate couldn't help but wonder why a child so young seemed so subdued. Children should laugh, run, and play—but life had dealt this family a hard blow, and it seemed even Ashley felt its weight.

Kate knelt in front of her and smiled while holding out her hand.

"Hi, I'm Kate. What's your name?"

Of course, she already knew, but she hoped the formality might help Ashley feel a little more at ease.

The girl's murmured reply carried surprisingly well in the stillness of the room.

Kate smiled again, reassuringly,

"It's nice to meet you. I wanted to talk with you a little bit about your bedroom. Is that okay?"

Ashley gave a hesitant nod.

"Do you and Emma like to sleep with your window open? I know I do when the weather's nice."

Ashley studied her toes, then replied softly, her voice flat and practiced. "We're not allowed to leave our window open."

"That makes sense," Kate nodded. "You want to be safe. I bet your daddy taught you that." She paused for a beat. "Did Emma like the window open, even though she wasn't supposed to?"

"No, Emma does what she's s'posed to. Sara doesn't. She always wants Emma to do stuff." Ashley said, glancing over her shoulder toward her dad.

Leaning closer to Kate, she whispered. "Emma told her no lots of times, but Sara didn't listen."

"What kind of bad stuff?" Kate asked softly. "What did Sara want to do?"

Ashley peeked behind her again, then scooted even closer. She cupped her hand around Kate's ear and whispered,

"She wanted to go catch fireflies. In the field, by the school."

Kate kept her voice calm.

"When did she ask Emma to do that?"

"The night she left," Ashley whispered, her voice wobbling.

"Do you mean Emma went to meet Sara in the field that night?"

Ashley nodded, lips trembling, eyes filling with tears.

Kate looked up to see Ashley's mother staring, frozen in horror. This poor girl had no idea of the weight of the information she held. Kate would bet money that the second she walked out the door, Emma's parents would be on the phone with the local police, repeating every word Ashley had just said.

Turning to Emma's mom, Kate asked gently, "Do you have contact information for Emma's friend Sara?"

"Uh—yes," she stammered, clearly rattled by her daughter's revelation. "Let me get it for you."

Kate's gaze slid to Mr. Personality for the first time since she began talking with Ashley. He looked stunned. She couldn't help but feel for them; this changed everything. Maybe it would ease some of their pain, but guilt had a way of lingering, even when it wasn't deserved.

A tingle of anticipation made her restless. She had to get to Sara before the Sheriff's Department did. If they got to her first, Kate would lose her edge. And after meeting with Agent Anderson, she found herself savoring the small satisfaction of being one step ahead. For now, at least.

"Here you go," Emma's mom said, returning with a scrap of paper. "Her name is Sara Hallis. She lives a couple of streets over." She looked Kate in the eye for the first time. "Will you let us know if you find out anything?"

Kate nodded, pocketed the paper, and turned to leave. She paused beside Ashley and knelt again.

"Thank you, Ashley," she said softly. "You helped in more ways than you know."

After gently squeezing the girl's shoulder, Kate stood and walked out the door.

The Hallis family home was the complete opposite of the Mathews'. Where the Mathews' house was neat and well-kept, this place sagged with neglect. The front lawn was littered with scattered toys, and the grass was overgrown. Paint peeled along one side of the house, giving the exterior a patchy, two-toned appearance.

Newspapers were piled on the front porch in a soggy tower. As Kate approached, the sound of kids screaming and laughing echoed from inside. She mentally braced herself and knocked.

After a few seconds of shouting from within, the door swung open to reveal a teenage boy, maybe eighteen. His hair was messy, and his clothes were wrinkled and torn at the knees. He leaned lazily in the doorway, looking her over with a grin that made Kate mentally roll her eyes.

"What can I do for you, sweet thing?" he asked in an exaggerated drawl.

"Hi. I'm Kate Millard," she said coolly. "I was just over at the Mathews' home. I was hoping to speak with Sara."

"Sure, come on in," he said with a shrug, already turning. "Name's Davey, by the way."

Kate stepped inside and found the interior no better than the exterior—cluttered, loud, and forgotten. She followed him through the mess.

"Sara!" Davey bellowed.

A young girl burst into the room, full of energy. "What?" she chirped, her voice bright as she eyed Kate with open curiosity.

Davey nodded toward Kate. "This lady wants to talk to you." Then, without another word, he turned and walked off.

Kate shifted to face the girl. Her dark hair hung in tangled strands around her face, and her clothes were faded and stained. Despite it all, she looked up at Kate and smiled broadly. Funny, Kate thought—two little girls, so different. Ashley had been timid and solemn, while this one radiated energy and openness.

Sinking to her knees, Kate offered a gentle smile. "Hi, Sara. I wanted to ask you about Emma."

Sara's smile widened. "Okay! Emma's my friend, but she's not around anymore. Nobody knows where she is." She said it matter-of-factly, her innocence underscoring the tragedy.

"I know, sweetheart," Kate replied softly, though she wondered if Sara understood what "not around anymore" meant. "I heard you two had plans to catch fireflies the night Emma went missing. Do you remember that?"

"Yeah, we talked about catching fireflies all the time. Emma said they were magical and might give us superpowers or something. I wanted to catch some in the field by the school. Emma said there were, like, *hundreds*, and if we were really quiet, they wouldn't even notice us, and we could sneak up and catch them with our nets."

Sara's voice lit up with excitement as she described their plan.

"We were supposed to meet at the end of the street and walk there together. But...she never came."

She shrugged, her smile fading.

Kids never seemed to grasp the gravity of a situation. Kate doubted Sara even understood that her friend was never coming back.

"What did you do when she didn't show up?"

"I still went to the field. I thought maybe she forgot we were meeting at the end of the street. The fireflies were everywhere, just like she said. I caught a few while I waited."

"Do you remember what time you were supposed to meet?"

"Yeah. After bedtime."

"And what time is bedtime for you?"

"Nine."

"What about Emma? Do you know what time *her* bedtime was?"

Sara shrugged again, looking unsure.

Kate pushed down her growing irritation. Turns out, nothing tests your patience quite like two back-to-back conversations with kids.

"So, you planned to meet... but didn't say exactly *when*?"

"We *did* say! I *said* after bedtime!" She crossed her arms, her face scrunching with annoyance. "I already told you that."

"Sara...if your bedtime is nine, and Emma's was earlier, maybe eight, that means she could've been waiting for you for an hour. Does that sound like a good plan?"

Sara blinked, her expression blank. The concept clearly didn't land.

Kate's heart sank. This child had no idea. One day, maybe, the truth of it all would hit her. She just hoped Sara wouldn't carry the weight of it when it did. Two little girls who'd snuck into the night with no clear time or plan. They'd never had a chance.

"Did anyone else know you were planning to meet that night?"

"Davey knew. He came into my room when we were talking about it," Sara said. "Davey and his friend laughed at us. They said we'd get caught, and I was gonna get my butt spanked when we did."

"Did you tell anyone else? Any grown-ups?"

Sara shook her head. "No. We didn't want to get in trouble, so we promised not to tell anyone."

"What about Emma? Do you think she would've told someone?"

Sara's answer came quickly. "No way. Emma was the best at keeping secrets. I told her how I broke my mom's favorite lamp and blamed it on our cat Toby, and she never told anyone."

A smile tugged at Kate's mouth despite herself. "Okay, Sara. Thanks for talking to me."

She rose to her feet and turned, startled to find Davey leaning against the wall, watching her. Kate's skin prickled. Brushing off the discomfort, she kept her tone casual.

"So, you knew the girls were planning to sneak out?"

Davey pushed off the wall and took a step toward her. "Yeah. I thought they were just messing around. I didn't think they'd actually do it." His usual smirk vanished, replaced by something closer to irritation.

"And the friend Sara mentioned, who was he?"

"Just a buddy from high school. Played football. Crashed here one night. I haven't seen him since he went off to college." There was an edge of jealousy in his voice. Kate clocked it instantly. Clearly, Davey had wanted to leave, too—but hadn't.

"And his name?" she pressed.

Davey looked away. "It was the week before Emma disappeared, I think. Look, I didn't remember any of this until she started talking. Otherwise, I doubt I would've even thought about it. It's not like my buddy and I talked about it. We were headed to a party that night. Why would we care about what two little girls were saying?"

"You still haven't told me your buddy's name," Kate reminded him.

"Yeah, and I'm not going to," he said flatly. "He had nothing to do with it. I told you—we were at a party."

Kate's jaw tightened at his stubborn refusal. Her hands were tied—what could she do? As tempting as it was to beat the truth out of him, that wasn't an option. Not yet. She leveled him with a cold stare. "Thanks for your help, Davey. Better late than never, I suppose."

Davey narrowed his eyes but didn't argue. He walked her to the door in silence.

Let him glare. She wasn't here to coddle anyone. Emma might still be home if he'd cared even a little and told his parents what the girls were planning.

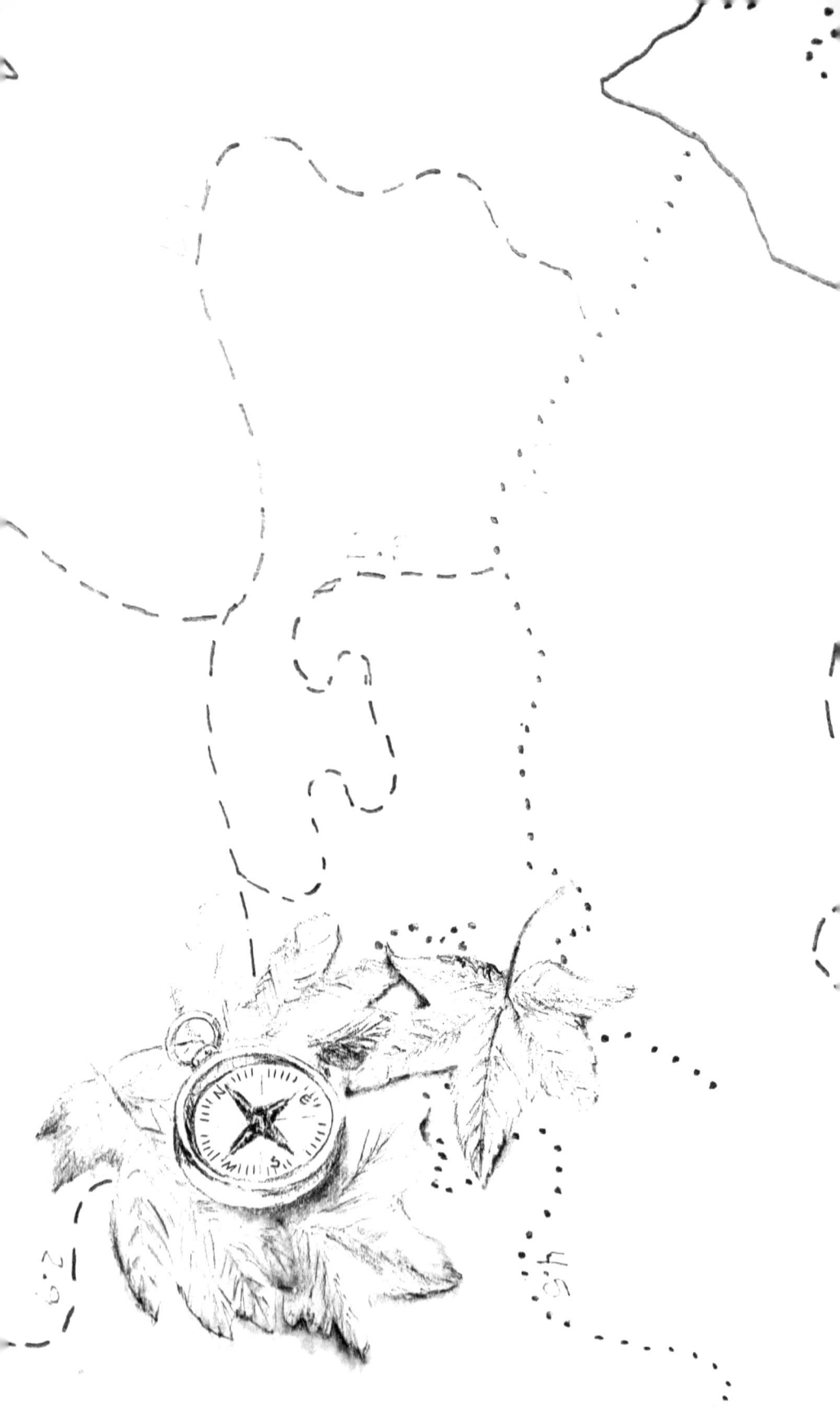

Chapter Eleven

Sherri's autopsy report lay open on the table, the same page staring up at him with brutal finality. The gory details were right there in black and white—information Fox had to absorb for the sake of the case.

Bile rose in the back of his throat as he read. The words were clinical, but the images they conjured were anything but. He was disgusted by what someone had done to a child and angry with himself for not being able to detach emotionally.

He shifted restlessly in his chair. Every instinct told him to close the file, but instead, he forced himself to read on, eyes scanning each neatly typed line. He took the violations, wounds, and cold medical descriptions in one sickening row at a time.

Years in the Bureau had trained him to process facts without reaction. Usually, he had no issue keeping his emotions on a tight leash. But when it came to kids...that was different.

Call him old-fashioned, but Fox believed every adult bore the duty to protect any child. So when he was forced to study the aftermath of someone who'd intentionally preyed on one, a cold rage burned in his gut.

He could feel his control slipping. Try as he might, he couldn't rein it in.

Fox began drumming his fingers on the tabletop—slow, steady, deliberate. The rhythmic tapping helped dull the heat in his chest. His mother had taught him the trick years ago after too many calls home from teachers concerned about his outbursts under pressure.

She'd enlisted his Uncle Tom, a child therapist, who'd shown Fox how to externalize stress—focus on the trigger, then tap in response to redirect the anxiety.

It had stuck.

Even now, all these years later, whenever a case threatened to pull him under, he fell back on that small, soothing habit. Tap. Tap. Tap. It helped. Barely.

The sudden buzz of his phone pulled him out of the spiral.

"Agent Anderson," he answered gruffly, grateful for the interruption. He'd welcome any excuse to close the file in front of him. Even if it was only for a few minutes of reprieve.

"Agent Anderson, this is Deputy Riggs. We just finished our interview with Susie Miller's mother. You're never going to believe what we found out," she said, her voice brimming with excitement.

Fox leaned back in his chair, already sensing her energy through the line. "All right, I'll bite. What did you find?"

"Guess which team the high school was playing the night before Susie was kidnapped."

Fox froze. "Don't tell me—Windsor Brooke High?"

Fox shook his head, a small rush of adrenaline spiking through him. It wasn't a smoking gun, but it was something. A tangible lead, finally. Up until now, the case had very few of those. This was a real thread they could pull.

"I don't know what it means," Riggs continued, her thoughts tumbling out, "but it has to mean something, right? This has to be the first real connection we've found. Do you think it was someone at the game? High school football's a big deal here. Not college-level, but still...Do you think it could've been a fan? Someone who saw Susie with her family?"

Reflexively, Fox tuned out Riggs's rambling and focused instead on what this new information could mean. Had a spectator spotted Susie in the stands? What were the odds someone followed her home and waited for the right moment to snatch her?

A flicker of elation stirred in his chest, but he tempered it quickly. This was no time for premature confidence. They were still miles from solving the case—but now, at least, they had a branch to shake and see what else might fall.

"Okay, here's what we need to do," he said, cutting Riggs off mid-sentence. "Talk to the high school. Find out if they keep any kind of attendee lists, season pass holders, volunteers, or even regulars who show up to every game."

"Got it. Unless something urgent comes up, we'll update you when we're back," Riggs said.

"Sounds good."

He ended the call and tossed his phone onto the pile of reports in front of him. Sherri's autopsy was momentarily forgotten as he crossed the room. Pulling a notecard from the stack, he scrawled **Windsor Brooke High – Football** in block letters and pinned it beneath the "New Lead" section of the case board.

The light clicking of keys drew his attention to the sheriff's surly assistant. "Sylvia, isn't it?" he asked, turning on his best good ol' boy charm. He propped a hip on the edge of her desk and flashed his trademark smile. "Any chance you could dig up the football schedule for Windsor Brooke High? Last two years."

Lifting her head, Sylvia stared at him, "When would you like to have the information?" she asked, pursing her lips.

"As soon as possible."

"I'll reach out after they get back from lunch," she said flatly, already turning back to her screen.

Fox nodded to the back of her head and tried not to let her obvious disdain bother him. He wasn't embarrassed to admit he wasn't used to women being cold to him. He never had trouble with the ladies. It didn't matter their age either. Old and young seemed to enjoy his company. Sylvia's standoffish behavior didn't make any sense.

His brow furrowed as he reached for his phone, just as it rang again, "This is Anderson."

"Hey, Anderson, Shane here. We just finished meeting with Emma Mathews' family. They had some interesting information to add to their previous statement."

"Really? What was that?" Fox strode to the case files, shoving the others aside until he unearthed Emma Mathews'.

"It turns out that Emma had planned to sneak out and meet a friend the night she was abducted. According to her sister, Emma had climbed out of the bedroom window just after their mother had checked on them."

"Why the hell are we just now hearing this?" Fox growled, raking a hand through his hair. "How long has the sheriff's department been sitting on this?" He could've strangled someone.

"The family said they just learned about it from their youngest daughter today. As it turns out, we weren't the first ones to talk with the family." Pausing for emphasis, Shane said, "Kate Millard spoke with them about an hour before we showed up. After leaving their house, she talked to the friend Emma was supposed to have met the night she went missing."

"Huh," Fox muttered. Looked like he'd be having another meeting with Kate Millard sooner than expected. "Is she still there?"

"No. We think she headed back to Windsor Brooke almost an hour ago. Do you want us to continue interviewing people down here? We thought about stopping by the friend's house too. Not sure if the girl's family will be willing to let us talk with her since Kate was just there, but thought it would be worth a try."

"Yes. Interview the friend and canvas the neighborhood again. See if anyone remembers seeing either of the girls the night in question."

"Will do."

Fox hung up the phone, reclining in the office chair he'd commandeered for his use. Kate Millard was proving to be just as intriguing as he'd expected. When they met, she claimed she was only trying to ease her friend's mind, but now it looked more like she was trying to track down the perpetrator herself.

At the pace she was working, it wouldn't surprise him if she reached the suspect before he did. And then what? What was she planning to do if she found them? He pictured the woman he'd met just hours ago—slim, lithe, delicate. Sexy. Not someone you'd imagine throwing a punch. She didn't strike him as the type to chase monsters, more silk than steel.

It would fall on him to figure out why Kate Millard was nosing around in his murder case, and he had no problem performing his civic duty. The idea of going toe-to-toe with her again had him rubbing his hands together in anticipation.

A glance at his watch told him he still had half an hour before she was likely to return to Windsor Brooke, just enough time to update the boards and grab a quick lunch from the bakery. The smell of fresh bread had been wafting through the air all day, and the temptation to sink his teeth into whatever was causing that mouthwatering scent was becoming harder to ignore.

Figuring this was another chance to grease the friendship wheel, he called out politely, "Hey Sylvia, I'm heading to the bakery for lunch. Want me to bring you anything?"

Without breaking stride, she waved a hand dismissively and kept typing.

Sighing at her cold shoulder, he figured maybe something sweet would soften her up. Some kind of chocolate dessert. If there was a better way to a woman's heart than chocolate, he didn't know it.

Whistling, he stepped out of the door. He was always happier when he had a plan.

Kate turned off Main and slipped down one of Windsor Brooke's winding side streets. Her store stood just behind the town square—prime real estate, thanks to the town's maze-like layout. Every road looped back to the center, and her cheerful shop sat right in the middle of it all.

She didn't need to stop in. Bridgette had things under control. But Kate couldn't help herself. The store was her anchor. A daily dose of normalcy in a world that was anything but.

She parked out back and unlocked the bright red door—her splash of rebellion in a town full of neutral tones. Even in a town like Windsor Brooke, she insisted the back door stay locked. You never really knew who the bad people were.

The quiet that greeted her as she stepped inside was troubling. Puzzled, Kate wove her way around piles of inventory stacked precariously throughout the back storage room, carefully skirting one particularly unstable tower she was sure would topple at the slightest provocation.

"Hello?" she called cautiously. "Where is everyone?"

"Up in the front window," Bridgette's slightly muffled voice called back. "What are you doing here? I thought you were on the hunt?" she added, teasing.

Kate rounded the last corner and found Bridget buried under a heap of throw blankets and some kind of gauzy fabric.

"What do we have here?" she asked, trying to stifle the laugh bubbling in her throat.

"Just got our shipment of throw blankets and sheer window panels for the winter stock. I was in the middle of hanging the sheers when the pile of blankets started to fall. Naturally, I tried to catch them, lost my balance, and—well, you can see how that ended."

Bridgette ended her explanation with a dramatic sigh. "Now that you are here, you can help me set up the display." She held up an armful of blankets. "Grab that stack and set it over by the shelf."

Kate bit her lip to hide her grin. "Right away, boss," she said, lifting the throws over her head to clear the way and offer a hand.

"Glad you know your place," Bridgette chirped as she reached up, hoisting herself onto her feet, letting the sheers fall into a pile on the floor. "When you finish with those, you can clean this mess up next," Bridgette teased as she worked on making some semblance of order out of her mess.

Picking up the stack of throws was easier said than done—half of them seemed woven together with sheer panels in some kind of malformed braid. After a few minutes and a minor tug-of-war, Kate finally managed to refold the throws and stack them neatly on the shelf.

"Come hold the ladder—and this panel—while I see if I can get this curtain rod in place," Bridgette instructed.

"Right away, boss," Kate laughed. It felt good to laugh—really laugh.

"Hold still," Bridgette called, wobbling precariously on the top step of the store's only ladder. "Just there—okay, hold it."

Watching the scene unfold with a mix of amusement and mild alarm, Kate made a mental note to pick up a taller ladder the next time she headed into the city.

"They're all done. Well, what do you think?" Bridgette beamed triumphantly.

"This looks fantastic! I love the colors—where did you find these?" Kate asked, running her fingers through the silky sheers Bridgette had hung so artfully in the window.

Waving a hand dismissively, Bridgette replied, "Oh, you know the one wholesaler I talked you into last year? This is from their new catalog."

Stepping out of the window display, Kate looked back at Bridgette, "Well, you certainly have great taste."

"Thank you. I do, don't I?" Bridgette said with a confident grin. "Let's get the throws arranged on the chair and this shelf. I'll grab the accessories I was thinking of adding to the display."

Bridgette scurried around the store, returning with her arms full of various trinkets—each surprisingly complementary.

"Now it's finished," she declared, stepping back to admire their work.

"Let's go out front and look at our handiwork," she added, grabbing Kate by the hand and dragging her outside.

"It looks perfect, Bridgette. You've outdone yourself again."

Bridgette beamed with satisfaction and nodded.

Kate's world froze. The hairs on the back of her neck tingled with awareness. Someone was watching her.

Casually, she lifted her chin and turned slightly, first to the left, then to the right. She studied the faces around her using her peripheral vision and the reflection in the store window. None stood out. No one seemed to be paying her any attention.

But someone was there. She could feel it. The prickling weight of a predator's gaze.

She reached for Bridgette's hand and gently tugged her toward the door.

"Bridgette, let's head back inside. I'm going to grab my purse, then run over to the bakery and get us a treat. A little reward for all our hard work," she said lightly, almost pushing Bridgette ahead of her.

"We really did a great job," she added, keeping her tone casual, not wanting to alarm her friend. What she needed were her sunglasses—then she could search without drawing attention.

"You don't need to do that; it isn't a big deal," Bridgette said with a wave.

"Oh, I insist," Kate smiled, masking the tension behind her words. "I'll be right back."

Slipping on her sunglasses, Kate stepped back outside, briskly scanning the square. A quick headcount told her there were about seventy-five adults milling about, ranging in age from early twenties to late seventies. No one appeared to be watching her. No one seemed out of place.

But the feeling hadn't gone away.

Someone was still out there—watching. Lurking.

Who was it?

The walk to the bakery took less than three minutes, not nearly enough time to study everyone. Still, she found comfort in knowing she'd have a new angle on the walk back. There was still a chance to spot them.

The bakery door swung open as she stepped inside.

"Hi, Sue; how is business going?" Kate said brightly.

Sue looked up from behind the counter and smiled. "Hi, Kate. Oh, you know, same old, same old." She grinned. "That FBI fellow came in earlier today. *Mmm,* he is a looker."

She licked her lips dramatically. "If I were twenty years younger, I might have to chase that one down myself."

Sue was the town flirt, sweet, bold, and famous for sneaking donut holes to the young boys who passed by her shop.

Scrunching her nose, Kate scanned the pastry display.

"I met him earlier, too. Seemed he was a little... stiff."

"Stiff?" Sue raised an eyebrow and gave Kate a *get real* look.

"Are we talking about the same man? I gave him a free donut, a muffin, *and* an eclair just because he smiled at me. Melted me to my toes."

Kate chuckled and shook her head. "Sue, you're hopeless. If you keep giving everything away, how are you going to stay in business?"

"Oh, honey, I'll just make more, of course!" Sue said with a booming laugh.

Then, playfully, "So, what can I get you today? And don't worry, I'll make you pay."

"Two of your blueberry muffins to go, please."

"You got it. Let me bag those up for you."

"Thanks, Sue. You're the best."

"That I am, my dear. That I am."

The moment Kate stepped outside again, she knew.

They were gone.

Her stomach sank a little. She'd hoped to spot them from a different angle on the return trip. Less guarded now, she scanned the square again, trying to recall who was missing.

Maybe ten people were gone. Three of the men she'd noted earlier among them.

It could've been a coincidence. But maybe not.

Maybe she'd swing by their homes later and see if any whistles went off.

The bench in the town square was ideally situated. He had a clear sightline of the sheriff's office, Miss Kate Millard's Store, and the playground. Sitting in the shade on a beautiful day, he had no complaints.

He watched Kate work in her store window alongside that kook, Bridgette. Watching her now didn't thrill him the way it had when he'd seen her in the woods. A shame—he'd hoped she'd become a new source of amusement.

Turning, he let his eyes settle on sweet little Chloe playing on the swings.

"Oh Chloe, sweet Chloe, won't you play with me, Chloe, sweet Chloe, won't you be mine..." he sang to himself, humming with delight. It would be time soon.

Movement caught his eye—Kate stepping out of the front door to admire her window display. He leaned forward, watching her back. He saw the moment she knew he was there.

Oh yes, there it was, that zing of anticipation. The jolt of one predator sensing another. He shifted in his seat, nearly giddy.

She was perfect.

Not yet, though. Chloe had to come first. He needed Chloe. He only wanted Kate. And that meant she could wait.

Like a siren's call, his eyes returned to Chloe. She leaped from the swing and ran to her mother, turning to wave as she left.

Soon, Chloe. Very soon.

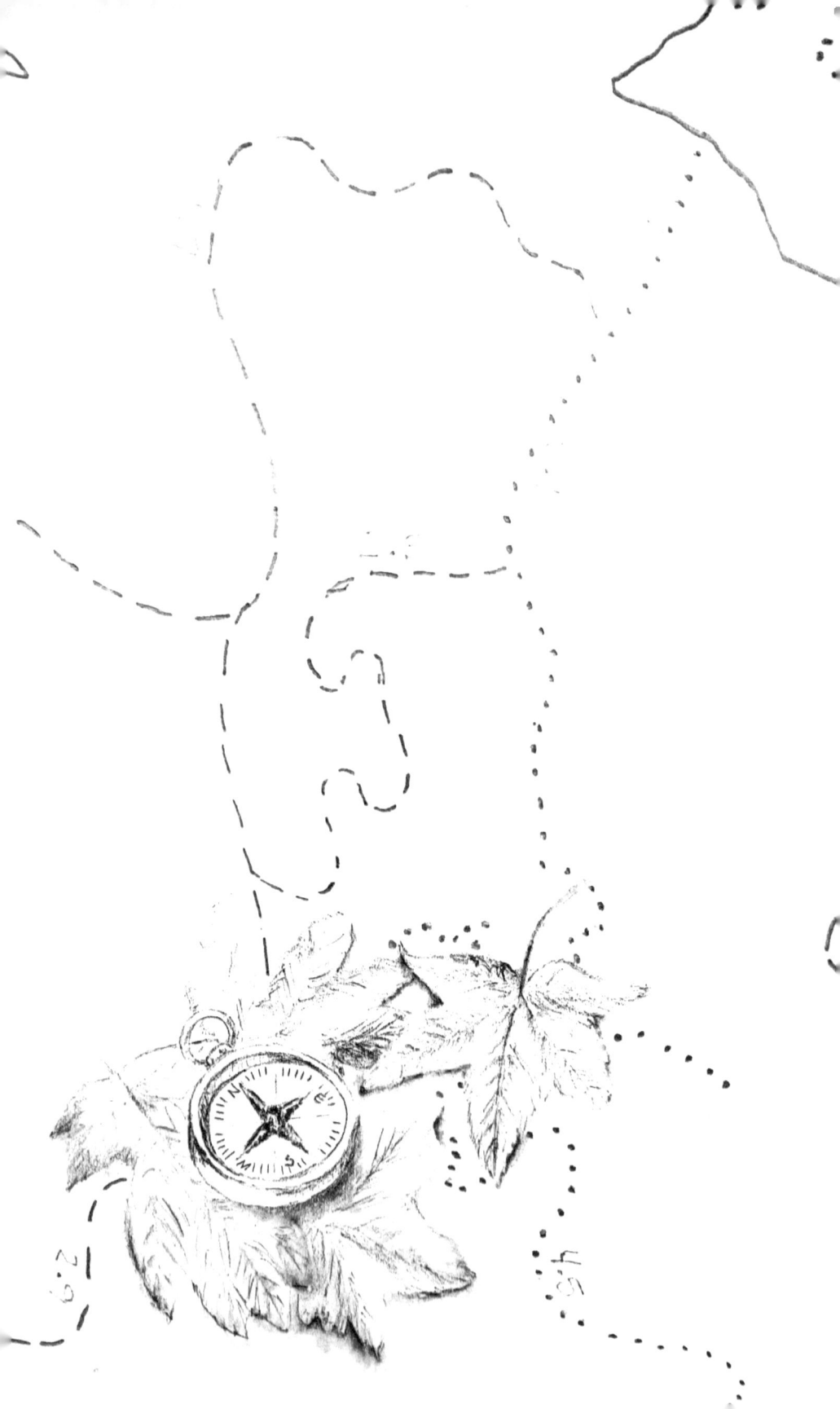

Chapter Twelve

F ox placed a chocolate éclair on the edge of Sylvia's desk, his peace offering still untouched fifteen minutes later. A brief flicker of delight was on her face before she quickly masked it. Then she nodded a thank you and turned back to her work without so much as peeking in the bag. The lack of reaction was a bit disappointing, but he wasn't ready to admit defeat just yet.

"Sylvia," he said, perching on the corner of her desk, with his most earnest tone, "do you have an address for Kate Millard?"

Sylvia's fingers paused over the keyboard before responding in her usual clipped way. "Yes, I'll print it out for you."

"Great, I appreciate it," Fox said, flashing his most charming grin.

The office door banged open, bouncing against the office wall. Turning toward the sound, Fox watched as a young man sauntered in. He looked around eighteen, muscular, an athlete probably, neatly dressed, face carved with sharp lines better suited for a sculpture. "Hi, Mom," he called cheerfully, though the smile didn't quite reach his eyes.

Fox blinked. *Mom?*

He glanced at Sylvia, who actually responded. Reason told him he shouldn't be surprised—there'd been no reason to assume she wasn't a mother—but still. Looking between them, he struggled to find a resemblance. Same eyes, maybe. That was it.

Sylvia glanced up, and for the first time since he'd arrived in town, her expression softened into something almost warm. "Hi Tuck, what are you up to today?"

"Not much, just walked around the square a bit; I'm heading to Mathew's to work on some homework, then I'll head home." He reached down with his left hand and fiddled with her stapler, squeezing and releasing so that tiny squished staples littered her desk.

Her lips thinned as she reached for the stapler, plucking it from his hands and tucking it away in her top drawer. Without a word, she proceeded to pick up every used staple off her desk and drop them into the trash.

"Okay, dinner will be on the table at six. Remember how your father doesn't like to wait?" she said with a motherly stare. Fox bit back a grin. He knew that look all too well. His mother had given him the same one countless times over the years.

"Yes, Mom, I won't be late, promise." Fox arched a brow at the condescension in the kid's tone. Sylvia didn't even blink.

Sylvia smiled softly at him, "Okay, then. Have a good time. Be a good boy."

"Love you." He said as he walked out the door.

Fox walked over to Sylvia, leaning with one hip on her desk, and watched as the young man left the office. "I didn't know you had a son," he said casually." He looks like a fine young man. Is he a senior in high school?"

"You never asked, nor is it any of your business. My private life is mine alone." Standing, Sylvia walked around her desk, indicating she was through discussing her personal life or perhaps her son.

"Before you get too far, did you happen to print out Kate Millard's address for me?"

"Yes, it is right here." She squeezed past him, moving quickly to a stack of papers near the edge of her desk.

A faint flush crept up her neck as she stepped back.

Without a word, she crossed to the computer. The printer hummed to life. Moments later, she handed him a warm sheet of paper.

Fox said over his shoulder, "Thank you, Sylvia; if any of the deputies make it back to the office while I am out, let them know I want to debrief with everyone, but only if it is before seven tonight. If not, we will meet first thing in the morning." He said on his way out, "And will you call me if anyone shows up while I am out?" Glancing back at her, he saw her nod and concluded she had heard him.

With the door swinging shut behind him, he relished the feeling of excitement building. Finally, he was heading out to meet with Kate. This was one interview he couldn't wait to get started.

Kate Millard's house had turned out to be surprisingly hard to find. What should have been a quick drive from town took twice as long, thanks to winding roads, dense brush, and more than a few wrong turns. When Fox pulled into her driveway, irritation was buzzing beneath his skin.

The house, however, was unexpected. A two-story mix of wood and stone, its front garden was wild with vines and flowers. Deep green shutters framed large windows, and a small balcony offered a cozy seating area that looked almost romantic, especially on a cold winter night.

Fox eyed the porch swing on his way up the steps—comfy cushion, inviting pillows. His mind, unhelpfully, offered up a few pleasant scenarios involving Kate and that swing.

He knocked twice on the door, then stepped back to wait, bemused to find his thoughts still circling back to the swing.

Fox scowled at the still-closed door. What in the hell was taking her so long? He was sure she would have been home by now.

After a few more minutes, he knocked again, this time harder.

He had just lowered his arm when the door flew open. Kate stood in the doorway, one hand on her hip.

"What do you want?" she snapped.

He lifted an eyebrow. "Well, hello to you, too," he mocked, grinning at her angry face.

Her eyes snapped with ire. In this light, he could see just how vivid they were, deep green, flecked with gold.

"Aren't you going to invite me in?" Fox asked.

"Why would I do that?" Kate shot back, shifting to block more of the doorway. "I already answered your questions earlier today. I don't see what more there is to discuss."

"Don't you?" He arched a quizzical brow. "I thought maybe we could talk about what you learned today from your visit with Emma's family."

Her eyes widened in surprise. She hadn't anticipated him finding out so quickly about the information-gathering trip.

"Oh. Well, I assume someone from the sheriff's department contacted you." She sighed something between resignation and a groan and stepped back to let him in.

"Might as well get this over with," she muttered.

Fox chuckled at her response; he didn't know whether to be offended or amused. He followed her into the front sitting room, his eyes drawn—unapologetically—to the sway of her hips.

"Have a seat, Agent Anderson. Would you like something to drink?"

"Sure, water would be great. Oh, and call me Fox," he said, flashing a smile. "Feels like we'll be seeing a lot more of each other before this is all over."

She stiffened, her eyes widening.

He gave her one of his most charming smiles. "Might as well be on a first-name basis, don't you think, Kate?"

She huffed, pure impatience etched across her face. "All right, Fox, was it? What kind of name is that, anyway? Last I checked, it was a small animal," she jibed.

"Why don't you go grab that water, and I will tell you all about why my mama thought *Fox* was the name for me," he said, easygoing as ever.

While Kate disappeared into the kitchen, Fox let his gaze drift around the house. He was curious about her—what kind of woman goes to such lengths for a friend? Her motives didn't quite add up.

The decor was typical, nothing flashy. But his eyes snagged on a trophy perched on the mantle, first place in sportsman shooting. That gave him pause. It's not totally surprising for a small Midwestern town, but still...not what he expected.

Kate returned and set a glass of water on the table beside him, then took a seat—noticeably at the far end of the couch. He didn't comment on it. Instead, he took a slow sip, using the moment to study her.

She'd slipped behind a mask, calm and unreadable. But Fox saw through it, or at least wanted to. Was she hiding something from him? Or perhaps he made her nervous for an entirely different reason.

"My mother's a conservationist," Fox began. "Loves animals, thinks man is the root of all evil. So, in tribute to her beloved creatures, she named us after her favorites."

"Buck is the oldest, then my sister, Raven. I'm next, and my baby sister's Dove." He shrugged, grinning. "Personally, I think I lucked out. My dad only had two boy-name options to pick from, and *Fox* beats *Buck* any day. Don't you think?"

Kate tried to stifle a laugh, covering her mouth with her hand.

"Agreed," she said, smothering a laugh. "At least your mom didn't go with Bunny or Birdie for your sisters. That would've set them on a very specific life path."

"Yeah, people are always a little awkward when they first hear our names, but after a while, they usually get used to it—and stop teasing us." Fox chuckled. "My brother figured out early on that he'd need thicker skin than most to survive school with a name like Buck. Now he's a fire chief in Baltimore, married with three daughters, all named after his wife's side of the family. Much to my mother's disappointment, not a single animal name in the bunch."

Fascinated, Kate leaned in a little. "What about your sisters? What are they doing with their namesake?"

"Raven is married and living with her family in a suburb about an hour from my parents' house. She likes to say they are close enough to visit but far enough away to avoid drop-ins. She has three kids as well, two boys and one girl. She, however, embraced my mother's love for animals and decided to continue the tradition; her boys are named Lark and Colt. Their little girl is a spoiled little spitfire named Vixen, but we call her Vixy. She looks like an angel but raises more hell than her brothers."

Kate smiled at the image. "And what about Dove? Where did she end up?"

Fox gave a small laugh.

"Dove? Being the baby, she'd decided life was too short to settle down. She only dates guys who spoil her, and when she gets bored, she moves on. I'm pretty sure she's cycled through more relationships than the rest of us put together. The only upside is she leaves the boy toys behind for holidays, those are strictly family-only. Mom thinks she'll figure it out eventually, but...I'm not holding my breath."

"Wow," Kate said, eyebrows raised. "She sounds like a handful. I am surprised she can find men who are okay with her treating them like that."

"When you look like Dove," Fox said with a shrug, "it doesn't take much to get people to do what you want."

"Oh?" Kate lifted a perfectly arched brow. "And what does she look like?"

Leaning back, Fox grinned.

"A lot like me, actually. Her hair's longer, or it was last time I saw her." He shifted, draping an arm along the back of the couch to face Kate more fully. "She's got blue eyes, and she likes to work out every day. Says she's making an investment in her future."

His pulse quickened at the sound of her lithe chuckle. He wanted to hear it again—wanted her to speak in that husky, rich voice that made his stomach tighten and his heart lift. "So that's my family," he said, then asked lightly, "How about yours?"

The shift was instant. The light in her eyes vanished like a match burning out. She sank back into the cushion, her body retreating as if the couch could shield her from the conversation.

"Sorry," she said, voice clipped. "Nothing to tell. They died in a car accident when I was a teenager. I was the only one who made it." She squirmed in her seat, brushing it off with a shrug that didn't quite land.

Fox froze.

Well, shit. How had he not known her family was gone? Just when he had her opening up, he went and shoved his foot in his mouth.

"I'm sorry to hear that," Fox said. "I lost my grandparents on my dad's side in a car accident. It's hard to lose someone you love—almost unbearable when you're young."

He lifted the glass to his lips, searching for a lighter topic. She seemed to enjoy hearing about others, maybe he could steer the conversation that way.

"What's up with Sylvia?" he asked, a crooked grin forming. "Does she have a stick up her ass, or what?"

Kate's eyes snapped up to meet his.

"I don't know," she said cautiously. "Everyone who's been around town for twenty-plus years says she's always been like that. No one's ever gotten close to her. I've heard she grabs the occasional lunch with a few acquaintances, but otherwise, she keeps to herself."

She paused, then added, "Some people say her husband's controlling. There are even rumors about abuse, but...I've never seen any signs of it."

Kate shrugged, letting the explanation trail off.

Fox was pleased to see the spark return to her eyes. It was faint, but it was there. If he could just ask the right questions, maybe she'd open up again. Let him see her.

That first genuine smile had stunned him. It had taken his breath away. Now, it was like a high he needed to chase for reasons he didn't quite understand; truly seeing her had become the most important thing.

He knew he should ask about the case, but at this moment, there was no case. There was only Kate—and the quiet flame in her he was dying to see burning bright again. "Tell me about the sheriff. What are your thoughts about him?"

"Sheriff Jacobs?" She questioned, looking at her hands. "He's a good man. I don't see him much, but the town seems to like him."

"Do you think he does his job well?" His tone was casual, his eyes searching. "Ever hear anything that might suggest he's not quite what he seems?"

"Like what?" she asked, tilting her head.

"I don't know. Does he seem like the kind of guy who really cares about what goes on in town? Or someone who'd keep things quiet if it meant protecting his position?"

"Honestly? I'm not sure." She picked up a pillow and fiddled with the corner. Her expression grew distant, pensive. "He's always struck me as your typical egotistical alpha male. He loves the status that comes with the badge. I doubt he'd risk that willingly."

The more they talked, the more he could see her body relaxing again. With each easy exchange, she opened up a little more. Leaning back, he stretched out his legs, surveying the room, not just as an agent now but as a man curious about the woman behind the walls. He liked the space and appreciated that there was plenty of room to stretch out.

"I had some time to talk with Deputy Shane," he said, "but I have only met the others for a few minutes. Anything I should know? Strengths I should be tapping into?"

If Kate thought his questions were strange, she didn't show it. She kept fiddling with the pillow in her lap, her expression serene, as if they were discussing nothing more interesting than the weather.

"Sina Riggs is their best interrogator," Kate replied. "But Johnson usually gets the credit because they're always partnered together."

"Why doesn't she call him out?"

"Because it's a man's world," Kate said bluntly. "The last time she spoke up about how things were being run, they accused her of menstruating. Needless to say, she learned her lesson. Now, she only gives her opinion if asked directly."

Her mouth tightened in a grim line, hardening her expression. "She's sharp, though. I've always thought her input was excellent. Not that they let her share it all that often."

Fox made a mental note to ask Riggs directly during their next debriefing. He was curious to see if Kate's assessment was accurate.

"Good to know," he said. "What about Johnson? Doesn't sound like much of a team player."

Kate shook her head. "It's not that. He just seems...clueless. I don't even think he realizes what he's doing. Probably thinks it's all part of being a team."

Fox raised a brow. "You really think he's that oblivious?"

"Maybe. That's just the vibe I get. More of a dumb jock than a diabolical mastermind."

He chuckled. "You're good at reading people. So, what kind of impression did Emma's family leave you with today?"

"I assume you already know Emma wasn't taken from her bed," she said, her tone suddenly distant. "She snuck out that night."

Fox noted the shift instantly. Her body closed off, her voice clipped. He frowned. What had he said? All he wanted was her insight, not to put her on the defensive again. He was beginning to hate the tightly drawn expression she wore like a cloak.

"What made you go question the family?" he asked lightly, trying to keep things easy.

"Same reason you would've," she replied. "It didn't make sense for Emma's file to be grouped with the others. Her case didn't fit the pattern."

"I agree. It was out of character for our guy." He leaned forward slightly. "How'd you get the sister to open up?"

"I asked if they usually slept with the window open. She said no, their parents didn't allow it. If that's true, someone would've had to break in—noise, glass. That would've woken the girls, at least."

Fox's frustration flared. He was tired of this push-pull game. Every time he got close, she shut down. He wanted to see her fire again, the passion she kept hidden behind that carefully constructed wall.

There might as well have been oceans between them for all the distance she managed to create in a single breath. And why the hell did it bother him so much?

It shouldn't matter. As long as he solved the case and she stayed out of his way, everything would be fine.

Only it didn't feel fine. It felt like something vital was slipping through his fingers, something he couldn't quite grasp, no matter how tightly he reached for it.

His gaze dropped to the pillow she held clasped against her chest, using it like a shield between them. He scowled. The joke was on her, she didn't need a pillow. She was doing a damn good job of keeping him at arm's length all on her own.

"Were her parents surprised to hear she had snuck out?" he asked, the bite in his tone unmistakable. Let her be offended. Let her glare. He was too damn tired of pretending he didn't care.

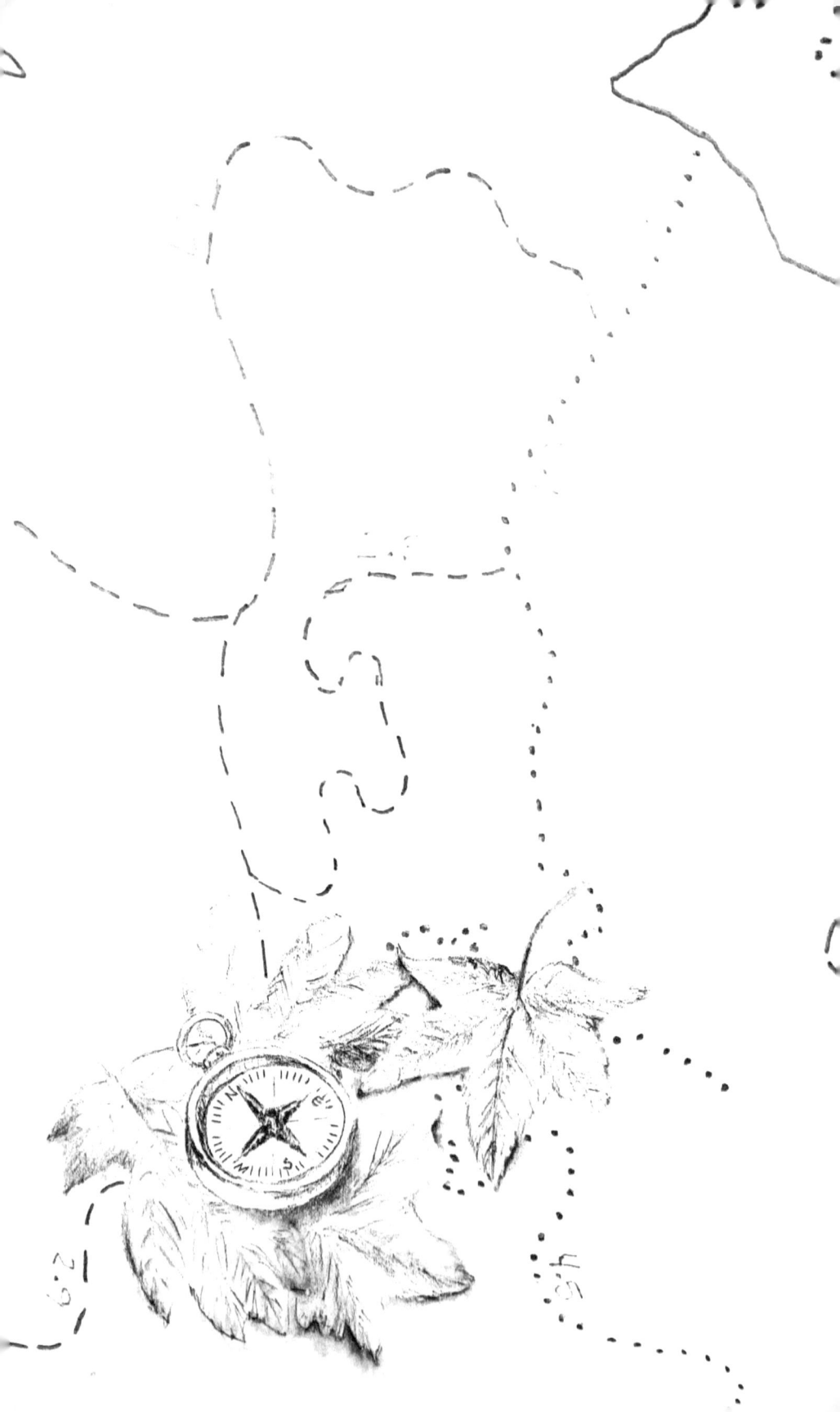

Chapter Thirteen

There it was—the real reason he had come. Kate had almost forgotten, slipping into a natural rhythm with him, letting herself forget. That was dangerous.

She knew he'd be a temptation from the start, but she hadn't expected to *want* to give in. That was worse than Fox himself. She needed to keep him at a distance. Otherwise, she might lose more than just control; she might lose herself.

His scent reached her—woodsy, musky, undeniably male—and unsettled her more than she wanted to admit. But worse still was her heart's reaction. It was racing. Skittering in her chest with excitement, she shouldn't *be* excited. Not by this man. Not by a stranger with a badge and the power to ruin everything she'd built.

She could feel his gaze, heavy and warm, and finally looked up, meeting his eyes. Everything she was trying to hide—the uncertainty, the confusion—was right there for him to see. She couldn't stop it. Couldn't hide it.

The silence between them stretched long. It couldn't have been more than a few seconds, but it felt like hours. She was wide open and exposed in that space. And she'd never felt more vulnerable than she did now, sitting with a man she barely knew.

Panic flared through her in white-hot pulses. She took a slow, steadying breath, forcing herself to push back the fear. Years of training kicked in. Focus. Regain control. She would play along. Bide her time.

"Well, were they?" Fox prodded, a taunting smile tugging at the corner of his mouth.

"Yes, of course, they were surprised," she finally answered. "Emma's mother was like a zombie the whole time I was there. The only moment she showed emotion, was when Ashley, Emma's little sister, said she'd snuck out to meet a friend."

"Did you talk with her friend? The one she was supposed to meet?"

"Of course I did," Kate muttered, glaring at him.

"And?" Fox prompted.

She rolled her eyes. "Why do I have to do all the work for you? Go talk to her yourself. Draw your own conclusions."

"Why would I do that," he said, flashing her a dazzling smile, "when I can get everything I need right here, right now—from you?"

To her dismay, her mouth curved into a matching smile. Laughing despite herself, Kate shook her head. He's more dangerous than she realized. He could make her laugh.

The irony wasn't lost on her. After a life built on solitude, keeping others at arm's length, Fox had slipped past her defenses with almost no effort. She hadn't even realized how close he'd gotten until it was too late.

"All right, you win," she conceded. "If I tell you what I learned, will you leave?"

"If that's what you want," Fox said easily.

"Of course it is," she snapped, irritation covering the mess of feelings underneath.

Ignoring her tone, he said, "First impressions of the friend's home. Family. Go."

"Okay...The house wasn't nearly as well-kept as the Matthews' place. The older brother answered, probably no older than twenty. Cute kid, kind of suave, devil-may-care. Had no problem letting me talk to his sister."

Kate shifted, leaning back slightly. "Sara, Emma's friend, came to the door like it was nothing. Said she and Emma had planned to sneak out and meet at the end of the street, then go catch fireflies in the field next to the school."

His brow lifted. "On their own?"

"Seems so. They were meeting up after bedtime. I asked what time exactly, and she said hers was nine. Emma's was probably earlier. That gave our guy a clear window. He could've taken Emma without anyone knowing. Sara would show up, think Emma bailed, and just go home. No questions asked."

"Did they tell anyone what they were planning?" Fox asked, musing aloud, "I wonder how our guy knew she would even be outside. Was it just a coincidence, or had he been following her for a while?"

"I'm not sure how he found her; I know Sara's brother heard them talking about it. He had a friend over; evidently, they had a good laugh at the girls' expense."

"Who was this friend? How long after they had overheard the girls talking was Emma's disappearance?"

"According to the brother, it was about a week. Supposedly, the friend had gone back to school the next day." Reflecting on the earlier conversation, Kate frowned at the memory, "It was odd." She admitted, "Davey wouldn't tell me the name of his friend. Even when I asked for it."

"Deputy Shane and Marcos canvassed the neighborhood, asking if anyone saw anything. Now that we know she wasn't taken from her room, our search has expanded. I'll have them talk to the brother again. Maybe a badge will motivate the correct response."

Fox turned, resting a hand on his knee, his impulsive nature taking the reins.

"I haven't seen much of Windsor Brooke," he said, then added with a wry smile, "Not that there's much to see, I imagine. What would you say to having dinner with me? Afterward, maybe you could show me what Windsor Brooke has to offer in terms of nightlife."

He watched as she slowly raised her eyes to meet his. Green. Vibrant. Beautiful. And staring at him like he'd grown two heads.

She snorted, an inelegant sound that cut through the silence like a bell.

"What?" he asked, cocking his head. "Do you have plans? We could do tomorrow night if that—"

She burst into laughter before he could finish.

She was mysterious, an enigma he couldn't quite figure out. And he liked the mystery she hid behind. However, he didn't like the loud, unrestrained laughter coming from her now. His frown deepened as he sank back into the cushion.

Kate tried to stifle a giggle, but one look at him sent her into another fit of laughter. He scowled at her glowing, laughing mouth. She looked radiant, but he wasn't particularly fond of being the punchline.

"Sorry," she managed between giggles. "I haven't had a good laugh in ages. You'd have to be crazy to think I would go out with you. You were joking, right?"

He arched a brow. "Why would I be joking?"

"Because...you're a fed."

"And?"

She sobered fast. Almost too fast. His eyes narrowed as a flush crept up her neck. Whoever Kate Millard really was, she was a puzzle. One he couldn't quite figure out. But that wasn't about to stop him.

After all, he thought wryly, he was never able to resist a puzzle, especially one as challenging as hers.

Despite his best efforts to keep things professional, Fox knew it was a lost cause. Kate Millard was a riddle he couldn't wait to solve.

Just as he was about to ask what she meant, his phone rang—a shrill, grating noise that made his jaw tighten.

"Someone had better be dead," he muttered, digging the phone from his pocket. He watched helplessly as Kate took the opportunity to slip away into the kitchen.

Glancing at the screen, he growled, "What?"

"Oh, sorry," Shane's hesitant voice crackled through. "Sylvia told me to let you know we're back at the office. Is this... not a good time?"

No, damn it. This couldn't have been a worse time. But duty was duty, and nothing took precedence over the job.

"No, it's fine," he said, masking his irritation. "Are Riggs and Johnson back yet?"

"Yes, sir. Just drove in."

"Good. I'll be there in half an hour."

He ended the call and slipped his phone back into his pocket. Then, with a glint in his eye and a renewed sense of purpose, he went to find Kate.

It didn't take long to find her. She was in the kitchen, scrubbing a pan with more vigor than necessary.

"Hey, sorry about that," Fox said casually, leaning against the counter, his long legs stretched out in front of him. He kept his posture intentionally relaxed and non-threatening. He'd made some headway with her—though not nearly as much as he wanted—and he wasn't about to lose any ground now.

"The deputies are back at the office," he explained. "I need to debrief with them, see if they turned up anything useful."

Kate hadn't looked at him since he walked into the kitchen. Her back was stiff, her movements mechanical. Fox wouldn't be surprised if her expression had returned to that same cool, unreadable mask.

He sighed. "I have to go. Will you be home later? Can I come back after the meeting?"

"I don't think that's a great idea," she said, her voice carefully neutral. "We should probably call it a night. I'm sure you'll have plenty to do...figuring out your next steps and all that."

Fox watched her try to empty her face of emotion, walling herself off again. He knew if he gave her too much space, she'd lock him out completely.

"I should only be a couple of hours," he said, ignoring the flicker of panic in her eyes. "I still have questions. I'll be back, and I'll bring dinner."

There was no room for debate. Her lips pressed into a stubborn line, but she didn't argue. He could tell she wanted to slam the door in his face, but she wouldn't. Not with him being a fed. Whatever that meant to her, he planned to use it, at least until he figured out what exactly she was so afraid of.

Stupid, stupid! How could she be so foolish? Sure, he was hot, but he was FBI, and her lifestyle wasn't exactly compatible with law enforcement.

She needed to breathe. Her life was fine the way it was. She had everything she needed; what she didn't need was some agent swaggering in, throwing his weight around, complicating things.

Kate dried the pan she'd been scrubbing, shoved it in the cupboard, and hung the towel with a sharp snap. She needed to get back to work. She didn't have time to waste thinking about Agent Fox Anderson.

Up in the loft—her makeshift case room—she curled into her favorite chair, tugged her worn blanket up to her chin, and tried to focus.

Okay, what did she know about the perpetrator?

Her mind wandered almost instantly, drifting back to Fox. The curve of his mouth. Those vivid, electric eyes.

Exactly the direction she shouldn't be thinking.

When she first opened the door to his persistent knocking, she wasn't surprised to see him standing there. She'd watched him from the loft window—saw him drive up, get out, and walk to her door.

Instead of answering right away, she waited, hoping he might give up and leave. Cowardly? Maybe. But he rattled her, which hadn't happened in a long time.

Of course, he didn't leave. He just knocked louder. Harder. Longer. Until she had no choice but to give in and open the door.

Squaring her shoulders, she steeled herself for the confrontation and put on her game face.

Much to her dismay, the cold shoulder wasn't working. Fox saw right through her, leaving her with no room to maneuver.

It was embarrassing to admit, even to herself, that she didn't have much experience in this area. Her last kiss had been right after high school, so long ago she'd nearly forgotten what it felt like. What to do, even. Those innocent kisses of youth hadn't prepared her for this.

Fox was a man who knew what he wanted. And Kate had no doubt he'd expect more than she was ready to give.

Some women used their bodies as weapons. She never had. That line mattered. She wanted to walk away from this life clean if she ever could. Until Fox, she'd never been tempted to cross it.

If she ever chose to be with someone, it would be for life, not out of convenience, not to satisfy a passing desire.

Fox was just here for the case. Once it was closed, he'd be gone. She doubted he was looking for anything beyond a good time.

The smart thing would be to end this now—before feelings and desires became obstacles they couldn't afford.

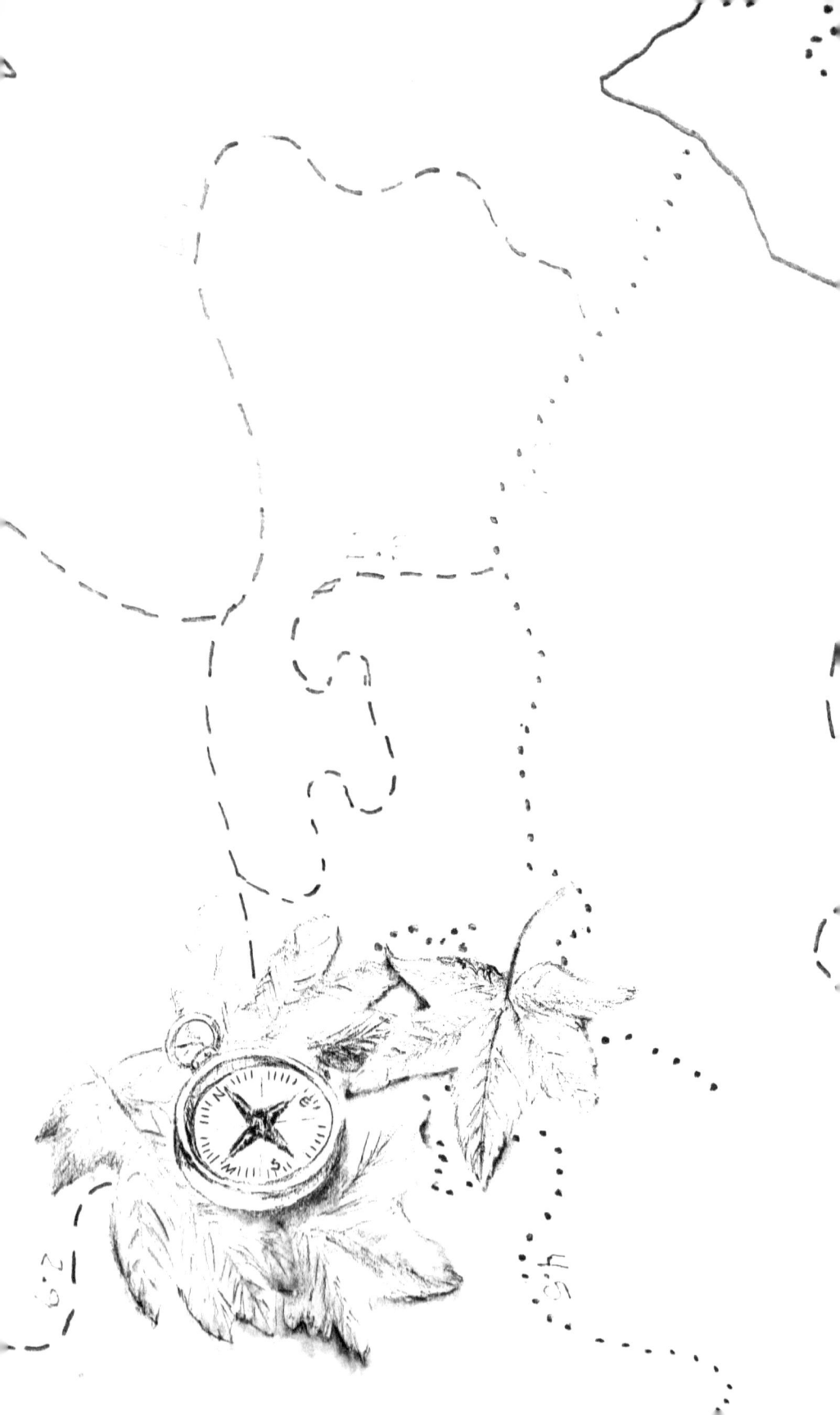

Chapter Fourteen

F ox walked into the Windsor Brook Sheriff's Office and, for the first time, took in the entire staff. It was underwhelming.

The sheriff stood apart from the team—a lone figure who made it clear that, although he was in charge, he didn't consider himself part of the crew. More politician than a police officer, Fox suspected he'd toss anyone under the bus long before admitting his role if things went sideways.

Shane, by contrast, was adequate—good enough but lacking the backbone necessary for this line of work.

Then there was Johnson, the youngest deputy, maybe twenty-five, with a baby face and an easy smile. Kate had called him a jock without a brain. Fox wasn't ready to agree—or disagree. Time will tell.

Marcos was middle-aged and quiet. He didn't seem to have much to say and nodded in response to any question directed at him. Fox could only hope he'd give an actual explanation if asked directly.

Riggs, however, was different. As the only female deputy, she had a knack for detective work. In a brief phone call, she sounded genuinely eager and committed. In a big city, her promotion might have been a given within a few years. But here in Windsor Brook, the only higher post was Sheriff, and that chair was occupied for the foreseeable future.

As Fox approached, the room buzzed—deputies talking over one another, their words colliding in a tangle of excitement.

"Let's begin." He sat at the head of the table, pulling out his notepad and pen. "Deputies, what've we got?" He scanned each face, waiting for someone to take the lead.

"I'll go first," Riggs said. "After speaking with the first victim's mother, we found out the high school her daughter's team was playing that night was Windsor Brook High. That detail wasn't in the original case file."

Fox raised a brow. "Any idea why it was left out?"

He let his gaze travel around the room, lingering on Sheriff Jacobs, whose eyes had gone flat and hard.

"We think it was considered common knowledge at the time, something no one thought to include."

"Wait a damn minute," Sheriff Jacobs snapped, rising from his chair, "I hope you aren't suggesting a football player is responsible for these missing girls, Riggs."

"No, sir," Riggs replied evenly. "No one's accusing a high school student. But football's a major event around here—big crowds, lots of out-of-towners. Maybe a parent, a staff member, or even a regular fan is involved. Or maybe the connection means nothing. But it's worth checking out, don't you think?"

She held his gaze, a quiet challenge in her eyes. Fox noted how her jaw had set—not disrespectful, just firm. She was making it clear: the case came first. Not Jacobs' legacy.

Clearing his throat, he tugged at his collar before finally answering, "No, of course not. I just want us to be careful, no sense in causing problems that don't need to be caused."

"Okay, let's get back on track." Fox turned to Sylvia. "I asked her to compile a list of football games the high school played over the last two years. Let's compare it to the victim timeline and see if there are any overlaps."

He held out his hand as Sylvia passed him a stack of papers, each listing game dates, locations, and team rosters. Fox thanked her as he held the list out to Riggs.

"Riggs, I want you to run point since you and Johnson uncovered this lead. Here's the list; cross-check it with the missing girls, and let me know what you find. If we see a pattern, we'll make a plan of action."

Before Riggs could reach for the list, Johnson snatched it up and turned to her with a cheesy grin. "Well, partner, it looks like you and I got a few more field trips to take."

Rolling her eyes, Riggs snatched the papers from his hand and smacked him upside the head. "No, dumbass. We're on desk duty. All we have to do is cross-check the case file dates and locations with the game schedule. Moron."

Johnson's face turned red as he sank lower in his chair. "Whatever," he muttered, glaring at her.

An awkward silence settled over the room.

Fox kept his expression neutral, though the tension was hard to ignore. That little exchange said a lot. No wonder Riggs wasn't climbing the ladder around here—she was sharp, but she didn't hold back, not even in front of an audience. And while the guy was clearly an idiot, publicly humiliating him only made things worse.

"Okay," Fox said, breaking the silence, "Let's hear from Shane and Marcos. Did anything new come up since we last spoke?"

Shane glanced at Marcos, who gave him a quick nod.

"I guess I'll handle the debrief for us," Shane said. "After talking with the fifth victim's family, we found out Emma had snuck out to meet a friend that night. The two girls had different bedtimes—Emma's was 8:00 p.m., and her mom checked on her around 8:30. Sara, the friend, had a 9:00 p.m. bedtime, and no one usually checked in on her. So it looks like our perp had about a thirty-minute window to snatch Emma before Sara showed up."

Fox leaned forward slightly. "Any new leads from canvassing the neighborhood again?"

Shane nodded. "Yeah. One potential lead from a house at the end of the street, where the girls were supposed to meet. The homeowner said they noticed a blue car parked out front around 7:45 p.m. It was gone by 8:45. They couldn't make out the make or model, just that it was an older vehicle and pretty nondescript."

"Why'd they notice it at all?" Fox asked.

"Their neighbor's dog was going nuts," Shane said. "Barking like crazy. When they looked out to see what the fuss was about, they spotted the car. But they didn't see the driver or anyone else on the street."

Leaning back in his chair, Fox let his gaze sweep across the room, settling on each deputy before he spoke.

"With this new information, I think it's fair to say we're looking at the same perpetrator across all the cases."

He paused, letting that land before continuing.

"Based on what happened to Sherri, I also believe the chances of finding any of the other girls alive are...highly unlikely."

A heavy silence fell over the room.

"I've been reviewing Sherri's autopsy report. She was severely tortured and raped. Cause of death: asphyxia. Strangled by someone right-handed, according to the bruising. All the injuries were inflicted on the lower part of her body—there were no marks on her face or upper chest."

Fox leaned forward now, his tone sharpening.

"There are three questions I want answered moving forward."

He held up a finger. "First—how did he know Emma would be on that specific street corner, on that specific night, at that exact time?"

A second finger joined the first. "Second—are the Windsor Brooke High football games linked to any of the other missing girls?"

"And third..." he paused, eyes narrowing, "if finding Sherri's body was an accident—then where was he planning to dispose of her? Is he using that same location to hide the others?"

Fox turned toward the bulletin boards, his eyes scanning the rows of photos, the girls' faces looking back at him in frozen innocence.

"Shane, Marcos—I want you on Emma. Talk to her friends, teachers, anyone at the school who might've known her plans that night."

He shifted his attention. "Riggs, Johnson—you already have your assignment."

"And I'll take point on the body disposal angle. There's something we're missing there...and we need to figure it out. Fast."

He looked back at the team, eyes hard but steady.

"Any questions?"

"When do we let the public know?" Johnson asked.

"We don't," the sheriff said, speaking for the first time since his confrontation with Riggs.

"What do you mean *we don't*?" Riggs challenged. "They have a right to know. They need to be prepared—on guard."

"The Sheriff's right," Fox cut in before it escalated. "We can't go public until we have tangible evidence linking all the cases. Right now, all we have is a theory. A weak one that wouldn't hold up in court. So we keep a lid on this, for now. Understood?"

"Yes, sir," they all echoed.

"Anything else?" Fox asked.

Everyone shook their heads.

"Okay, let's call it a night. Head home and get some sleep. We'll hit it hard first thing in the morning."

Fox stood, eager to be on his way. He had left some business unfinished, and he hated loose ends.

Kate sat in her loft, poring over the case files, cursing herself every time her eyes drifted to the clock.

Thirty minutes to go. If he didn't show up by then, he wasn't coming at all.

She told herself she should feel relieved, but the truth was, she felt disappointed, and that made her feel even worse.

Shrugging it off, she tried to focus. A clean break was better—easier, safer—before things got complicated.

Besides, she had work to do.

She had just taken another job, this time in Morocco. The mark was supposed to be on his yacht, docked off the coast of Rabat, in three weeks. That gave her maybe two weeks to find this sick bastard and put him down.

Good thing she thrived under pressure. Otherwise, she might've started to worry.

A knock at the door made her jump.

She'd been so deep in thought that she hadn't noticed anyone pulling into the drive.

Her heart kicked up. Instinct or anticipation—she couldn't be sure.

She smoothed her clothes, gave herself a quick once-over in the mirror, and reached for the door.

Taking a deep breath, Kate swung the door open, only to find Cara standing there with a box of cookies.

The smile she had prepared faltered. She forced it back into place.

"Hey, Cara. I didn't know you were coming over."

"I figured you'd be working on this all alone," Cara said, lifting the box with a grin. "Thought I'd surprise you with a little treat."

"Do you have any milk?" Cara asked over her shoulder, already heading for the stairs. "We're going to need it with this yummy goodness."

"Yeah, I'll grab us a couple of glasses. Go on up, I'll be there in a sec."

Kate walked to the kitchen, muttering under her breath. Normally, she loved it when Cara stopped by. But tonight, after that tense, charged moment with Fox Anderson—the *too-sexy-for-his-own-good* FBI guy—she was on edge. And still unsure if he was going to show up.

If he did? And Cara was still here?

She winced. Cara was sweet, sure, but also the local megaphone when it came to gossip. The last thing Kate needed was more attention.

"Here we go," Kate said brightly as she returned, two glasses of milk in hand. "Now, hand over the cookies."

But Cara didn't move. She sat staring at Kate's wall, frozen.

"Cara?" Kate asked, concern edging her voice. "You okay?"

Cara didn't look away from the photos. "I thought it was just Sherri," she said quietly. "I mean, I knew what you told me...but I didn't *see* it. Not like this."

She turned, eyes wet, and handed over the cookies with a weak smile. "Sorry. You asked for these, and I'm just...hogging them."

Kate took them gently. "It's okay. Really."

"I *should've* believed you," Cara whispered. "They all look so much alike...it's horrifying. And you're good at what you do, Kate. I should've known that."

"You don't have to stay," Kate said softly. "I've got this."

"No." Cara shook her head. "I asked you to look into this. I'm not bailing. I'll help however I can."

Kate gave a tired smile. "Then help me take a break. Come on, let's sit out on the porch swing. You can catch me up on all the juicy gossip."

"If you really need a break," Cara said, hesitating.

"I do," Kate said firmly. "You grab the cookies. I'll get the milk."

It was a beautiful night. The sun had set over an hour ago, and the stillness of the woods was broken only by the soft hum of insects calling to each other in the dark. Kate stared past the driveway toward a small clearing where grass and wildflowers swayed gently in the breeze. Over the blooms, fireflies blinked in slow, golden pulses.

Poor Emma. So young. So innocent. Just a little girl who wanted to catch fireflies with her friend.

She had no idea there were monsters lurking in the dark.

Kate's jaw tensed.

Whoever did this didn't know it yet, but they were already dead.

"What's wrong?" Cara asked, frowning.

Kate blinked and looked over. "What?"

"You had this...creepy expression on your face. What were you thinking about?"

Just another reminder of why she had to keep this side of herself separate.

Cara was okay with what she *did*—but not with *seeing* it.

"Oh, nothing," Kate said lightly. "So...what's new in town? Has anyone done anything crazy lately?"

"Well, let's see," Cara said, thinking aloud. "The Fredricks moved to Ohio to be closer to his mom. Apparently, she's been having some health issues, and since he's an only child, they decided to move in together to take care of her. That's a big responsibility if you ask me. I'm not sure how well Amy gets along with her mother-in-law, but I wish her luck."

She tapped a finger to her chin. "What else... Oh! Sylvia's been crowing about her son lately. First, he got a scholarship to the state university. Then he came home for fall break and dropped the news—he's the new starting quarterback. They love that he's a lefty who can throw just as well with his right. Sylvia won't stop bragging about how her husband spent hours working with him, day and night until he mastered it. Honestly, I think her husband's a tyrant. That boy's lucky to have made it out of that house in one piece."

"I forgot about Sylvia's son," Kate said thoughtfully. "I see her daughters around town sometimes, but I'm not even sure I'd recognize him."

"Not surprising. He was always working side jobs or out on the field. I only know because David's obsessed with football. He follows the college and high school teams, too. And he never misses a game."

"He never misses a game," Cara said.

Kate tilted her head. "Just the home ones?"

"All of them, I think. I mean, I only half-listen when he talks about football, but yeah, he travels too."

Kate raised an eyebrow. "Really... Do a lot of men around here follow the team that closely? I mean, do any of them travel with the team? Go to the away games too, not just the ones at home?"

"I'm not sure," Cara said, pausing for a moment before adding, "David would probably know more about that. I only half-listen when he gets to rambling like he does."

"Think I could stop by and talk to him tomorrow? What time does he usually get home from work?"

"Around six, usually. Why don't you stay for dinner too? The kids love it when you visit, especially JT," Cara snorted. "Pretty sure he's got a crush on you."

"Oh, shut up," Kate laughed, giving her a playful shove. "He does not. He just likes hearing my awesome stories."

Headlights began winding their way through the trees, and Kate's stomach knotted.

"Holy crap," she muttered. He was coming. She glanced at her watch, over an hour late.

Men.

Oh hell. Cara shifted beside her, drawing Kate's gaze. She was *still* here. Kate's eyes flicked back to the looming headlights—Fox was getting closer. Panic bubbled in her chest. She hadn't figured out what to say to him yet—if anything. Her brain stalled, blank. But her heart? It was thumping out a happy little rhythm all its own.

"Who's that?" Cara asked, sounding genuinely puzzled. "Were you expecting someone?"

Kate shot her a look, mildly annoyed. It wasn't like she wasn't allowed to have other friends. She just... didn't.

"Not really," Kate said with a shrug. "Agent Anderson from the FBI mentioned he might stop by to talk about the case. I wasn't sure he actually would, but—" she gestured toward the headlights—"I guess he is."

Cara's expression lit up instantly, voice pitching up into full gossip mode.

"Oh *really*," she said, drawing the word out. "Is this the same FBI guy Sue said looks all tall, hot, and steamy?" She wiggled her eyebrows playfully.

Kate sighed, unwillingly watching the headlights cut through the trees. "Yes, it's the same FBI guy. Really, Cara—you already know there's only *one* FBI guy in town. Besides, Sue thinks *all* men are hot and steamy."

"Are you saying *you* don't think he's attractive?"

"Of course, he's attractive," Kate muttered. Heat flooded her cheeks. "I am just saying not all of Sue's observations are accurate. Just trying to keep it in perspective."

"Oh, wait, I get it. It's not that you don't think he's attractive—it's that you don't want *me* to know you think he is." Cara grinned, perfectly summing up what Kate had been trying to hide.

Kate shot her a glare, refusing to answer.

Cara studied her profile, and then her eyes lit up with realization. "It's more, isn't it? Oh, Kate—do you have a *crush* on him?" she teased, giggling.

"I do *not*," Kate blustered. "He's attractive, that's all." She tried to explain, but Cara was already doubled over, laughing.

"I can't believe *you*, of all people, have a *crush*," Cara gasped, not even trying to hide her amusement.

"Oh, shut up," Kate said, throwing a pillow at her.

Cara held up a shaky arm to block it, still laughing and singing some ridiculous childhood rhyme about sitting in a tree. Kate couldn't help it—her own laughter bubbled up and spilled out. Cara was right. She *did* have a crush on the dumb hunk.

Chapter Fifteen

T he small luxury SUV parked in Kate's driveway looked out of place against the dense forest backdrop, mostly because it hadn't been there when he left.

Irritation flared, sharp, and sudden. Someone else was here. Someone she hadn't mentioned.

He leaned across the front seat, grabbing the takeout bags from one of the two dining options in town. Then, maybe a bit too deliberately, he slammed the car door shut—hard enough to rattle the windows.

He strode up the gravel drive, boots crunching with each step, and froze at the bottom of the porch stairs.

There she was—Kate—seated on the porch swing with another woman. A friend, probably, judging by how they leaned into each other, howling with laughter.

A box of half-eaten cookies was squished between them, and two glasses of milk sat nearby—one of which had toppled during the chaos. A slow trickle of white liquid oozed between the deck boards, dripping down into the shadows below.

Fox's jaw tensed as he took it all in—the scene, the comfort, the inside joke he wasn't a part of. He narrowed his eyes, watching, waiting. But neither of them even glanced his way.

After a long beat, he rolled his eyes and climbed the steps. He stopped just in front of the swing, looming over them. When they still didn't acknowledge him, he casually checked his watch, then looked pointedly at Kate.

After a beat, Kate calmed herself, wiping tears from her eyes. She looked up at him with a smile so open and carefree it knocked the heat right out of his anger.

Something fluttered in his chest, and just like that, he wanted to kiss her. Right then. Right there.

His gaze shifted to the other woman on the swing. And for a beat, Fox hated that she was the one who'd made Kate laugh like that. He promised himself: *Next time she smiles like that, it'll be because of me.*

"Hi, Agent Anderson," Kate said, a notable coolness in her voice. "This is my very good friend Cara."

Fox didn't miss the subtle emphasis; the message was loud and clear: *Play it cool. We're just colleagues.*

Cara snorted. "*Very good friend?* My ass. Try, *best* friend." She glared at Kate, shoving a sharp elbow into her ribs. "What the hell, am I being demoted?"

"Ow," Kate muttered, rubbing her side. She gestured toward Cara with mock contrition. "Apologies, Agent Anderson. This is my *very best* friend, Cara."

"Ma'am," Fox said, giving her a polite nod before lifting the takeout bags. "Sorry to interrupt—only brought enough for two."

He looked at Kate, letting her decide how she wanted to handle it.

"Oh," Cara said, nudging Kate with her elbow. "He *only* brought food for two."

She laughed again, then stood and handed Kate her empty glass.

"I should get going anyway—David's probably wondering where I am." Cara flashed a sly grin. "Keep the cookies. You can have them for dessert." She gave Kate a wink full of unspoken meaning.

"I didn't think you would make it," Kate said over her shoulder as she gathered up the glasses of milk and what remained of the cookies before heading inside.

Fox followed her inside, the smell of takeout mingling with the warmth of her home.

"Yeah, well..." he paused, watching her fuss with the glasses, "you invited someone over?"

Kate turned, brows lifting. "So?"

Fox held up a hand, his voice cooler than he intended. "Just...wasn't expecting you to have company, that's all."

Silence stretched between them, thick and uncomfortable. A dozen thoughts raced through his mind, but none were right—at least, not the ones he could actually say. And the one thing he *wanted* to say? He didn't dare.

So instead, he settled for something safer—half true, gentle, and stripped of the edge he'd been feeling.

"If you're trying to tell me something, Kate, just say it," he added, softer this time. "I get it—maybe you didn't want to be alone when I didn't show. Maybe you didn't want to be alone with *me*."

"What's that supposed to mean? You're over an hour late, and now you're acting like I stood you up."

Kate huffed, color rising in her cheeks—embarrassment? Frustration? Maybe both. She crossed her arms quickly, almost defensively, like she was trying to put space between them. Or maybe shield something she didn't want him to see.

Fox stepped closer until they were nearly nose to nose, glaring at each other, the heat of anger and attraction simmering in the narrow space between them. She was right—it wasn't his business who she had over. And yeah, he was late. But still, it grated that she hadn't waited.

He hadn't been able to stop thinking about her since he left. He'd driven back like a man on a mission, stupidly picturing her alone on the couch, watching the clock, willing time to move faster—just like he had.

Gruffly, he admitted, "It took longer than I expected to pick up the food."

The truth was, he probably would've been on time if he'd ordered the food first, *then* gone back to his motel to shower. But he'd felt grungy, and he'd been hoping—maybe stupidly—to pick up where they'd left off. At the time, a shower had seemed like the smart move.

"Well, you should plan your time better," Kate said, not giving him an inch.

"I'll take that into account." He grinned, leaning in until their noses were nearly touching.

Kate's eyes widened. She was bluffing. That realization nearly made him laugh—she wasn't as indifferent as she pretended to be. Not even close.

He'd expected they'd eat at the kitchen table—and he'd been ready to nudge Kate into letting her guard down. So when she turned and headed upstairs, he blinked, surprised, then followed. Curiosity piqued, he trailed behind her, letting his gaze drift over the space—and linger on her—with unfiltered interest.

The stairway opened into a spacious loft. A sofa and armchairs framed a large square coffee table, but Fox's attention snagged on the far wall.

Photos. Dozens of them—taped up with the kind of precision that only came from obsession.

He walked past the takeout bags, setting them down without a glance. Every image was tagged with notes, lines of connection, and theories. She even had a copy of Sherri's autopsy report.

How the hell had she gotten her hands on that?

"I figured since you wanted to talk about the case, we might as well eat up here," Kate said, curling into one corner of the sofa.

Fox shrugged off his jacket and hung it on the nearest chair. He hadn't bothered putting on a tie and left the top few buttons of his shirt undone, but he still felt confined. He thought about just throwing on a T-shirt and jeans but thought Kate might find his casual attire threatening.

Rolling his sleeves up to his forearms, he sat beside her. She could've taken the armchair if she wanted space.

Fox reached for one of the bags and pulled out a few takeout boxes, opening them and setting them on the coffee table. He handed Kate a set of silverware.

"I didn't know what you liked, so I went simple—pasta, bread, salad."

"Did you order from Angelo's off the square?" Kate asked, accepting the pasta dish. She smiled. "I love their spaghetti. Good choice."

"Yeah, everyone said it was a fan favorite, so I doubled up—two of everything. Glad I guessed right."

"How did your meeting go? Learn anything new?" Kate asked, curling pasta onto her fork.

"A few things. You already know about Emma Mathews," Fox said, then hesitated. He debated how much to tell her. On one hand, she'd already helped push the case in new directions. On the other hand, she wasn't law enforcement, which made her a liability.

He watched her out of the corner of his eye as she ate, calm and focused, at least on the surface. Who *was* she, really?

Earlier, he'd fielded an unexpected call from HQ. It had only made things murkier. They hadn't told him to keep her informed—but they hadn't told him to shut her out either. Give her a wide berth, they'd said. It was clear that even his boss didn't know what her role was supposed to be. The whole thing left him uneasy.

So where did that leave him?

He couldn't tell her everything. It went against the grain of his conscience. But if he kept her in the dark, she'd go rogue again. That much he was sure of. And a wild card was dangerous in any case.

Better to keep her close. At least then, he'd know what she was up to.

"We canvassed the Mathews' neighborhood and found a witness who saw a car parked in front of their house between 7:45 and 8:45 that night."

"Really?" Kate lit up, the excitement vibrating off her. "What kind of car? Did they see the driver?"

Fox bit back a grin. "Basic description—older model sedan. That's about it. No ID on the driver."

"Too bad. That could've sped things up," she said, her eager excitement from a moment ago deflating.

Fox glanced at her, curious. "Speed things up? You in a hurry for some reason?"

She just slipped up—and she knew it. Her eyes widened, not much, but enough to give her away. He got lucky but wouldn't again. She was too smart to make that same mistake again.

"Nothing. It would be nice to get some momentum on this thing, don't you think?"

He gave her a long, skeptical look but let it drop for now.

"Anyway," he said, shifting gears, "we also learned from Susie's mother that the team they played the night before she disappeared was Windsor Brooke High."

Kate's head snapped up. "Windsor Brooke High?"

"It's the first solid link between the girls," Fox said. "Six cases and this is the only common thread we've got."

"Is it possible he's from Windsor Brooke?" she asked. There was an edge in her voice now, something sharper.

Fox didn't answer right away. Her reaction was...interesting. He wanted to sit with it for a while. Rewind and replay every nuance. Something about her response was telling, but he couldn't quite put his finger on what.

"I'm not sure yet," he admitted. "I've got Riggs and Johnson looking into it. We'll know more soon."

He leaned back and gave her a crooked grin. "You were right about Riggs. She's sharp. Humiliated Johnson today—I almost felt bad for the guy."

Kate smiled around a bite of breadstick. "What happened?"

"I asked them to check if any of the victims' teams had played Windsor Brooke. Johnson figured they'd have to drive to each school and ask in person." He chuckled. "Riggs called him an idiot and told him to just pick up the phone."

Kate winced, but she was laughing. "Ouch. Brutal. I never said she was diplomatic."

"She's not. Makes for an awkward pairing."

"Very perceptive. Did you change their assignment?"

"Nope. Figured I'd leave the personnel issues to your Sheriff."

Kate rolled her eyes. "Good call. I'm not sure Sheriff Jacobs has ever handled anything uncomfortable head-on in his life."

The silence that followed stretched a beat too long. Fox watched as she reached for the takeout bag, a little too eagerly, gathering trash and stacking containers. Her hands moved quickly, almost anxious. He had to jerk his hand out of the way when she reached for his plate.

"Ah—seems I'm finished," he said, smirking.

A flush climbed her neck. "Sorry. I just thought we could wrap up so I can get to bed. Early morning tomorrow."

Her tone was off—too light. Too rehearsed. The excuse was laughably transparent.

Fox tilted his head, letting a slow, knowing smile pull at his mouth. "Well," he said, voice low, "when you put it that way, bed does sound tempting."

She sprang to her feet, jittery as a rabbit. "NO! I mean—" she stammered, her cheeks scarlet, "I meant *me* to bed. Not *we*." She took a step back, clearly rattled, casting around for an exit.

Fox rose, his movements slow and deliberate. He matched each step she took with one of his own until her back hit the wall. He planted his hands on either side of her, boxing her in. She stared up at him, wide-eyed.

"I know what you meant," he said, voice teasing. "I was only playing."

He reached up, running his fingers through her hair, tugging lightly on the ends.

Her reaction was instant—a breathless "oh," her gaze fixed on his chest because it was easier than looking into his face. But Fox didn't miss the shift. She wasn't scared. She was overwhelmed.

He slipped a finger beneath her chin, gently guiding her face up until their eyes met. She resisted until the last second, then gave in, reluctantly.

What he saw there stopped him cold.

It wasn't indifference. It wasn't flirtation. It was uncertainty. Vulnerability.

She didn't know what to do with him.

It hit him all at once—Kate wasn't playing hard to get. She wasn't sure *how* to play. Her reactions, her awkwardness, the way she kept him at arm's length... it wasn't rejection. It was inexperience.

And suddenly, everything about her made sense.

He wouldn't be able to approach this as he usually did. He'd have to be clearer in his intentions and more deliberate. There was only one problem: he wasn't sure what he wanted. A relationship didn't fit his life. He was always on the move, his schedule a mess. He didn't know what this *was* or what it could become.

But he knew one thing.

He wanted her.

And he'd do whatever it took to have her.

"Kate, case aside," Fox said, voice calm, "I like you. I want to get to know you." He studied her face. "The question is—do you like me?"

Despite the even tone, his heart pounded beneath the surface, the rhythm just a shade too fast. Everything hung in the balance—this room, this moment. And Kate, without even realizing it, held all the power. One word from her could tilt the scales.

She looked dazed as if the question had thrown her. Her gaze flicked away.

"Yes, I do," she said hesitantly. "It's just...I don't date. I don't have time. I'm barely ever home, and when I am, I'm buried in paperwork. Men are a low priority."

"Hey," he said, lifting his hands in mock surrender. "I'm not asking for a commitment. Just some time. See if there's something here. What do you say?"

She went still, obviously torn. He could see it—the tug between her desire and her instinct to shut it down. Finally, she gave a small nod. "I guess that would be okay." A beat passed. "But... no sex."

Fox blinked. His brain stalled.

No sex—not exactly subtle.

Women had asked to take things slow before, but never this clearly. Never this direct. He opened his mouth, then closed it again. What was he supposed to say to that?

His thoughts spiraled. Was it trauma? Religion? A bad past experience? Hell, did she just not *like* sex?

That last one scared him the most.

Still, she'd said it with such conviction he didn't dare argue. If anything, it made him *more* curious. More interested. She was serious about this.

He was bungling this. But silence wasn't going to help. He needed to say something, anything. The longer they stood in this standstill, Kate's posture stiffened. Her expression hardened as she stood her ground. Even with her back against the wall, she crossed her arms, daring him to...argue? Taunt?

"When you say *no sex*..." he began slowly, "do you mean...not ever?"

"No," she snapped, "I mean, I don't have casual sex. *Ever.*"

As her words sank in, his eyes widened. Realization struck—a slow, dawning truth he hadn't seen coming.

"Are you telling me you're a virgin?"

The color rising in her cheeks gave him his answer.

He stared, trying to process it. She had to be what—early thirties? And still untouched? It was... unexpected. Maybe even admirable. But damn.

"There's no need to act dumbfounded," she said, arms tightening across her chest. "It's not unheard of for an adult to be a virgin. Just because society treats sex like an all-day pass to an amusement park doesn't mean I have to go along for the ride. My body matters, and not just anyone gets a ticket. Thank you very much."

He wished she'd stop referring to her body as a ride. He was having a hard enough time with this conversation, and just hearing the words "all-day pass" made his heart race. When he finally managed to wrestle his thoughts back in line, the implications of what she'd said sank in.

A slow, satisfied smile tugged at his lips. He had no doubt—Kate would be worth the wait.

He slid an arm around her waist and pulled her close. "Hey," he murmured, "I'm all for saving yourself. And for the record—I don't like sharing either. So, having you all to myself? Not a bad place to be."

She raised a brow. "What makes you think you'll be my first? Seems a mite cocky."

"Not cocky. Just confident," he said with a wink. "Give it time. You'll see."

Kate snorted. "We'll see," she said, but her tone had softened.

Then she pulled away. "If we're done talking about the case, I think it's time you headed out."

"Already kicking me out?" he teased. "How about we finish the night on the porch swing? I admit—I was a little jealous seeing you out there earlier without me."

Before she could protest, he was already leading her downstairs. Her hand nestled in his.

A moment later, she was nestled into his side, his arm draped comfortably along the back of the swing. The plush cushions made it easy to sit close—something he wasn't above taking advantage of. If he had any hope of earning Kate's trust, he'd have to use everything at his disposal. Time was short, and he had to make every second count.

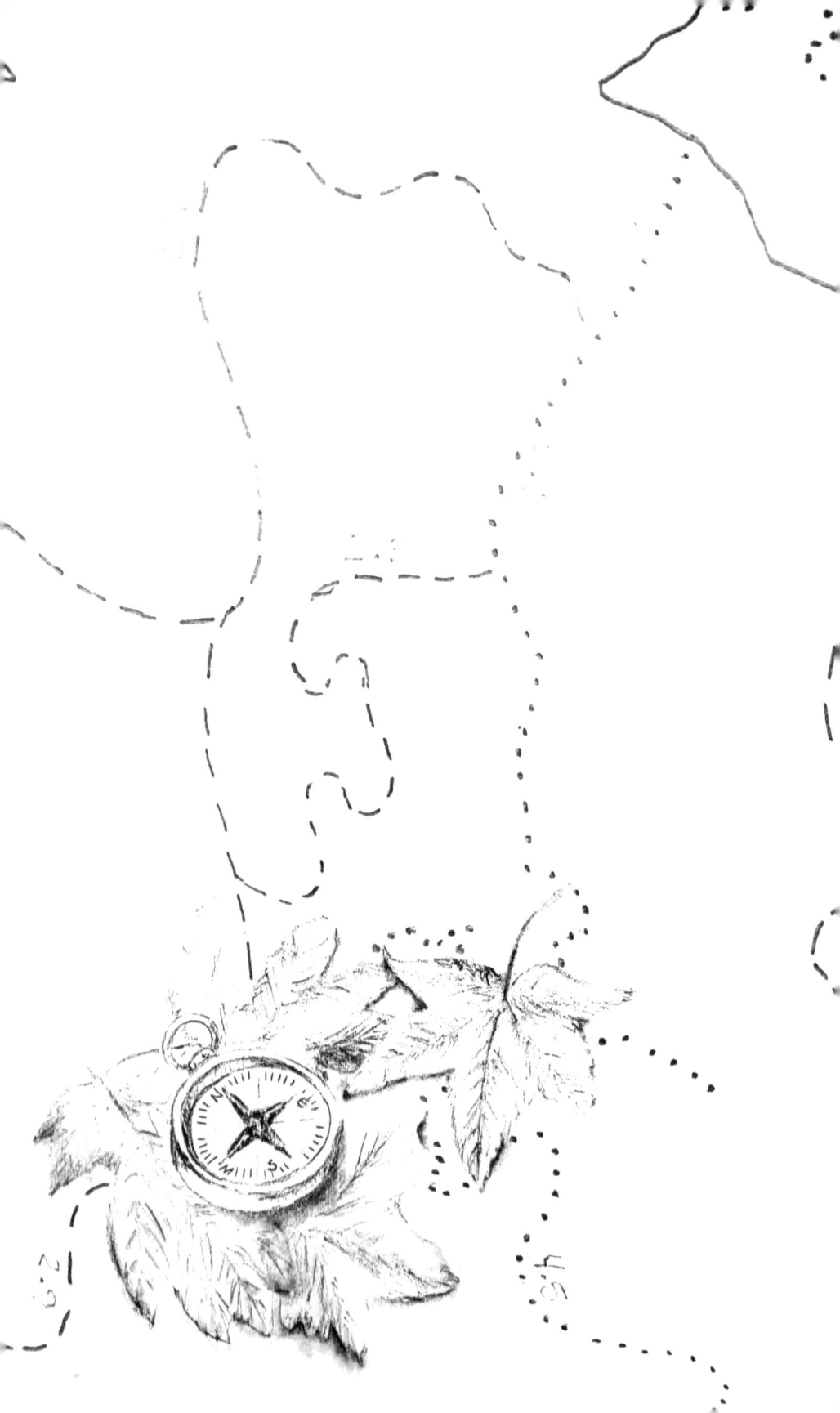

Chapter Sixteen

Well, well, well, what do we have here?

Looked like Kate had gone and gotten herself a little boyfriend. How sweet. Too bad it won't last.

Kate was different. Special. A treasure. The waiting was torture—but he had to be careful. She wouldn't be on the market much longer. *Everything had to be perfect before he took her.*

Maybe he'd hold on to little Chloe a bit longer than usual. Then, when the time was right, he could show Kate exactly what happened to his other treasures. She'd be terrified then. Humbled. She'd understand his power.

Just thinking about her begging and pleading had him hard. He watched as her boyfriend rubbed her leg. His hand reached down to mimic the motion. Soon, she would belong to him, and it was going to be perfect. He just knew it.

Kate stiffened, her body tightening like a drawn bowstring.

Her gaze swept the yard, eyes narrowing at the shadows between trees. He was here—she could feel it.

Her brow furrowed. She didn't bother to hide her reaction. What was the point? If Fox saw the darker side of her, let him. Let him walk away like everyone else eventually did.

Right now, her quarry was here.

Nothing else mattered.

She scanned the woods in one slow, deliberate pass.

Dark shadows. That was all her life was made of—just darkness lurking in the background, waiting. It clung to her like smoke. It *followed* her. She couldn't escape it.

But how did he find me?

No headlights. No engine. He must've walked in. Which meant he'd known where she lived. Very few people had that information. Her private sanctuary was violated.

"What is it?" Fox asked, his voice low.

She didn't answer, eyes still locked on the tree line.

A beat later, he turned his head, following her line of sight, scanning the dark woods to see what had triggered her reaction.

She felt him.

She knew he was watching.

A tingling thrill ran up his spine—a glorious sensation. He knew the minute she sensed him. It was when he was planning the fun they would have together. It was perfect, this connection they shared. As if all the little angels he had taken had led him to this very moment—his soul mate.

He was tempted to walk up and introduce himself. Maybe she'd recognize him for what he was. Maybe she'd see what they both shared, the darkness within.

Shame her boyfriend was sitting next to her.

He could wait.

A little longer.

Kate knew the moment he left—the monster knew where she lived.

She hadn't wanted to install security cameras. Too much wildlife. They'd trigger every time a rabbit darted past. But after this? It might be time to reconsider.

If he was going to start stalking her, this could be her chance to get a look at him.

Leaning back into the swing, she turned to Fox. He was watching her with an intensity that told her something important—he'd seen a glimpse of who she truly was. A hunter.

"What was that all about?" Fox asked, his eyes watchful.

Careful.

She exhaled and cleared her mind, relaxing her face. "It felt like someone was watching us," she said. "Didn't you feel it?"

"No," Fox replied. "Not until you tensed up."

"Whatever it was, it's gone now." She rested back, hoping he'd let it go.

But then, softly, "Kate?"

"Yeah?"

"Are you ever going to let me see all of you?"

She pulled away, startled. "I *told* you. No sex. Jeez—is that all you think about?"

He laughed and set the swing in motion. The chains creaked under the weight.

"I meant who you are inside," he said, then added with a grin, "But yeah... I'd love to see you naked, too."

"Fox." She tried to sound scandalized but couldn't quite pull it off.

"Okay, okay, one last thing before I go." He stood, grabbing his coat. "What are you doing tomorrow? Want to check out the disposal site with me?"

Kate had already been there, but there was no way she would tell Fox that. Besides, maybe he might see something she hadn't. "Sure, what time?"

"How about 9:00 am?"

"Okay, I'll be ready."

Fox grabbed his coat and walked to his car. "Tomorrow, Kate."

She watched him drive away.

It was good that he'd only be here for a little while because she was in trouble. She just had to stay strong. A week. Two tops. She could handle that.

Fox sat at the small table in his room, Sherri's folder open in front of him. But his mind wouldn't focus.

The first should've been simple enough to fix. The problem was that it depended heavily on Sheriff Jacobs. And so far, Jacobs had failed to impress. The man was a peacock—flashy, loud, and completely useless unless a distraction was needed.

Jacobs might prefer to let things go on as they always had, but Fox wasn't about to let that happen. A little verbal sparring was expected—it was part of the job. In law enforcement, men had to blow off steam somehow. Usually, the women stayed out of it, letting the guys run their mouths.

But Riggs hadn't just joined in—she'd gone too far. Jacobs might refuse to see it, but Fox knew the truth: Johnson hadn't just been embarrassed. He'd been pissed.

That kind of anger between partners wasn't just dangerous, it was a setup for betrayal. And when one partner stops trusting the other, someone gets left out to dry.

He needed to speak with Jacobs, but only when no one else was around, especially not Sylvia. Jacobs' little watchdog heard more than she should.

Fox didn't trust her. She was too standoffish, too remote. Whatever needed to be said was for Jacobs' ears only.

Fortunately, with Jacobs working the graveyard shift, Fox could drop in later and have that little talk—just the two of them.

Office dynamics were a problem, but they weren't the reason he couldn't focus.

That problem rested squarely on Kate's shoulders.

He hadn't expected things to unfold the way they had with her. For one, he'd hoped to have a clearer idea of where he stood. But that wasn't going to happen anytime soon, not after learning how completely she'd removed herself from any kind of social life.

And he doubted it was just dating. A woman like Kate didn't simply keep men at arm's length, she kept *everyone* out.

That insight should've sent him running for the hills. But it hadn't.

Instead, it had only fueled his need to understand her, not just physically, but on every level. She was intriguing. Complex. A puzzle box he couldn't wait to unlock.

But then there had been her reaction on the porch.

Fox frowned at the table, his eyes unfocused.

He'd been toying with the idea of asking for a kiss—just to see how she'd react—when she'd turned to stone. Completely still. He thought she'd stopped breathing.

And then he'd felt it—the danger.

It was like she'd heightened *his* awareness, pulled him into whatever she was sensing. Until that moment, he hadn't realized it, but someone *had* been watching them. His hand had instinctively gone to his gun.

But there was nothing. Just woods. A wall of darkness. Impenetrable.

Anyone could've been out there. And he would never have known.

Except...Kate had.

Now that he thought about it, not only had she known, but her face had changed. That softness from just moments before had vanished. In its place was something sharp, carved from steel.

The light had drained from her eyes, replaced by something cold and endless.

Fox shuddered.

Kate wasn't what she seemed. It was another piece of a puzzle he only had half the picture of.

Fox twirled a pen between his fingers. He pressed the end, releasing a soft *click*. Then, he tapped it against the tabletop as he scrawled a few notes. After a moment, he picked up his phone and called Keller.

Keller worked in the basement, but he was a genius at uncovering things only someone who saw the world in ones and zeros could. It didn't matter that it was well past midnight. As far as Fox knew, Keller never slept.

The line picked up on the second ring.

"Do you know what time it is?" Keller snapped, though it sounded more like distracted irritation than real anger.

"Yeah," Fox said, grinning. "Figured you wouldn't mind. I need a favor."

Keller snorted. The soft clack of keys sounded in the background. "What kind of favor?"

"I need you to look into someone for me. Quietly. This hasn't exactly been cleared—and based on the call I got earlier, it won't ever be. If you do this, it's for your eyes only."

The tapping stopped.

"Anderson," Keller said, a gleeful hitch in his voice, "you always bring me the best puzzles. Who is it?"

"Her name's Kate Millard. I need anything you can find. But be careful—this kind of search might get flagged."

"Right," Keller said, already typing again. "The day I get flagged is the day I turn in my badge. I'll call you when I have something."

Fox set his phone down and picked up Sherri's file once more. Tomorrow was bound to be full of surprises.

The biggest one was Kate.

Anticipation flared—hot and fast.

Sleep had never felt so far away.

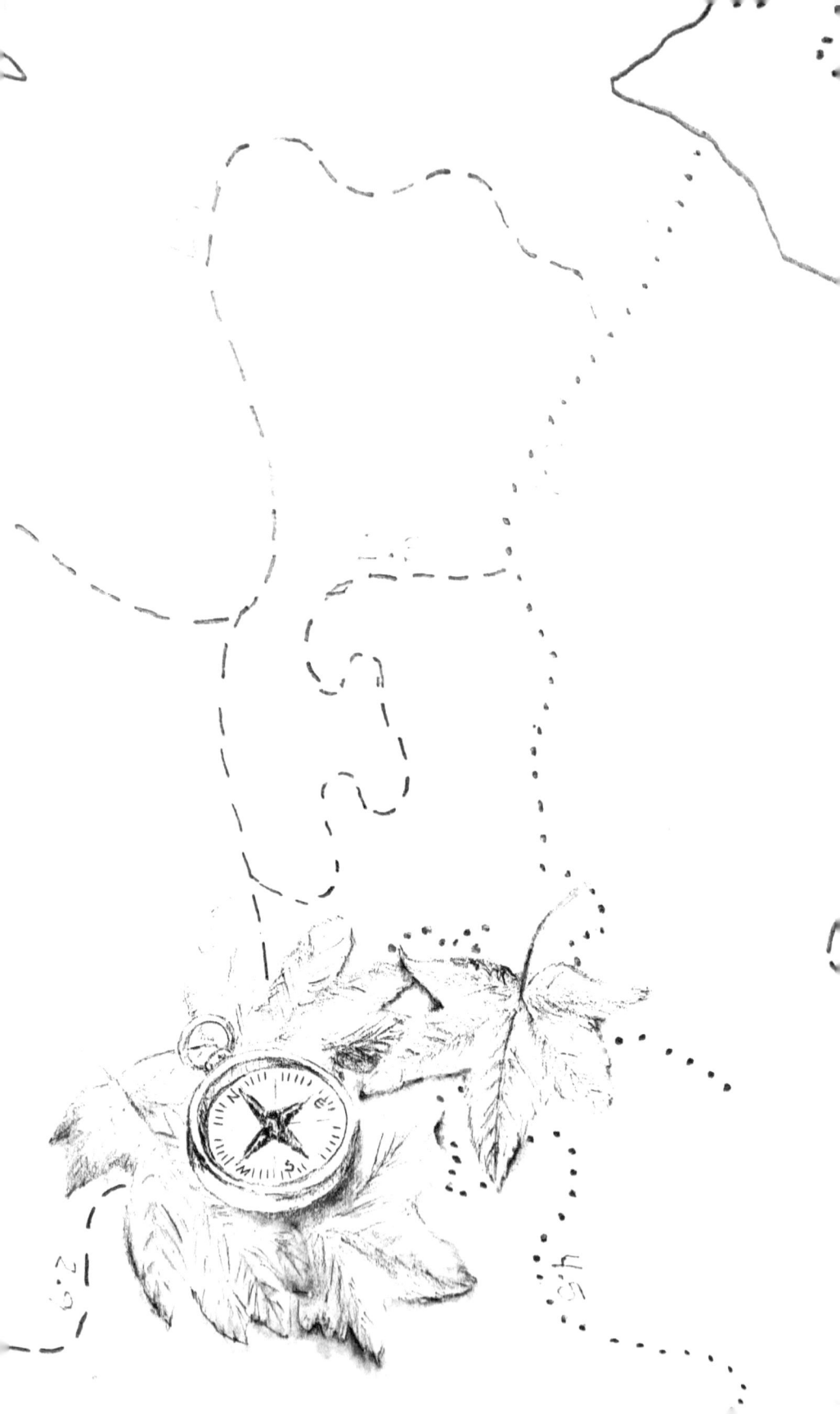

Chapter Seventeen

Sheriff Jacobs sat in his office, staring out at the empty bullpen. With all his deputies tied up on Sherri's murder, he'd been stuck covering the graveyard shift alone.

An empty coffee cup rested at his elbow. He couldn't stomach another. The pot had long gone cold, the dregs turning sour.

He rubbed his eyes and glanced at the clock, scowling. He hated these early morning hours. They messed with his whole rhythm.

No time for his favorite bar. No time for a drink. And worst of all, he had no time for the company he really missed.

He was in a dry spell—but that was just bad luck. The graveyard shift wasn't helping.

He had a couple more hours before Riggs showed up, and he could finally get out of here. She was always at least thirty minutes early and stuck around long after her shift ended. Normally, he'd raise hell about the overtime, but true to form, Riggs never clocked in early or stayed on the clock late.

Ambitious as hell, that one. She might even take over if she ever learned to watch her mouth when he retired.

But yesterday? He shook his head, a cruel smile tugging at his lips. She'd handed Johnson his balls in front of the whole department. Again.

It was awkward and not great for morale—not that their "department" was more than a handful of people. Still, it stung. Johnson wasn't the only one she'd gone after, but she sure seemed to have a special taste for him.

Jacobs sighed. It was probably time he stepped in. Just not while Anderson was around. No need to air dirty laundry in front of the feds.

Pulled from his thoughts, Jacobs blinked in surprise as the door opened, and Anderson walked in.

What was he doing here so early?

He frowned, watching as Anderson crossed to the bulletin board, pausing by the case files. He shuffled through a few pages, pulled a couple from a folder, then turned and headed toward Jacobs' office.

Jacobs sprang up from his chair, rushed to the window, and quickly slid the art piece back into place. Then he hustled to his seat just as a light knock sounded at the door.

"Come in," he called.

"Morning, Sheriff. Got a minute?" Fox asked as he stepped into the office and made his way to the empty chair across from Jacobs.

"Sure. Have a seat. What can I do for you?"

"I wanted to see if you have heard anything new from any of the other police departments we've been consulting with?"

"No, nothing since our meeting yesterday morning. You hoping for something in particular?"

"Not really. Just trying to keep a thumb on the pulse of the case is all."

"I see." Jacobs shifted in his chair, sensing there was something more on Anderson's mind. The man always seemed to be watching, quiet, calculating, and making assumptions. It made Jacobs uneasy.

He didn't like being challenged, and Anderson did nothing *but* challenge him. The constant pressure was getting old. He was damned tired of walking on eggshells.

Tension crept into his shoulders and neck, but he resisted the urge to rub at the tightness.

"Is there something else you wanted to talk about?"

"Riggs," Anderson said, pausing, his eyes steady. "Does she make comments like that often?"

Jacobs hesitated, weighing his options. Edging the truth seemed the safest route, so he went with vagueness.

"Has it happened before? Yes. Often? No, I wouldn't say that."

"Well, Sheriff, I don't think I need to tell you how damaging bad morale can be to a case. If your deputies can't work together, we might need to talk about removing one or two of them."

Jacobs sighed and rubbed his forehead. This was the last thing he needed right now.

"Listen, Anderson, I appreciate your concern, but the internal dynamics of my team are *my* problem. They have nothing to do with you or solving this case. I'd already decided to speak with Riggs once this is over."

He met Anderson's eyes, his tone firm.

"Now, if there's nothing else, I've got work to do."

Jacobs scowled at the stubborn set of Anderson's jaw. Damn, fed didn't even blink at his tone.

"Sorry, Sheriff, but that's not good enough. I won't let this case get compromised because one of your deputies thinks it's okay to humiliate her partner. You may want to brush it off, but I guarantee Johnson didn't walk away from that exchange feeling good about working with her.

Tell me—what do you think he'd do if it came down to protecting her? Would he take a bullet for her?" He arched a brow.

Jacobs scoffed. "Windsor Brooke's a quiet little town. Nothing violent ever happens here. I can't imagine a situation where that'd be tested."

Anderson narrowed his eyes. "I think you mean it *used to be* a quiet little town. Or have you already forgotten about Sherri?"

"Yes, well..." Jacobs shifted in his seat. "That was an isolated incident. I'm sure we'll sort this out soon enough, and everything will go back to normal."

"Hmm." Anderson stood. "Sheriff, I hope you're right." With that, he turned and left.

Sheriff Jacobs waited for the door to close before crossing the room and removing the art piece again. He stood at the window, watching Anderson grab another file from the table and exit the building.

Asshole. What did he know about running his team? He couldn't just waltz in and start telling him how to run his department. Sure, Riggs shot her mouth off now and then, but it was manageable.

Jacobs knew his team. They had to keep functioning after Mr. Hotshot Fed packed up and left. The last thing he needed was some outsider stirring up drama better left buried.

Riggs stifled a yawn, fingers tapping the counter as the coffee pot filled. The rich aroma already coaxed her body toward the caffeine fix it craved. A small smile curled her lips as she took the first sip, the silence of the office wrapping around her like a cocoon of routine.

She huddled at her desk, hunched over her mug like it was a lifeline. The computer hummed to life just as the back door creaked open.

Perfect.

The last thing she wanted was someone intruding on her sacred morning ritual. These early hours were hers—her time to center herself, to plan, to brace for whatever idiocy the day would bring.

Her scowl deepened when Johnson strode in, his jaunty step earning a quiet curse under her breath. She glued her eyes to the monitor. Maybe he'd take the hint if she didn't look at him.

He didn't.

As he passed her desk, he gave her a wink. "Morning, Riggs."

"Morning," she grumbled, not looking up. Her voice was muffled by the rim of her cup.

Johnson settled into his chair, ignoring her brush-off. "So," he said casually, "I thought we might check out a few spots this perv could've used to hold up with the girls he took."

She'd planned to ignore him, but that bait was too tempting to pass up. She looked up, brow lifting. "Where'd you come up with this list of possible locations?"

His eyes narrowed for a beat, then crinkled at the corners as he grinned. "Asked around a bit. Focused on remote spots—old hunting cabins, that sort of thing."

"Not bad, Johnson. We'll head out once Sylvia gets in."

Johnson stood and moved to her desk, resting a hip on the edge. "I already gave her a heads-up. She said she'd come in early to cover us."

Riggs didn't like the idea of leaving the office unattended, even for a few minutes. What if someone needed help and no one was here? But still... if she was the one to find the perp's hideout, it could be the kind of break that elevated her career. She'd be a shoo-in for the sheriff position when it opened up.

In the end, ambition always won.

"All right. Let's go." She grabbed her purse and locked her desk.

She led the way to the parking lot. Pulling out the patrol car keys, Riggs headed for the driver's side. Her hand was on the door handle when Johnson called out.

"Looks like we need to take your car." He nodded toward the front right tire. "Unless you feel like changing a flat?"

Riggs came around the front, frowning. Johnson was right—not only was the tire flat, but a three-inch nail jutted from the sidewall.

"Why can't you change it?" she asked.

"Not in my job description."

"And it's in mine?" She shot him a look. "I thought you were supposed to be a man's man. Isn't this like... rolling in the mud for you?"

He held up both hands and took a step back. "If you don't want to go check out this lead, no big deal. I'm sure Marcos will go with me."

Riggs glanced at her SUV, parked a few spaces away. It gleamed in the rising sun, the recent wax job catching the light. She turned back to Johnson.

"Why can't we take yours?"

He hitched his chin toward his motorcycle. He didn't ride it to work often, but of course, the one day his truck would've come in handy, he'd left it at home.

"Fine." She huffed, digging out her keys as she stalked to her car. Then she stopped, spun on her heel, and poked him in the chest. "If there's one scratch on my baby after this, you're dead."

"Sure," Johnson said with an easy smile as he slid into the passenger seat.

With the car in gear, she checked the rearview as she backed out. "Where's the first spot?"

Johnson held his phone in his hand. "Out on the state route, just past Williams Boot."

She frowned. "That's kind of out of the way, isn't it? Not exactly near the drop site."

"No, it's not," he said, "but I figured we'd start furthest out and work our way back in."

She shot him a look as a thought struck her. "How many places are we talking?"

"Just four for now. Figured we'd hit these today. If they don't pan out, we can check others tomorrow."

Riggs narrowed her eyes. "Interesting you'd start with the furthest ones. Most people would begin closer to the dump site and expand outward."

Johnson's gaze turned straight ahead. His mouth thinned. "I looked more at the remoteness of the location," he said, his tone even, "How difficult it was to get to, and whether the place had resources available."

"Resources?"

"Yeah, like running water, a power source, things like that."

The more he explained, the more impressed she became. She'd pegged him as the village idiot, but this gave her pause. Maybe she'd been too quick to judge. She might need to rethink her strategy, especially if she hoped to sit in the big chair one day.

"Not bad, Johnson. Looks like you thought this through." She gave him a sideways glance. "I'm impressed. If this pans out, I'll make sure the sheriff knows it was your idea."

"Thanks, Riggs. Glad you think it's a solid plan." He glanced at his phone, then back to the road ahead. "Oh, make a right here."

"Here?"

"Yeah. The directions say in about a mile, you'll make a left."

After the turn, the SUV lurched and bounced over the dirt road with each rut. Her fingers tightened on the steering wheel as she struggled to keep her car on the path.

"Wow, this road's rough. Good thing I brought my SUV."

He ignored the comment. Like it had been her idea.

"Here it is—up on the right. Do you see it?"

"Yep, I see it." She pulled into a gravel driveway, shut off the car, and climbed out.

"You want to take the back, and I'll check the front?"

"Sure." Riggs made her way around the back of the small hunter's cabin. She doubted the place was more than three hundred square feet. Peeking into the windows as she went, she saw sparse furnishings—a cot in the corner, a small table and chair in the center, a cast-iron fireplace, and a sink with a tall cabinet beside it.

There was no dust buildup or cobwebs, meaning someone kept the place up. She continued around until she reached the front again, where Johnson stood waiting.

"Any luck?" she asked Johnson.

"No. The door's locked, and I didn't see anything that gives us probable cause. You?"

"Same."

Riggs put her hands on her hips and took a step back. "Looks pretty well maintained, considering how remote it is."

"Suppose so," Johnson said from behind.

"Weird that your contact would send you to check out this place," Riggs said, frowning. "The only thing it meets is that it is remote.

Otherwise, nothing about this place would provide a reliable place for someone to—"

Her words cut off in a startled cry.

A hot, searing pain tore through her back, stealing her breath. She reached instinctively for her weapon, but her arm dropped uselessly to her side. Her knees buckled. Blinded by pain, she stumbled, trying to stay upright, but collapsed to one knee.

Her mind spun in a fog of confusion. She reached out for Johnson—only he wasn't there.

He was circling her. Slowly. A five-inch blade in one gloved hand.

Gloved?

Her gaze locked on the black leather, confused. *Was he wearing those earlier?* She didn't think so. Her eyes lifted to his face, searching for something to reveal the joke—some sign this wasn't what it looked like.

"What are you doing?" She pressed a hand to her wound, breath ragged. "Why do you have a knife?"

Each question drained more energy from her until the last came out in a gasp.

"What's going on?"

An odd glint entered his eye—something she'd never seen before. She shivered. Her muscles quivered as she tried and failed to stand. A sick, hollow panic twisted in her gut.

Johnson stopped in front of her, gripping her left shoulder. His fingers biting into her flesh. Slowly—deliberately—he drove the knife into her stomach, his eyes locked on hers. Her body jerked, trying to recoil, but he held her firm.

The first stab had just been a taste, barely grazing her kidney. This one went deep—blade to the hilt. She felt her blood spill over his hand, warm and slick as it hit the ground.

He watched her face, savoring the shift: shock... confusion... and finally, fear. The moment her eyes filled with the knowledge she was going to die—*that* was the moment he wanted to remember.

Riggs lay stunned, no longer feeling the cold, hard ground beneath her. Her eyes focused on Johnson, mirroring the horror consuming her. Only one word echoed in her mind until it broke free in a gurgled breath, "Why?" She demanded. "Why?"

Johnson crouched beside her, a cruel smile stretching across his face.

"Because you humiliated me in front of everyone and thought there wouldn't be consequences. Because I've dreamed of this moment for *years*. Yesterday, you gave me the excuse I needed."

He leaned in, his voice lower, darker.

"Because if I couldn't fuck you... this was the next best thing."

He laughed then—sharp and jagged. He pressed two fingers into her open wound. Beyond feeling now, Riggs couldn't move, numb to the torment of his probing fingers. Limp from the loss of blood. Cold. So very cold.

He's trying to kill me.

Over what? A few jokes? A bruised ego?

Was that all her life had been worth?

Her thoughts slowed, muddled by shock and blood loss.

Sylvia... he said he told Sylvia.

Someone would know. Someone had to.

He wouldn't get away with this.

He couldn't.

Her final thought, faint as breath: *No.*

Johnson watched her last breath release before standing up.

He peeled off his gloves, shoved them into his pocket, and walked to her car to retrieve his bag. Blood clung to his uniform, tacky and warm. He peeled it off piece by piece and slipped into a clean one—same department badge, same name patch. Just... not soaked in her.

Shoes, clothes, knife—all of it went into the bag.

He zipped it shut and started jogging north, back toward the dirt pullout where he'd left the truck he'd borrowed from his buddy. His pace was steady and practiced. Not rushed.

He'd timed it all.

Forty minutes. That's how long he had before Sylvia clocked in.

No one would know he and Riggs had left early this morning. Once he was back in the office, sitting at his desk, his alibi was locked in. He'd been there all day.

As long as nothing got in his way...

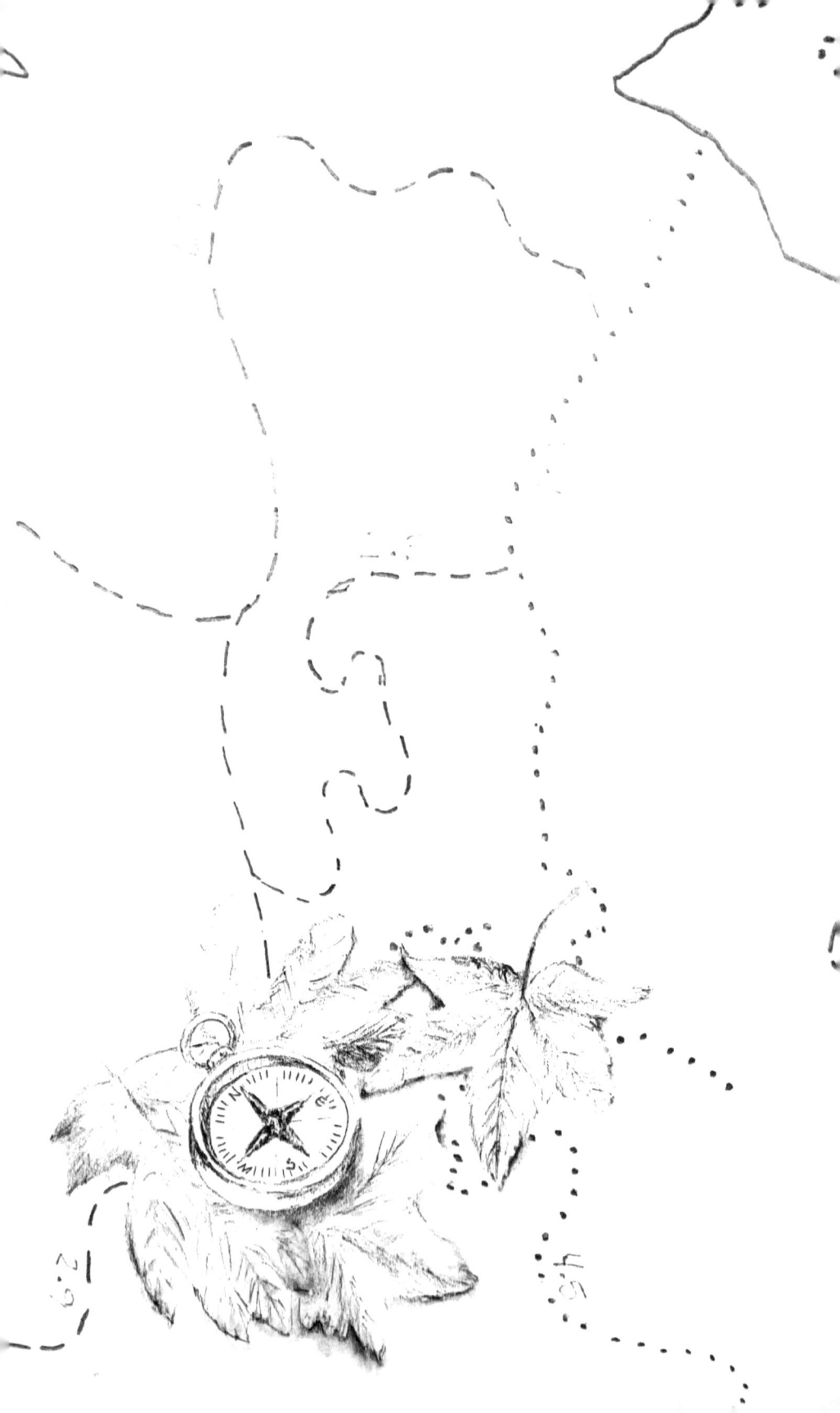

Chapter Eighteen

Sylvia walked into the office five minutes early, just the way she liked it, nodding to Johnson as she headed to her desk. She unloaded her arms and pressed the button on her outdated answering machine. Three messages were already waiting. This place would be lost without her. She arranged her things, grabbed her notepad and pen, and began jotting down notes from the messages.

Only one seemed important enough to consider waking him: the school district in Prior County had called with information for Deputy Riggs. They hadn't been able to reach her and wanted to make sure the sheriff's office had received the message.

"Deputy Johnson?"

He looked up from his computer. "Yes, Sylvia?"

"Have you heard from Riggs today?"

"Yeah, she came in early but said she wasn't feeling well. Called it a day. Why—something I can help with?"

"Not really. I've got a message for her, and if she's out, it should probably go to the sheriff to decide what to do with it."

"Come now, Sylvia," Johnson coaxed. "Why don't you give it to me? No reason to wake the sheriff over something minor like a missed call." He flashed one of his charming smiles and gave her a playful wink.

Sylvia wavered. Johnson always reminded her of her son, Tuck. The same flirty grin she could never quite resist.

"I suppose you're right. Let me write it down again so the sheriff has a copy. Here you go, says they've been trying her all morning. Hope she feels better."

"I think it was a stabbing pain or something. I'm sure it'll pass. These things usually do, you know." Looking at the note, Johnson added, "I'll call them back, see what they have to say."

He walked back to his desk, whistling cheerfully to himself.

Kate sat at her dining room table, staring at her cereal. She couldn't eat—her appetite had given way to worry. Her mind kept drifting to the woods beyond her front door. The dense foliage had never bothered her before, but now, knowing someone had been hiding in those shadows made her painfully aware of how vulnerable she was.

Too many places to hide. The thought of being stalked set her teeth on edge. She was used to being the hunter, not the prey, and the role reversal left her raw and exposed.

After this little outing with Fox, she needed to look into a monitoring system for the house and the surrounding woods. Something with infrared. She didn't want to miss him the next time he decided to drop by uninvited.

A light knock sounded at her door. Shoving her uneaten cereal aside, Kate rose to answer it. Fox stood on her porch, smiling. His stance was casual, but she could feel the energy simmering beneath it.

She gave him a quick once-over, surprised to see he'd chosen a suit and tie. She arched a brow in silent question. Meanwhile, she wore yoga pants, a light sweater, and tennis shoes. Oh well. She gave a mental shrug and stepped outside, forcing him to step back.

She'd hoped this morning wouldn't be awkward. She'd shown her hand—overstepped. Now, she wasn't sure what to say and was already on edge; remembering the night before wasn't helping. She struggled not to blush.

As she turned to lock the door, a warm, solid arm slipped around her waist, drawing her back against an even warmer, more solid chest.

"Good morning, beautiful," he murmured, nuzzling her ear.

A small smile tugged at her lips. "Good morning yourself," she said, elbowing him lightly. "A little overdressed, don't you think?"

"Not at all," he said, rubbing the rib she'd elbowed. "I need to follow up on a few leads after we finish at the crime scene. Figured it made more sense to head straight to the office instead of doubling back to the motel for a change of clothes."

"You could've brought them with you," she said, arching a brow. "I do have a bathroom, you know."

"Believe me, I thought about it. But I didn't want to waste the time." He stroked a finger down her cheek. "The clock's ticking. It won't be long before this guy strikes again."

Kate knocked his hand away. "Really, why do you think that?"

"Sherri," he said, his tone going pensive. "How she was found tells me something went wrong—something that disrupted his M.O. And that kind of deviation? It eats at them. When they don't get what they want, they escalate."

Kate hesitated. "Won't it be easier to catch them if they take another girl?" She tried not to sound insensitive, but gauging Fox's stare,

"Only if we know the moment she goes missing and she's nearby. But even then..." He laced his fingers through hers as they walked to his car. "We still know next to nothing about this person. They could slip right through our fingers."

She frowned at their joined hands. It was a harmless gesture; she'd held hands with others before, but this felt different. As though there was an underlying meaning to it that she didn't want to know.

"Why did you want to see the dump site? I'm sure you've reviewed the crime scene photos; what more do you hope to find?"

"I want to see it for myself. There's something about it—something the photos aren't showing me."

"What makes you think there is more there than just a dump site?" she asked, her curiosity slipping out before she could stop it. She thought about telling him she'd already been out there... but didn't. She had a feeling he'd find a reason to be upset about it.

"If this person likes to dump bodies, then where are the others? Why haven't they been found?"

"Wild animals?" Kate offered. "I mean, bodies left in the open can disappear pretty fast, right?"

"Sure, animals can scatter remains and make a cause of death hard to determine—but it takes *weeks*. That's still plenty of time for someone to stumble across it."

"Okay. What else?"

"It's how she was left," he said. "Just lying there, out in the middle of a meadow? If this was just about disposal, why was it done somewhere so open, so easy to find? They've been careful this long—why slip up now?"

"You think they *didn't* want her found?" Kate was surprised. She'd assumed it had just been a careless drop, maybe meant for animals to finish the job. *Not that she'd ever worried about body disposal herself.*

Proof of the kill was usually required in her line of work. Otherwise, clients get upset.

"No," Fox said. "I think they had something else planned. And when the deputies stumbled on her, they had to abandon whatever that was. Which means, for them, the ritual wasn't complete."

"But why would that set them off? Why not just walk away and move on?"

"Because people like this aren't wired right. They can't form real attachments, so they create twisted ones with their victims. That's why they keep trophies, pieces, and possessions. It's all part of the ritual. And when that ritual gets interrupted..." He shook his head. "It messes with them. I may not have the proof yet, but there has to be something at that site. For some reason, they left her there. Something they didn't get to finish."

Fox turned down the narrow lane to the meadow where Sherri had been found. As soon as he parked, he was out of the car and opening her door before she could unbuckle. He held out a hand, leaving her no choice but to take it.

Why he thought she needed help getting out of a car was beyond her. But once she was on her feet, he didn't let go. Instead, he turned and started weaving through the trees, stepping over roots and ducking low branches—her hand still in his.

They walked together into the clearing. Everything looked just as it had the last time she'd been there: quiet, undisturbed, untouched by anything but memory.

Fox moved silently, leading her in a slow circle, stopping now and again to study the ground, the trees, and the slope of the land. Neither of them spoke. Fox looked just as lost in thought as she felt.

Kate looked down at their joined hands. It felt out of place—too soft, too intimate for a place like this. She couldn't remember the last time she'd held someone's hand. Maybe that boy she dated for a while after high school. His name escaped her now.

But it wasn't the hand-holding itself that unsettled her. It was the way it felt *forced*, like she was being drawn into something she hadn't agreed to—something warm and safe and close.

She lived in solitude. It was her shield and her comfort.

So what was she supposed to do with a man who didn't ask for anything yet still managed to want something from her?

Kate gave her hand a subtle twist, testing if she could slip free without making a scene.

Without breaking stride, Fox spun her toward him, catching her with a firm, almost theatrical pull. Their bodies collided with a soft thud, and before she could protest, his arm curled behind her back, fingers still laced with hers. The warmth of his chest pressed against her, stealing her breath.

"What the hell are you doing?" she muttered, placing her free hand on his chest.

He just grinned, easing his face close to hers. "Dancing," he said, swaying slowly as if the forest itself had cued up a song only he could hear.

"You're ridiculous."

"What's wrong?" he crooned.

"You're smothering me," Kate muttered against his neck, irritation threading through her voice. She couldn't believe he was dancing with her in the middle of the forest.

"Aw, honey, don't you like touching me?" he murmured, brushing his lips against her neck in an infuriatingly gentle kiss.

A strangled sound escaped her as she tried to focus on her breathing, willing herself to ignore his slow, relentless assault. They were here to do a job. If she kept repeating that, maybe she could resist the liquid heat he was stirring inside her. Damn him—he was making a mess of everything. And yet, her body betrayed her, leaning into him, her head tilting to give him better access to the sensitive line of her neck—one she hadn't even realized existed until now.

He released her hands and gripped her hips, pulling her firmly against him. His mouth claimed hers in a kiss that left her reeling, her pulse quickening in response. She melted into him, arms wrapping around his neck, drawn by something deeper than desire—need.

Their bodies moved together, her hips instinctively seeking relief from the tension coiled tight inside her. He made her burn—there was no other word for it.

Somehow, they'd danced out of the clearing and against a tree. The bark scraped against her back, sharp and real against the warmth of his body pressing into her front. She reached for his mouth again, needing the connection, the heat, the grounding. Their lips met, and the world narrowed to the taste of him, the feel of him.

Her sense of control frayed, unraveling one thread at a time. She was losing herself, and for a breathless moment, she didn't care.

Then, the hairs on her neck prickled. A chill slithered down her spine, extinguishing the fire.

She stiffened in his arms, breaking the spell. Fox lifted his head. Puzzled, he looked down at her. Quietly, she whispered in his ear, "We aren't alone."

She felt him draw closer, his breath warm against her ear as he whispered, "Where? Can you tell?"

"No," Kate whispered, shaking her head slightly. "I can't see anything, but the forest feels different. There's something out there."

Fox didn't question her instincts. "I'm going to lift you up—wrap your legs around me. Look over my shoulder, see what you can spot."

His hands moved to her waist, lifting her with ease. She wrapped her legs around him, holding tight, scanning the woods behind him. The position was intimate—too intimate—and her body betrayed her, recalling the heat from moments ago.

But she forced her attention outward, narrowing her eyes at the tree line and searching. She caught a flicker of movement—a shadow slipping between trees—but nothing clear enough to call out. Her body remained taut, caught between fear and lingering desire.

Fox's breath was warm against her chest. "Anything?"

Kate swallowed hard. "No. Just... wolves, I think. They were watching. But they're gone now."

"Wolves?" he asked, glancing toward the brush. "You sensed them before you saw them?"

Still perched in his arms, Kate nodded, her face pressed against his shoulder. "I didn't know what it was. I just knew something was off."

Fox didn't say anything. He just held her tighter, his hands warm and steady, grounding her as her racing heart slowly began to settle. When he finally loosened his grip, she slid down the length of him, her feet finding the forest floor again. The contact should've made her feel steadier—but it didn't.

He didn't step back. His arms stayed around her, one hand gliding up and down her back in slow, soothing strokes. The intimacy of the touch, the tenderness in it, unraveled something inside her. She hated that it felt good. Hated that she wanted to lean into it.

"Kate," he murmured.

The way he said her name—it was too much. Too gentle. Too real. It slid under her defenses like a knife wrapped in silk. She couldn't face him. Not now. Maybe not ever. All she wanted was to go home, reset, and get her mind back on the job—on something she understood. This... this mess between them? It wasn't something she could make sense of.

She stayed quiet, unsure of what her voice might betray if she tried to use it.

"Are you ready to go home?" he asked.

Kate nodded, not trusting herself to speak. She felt the shift in his body as he accepted her answer. Then, carefully, she pulled away from him. She didn't look at him, not really. Just enough to see the edge of his expression, and that was more than enough. She didn't need to see the whole thing to recognize it. Disappointment. Maybe something more. She didn't want to know.

Her body moved on autopilot, stiff and awkward in ways she hated. Every step felt like it broadcasted her confusion, her shame. She knew he was watching. She could feel his eyes on her, warm and heavy. And even though part of her wished he'd say something—anything—to make it less terrible, the rest of her was grateful he didn't.

Whatever had just happened, she'd have to figure it out on her own.

Desperate to distract herself from her spiraling thoughts, Kate focused on the forest floor as they walked. A sudden glint of light bounced off something half-buried in the leaves, catching her eye. As they neared it, she saw it was just a crumpled foil wrapper—gum or candy, probably. But the sight triggered a memory.

The pendant.

She'd found it that day in the woods, the same day she'd felt eyes on her. The same day, she'd been too rattled to think straight. In all the chaos, she'd shoved the charm into her pocket and completely forgotten it.

Well, shit.

How was she supposed to explain that to Fox? That she'd had a potential clue for—how many days now?—and hadn't said a word? It could be nothing, sure. But it could just as easily be everything. She needed to make sure she still had it. Hopefully, it was buried somewhere in her laundry. She'd deal with that later.

She was so caught up in the thought that she didn't notice the root until it snagged her boot. She pitched forward with a yelp, bracing for the forest floor—but Fox caught her, arms around her waist before she hit the ground.

Great.

She hated that he'd caught her. Hated needing his help. She would've loved nothing more than to shove his hands off her, but she knew that was childish, and it wasn't his fault her body and brain weren't syncing up today. Grudgingly, she gripped his hand and steadied herself. "Thanks," she muttered.

"You okay?" Fox asked, easing his hold.

"Yeah," she grumbled. "I wasn't paying attention. Tripped on a root."

The awkwardness between them flared again, and she hated how unnatural everything felt now.

Fox tried to lighten the mood. "Hey, that's what I'm here for—to be the hero who saves you."

She bristled. "I don't normally need saving, so don't get used to it." Her tone came out sharper than she intended, but she didn't bother to soften it. He needed to understand—she wasn't someone who fell apart just because things got messy.

Fox didn't rise to the bait. She could feel him watching her, amused, unbothered. If anything, her outburst seemed to amuse him more.

"You good to walk, or should I carry you?" he asked, a teasing edge in his voice.

She shot him a look. "I can walk." She yanked her hand free and stalked ahead of him, not trusting herself to stay close. He let her go, following behind with a low chuckle.

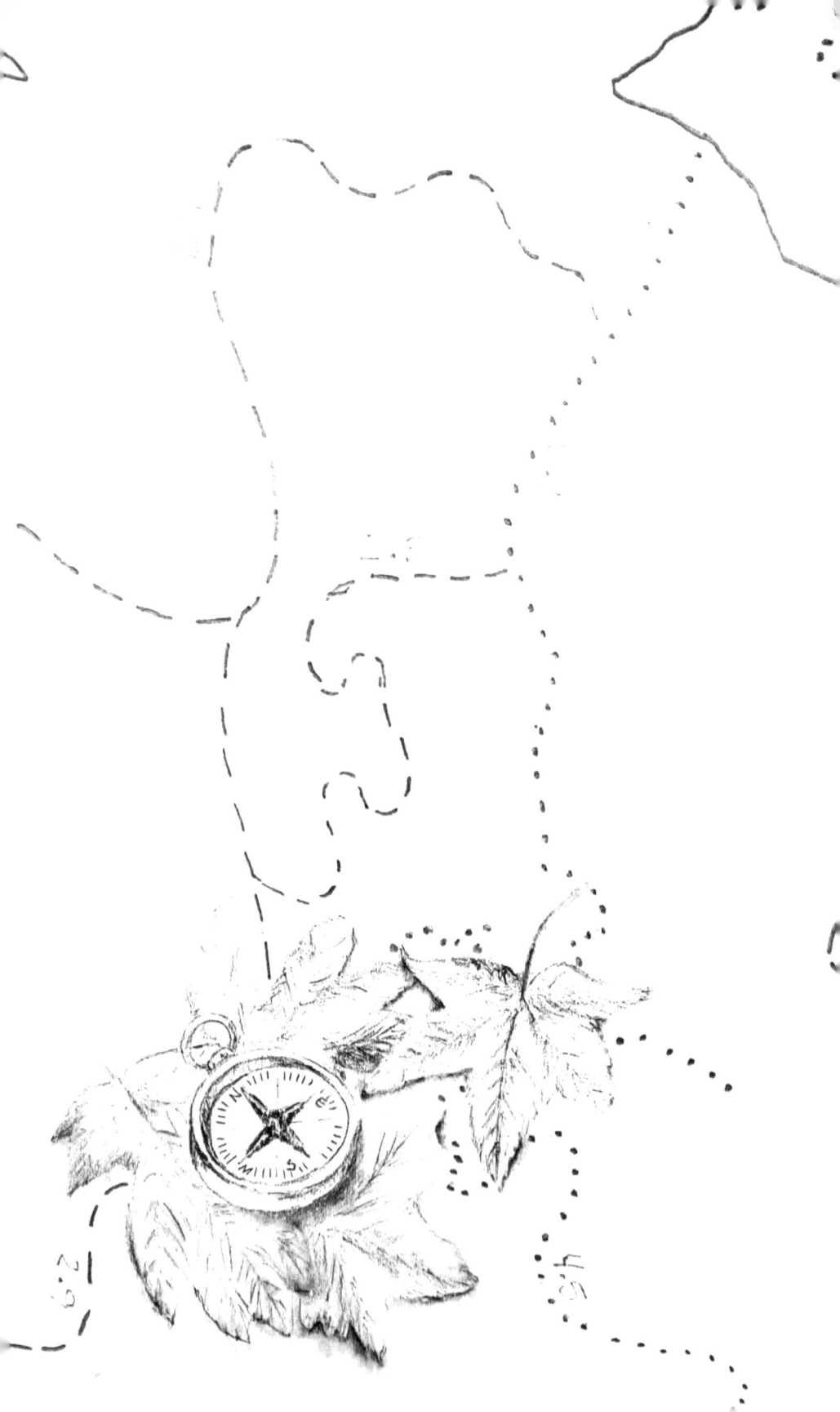

Chapter Nineteen

K ate slammed the door behind her, tossing her keys onto the entry table with a clatter.

Fox's parting words echoed in her head like a taunt: *"I'm coming over tonight. I'll pick up dinner."*

Then, like he had any right, he'd grabbed her by the back of the neck, kissed her hard, and practically shoved her out of the car before she could argue.

Presumptuous ass.

Kate stomped to her room, muttering under her breath.

She needed to get out of her dirty clothes. Her pants were caked with mud at the knees, her back still covered in dirt and bark from where Fox had pressed her against the tree. She peeled off the layers, striding to the closet, and tossed them into the hamper.

That's when she remembered the pendant.

A smug smile tugged at her lips. This was one thing Fox didn't know about—her one-up on him. It wasn't much, but it was hers. And it might just lead her to the killer first.

Digging it out gave her the perfect excuse to dump the rest of the laundry onto the floor and shove it back in with more force than necessary.

"Well, take it nice and easy," she mimicked, rolling her eyes. What if she didn't want to take "it" anywhere?

"One step at a time," he'd said. Ha. Maybe for now, but when this case ended, they would also. His job would take him away, and he'd blow out of her life as quickly as he'd blown in.

She shoved her dirty clothes in one by one, still muttering. Only when she reached the bottom of the pile did she find the pants she'd worn the day she'd first felt his presence.

An eerie ripple of unease crawled down her spine.

He'd been there again.

Either he'd followed her... or he'd come because of Sherri. Which only made sense if Fox was right—if there was something else. Something that pulled him back.

She sighed when her fingers closed around the cold metal, the small pendant still tucked in the front pocket of her pants. It was a stroke of luck that she hadn't lost what might be a key piece of evidence. At least if she had, she wouldn't have to figure out how to explain to Fox how she'd come to have it.

Kate tossed the pendant in the air and caught it, her mind cycling through idea after idea. None of them felt right. She had to figure out how to tell Fox—not just that she'd found a potential clue days ago, but that she'd kept it quiet. A little finesse wouldn't hurt. Maybe she could cross-reference it first and make sure it meant something.

She pulled out her case file box, perfectly alphabetized like always, and flipped to the "M" tab. Megan Sanders. Her finger scanned down the list of what the girl had last been seen wearing.

Red t-shirt. Blue jeans. Pink jacket. Pink polka dot shoes...

Kate's breath caught.

"Gold locket engraved with initials' MK.'"

Bingo.

Fox walked into the sheriff's office, his arms full of baked goods fresh from Sue's bakery. He knew they were in for a long day, and a little bribery never hurt when it came to morale.

Shane clocked the bags in Fox's hands and wasted no time relieving him of the load, sneaking a peek as he carried them to the center table. Without ceremony, he pulled out muffins, bagels, donuts, cupcakes, and brownies, lining them up like they were about to be judged.

Fox surveyed the spread, thinking wryly that he was fast becoming one of Sue's best customers.

"This all looks great," Shane said, grabbing a cream-filled donut. "What's the occasion?"

Fox took a muffin for himself. "No occasion. Just figured we could all use a little extra fuel. It's going to be a long day."

Marcos and Johnson each helped themselves to muffins.

"Thanks, Anderson. That's awfully kind of you," Marcos said around a mouthful of blueberry.

Satisfied that everyone was settled and the sugar was kicking in, Fox straightened. "All right, let's get to work. I want to know where we're at. Marcos, Shane—were you able to find out if anyone else knew Emma was planning to sneak out?"

"No. The only other people who knew were her friend Sara and Sara's brother, Davey," Shane said. "We're planning to head back out there to speak with a couple of her closest friends in person. We've been working with the local sheriff's department, but they haven't offered anything new so far."

"Any link to the Windsor Brooke football team?"

Shane shook his head. "Nothing. We couldn't find any connection between the team and the night she went missing."

Damn. Fox had been hoping they'd turn up something—anything—that tied the team to the cases.

He began to pace. "That'll do for now. Stick with it. Johnson—" he looked around—"Where's Riggs?"

Johnson shrugged. "No idea. She left this morning and said she wasn't feeling well. Haven't seen her since."

"Okay, then, can *you* fill me in?" Fox asked, fixing Johnson with a look. "What links have you found so far?"

"April Davis was taken the same night the high school played Windsor Brooke's football team. Becky Larson disappeared a week after the playoff game against Windsor Brooke. Megan Sanders went missing two weeks after our school played them. We're still trying to confirm whether Megan or Becky attended those games," Johnson said. "Riggs had a note to call one of the school districts back. I assume she'll handle it when she comes in."

Fox shook his head. "No—I don't want to wait on any potential leads."

He stepped in closer, his tone sharpening. "You follow up with the school district. Find out what they wanted to tell Riggs. Then, get on the phone with both families. I want to know if either girl went to any of those games—and if they did, which teams were playing. There's a connection here. I can feel it. We just have to find it."

He turned back to Marcos and Shane. "Shane, forget the road trip. Stay here and start calling. Get the sheriff's department to interview

Emma's friends, her teachers, and anyone who might know something. We don't have time to waste."

Then, more pointedly, "What do we know about Sara's brother? Any weird vibes? How old is he again?"

"I'm not sure," Shane admitted. "We didn't talk to him. We were mostly focused on Sara."

Fox caught the glance exchanged between Shane and Marcos and didn't like it.

He narrowed his eyes. "What do you mean you didn't talk to him?"

Shane shifted uncomfortably. "He just came off like one of those dumb jock types. You know the kind—too into himself to notice much else."

Fox stared at him, stunned. That wasn't just lazy—it was reckless.

Before he could respond, Sylvia spoke up, her tone cutting through the room like a blade. "Deputy Shane," she said firmly, slipping into the voice of someone who'd raised a few kids of her own. "I suggest you keep your unkind opinions to yourself. Just because that boy plays sports doesn't make him stupid. I find your assumption insulting."

Fox watched as Shane immediately backed down, shoulders folding in like a reprimanded teenager. No one wanted to get on Sylvia's bad side.

"Sorry, Sylvia," Shane mumbled. "I didn't mean it like that. I wasn't talking about your boy. I know he's smart. We talked the other day, and he mentioned some of his classes. He's doing great."

Fox didn't care about Shane's apology. He cared about missed leads and sloppy instincts. If Davey had been in the house that night and they'd overlooked him because of a lazy stereotype, that was unacceptable.

He folded his arms and stared Shane down. "Scratch what I said before. I don't want anyone else interviewing him but you two. You're going back today. I want a full write-up—no assumptions this time, just facts."

Fox glanced at his watch. "If you leave now, you should make it there and back before five. Use the drive to make those phone calls we talked about."

Fox walked up to Sylvia's desk and placed a chocolate muffin in an open spot, hoping to sweet-talk her into a few assignments.

"Sylvia, will you give Riggs a call? Ask her to check in when she can. I want an update on her status—and, more importantly, when she'll be back at work."

"Okay, I'll give you a call as soon as I talk with her."

"You're a pearl. Would you also give the sheriff a call? I want to talk with him about this weekend."

Sylvia looked past him, eyeing a chocolate-glazed donut. Taking the hint, Fox grabbed it and placed it next to the muffin.

"Of course. Anything else?" she asked.

"Not that I can think of—at least not right now," he said, giving her a wink.

Now, it was time to reassess the case. He was missing something. He could feel it just beneath the surface. He'd hoped for a clue at the site where Sherri's body had been found, but nothing had stood out.

He needed to start at the beginning, work his way through, and see where it led. And the beginning, for him, was Sherri.

Why would she go with a stranger? What would cause her to walk away and leave her home behind?

Maybe she hadn't gone with a stranger at all. Maybe she'd known the person—a family friend, a neighbor, someone she'd seen often enough to trust. That would mean they were local.

And if they were local, the real question became: how were they finding the other girls? Girls across state lines, miles away.

How were they chosen? And why were they going with them?

He needed to talk to Sherri's mom. If anyone could give him a list of people Sherri trusted enough to follow, it would be her.

"I need one more thing, Sylvia. Can you give me the address for Sherri's mother?"

Fox pulled on his jacket, grabbed the slip of paper, and headed for the door. Adrenaline surged through him.

Sherri had the key.

He just had to find it.

Kate pulled her phone from her pocket and silenced it again. Cara had been calling all day, probably to talk about Fox. But Kate didn't have the energy—or the clarity—for that conversation.

She lined up her throwing knives on the tree stump she'd cut specifically for this purpose. Physical exertion had always been her escape. The push and pull of her muscles, the precision in her movements—it was the one place her mind went quiet.

She'd had the training area built in secret, hiring over twenty different contractors from out of town to ensure no one saw the full scope of it. What looked like a simple wood-cutting space was actually a concealed target range. Six massive stumps stacked in a pyramid stood across from a single stump thirteen feet away. Beyond that, an obstacle course snaked into the woods—climbing walls, balance beams, and natural hazards designed to keep her sharp.

She spent the first hour running the course over and over, driving herself into that sweet spot of exhaustion. Then, as always, she ended with knives.

The rhythmic sound of steel sinking into the wood was its own kind of meditation. Throwing knives had become a part of her. Weighing in at only one twenty-five, most of her opponents outweighed her. Speed and accuracy were her weapons. And when hand-to-hand couldn't be avoided, she didn't hesitate. The blade had become an extension of her, one she'd honed to deadly precision.

With her body humming and her mind finally still, she let the first knife fly.

She squared up with her target again, relishing the familiar feel of smooth, cool steel between her fingers. The cadence of blades slamming into the wood was almost musical.

Her hip vibrated—again.

Sighing, Kate pulled her phone from her pocket. "Hi, Cara."

"Oh my *goodness*, where have you been?" Cara's voice practically screeched in her ear.

Kate rolled her eyes. "What do you mean, where have I been? I've been working—trying to track down the asshole you *asked* me to hunt, remember?"

"I *know*, I know. But why haven't you been answering your phone?"

Because I know exactly what you want to talk about, and I don't want to talk about it.

"I've been busy," Kate said aloud. "Didn't want to stop and chat, is all."

"Well then, *tell me*—why was that agent at your house last night? Is there something going on with you two?"

"No, of course not." She kept her tone even. "The sheriff told him I was looking into what happened to Sherri, and he wanted to ask what I knew."

Kate hoped that would be enough to end it.

Cara snorted. "Yeah, right. Like I was born yesterday. The way he was looking at you? He *couldn't wait* for me to leave. Come on, I'm your best friend. You can tell me."

Kate moaned in defeat, "All right, he might be interested in me too. Honestly, I have no idea what is happening with him. All I know is he will leave when this case is solved."

With a giggle, Cara exclaimed, "I knew it! This is great, Kate. When do you see him next?"

"Didn't you hear what I said? He's leaving. Why would I get involved with someone who'll be leaving soon?"

"Oh, I don't know, maybe because he's hot!"

Laughing, Kate admitted, "He is that, isn't he?"

"Come on, Kate," Cara urged, "he's drop-dead gorgeous, and honestly, it's been ages since you've even had a date. Why don't you take him for a spin? What is the worst that could happen?"

Kate could think of at least five bad things that could happen: "Oh gee, I don't know. Maybe he would figure out what my *real* job is, which could complicate things."

"So," Cara said, "You usually work with the government. You're going to have to do better than that."

"Okay, how about when he realizes I'm going to kill this pervert I am currently hunting. I don't think the FBI would look kindly on my killing someone who wasn't a sanctioned hit."

"Okay, you may have a point there," she conceded, "But you've been fooling the town for years. I'm sure you could fool him, too."

"I'm glad to hear you're so cavalier with my freedom. How about I develop feelings, and he leaves and breaks my heart?"

"You should know better than anyone that life is meant to be lived, and with living comes hurting. Besides, who says he doesn't fall in love with you too? Then you'd just have to figure out how to make it work."

"Don't you think I would have to be honest with him about who I am if we were in love?"

"Eventually, I wouldn't worry about it. Why borrow trouble? You should enjoy the ride for as long as it takes you."

Easier said than done, Kate allowed. "We will have to see, I guess. In the meantime, I need to get back to work."

"Okay, okay, I understand. You'll fill me in on how things go with him, right?"

"Yeah, sure."

"Oh, by the way, what's his name?"

"Fox Anderson."

"Did you say, Fox?"

"Yes, his mom loves animals," Kate said, smiling.

"Kate Anderson has a nice ring to it, don't you think?" Cara teased.

"Sure, whatever you say. Bye, Cara." Kate hung up, sliding her phone into her back pocket. Picking up another knife, she threw it with lethal precision, hitting the center of her target.

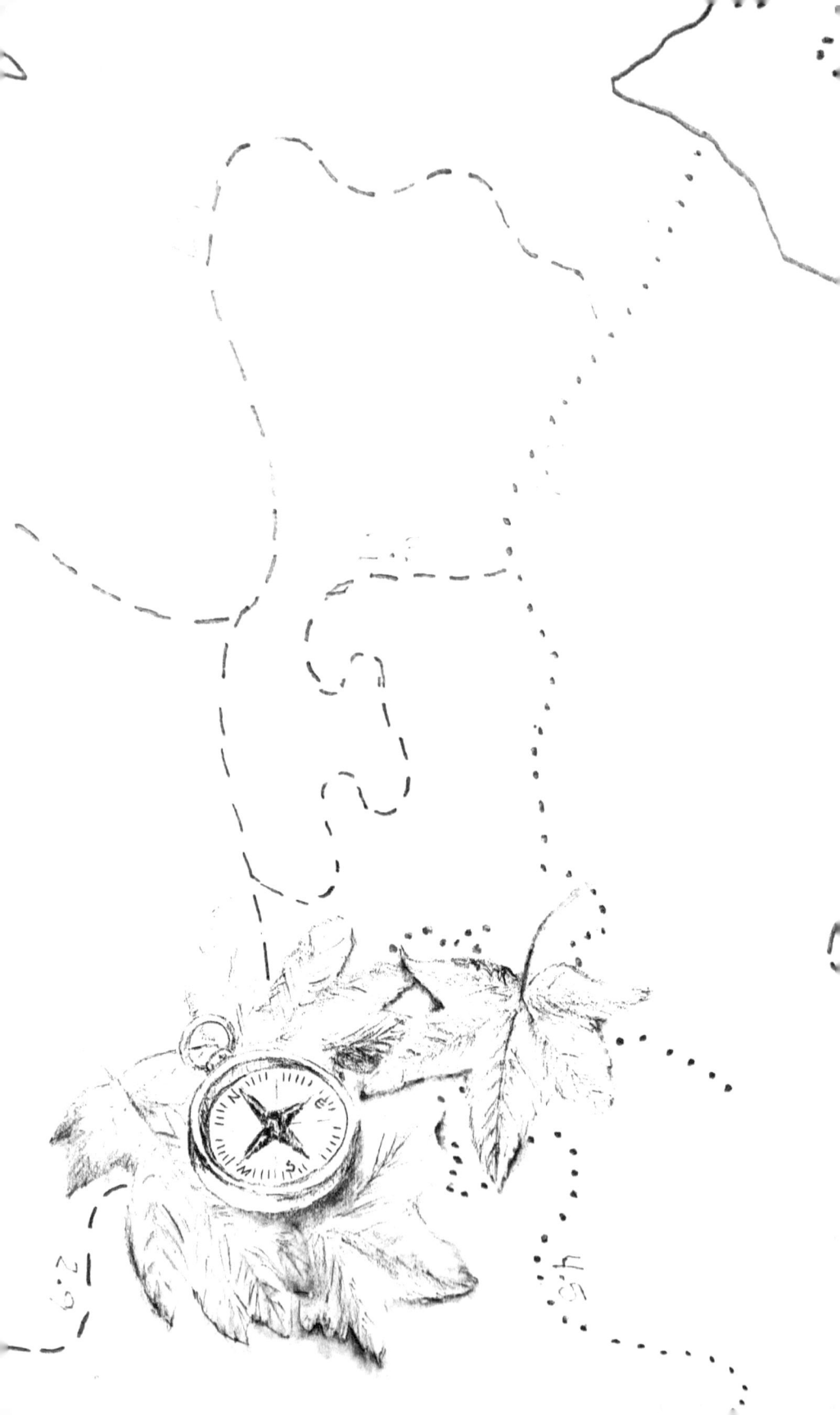

Chapter Twenty

Marcos and Shane pulled up alongside the curb of Sara's home. Shane was still kicking himself over the mistake they'd made. He couldn't believe he and Marcos had messed up so badly. There would be no screwups this time—he'd handle the questioning, and Marcos would take notes. Striding up to the front door, Shane knocked hard, then took a step back, jaw tight.

The door swung open, and Sara smiled up at them, holding a melting popsicle. "Hi Sara, do you remember us?"

"You're the police looking for Emma."

"That's right, we wanted to see if we could talk to your brother again."

"He isn't here anymore."

"What do you mean?" Shane asked. "Did he just go out for the day?"

Shaking her head, she slurped on her popsicle, licking the side of her hand where the red juice dripped.

"Where did he go, Sara?"

"Dad said he had to move out. Said he was tired of paying for his lazy butt to sit on the couch all day."

"He moved out?" Frowning, Shane glanced at Marcos, "When did this happen?"

"Last night. Dad was drunk," Sara explained, scrunching her nose, "and mad like usual. He tripped over one of Davey's shoes and lost his temper."

"Do you know where we can find him?"

Sara shrugged her shoulders, swaying as she finished her popsicle.

"How about your father? Where can we find him?"

"Work."

"Where does he work?"

"Over at the shop in town."

"Do you know the name of the shop?"

"Joe's shop."

Kneeling in front of Sara, Shane held her gaze, "Thank you, Sara," he said, "Now, Sara, this is very important. Are you sure no one else knew what you and Emma planned to do?"

"No," Sara said, shaking her head. Then she paused for a moment, looking at her feet. Well...maybe I did tell someone."

Holding his breath, Shane asked, "Who?"

When she didn't answer right away, he grabbed her hand. "Who, Sara?" he urged.

"Uncle Johnny." She whispered.

"Who is Uncle Johnny?"

"He lives down the street. He's really nice. He always gives me change for the ice cream truck. Says I can sit with him on the porch and tell him all about my day."

"Does he ask you a lot of questions?"

"Sometimes, but sometimes he can't talk."

"Why can't he talk sometimes?"

"He has special friends who come and visit him. When they're there, I'm not supposed to say hi."

Shane looked over his shoulder at Marcos. This guy, Johnny, sounded promising. "Which house is Johnny's?"

"You won't tell him I told you, will you?" Sara asked worriedly, "It was supposed to be a secret."

"No, you don't need to worry. Now, which house is his?"

"It's the blue one with the big train set out front."

"Okay, Sara, this is very helpful. Thank you."

Shane and Marcos headed back to their car.

"I think we should talk to this Johnny character, then track down the dad," Shane said.

"Agreed," Marcos replied, sliding into the driver's seat.

They rolled slowly down the street, scanning house numbers until they spotted the blue house five doors down from Sara's. Just as she'd said, a sprawling, intricate model train setup filled the front yard. The setup was no kid's toy—it was clearly the work of a serious hobbyist. A miniature town sprawled across the lawn, complete with hand-painted storefronts, tiny lampposts, and a delicate bridge that arched over a small koi pond. Fish darted lazily beneath the surface as the train curved toward the bridge.

They followed the decorative stone path toward the front door, stepping over a wooden bridge built right over the train tracks. The train passed beneath their feet as they crossed and rattled toward the pond.

Shane had to admit—it was impressive.

Marcos knocked.

A few moments later, the door opened, revealing a man in a plaid button-down shirt and neatly pressed pleated pants. He looked like he'd stepped off the set of an old kids' show—smiling, clean-cut, and just neighborly enough to feel off.

"Can I help you?" the man asked, standing in the doorway.

"Yes, sir," Shane said. "We were hoping to ask you some questions about your neighbors a few doors down."

The man hesitated, just for a moment, before stepping aside. "Yeah, sure. Come on in."

He led them into a surprisingly pristine home. Everything was neat and spotless. The only clutter was the shelving on one wall, filled with a collection of old toys. Shane recognized a few from his own childhood—action figures, tin cars, and comic books.

"Nice collection," Shane said, nodding toward the display.

"Thank you. I like vintage things." The man motioned toward a pair of armchairs. "Please, make yourselves comfortable. I also collect model trains and cookie jars."

"Cookie jars?" Shane raised a brow.

The man chuckled. "I know—it's a bit odd. But they were my mother's. She had a passion for them, and she left the whole collection to me when she passed. Over the years, I've added a few, but hers are still the real gems."

He folded his hands in his lap, smiling politely. "Now, you mentioned my neighbors?"

Shane nodded. "First, may we ask your name?"

"Of course, my apologies," the man said. "John Myner. And you gentlemen are...?"

"I'm Deputy Shane, and this is Deputy Marcos. We wanted to ask you a few questions about the Hallis family. They live a few houses down. Are you acquainted with them?"

"Not particularly," John said, his tone easy. "Why? Is something wrong?"

"No, not at all." Shane assured him, "We are just looking for some character references."

"No, not at all," Shane assured him. "We're just looking for some character references."

"Ah, I see." John nodded thoughtfully. "Well, I don't know how helpful I can be. I don't talk with the father much—he works long hours and drinks a bit too much. I've never seen the mother, come to think of it. The boy's around a lot these days, ever since he graduated. And I see the little girl, Sara, walking home from school most afternoons. Always has a big smile on her face. Sometimes, she's with a friend, laughing and chatting. Thick as thieves, those two."

A small smile curved his lips.

"Do you know the friend's name?" Shane asked.

"Can't say for certain," John replied, tilting his head. "Might've been Emma. I've heard Sara say that name once or twice."

"You know Sara pretty well, then?"

A little more guarded now, John replied, "No, not really—just what I overhear when they walk by."

Shane studied him; there wasn't even a hair out of place. "Is there anything else you can think of that might help us?"

"No, sorry."

"Okay. Thanks for your time." Shane pulled a card from his wallet. "If anything comes to mind, give me a call."

"Sure, of course." John took the card and walked them to the door. "Hope you find what you're looking for."

"Thanks—we appreciate it." After a quick handshake, Shane and Marcos made their way back to the car.

"John's an interesting character, don't you think?" Shane asked as he climbed in.

"Definitely," Marcos said, starting the engine. "We should have Sylvia run a background check."

"Already on it." Shane pulled out his phone and hit dial.

"Windsor Brooke Sheriff's Department, this is Sylvia."

"Sylvia, it's Shane. Can you run a name for me?"

"What's the name?"

"John Myner. Lives a few houses down from Sara Hallis—the address is 635 East Permis Lane."

"Got it. I'll call you when I find something."

"No, just print it and leave it on my desk. I'll check it when we get back."

"All right, will do."

The line went dead. Shane hung up and turned to Marcos. "She's on it."

Marcos nodded. "Let's look up Joe's Shop—see where we're going next."

Shane tapped his screen. "Okay, looks like it's on Main Street. Left at the light, then a right."

"Got it. Let's go talk to Sara's dad."

Fox sat on the couch across from Sherri's mother, accepting the glass of homemade lemonade she insisted on bringing him. She looked like she was holding it together by a thread.

"Mrs. Price, I know this is a difficult time, but I need to ask you about the people in Sherri's life."

She frowned. "What do you mean—the people in her life?"

"More specifically, who she spent time with. Did anyone ever make you uncomfortable? Anyone she talked to that gave you a bad feeling?"

"Besides family, I don't know who else there could be," she said, her brows knitting in confusion.

"What about neighbors?"

"She knew them by sight, but I don't think she ever really spoke to them."

"Would she have felt comfortable walking away with any of them?"

Her face tightened, voice fraying. "Wait—are you saying one of my neighbors took her?"

Fox raised a calming hand. "No, not necessarily. We're just exploring every possibility."

She nodded, dabbing her eyes with a tissue. "I don't think she would've gone with anyone. We talked about that a lot—she knew not to leave with anyone unless I said it was okay."

"Understood. Could you make a list of any adults she interacted with regularly? Teachers, neighbors, family friends. Anyone she might've trusted."

"Yes... I'll start working on it right away."

"Good." He handed her a card. "Here's my number. Call me when you've finished, and I'll come pick it up."

"I will."

"Thank you, Mrs. Price." Fox stood. "And please—call me anytime.

Outside, Fox sat in his car, drumming his fingers on the steering wheel. He was restless. His hands were tied until he had that list from Mrs. Price.

And his mind—well, his mind kept going back to Kate.

He'd been trying to push her out of his thoughts, convince himself this was just physical. Just something he needed to scratch and move on from. But the more time he spent with her, the harder it got. She was in his head, under his skin. Hell, his body was already reacting just thinking about her.

He still couldn't believe she was a virgin—though every time they were alone, it was more obvious. There was something wildly intoxicating about her innocence, paired with that fire. And she'd been liquid flame in his arms this morning—scorching and addictive.

He didn't stop to think. He pulled away from the curb and pointed the car toward Kate's house.

Kate stretched up against the tree, balanced on the top step of her ladder. One arm gripped a thick branch above her in a death hold as she tightened the last screw on the new security camera. She adjusted the lens, angling it for the best view.

She'd been installing cameras all over the property, carefully selecting spots to monitor the house and the tree line. Next time the creep showed up, she'd see him coming.

The rough bark scraped her cheek as she shifted, tossing her tool to the ground. She began to climb down, letting her foot slide to the next rung—when two hands suddenly closed around her waist.

Her mind flared. He's here.

Her body reacted before she could think. She twisted sharply, throwing her weight backward. One leg looped around the intruder's waist, her body flipping through the air and dragging him down with her. In a blink, she was on top, straddling his torso, hands pressed hard to his throat.

Vivid blue eyes blinked up at her in stunned confusion.

Slowly, recognition sank in.

"Oh shit! Fox!" she gasped, quickly lifting her hands. "What are you doing here? You scared me to death."

Kate blinked down at Fox, heart still pounding like a war drum. His body was sprawled on the ground beneath her, breath ragged, eyes narrowed—but not with pain. With confusion, maybe a little awe. Definitely a lot of heat.

Oh no.

Her knees pressed into his sides, and her hands were still planted near his throat. She hadn't meant to hit him that hard—hadn't even known it *was* him. Just hands on her waist, a sudden invasion, and her body had done the rest.

Fox lay there, stiff and silent, like he was waiting for his brain to catch up to what had just happened. She could practically feel the string of curses he was holding back.

And then he spoke.

Her cheeks burned, but she couldn't help the smile tugging at her lips.

"Not that I mind, of course," he added, and his hands found her thighs, giving them a slow, unmistakable squeeze.

She smacked his hands, grinning now despite herself. "Stop that."

Laughter bubbled up before she could stop it, spilling out as she looked down at him. His expression was caught somewhere between amused and annoyed, and that only made her laugh harder.

"What are you doing here?" Kate asked again. "I wasn't expecting you. I thought you were someone else."

Fox's brows furrowed. "You were expecting someone else?"

Kate blinked, her heart still not quite back to normal. "No. Why would you think that?"

"You said you thought I was someone else."

"Oh." Her eyes darted to the side for a second before settling back on his face. "I just meant... You weren't supposed to be here, so when someone grabbed me around the waist—unexpectedly—my brain filled in the worst-case scenario. And the only reason someone would be touching me like that was, well... not good. So I reacted." She paused, looking him over with real concern now. "Did I hurt you?"

She ran her hands down his ribs, pressing lightly, then across the flat plane of his stomach, checking for any sign of injury. His muscles tensed beneath her fingers.

Fox's jaw tightened. "Don't worry about it. I'll be fine," he said with a low groan. "How did you learn to do that, anyway?"

"Self-defense classes," she said, trying to keep her voice casual, even as her fingertips continued tracing soft circles across his abdomen. "I try to take a new one every few months. Just to stay sharp."

His body twitched under her touch, and only then did she realize she was still rubbing his stomach. She stilled her hand, suddenly aware of the intimacy of their position. His hands were still resting on her thighs. Not in a possessive way, but not casually, either. There was a slowness to the way his thumbs began to move, stroking gentle circles that mirrored hers.

She should move. She knew that. But she didn't.

She watched the way his eyes flicked over her face—curious, cautious, maybe a little amused. This wasn't like this morning. There was no rush, no shock. Just closeness. A different kind of tension threaded between them, warm and quiet and—heaven help her—*welcome*.

"Self-defense?" he murmured, breaking the silence. "That was some training they gave you. I didn't even realize what was happening until I landed on my back."

She smirked just a little. "That's the point. You shouldn't sneak up on someone. You never know what might happen."

"Well, I learned my lesson," he said, still pinned beneath her.

"I thought you weren't coming over until tonight?"

He hesitated, and for a moment, she couldn't read his expression. Then his voice softened.

"I missed you. Did you miss me?"

Kate froze. *Miss him?* Her stomach fluttered in surprise, then twisted. The question felt like a spotlight, catching her in the open. Vulnerability was a luxury she couldn't afford. So, instead, she deflected. So instead, she said, "It has only been a couple of hours since I saw you."

His scowl told her he didn't buy it.

"You didn't miss me even a little?" he asked, probing.

She shrugged, trying for casual, eyes fixed on the fabric of his shirt as her fingers fidgeted with a loose thread. She couldn't look at him. If she did, she might give herself away.

Then his hands shifted.

She noticed the change instantly, the way his touch went from idle to intentional. He wasn't trying to tease, not exactly. His palms slid slowly along her thighs, smoothing over the shape of her legs in a rhythm that felt... grounding. Like he wasn't trying to seduce her—just *reach* her. A quiet insistence. A reminder.

Her breath caught.

It wasn't just his hands, though they were warm and sure. It was the way he focused on her, the way everything else seemed to fall away when he touched her. Like he wanted her to memorize the feel of him. To trust it. To trust *him*.

"Come on, Kate," he coaxed, his voice low and warm. "Admit it. You'll feel better once you do."

She paused, weighing her response, and he could see it. She hated that he could read her so easily. Fox shifted their positions before she could react. In one smooth move, his thigh slid between hers, locking her in place as he rolled her onto her back.

Her breath hitched.

Now pinned beneath him, his hands cradled her face, his eyes searching hers. Then he leaned in, brushing a kiss over the tip of her nose—soft, maddening. His lips pressed to hers, gentle at first, then deeper, fuller. Just when she began to melt into it, he pulled back.

"Kate," he murmured, his weight resting on his elbows, his lips a breath away from hers. "Tell me you missed me too."

She frowned up at him. He was infuriating. Why couldn't he just let her be?

He wanted more than she'd ever given, and she couldn't do it. Not now. Not with everything so uncertain.

"Why do you want me to say that?" she grumbled, wiggling beneath him. "Just so you can say you were right?"

He smiled. That lazy, teasing smile made her want to slap him and kiss him senseless.

His mouth hovered over hers. "Because I need to know I'm not in this alone."

The sincerity in his voice hit her harder than his kisses. Her heart responded before her mind could catch up, emotions rising fast and wild.

Unwilling to face what he stirred in her, she leaned in again, trying to capture his mouth, desperate to turn this into something purely physical, something safe.

But he dodged her just enough to make her whimper with frustration.

Then he grabbed her wrists and pinned them above her head. Her breath caught.

His body pressed tighter, harder, and she felt completely at his mercy. She could get out of it. Throw his weight, hurt him.

But she didn't.

Because, despite herself, she wanted this. She wanted him.

Instead, she felt herself sinking into the moment, breathless as he kissed her again—teasing at first, then deeper, more demanding. His lips traveled to her jaw, down her neck, drawing little gasps from her throat.

"Kate," he whispered against her, "admit you want me too."

"Yes," she breathed.

"Yes, what?" His voice rasped against her skin.

She couldn't think straight. All she knew was him, the feel of his body, the way hers responded to his presence without her permission.

He lifted his head to look at her, eyes blazing.

"Kate," he said again, slower this time. "Tell me you want me."

Something in his tone stopped her. The rawness. The way he needed it, not just physically but emotionally.

And that terrified her.

She looked up at him, heart pounding. Her desire tangled with fear—because she *did* want him. And that kind of wanting never ended well.

Fox still had her pinned, but something in her eyes must've betrayed her retreat. His expression shifted, sharper, more determined. She saw the storm gathering behind his gaze before he even moved.

Then he locked her wrists in one strong hand and tangled the other in her hair. His fingers threaded through it like he meant to memorize every strand. His face hovered above hers, a breath away, eyes blazing, voice low and commanding.

"Give me what I want, Kate," he said, the words rough with need. Then softer, almost broken, "Don't pull away from me. I need to hear you say the words."

That voice—earnestness of it—hit harder than any kiss he could give. She wasn't ready for this. Her heart was moving faster than her mind could follow, and she hated how easily he cracked through her armor.

"Fox," she groaned, her chest tight with emotion. "But it changes nothing," she said, fighting the tears threatening to rise.

"Tell me," he said again.

"I want you," she breathed. The words tore out of her like a confession. She narrowed her eyes at him. "Happy now?" she bit out.

Smug and satisfied, he smiled and sealed her admission with a kiss that stole her breath. Then, with that same smooth confidence that always drove her a little crazy, he rolled them over again, putting her on top. His hands stroked up and down her arms with lazy, pleased affection.

"Tell me where you take your self-defense classes," he said with a grin. "I think I might need to brush up a little myself."

"Ha, ha. Very funny. I told you I was sorry," she muttered, punching him lightly in the chest. She braced her hands on him and stood up.

"Hey, where are you going? I thought we could lie here in the sun a little longer."

"Unlike you, I have work to do." She brushed off her pants and reached for her fallen tools. "I was just getting ready to head into town."

"Oh yeah? What for? Want me to take you?" He propped himself up on his elbow and grinned.

She barely stopped herself from rolling her eyes. Why did he always have to ask so many damn questions?

"Oh, you know," she said lightly, "check on my shop, that sort of thing. I'll drive myself. Not sure how long I'll be, and I don't want to worry about getting back."

Fox didn't budge. "My day just opened up. I'm waiting on a list from Sherri's mom," he said, "So until then, I've got time. Consider me your personal driver. I aim to serve."

Well, *shit.*

So much for quietly following up on her investigation; there was no way she could visit the square and poke around with him trailing after her. And knowing Fox? He'd be suspicious the second she started chatting up strangers.

Then she remembered the pendant. Her stomach clenched. She still hadn't told him.

Fox watched her closely, his brow creasing. "What's going on in that head of yours?"

Kate shifted, then sighed. "I just remembered something I forgot to show you." She reached out her hand. "Come on. It's up at the house."

He took her hand, rising easily to his feet. "What did you forget to show me?"

She swallowed hard. "Before you got here, I went to the site where they found Sherri's body," she admitted. "Just to look around. See if there was anything... anything that might help me figure out who this guy is." She stared down at her shoes. "And I found something."

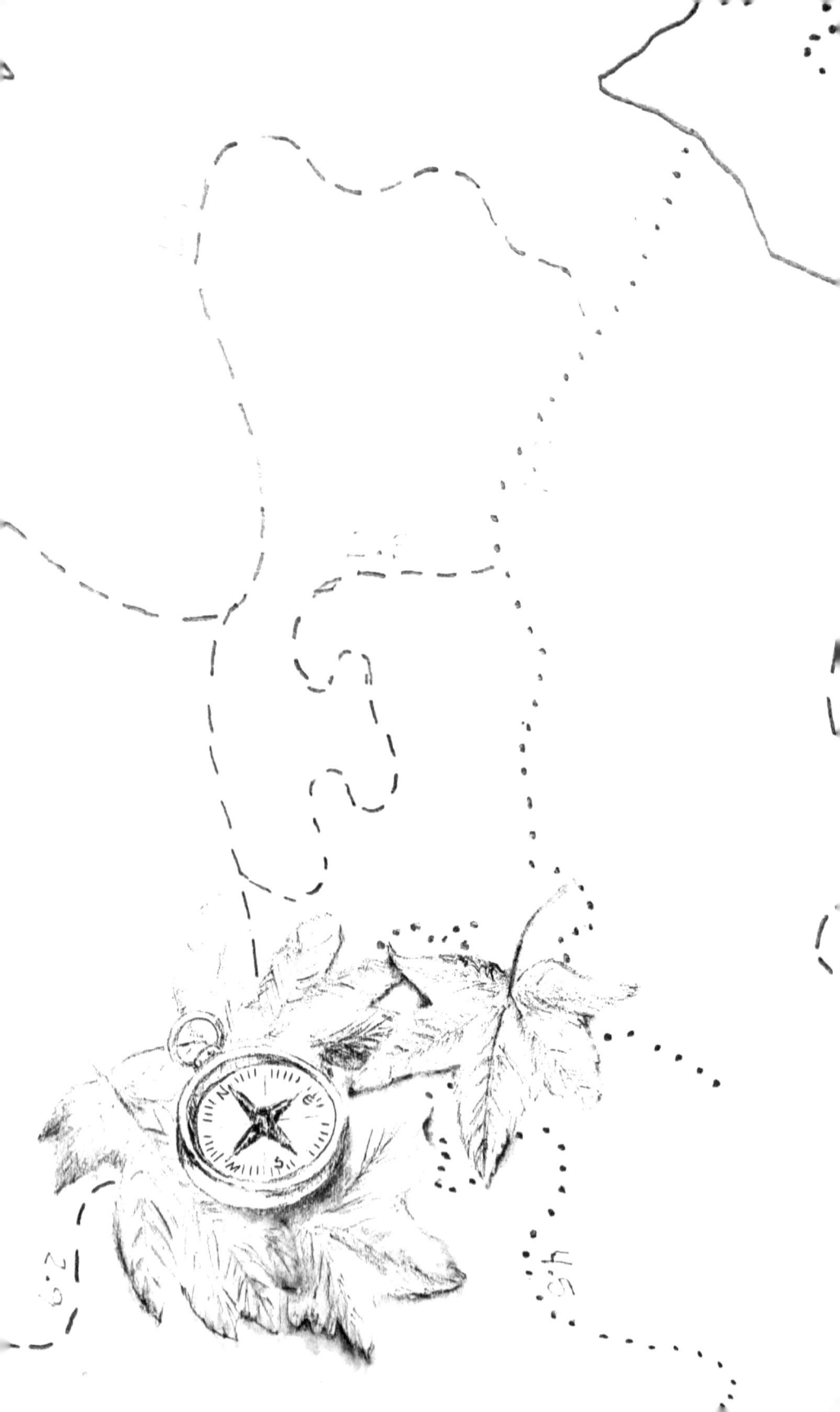

Chapter Twenty-One

F ox turned abruptly, jerking Kate to face him.

"What do you mean you found something?" He asked between clenched teeth.

Before she could respond, the questions started—rapid-fire, like bullets.

"What did you find? Why didn't you tell me sooner? Don't you know you could be charged with evidence tampering? How could you be so—"

His grip on her arm was like a vise. He wasn't hurting her, not really, but the pressure of his hand carried something worse than pain—anger. The kind that made her muscles tense and her instincts flare to fight. She struggled to keep calm, even as his words hit harder than his hands.

"I—" she began, but he cut her off again. His voice was sharp now, cold, laced with something that stung more than it should have.

Her eyes narrowed in warning.

"Dammit, Kate," he bit out, "do you even understand what this means? You could've compromised the case. What the hell were you thinking?"

He grabbed both her arms this time and gave her a quick, frustrated shake.

That was it.

She slapped his hands away, her voice rising to match his. "I wasn't *intentionally* keeping it from you!"

He opened his mouth, but she pushed through.

"I forgot, okay? I *forgot*. I only just remembered this morning."

Fox narrowed his eyes, fury still flickering in them. "By *this morning*, do you mean when we were together in the woods? *Searching for a clue?* For something the killer might've left behind?" His words grated out, low and furious.

"Yes," she snarled, scrunching her hands into fists, "That's when I realized my mistake."

"And why didn't you say something to me then?"

"I wanted to make sure I still had it."

"What's that supposed to mean?" His voice pitched higher, edged with disbelief. "Did you think you'd lost it?"

"Honestly? I wasn't sure." Kate gave a casual shrug, though her eyes didn't quite meet his. "Last I remember, I slipped it into my pocket."

Fox released his grip on her arms, and suddenly, she staggered before catching her balance. He slapped a hand to his face, dragging it down in an exaggerated gesture. "All right. Show me what you found."

Kate squared her shoulders. She would love nothing more than to tell him to take a flying leap, she seethed. It amazed her how she could swing from warm, fuzzy feelings to wanting to cause him bodily harm in a matter of seconds. No one else in her life had ever triggered such swift, violent mood swings. For now, she'd do what he asked—but only because she had made a mistake. This was not going to be the status of their relationship, she thought caustically.

She spun on her heel and led him into the house. He matched her stride in silence up the stairs and over to the coffee table. The pendant was lying in the center, just where she'd left it.

"Here it is," she said, picking it up and handing it to him.

He held the small heart-shaped pendant in the palm of his hand, starting at the engraved initials on one side. He stood motionless. He knew exactly what he was holding—Megan's locket. Victim number four. He remembered it listed among the items she'd last been seen with.

If Kate found this in the meadow where Sherri's body was discovered, the chances were high—they'd found his burial site. The killer's dumping ground. A chill crept down his spine. Without realizing it, Kate had just turned this entire case on its head.

Fox's mind snapped into motion. He needed to get a team out there. Immediately. Ground-penetrating radar, cadaver dogs, grid coordination—the works. But first, he needed Kate to show him exactly where she found the locket.

"Fox, do you know what that is?" Kate asked, her voice quiet, wary.

He had been standing still, staring at the pendant for several minutes without saying a word.

He didn't answer. He was still staring at the pendant, his thoughts racing. When she started to move toward her files, maybe to show him the matching description from Megan's inventory, he finally put the locket down and met her eyes.

Anger flickered in his gaze, a flash that made Kate's stomach twist.

"Fox?" she asked again, her voice uncertain.

He didn't answer. Couldn't. Not yet. His eyes locked on hers, refusing to give away the storm building inside him, though he knew she could see some of it anyway. Rage. Frustration. Something dark, curling beneath the surface.

She flinched, and the air between them shifted. Her pulse practically echoed in the space, loud and frantic. It wasn't just fear, not entirely. There was something else. Her cheeks flushed a deep crimson, and Fox's breath caught.

She's turned on.

The realization hit him like a bolt of lightning—hot and fierce. The rush of male satisfaction that followed was undeniable. So he wasn't alone in this. She felt it too—the pull, the heat, the chaos. That fire burning under the surface hadn't just been his.

A slow smile curved his lips, predatory and unrepentant. He took a step forward. Then another. Every time she backed away, he followed—deliberate, silent. Until her shoulders bumped into the wall behind her.

Her wide eyes locked on his, confusion swimming in their depths. Maybe fear, too. But she wasn't the only one caught off guard by the shift between them. He couldn't bring himself to step back, either. The need thrummed inside him—angry, raw, desperate to take.

Fox stood motionless, his breathing ragged as he fought to steady himself. He couldn't remember the last time someone had pushed him this close to the edge. It wasn't just lust anymore—he was sure of it. He'd thought that time with her would cool the fire, but it only burned hotter.

He wasn't a man who believed in love at first sight, but since they met, she'd turned his world inside out. And now, standing here with her, he realized how far he'd go to protect her—even if it meant covering up her involvement in tampering with evidence. Even if it meant jeopardizing the case.

His gaze drifted to the photo pinned to the wall behind her—an innocent face, a call for justice. But even that wasn't enough to sway him. Not if it meant losing Kate.

The wildfire of anger that had consumed him moments ago faded into quiet acceptance—of her, of everything. He released her arms and gently cupped the back of her neck, his fingers threading into her hair. Resting his forehead against hers, he breathed her name.

"Kate."

His lips brushed hers—soft, tentative—before claiming her mouth in a kiss that was anything but.

No longer interested in restraint, Fox let go. She belonged with him—no one else. As his hands explored the fire between them, he relished the feel of her body pressed intimately against his. His grip on control slipped, desire overriding thought. Kate's earlier vow of celibacy slipped from his mind, replaced by the primal rhythm of longing.

His fingertips skimmed the edge of temptation, his thoughts spiraling—just a little further, just a few more inches, and then—

She stiffened.

The sudden tension in her body struck him like a cold slap. Her hands pressed against his chest, shoving with surprising force. He pulled back, startled, searching her face.

"Kate?" he asked, voice low, hands frozen. "What's wrong?"

"I need you to let me go," she said, trembling. A flush of color burned across her cheeks—anger, embarrassment, maybe both.

Fox stepped back immediately, his arms dropping to his sides. "Did I hurt you?"

"No," she said quickly, then faltered. "I just need some space. Things got...too intense."

He caught the slight hitch in her voice and noticed how she avoided his gaze. A tight knot formed in his chest—was she crying? The thought unsettled him more than he expected. He couldn't understand it. She had been right there with him, her passion mirroring his. He hadn't forced anything. So why was she acting like he'd crossed a line?

Frustration surged through him. "Why do you do that?" he asked, his voice low but sharp. "Why do you pull away every time I try to get close to you?"

"I already told you," she snapped. "I can't do this with you."

Her words stung, laced with indignation.

"Besides," she added, crossing her arms, "aren't you leaving as soon as the case is over? Why even pretend this could be something?"

Fox stared at her, his expression turning to stone. "Fine," he said, the word coming out as a growl. "You win. I'll back off. If anything is going to happen between us, it'll have to come from you."

He was done being the one chasing, done being punished for something neither of them could control. Let her come to terms with what they had—because it wasn't just some fleeting spark.

No, this was a slow burn.

And he wasn't going anywhere until she realized it.

Fox studied her, watching the way she avoided his eyes, the stubborn tilt of her chin. She was retreating again, shutting him out just when he thought they were making progress. Anger simmered beneath his skin—not just at her but at the mess they were both tangled in. Dammit, he wasn't trying to push her into anything she didn't want. But she responded to him, *matched* him, and then ran from it like it meant nothing.

She thought this was some fling. That he was just after a few fun nights. And he didn't know how to make her see—this was more than that. So much more.

"Fair enough," she said at last, her tone distant, dismissive. She was trying to close him out. Again. She needed space—he could respect that. But she couldn't just walk away from what she'd done.

She turned toward the door. "Now, if you'll leave, I'll lock up and head into town."

Fox didn't move. His jaw tightened as he crossed his arms. "Sorry, no can do," he said, letting just a trace of satisfaction slip into his voice. "You're in this up to that pretty little head of yours."

Her shoulders tensed.

"That means you and I are going back to the crime scene. You're going to show me exactly where you found the pendant. Then we're heading to the sheriff's office so you can give an official statement."

She opened her mouth, probably to argue, but he cut her off with a look.

"If we're lucky, we can still salvage this evidence. If we don't? It gets tossed for mishandling. So, unless you *want* to see this whole case fall apart, you'd better cooperate."

He didn't want to be the one barking orders. But right now, it was the only way to keep her safe and keep this investigation from spiraling any further out of control.

It was amazing how much had changed in just a few hours.

Here they were in the same spot they had been hours earlier, only this time he was behaving like they were strangers. On the drive back to the crime scene, he hadn't looked at her once. He sat in stony silence the entire way.

Now, he was several paces ahead of her, moving briskly through the forest without so much as a glance over his shoulder. Kate watched the way his muscles shifted as he stepped over roots and stones, his body sure and controlled while tension rolled off him like heat.

She let out a sigh, trudging behind. If he was going to sulk, fine. She wasn't about to go out of her way to smooth things over.

In fact, wasn't this what she wanted? Distance? Detachment? If she stayed guarded, this thing between them would burn out as quickly as it had sparked—right?

She studied him with quiet curiosity. This was a new side of Fox. She knew him playful, she knew him serious. She even understood his anger. But this—this cold detachment was something else entirely.

Yet it seemed this was the version of him she'd have to face from now on. And she didn't like it.

A chill settled deep in her bones, the kind that had nothing to do with the air around her. She rubbed her arms as if the motion might summon back some of the warmth that had been quietly drained from her world.

They'd only known each other a few days, yet somehow, he'd carved a place in her life deeper than anyone had in years since she lost her family. Watching him walk ahead, stiff and hurting, made her want to close the gap between them. To take back the words, to undo the damage.

But if she did...they'd be right back at the edge of something she wasn't sure she could handle.

Being alone wasn't new to her. It was what she knew best.

But for the first time...she wasn't sure if she could bear it.

"Where did you find the pendant?" Fox's voice cut through the quiet, sharp enough to jolt her from her thoughts.

Kate turned, scanning the forest floor until her gaze landed on the familiar grouping of rocks. She walked a few feet to the left, stopping just short of them. "Right here," she said, pointing to the spot where she remembered seeing the glint of gold.

Fox knelt on one knee, shifting the dirt with practiced hands. After a few minutes, he stood and used his shoe to dig into the ground, marking the spot with a misshapen X. He stepped back and studied it from one side, then the other, before turning and heading back toward the car.

Kate watched him stalk away and realized that if she didn't want to be left behind, she'd need to hurry after him. The whole situation was getting ridiculous—he was acting like a child, ignoring his friend because he didn't want to share his toy. Well, she wasn't a toy, and she was damn tired of his juvenile stunts. They were two reasonable adults. There was no reason they couldn't maintain a professional relationship.

The sound of Fox stomping through the forest was impossible to ignore, each step louder than the last. Kate glowered at his back. She'd been upfront from the start—if he didn't like the terms she'd set, he could take a hike. She wasn't going there and was sick of him trying to push her into it.

A flare of rage sparked inside her, her thoughts fanning it into a blaze. His tantrum, the cold shoulder, the guilt-tripping, dragging her into situations she never asked for—it was all too much. Without thinking, Kate snatched a dry-rotted branch from the ground and flung it at the back of his head. It shattered on impact, but not before hitting its mark.

Fox froze, slowly turning his head to look back at Kate, his expression a storm of rage and disbelief.

"Did you just throw something at me?" he roared, squaring up to her, his fists clenching and unclenching.

Kate was less than impressed. Her temper was burning hot enough to match his. She squared her stance, hands flexed on her hips. "Damn right, I did, you ass!" She sounded unhinged, furious—and didn't care in the slightest. Right now, she *wanted* to scream—and damned if she wouldn't let him know exactly what she thought of his behavior.

"What did you call me?" he barked, the cord along his neck bulging.

"I called you an ass!"

He stood there, stunned as if it was the first time anyone had dared throw something at him. Please. She doubted he'd made it through grade school without someone chucking a shoe at his egotistical, hardheaded skull.

"What the hell are you throwing things at me for?" he growled, his voice tight despite the tic pulsing in his cheek. "And why the hell did you call me an ass?" His eyes blazed with raw emotion.

"Because you're stomping around, throwing a fit, ignoring me—and I'm sick of it. If I wanted to hang out with a child, I'd be with Chloe!" Kate snapped, glaring at him.

"I'm not throwing a fit!" Fox bellowed. "You said to back off—so this is me backing off. What more do you want from me?" His lip curled in a sneer. "Typical."

"No," she shot back, her voice rising. "What you want is sex, just like every other man. And when I pump the brakes, you sulk. Stomping around like some wounded teen—it's pathetic." The words were cruel, and she knew it—but pushing him away was safer than pulling him closer.

"Now, hold on a damn minute." His voice dropped, controlled but seething. "Have I asked you for sex? No. All we've had are a few hot moments—barely even heavy petting. Believe me..." His jaw clenched. "I wouldn't be this damn frustrated if we had."

"Oh, right," she scoffed. "So you're saying if I hadn't stopped things, you would've pulled back all noble and selfless?"

"You told me upfront—no flings, no sex. I knew what I was signing up for." His voice dipped lower, less angry now, more wounded. "And yeah, it's frustrating. But I was willing to wait to see where this might go. You think I'd risk a future with you for a quick toss in the sheets?" He stepped forward, his tone softening. "You really think I'm that stupid?"

Kate's righteous anger started to feel a little less righteous. What if he was telling the truth? Had she screwed everything up because she panicked? She dragged her fingers through her hair, frustration giving way to confusion.

"I don't know what to say. What to do," she murmured, eyes scanning his face for an answer she couldn't name. "What happens now?" Her voice cracked, the heat of anger cooling into something softer—uncertainty. The fight drained out of her, replaced by something far more terrifying: need.

Fox reached out to her, breaking his own word. He pulled her gently into his arms. She didn't resist. She stepped into him like it was the most natural thing in the world—because in that moment, for her, it was.

"I'm sorry I lost my temper," he said, voice roughened with honesty. "I seem to be a little on edge when it comes to you."

He kissed her temple, her cheek, and the soft spot just behind her ear, drawing a shiver from her, before tucking her beneath his chin, where she fit like she belonged.

All her anger, all her bravado, cracked under the weight of his tenderness. And just like that—she broke. Burying her face in his chest, she breathed in his scent. He smelled so good it almost hurt. Tears welled in her eyes, and before she realized it, they were sliding down her cheeks. She couldn't believe she was crying all over him. What was wrong with her?

She tried to pull away and hide her face so he wouldn't see the tears, but he wouldn't let her. He lifted her chin, wiped them away with the pad of his thumb, and kissed any lingering signs from her cheeks. Still silent, he tucked her head back beneath his chin and began to sway gently, offering comfort with nothing but his touch.

Fox let out a silent curse when his phone buzzed against his hip. The spell broke. He pulled it from his pocket.

"This is Anderson." After pausing to listen, he said, "I understand. I am on my way in now." He ended the call and slipped it into his pocket. "Time to go."

"Who was it? Where do you have to go?" Kate asked, alerted by the tension in his body.

"Another girl is missing," he said grimly.

Dread filled her. He'd taken another girl? Already?

"Who?" she asked, the words barely making it out. "Who did he take?"

"Chloe. The little girl's name is Chloe."

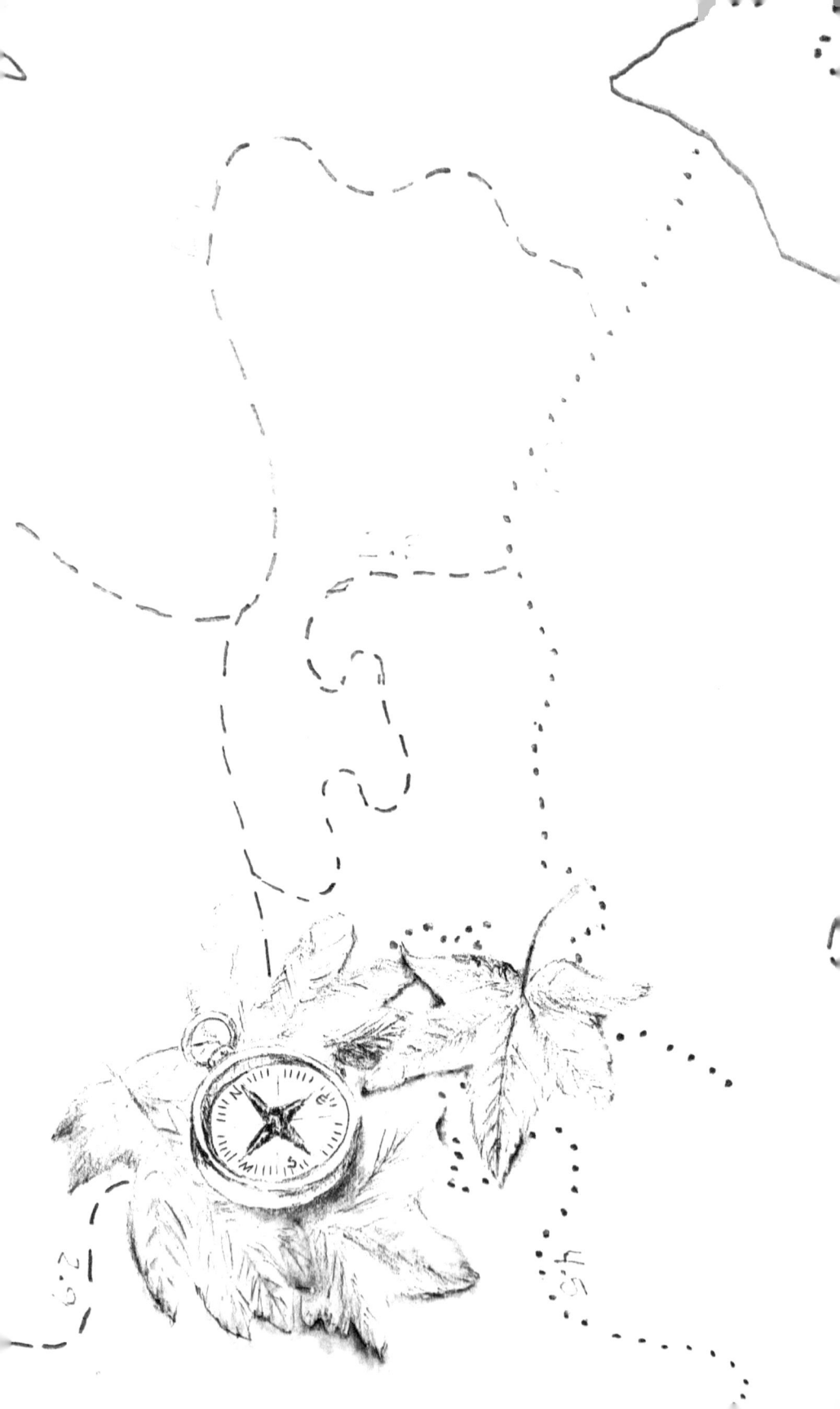

Chapter Twenty-Two

"*H*i *Chloe, do you remember me?*"

The small park had been buzzy with activity all morning. He'd waited patiently. He knew it was just a matter of —kids would get hungry, cranky, tired. And when they did, mothers would pack up their things and head home.

One by one, they left.

He wasn't interested in those children. He only had eyes for Chloe.

Once her mother kissed her and reminded her not to talk to strangers, he knew it was time. That simple warning didn't worry him. Parents always misunderstood the real danger.

To a child, a stranger wasn't someone dangerous. It was just someone they hadn't seen before. After a few brief conversations and a couple of friendly waves from across the park, he suddenly wasn't a stranger anymore. Just the nice man from the swing set. Or the grocery store. Or the library.

They almost made it too easy.

For him, grooming was never just about touch. It was about trust, building something out of nothing, showing up, being seen, and becoming familiar. Consistency was the key.

Now, all he had to do was reach out his hand. And Chloe would follow.

"Yeah, why are you here?" Chloe asked, kicking her legs higher on the swing.

He leaned casually against the frame, watching her hair flutter in the breeze. He imagined the silky strands slipping between his fingers.

"I saw you swinging," he said, smiling warmly. "Thought you might want some ice cream. I was just heading over to get one."

"I like ice cream," she grinned, face radiant.

Anticipation bloomed in his chest like fire, adrenaline pounding in his ears.

"I thought you might," he chuckled. "What kind do you like?"

He had to let her suggest it herself. If he asked directly, she might remember her mother's warning. But if she thought it was her idea...

"Oh, I like all kinds. What do they have?"

"Hmm, not sure. I could just pick one—maybe pistachio?"

"Yuck. The ugly green one? No way. That's gross."

He gasped playfully. "Uh-oh. That's a problem. How will I know what to pick for you?"

He rubbed his chin, feigning deep thought. Chloe swung back and forth, brows drawn in concentration. Then, her face lit up.

"I could come with you! That way, I could tell you which one I want!"

Hook. Line. Sinker.

He smiled again but didn't rush her. Let the line go slack. Let her feel safe.

"That could work. I'm going now, so if you want to come..." he let the words trail off and stepped away from the swing set.

Chloe launched herself off, landing solidly in the sand. She dusted off her legs and took his outstretched hand. He squeezed it gently, reassuringly, as they walked side by side down the sidewalk toward his car.

Once they reached it, he pulled a cloth from his pocket. Concealed between his palm and her hair, it looked like nothing more than a hug. When her body went limp, he lifted her and tucked her gently into the back seat.

Sliding into the driver's seat, he buckled in. Safety first. You never knew when a seatbelt might save your life.

Whistling softly, he pulled away from the curb.

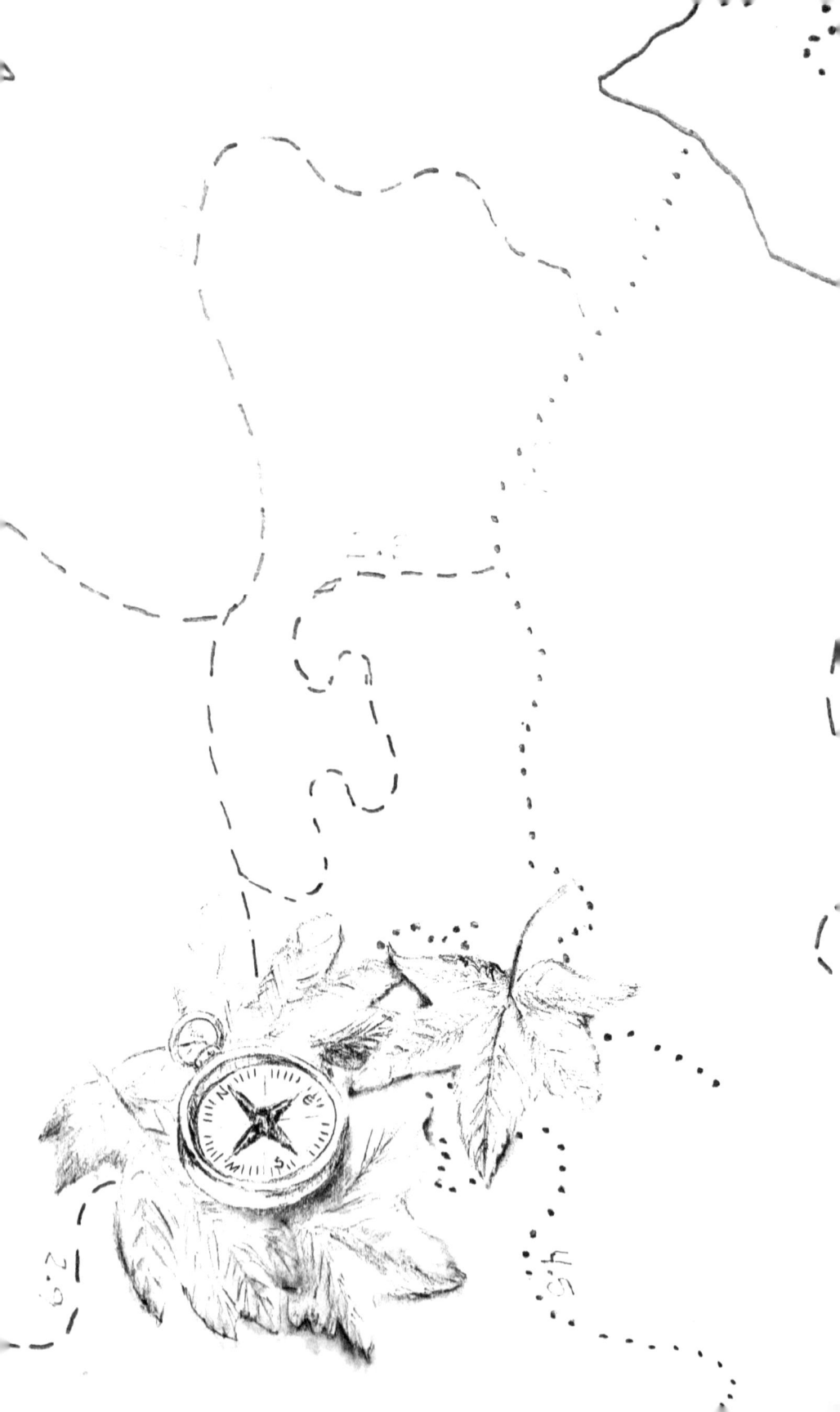

Chapter Twenty-Three

T he last two hours had been a logistical nightmare. Jurisdictional red tape, egos, and court orders had cost them precious time—time they didn't have. Since the moment his phone rang, the afternoon had slipped through Fox's fingers like smoke. Now daylight was bleeding out fast, and another girl was missing.

He pushed through the door of the sheriff's office, jaw tight. "Where's the sheriff?" he asked Sylvia without preamble.

"On his way in. Should be here in fifteen minutes for shift change."

"Have Shane and Marcos made it back yet?" His voice was sharp with urgency.

Silvia stiffened. "They're on their way, too. Should be here any minute."

Fox turned to Johnson. "Sit tight. As soon as everyone's in, we move."

Johnson cocked a brow. "What happened? You look like hell."

"Another girl's been taken. Near the state college."

A heavy silence followed before Fox turned to Sylvia. "Anyone talk to Riggs today? I want her on this."

She shook her head. "Left her a couple of messages. But she hasn't returned any."

"All right," Fox said, scowling at Riggs' empty desk. "Try her again. And Sylvia, call in a food order—pick the place and get enough to feed everyone."

Johnson groaned. "Guess I better call and cancel my date for tonight," he muttered, pulling out his phone.

Shane and Marcos strode in thirty minutes later, fatigue lining their faces. They moved over to the table, grabbing a plate of food. "What's the occasion?" Shane asked around a mouthful of food.

The office door swung open with a loud *thud*.

"What's everyone still doing here?" Sheriff Jacobs asked, frowning at his entire department huddled around.

Without missing a beat, Fox answered, "Another girl's missing. Her name is Chloe. Local PD is still determining if it's the same perp." He handed over the slim case file HQ had forwarded.

Jacobs flipped through the sparse pages, his jaw tightening. Then, without a word, he tossed the file on the table, dragged over a chair, and dropped into it.

"Okay," he said grimly, "what do we do?"

"About Chloe?" Fox clarified.

"Nothing yet. The local boys are handling it. Until we know more, we're focusing on a new lead from earlier today."

He tossed an evidence bag onto the center of the table. "A pendant—possibly the one missing from our fourth victim—was found in the meadow where Sherri's body turned up."

The bag landed softly in front of the sheriff.

"I've got a team coming in with ground-penetrating radar. We'll be sweeping the meadow tomorrow. I don't think it's just a dump site. I think our unsub's been using it as a burial ground."

Sheriff Jacobs shot to his feet. "Wait a damn minute."

His face drained of color. "You're telling me you think the bodies of the other five girls are buried in the woods outside my town?"

He stared at Fox like he'd been punched. "You need to be real careful about throwing around talk like that. If word gets out that a serial killer's been planting bodies near Windsor Brooke, I can kiss my career goodbye."

Fox didn't bother acknowledging the sheriff's callous remark. "Yes," he said plainly. "That's exactly what I think is happening."

Sheriff Jacobs exhaled and gave a reluctant nod. "When do you expect your guys to get here?" he asked, barely masking the resentment in his voice.

"Early tomorrow morning." Fox didn't give him the satisfaction of a glance. "Tonight, I want to review our new leads and plan our next move." He turned toward the two deputies.

"Shane, Marcos—let's start with you. What did our boy have to say?"

Shane picked up a thin file from Sylvia's desk.

"When we got to the Hallis residence, Davey wasn't home. His little sister, Sara, said their father kicked him out last night. She had no idea where he went or how to reach him."

Fox frowned, not happy with the delay but knowing better than to waste time stewing over it. "All right. So what'd you do next?"

Shane handed him the file.

"What's this?" Fox asked, flipping it open.

"We asked Sara if she'd talked to anyone else about her and Emma's plans," Shane said. "She told us she mentioned it to her Uncle Johnny—a neighbor who lives just down the street. We also got her dad's work info and figured we'd stop by after checking in with the neighbor."

He gestured toward the folder on the table.

"Let me tell you, walking up to Uncle Johnny's house felt like strolling into a damn theme park. The guy's clearly spent years building curb appeal—only his target audience is kids. There's a massive train set in the yard, shelves full of toys in plain view through the windows, and he answered the door dressed like some off-brand cartoon character." Shane's expression soured.

"If I had to guess, I'd say he prefers little boys to girls, but so far, they've never caught him with anything but an unsettling variety of photos. Still, we figured it was worth running a background check."

"And?" Fox asked, flipping open the report.

"We called Sylvia on the way out. She pulled this."

Fox scanned the page.

John Myner. The name was already setting off alarm bells. A prior arrest for possession of child pornography. He had no convictions, but he'd been questioned in at least three missing children's cases. Nothing had stuck. No charges. No closure.

Fox frowned. The guy fits the profile *too* well.

But there was one glaring issue—he didn't live anywhere near the meadow where Sherri's body had been found. Nearly two hours away. That distance didn't sit right with Fox.

"What about the father?" he asked. "Were you able to talk to him?"

"Yeah, he's a real charmer," Shane said bitterly. "Told us he was tired of his lazy-ass son mooching off him, so he kicked him out. Claimed he didn't know where the kid went, and even if he did, he wouldn't tell us. He said if we couldn't do our jobs, he sure as hell wouldn't do them for us."

Shane shook his head, disgust plain on his face. "Like I said—real class act."

"Were you able to get any idea where Davey might be?" Fox asked, tossing the folder back on the desk.

Shane shifted in his seat, clearly uncomfortable.

"We thought..." he began hesitantly, "we could try combing through social media. See if he's posted anything useful."

Fox gave a short nod.

"Not a bad angle. Let me know if it pans out." He leaned back, thoughtful. "As for John Myner—I'm going to have the Bureau dig deeper. Run a full background check, see what else turns up."

He paused before asking, "What time did you guys talk to him?"

Shane looked at Marcos, who replied, "Around one this afternoon."

Fox frowned, rubbing the back of his neck as he paced slowly.

"Chloe went missing just after three... which gives about a two-hour window from the time you left his house. With Myner living an hour and a half from the abduction site, it's a tight timeline. Not impossible, but tight."

He sighed, still pacing. "My gut says he's dirty, but probably not our guy—not for this. Still, I want the analysts at Quantico to take a look. If nothing else, he's worth keeping tabs on."

He turned back to the table.

"You guys did good work tracking this down," he said, meeting Shane and Marcos's eyes. "Now put everything you've got into finding Davey. I want updates the second you get anything."

"Yes, sir," they answered in unison.

"Sylvia, anything on Riggs?"

"No. I've tried calling again, but still no answer."

Sheriff Jacobs, who'd been quietly observing, finally spoke up, his brow tightening with concern. "What's going on with Riggs?"

"Not sure. She went home early—Johnson said she wasn't feeling well. No one's been able to get a hold of her," Fox replied.

"She looked fine this morning. What time did she leave?"

All eyes turned to Sylvia. She was the heartbeat of the department—nothing happened without her knowing.

Sylvia frowned and glanced toward Johnson. "I'm sorry, I don't know. She was already gone when I came in."

Everyone's attention shifted to Johnson.

"What time did you say she left?" Fox asked him.

Johnson leaned back in his chair with a casual shrug. "Oh, I don't know... maybe around six? A little after?"

Sheriff Jacobs's frown deepened. "She seemed fine when I saw her earlier. Did she say what was bothering her?"

"Said it was her stomach, I think. Honestly, I didn't really pay that much attention," Johnson said, a little too casually.

"Shane, swing by Riggs's place on your way home, would you?" the sheriff asked, making his first real directive in days. "Let me know if she's home and if she's okay."

"Sure thing, Sheriff," Shane said with a nod. "No problem."

Johnson suddenly straightened in his chair, the casual slouch vanishing.

"Whoa, wait a minute. She's my partner. Don't you think *I* should be the one to check on her?"

Sheriff Jacobs barely looked at him. "There's no need for you to go out of your way. Shane drives right by her place—it's easier this way," he said dismissively, already turning back to the file on the table.

"Sure, no problem. Just say the word if you want me to stop by instead," he added mildly.

Fox listened absently to the exchange between the sheriff and Johnson. A missing deputy was the last thing he needed right now. Once the two men had finally reached an understanding, Fox pressed on.

Johnson cleared his throat and tugged at his collar. "Uh..." His eyes widened slightly. "I couldn't get any further with it today. Left loads of messages but haven't heard back from anyone yet."

Fox looked at him, a flicker of disgust crossing his face. "All right. Follow up tomorrow. I want something by the end of the day."

He glanced around the room, noting the exhaustion etched into everyone's faces. "I know it's late. We've got a decent handle on things for now. Let's call it a night. Get some rest—tomorrow's going to be a long one. And believe me, you're going to need it."

A sigh of relief swept through the room as everyone grabbed their things and filed out. Fox remained behind, watching them go. It had been a long day—he needed rest as much as anyone—but all he could think about was Kate.

When he'd told her the missing girl's name, the color had drained from her face. Her eyes filled with terror, and then she collapsed into his arms. Sobs wracked her body. She beat against his chest, screaming that it couldn't be true, that he had to be wrong.

Only after she'd quieted had he understood: her friend's daughter was named Chloe, too. She'd thought it was *that* Chloe who had been taken.

Once he reassured her, she regained control fast—almost *too* fast. One moment, she was crying in his arms, the next, she was practically pushing him out the door, saying she had errands in town.

That shift still sat uneasily with him.

He glanced at the clock. It wasn't too late. Maybe he'd just swing by—check on her, make sure she was all right.

"I'm heading out, Sheriff," Fox said, grabbing his jacket. "I'll keep you updated tomorrow if we find anything."

"Good, thank you. I'll head home after my shift and catch a few hours of sleep before coming back in."

Fox gave a quick nod and a wave, then headed for the door. A weight lifted from his shoulders. He was going to see Kate—and somehow, that made everything feel a little more manageable.

After Fox had left her on the front step of her house, Kate took a second to collect herself. She hadn't expected to fall apart like that.

Not in front of Fox. Not at the mention of a name.

But Chloe wasn't just a name. She was a promise.

That moment—collapsing in his arms—wasn't just grief. It was guilt. Fear. Rage. The helplessness she'd kept buried for years cracked wide open.

And when she realized it wasn't *her* Chloe? That rage didn't fade. It shifted.

She wasn't going to lose control again.

Failure wasn't something she was used to. She lived her life by rules, strategies, and calculated plans—all things that kept her in control and brought her success. The thought of failing—of being powerless—was unbearable.

She'd been playing defense since this started. That was over. It was time to take control. Time to go on the offensive

The first thing Kate needed to do was check on the men who'd been in the square the day before. No one else knew what she was looking for—but *she* did. It was a man. She'd felt it in the way he watched her. Every instinct she had screamed predator, and somewhere deep inside, she knew—*it was a man*.

Grabbing her purse, she headed out. If any of them were home during the abduction, they couldn't have taken Chloe. That left only the ones she couldn't find.

It took almost three hours to knock on all seventeen doors. Of those, six were missing—supposedly at work. After a few more calls and a lot of running around, she confirmed each of them had been where they said they'd be.

Frustration bubbled up. She'd been so sure she was close—that this would lead to him. She *knew* he was out there. She'd felt him watching her. But he still slipped through her fingers.

This detective thing was becoming a pain in the ass. She needed a new angle, a new perspective. And she knew just where to get one.

Kate turned onto Main Street, weaving through traffic until her storefront came into view. If anyone could help her reset her thinking, it was Bridgette.

"Well, look at what the cat dragged in," Bridgette said with a big smile. "How is the investigation going?"

"It's not," Kate grumbled, tossing her bag on the counter. "I'm going nowhere fast. And to make it worse, I have to go out of town again in two weeks."

"Oh? Where to this time?"

"Morocco. I've got a line on some great finds for the store."

She didn't—but the lie came easily. She didn't feel bad about it either. She always found something worthwhile once she got there.

"Fun. Don't think we've had anything from there before. Let me know if you want my opinion before you buy."

Bridgette's voice had a hint of longing that made Kate feel a twinge of guilt. Maybe one day, she could take her on a trip. Then again, Kate wasn't sure she could spend that much time with someone and *not* want to kill them.

"Sure. I'll let you know."

Kate wandered the store, eyeing the inventory. "Everything looks great, as usual."

"Don't I know it," Bridgette said with her usual sass.

"Need anything from me? Paperwork?"

"Nope."

Bridgette leaned on the counter, tilting her head as she studied Kate. "You seem tense. What's up?"

"I'm just stumped. I need to figure out who this guy is, and nothing's clicking."

"Hmm. Wish I could help, but that's all you."

"Yeah, I know."

Kate fiddled with a pen on the counter. "By the way... has anyone in town ever made you feel uneasy?"

Bridgette raised an eyebrow. "What a weird question. Let me think..." She tapped her fingers against the counter. "Well, Bobby Jean's husband has always given me weird vibes. And Chris—Stacey's husband—he stares too much. Creeps me out a bit. No one else comes to mind, but maybe I'll think of more."

Kate mentally crossed them off. Both had been in the square, and both had been home when she stopped by. They were dead ends. Again.

The whole day had turned into one big disappointment. She wanted to go home and rest—but how could she, with another girl missing and no answers?

"Thanks, Bridgette. You're the best. Let me know if you think of anything else, okay?"

"Sure," Bridgette said as Kate turned to leave.

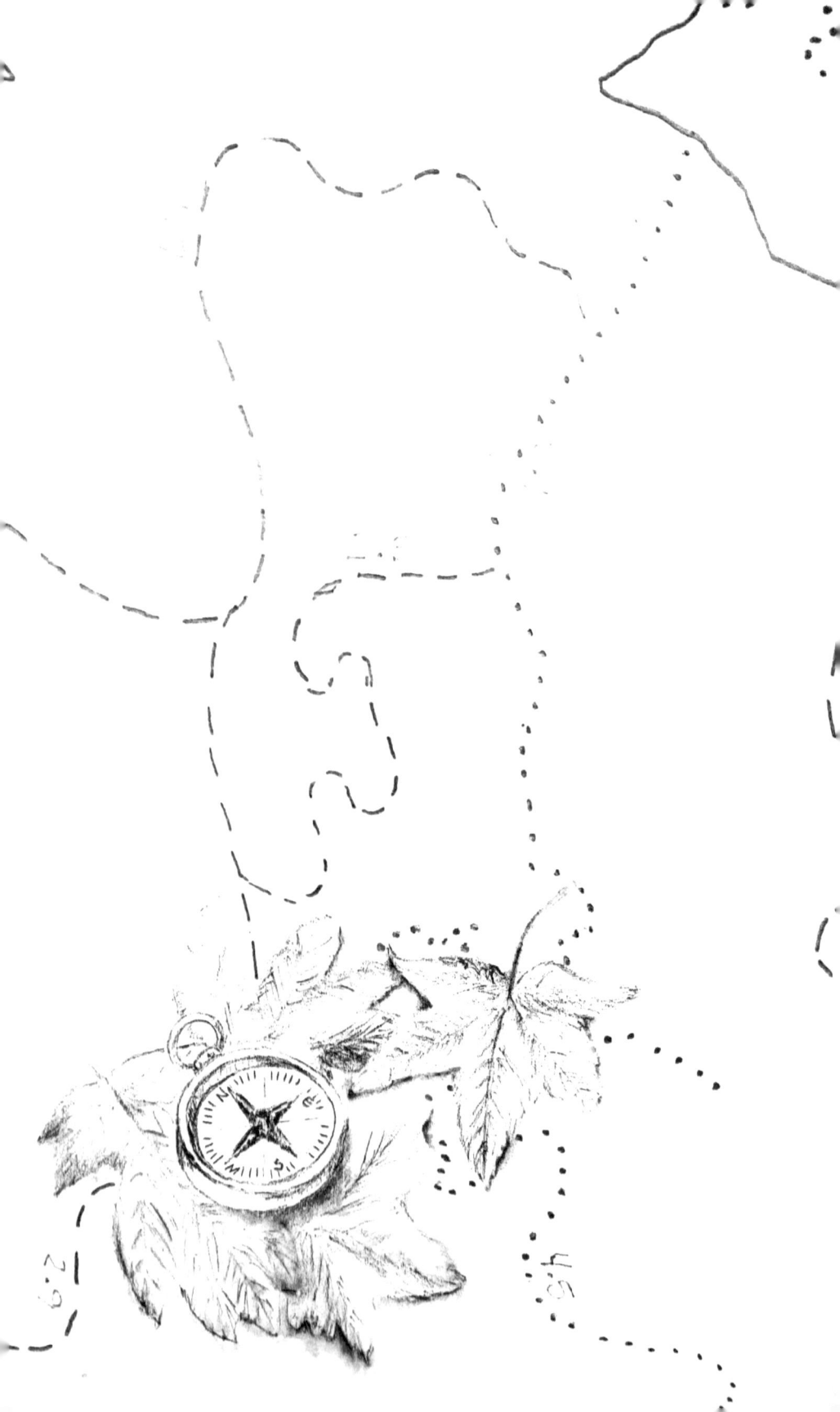

Chapter Twenty-Four

F ox was sitting on her porch swing when she pulled into the drive. She hadn't expected him to come back after dropping her off earlier, and definitely not tonight.

As she walked up the front steps, Kate ignored the flutter in her chest. She refused to think about how she'd acted before or how close she'd come to letting her guard slip.

He looked maddeningly relaxed as if he belonged there. She hadn't expected him to come back tonight. She might have braced herself if she'd known, but of course, he would just show up. She should have known.

What was dangerous was that she *should* have known he would. She was slipping, and her instincts were sluggish.

Her boots hit the porch boards with deliberate weight. She walked straight to the door, letting herself steal one quick look at him as she passed, just enough to catch the shift of his eyes following her.

A prickle of energy crawled over her skin. She swung the door open and turned, only to find Fox behind her, close enough to steal her breath. She was surrounded by his heat and scent. Her head whirled.

Instinct took over. She stepped back.

She had to tilt her head all the way up to meet his eyes—something she instantly regretted. His expression was guarded, unreadable in a way that made her leery of knowing what he was thinking.

"I'm surprised you came back," she admitted.

He studied her face through hooded eyes. "Really?" His voice was tight. "I told you I'd be coming by tonight."

"Yes, but that was before. I assumed you'd have more work to do now. I don't want to keep you from your job," she said, offering him an easy out.

"You don't need to worry about me. I'm a big boy." He paused. "Did you get your errands done in town?"

"Yes, I did. Thank you."

But something was off. She felt it—felt him. Crowded and uncomfortable, Kate backed into the doorway, each step carrying her further into her house. Fox followed without hesitation, matching her pace exactly, stride for stride. They moved in a quiet rhythm, one she hadn't agreed to and wasn't sure she wanted.

His mood puzzled her. When they'd parted ways earlier, everything had seemed fine. Now, he felt distant. Austere. She couldn't tell if he was still upset with her, yet he didn't *seem* angry. Just...off.

"Fox," she said carefully, "are you okay? You're acting strange."

Instead of answering her, Fox shrugged off his jacket and tossed it over the arm of the couch. He loosened his tie, pulled it free, and laid it beside the coat. With quick, practiced movements, he rolled up his sleeves and unbuttoned the top few buttons of his shirt. Then, as if he belonged there, he sat down on her sofa.

"It feels good to stretch out," he said. "I'd just gotten home when they handed me this case. No time to relax or unwind."

Without waiting for permission, Fox kicked off his shoes, claimed her remote, and dropped onto the couch like it was his. He patted the cushion beside him as if this were routine.

Kate wasn't sure whether to be offended or amused by the liberties he was taking. But with a sigh of acceptance, she grabbed her favorite throw and sat down next to him.

Fox slipped his arm around her, tucking her into his side, her head resting on his shoulder.

It did feel good, she admitted to herself, to just sit and do nothing but stare at the television. Even if it could only be for a little while.

Kate stole a glance at Fox, trying to read the rigid set of his jaw and the way his brows pulled together, even as he stared at the TV. He hadn't said much since she got home, and though he tried to act relaxed, something in him was off. Coiled. Agitated.

Had he really been waiting for her this whole time?

Unlike Fox, she had hoped for a reprieve—maybe to put off the necessary, if unwanted, confrontation for another time. She'd needed those few hours to clear her head. To breathe. But judging by his mood, he hadn't taken her absence lightly.

She wondered what exactly he'd expected to find. Her pacing the living room, waiting for him like some heroine in a melodrama? Kate bit back a sigh. Fox was used to being needed, maybe even wanted, in a way she wasn't sure how to offer.

He didn't say a word, but the way he leaned into her now, head bowed and face buried briefly in her hair, said everything. Something in him had softened, his breath slower, his body heavier against hers. She felt the shift—the anger ebbing, the tension bleeding out of him.

It was strange, this moment. Quiet. Intimate. And completely unexpected.

The sound of Fox snoring caught Kate by surprise. She turned to look at him, incredulous. To her dismay, he'd fallen asleep.

What was she supposed to do with him now?

Somehow, waking him felt cruel. Still, it didn't speak well to her appeal if men just passed out in her presence.

A little miffed and even more charmed, Kate was reminded of Danny—her first real crush. It was just before the crash that changed everything. Back then, she'd been carefree, sneaking time with him at the mall or driving around for hours, talking about everything and nothing. Her mother had been wary at first, but Danny quickly won her over.

They used to sit like this, hands entwined, watching movies with her family. Life had felt so simple.

Then came the crash. Tragedy swept in and reshaped everything. Friends drifted. Danny faded, too, unable to handle her grief. Only Cara had stayed.

By senior year, Kate had perfected the act. Most believed she was back to normal. A few boys asked her out, but nothing stuck. She couldn't fake the spark. Her final date—some jock whose name she couldn't remember—pushed too far. One well-placed knee and a long walk home ended that.

No one asked her out again. Not even to prom.

She remembered helping Cara get ready, smiling for her best friend while something inside her quietly ached. A small part of her—the girl she used to be—had mourned that loss.

But memories like that were dangerous. They stirred up sorrow that clung too tight. With a practiced breath, she let it go. There wasn't time to get lost in what might've been.

Things were different with Fox. Her feelings for Danny had been sweet, almost delicate in their innocence. But Fox stirred something deeper, something that filled the empty places inside her. He'd opened parts of her she thought were closed for good.

Careful not to wake him, she stroked her fingers softly along his chest, savoring the solid warmth of him. He felt strong. Safe. She wanted to sink into him, lose herself there.

With a quiet sigh, she let go and drifted into sleep.

Shane had to get up earlier than usual before his shift. He'd been so exhausted after spending the day in his car that he'd forgotten to stop by and check on Riggs. He didn't even understand why the task had fallen to him or why they couldn't wait for her to show up when she was good and ready. Shaking his head, he threw off the covers and sat up.

"What's wrong, Kyle? Why are you getting up so early?" Molly murmured, reaching for his hand.

He turned his hand over, clasping hers gently. "Sorry, didn't mean to wake you. I forgot to run an errand for the sheriff last night. Gotta do it before I head in."

She blinked sleepily at him, and he leaned down to kiss her forehead. "Go back to sleep. I'll see you tonight."

Smiling down at his wife, Shane knew he was a lucky man. He'd married his high school sweetheart at eighteen, and though everyone said they were too young, he never had a doubt. They'd had their ups and downs but always found their way back to each other. It was Molly who had suggested he join the sheriff's department, and she'd never once complained about the long hours or late nights. Always supportive. Always steady. Yeah, he was lucky.

Riggs's house sat along Shane's daily route to work, so stopping by in the morning was just as easy as catching her after his shift. Hopefully, the

sheriff wouldn't ask too many questions, no one needed to know he'd
forgotten to check in on her last night.

He pulled into her driveway and immediately noticed her SUV was
missing. Maybe she parked it in the garage. Taking the cobblestone path
to the front door, he knocked a few times, then rang the bell.

He glanced around as he waited. Her house always looked
nice—neatly trimmed bushes, a tidy lawn. He remembered when she'd
brought paint samples into the office, asking everyone's opinion. The
sage green had won and looked sharp with the white trim and shutters.

He rocked back on his heels, whistling quietly. But a crease formed
between his brows after a few minutes with no answer. Riggs wasn't
usually this hard to reach. Pulling out his phone, he decided to try her
number again—right there on the porch, listening as it rang.

Fox woke up in a precarious position.

The first thing he noticed was the stiffness in his body, typical of a
night spent on a couch. Then it all came back: he was at Kate's house, on
her couch, and apparently, they'd fallen asleep together.

Judging by the light seeping through the curtains, it was still early. His
phone hadn't gone off yet, so he hadn't missed the FBI forensics team's
arrival—a relief. If he had, he'd never hear the end of it. He didn't screw
up often, which made it all the more enjoyable for the guys when he did.

Carefully shifting, he glanced down. Kate lay tucked beneath him, her
body curled against his. Sometime during the night, he'd stretched out
along the couch, one leg draped over her, pinning her in place. His hand

had slipped under her shirt, resting high on her stomach. A few inches higher and—he shuddered at the thought.

He needed to go. A long day waited for him, and he still had to shower and change back at the motel. But he wasn't ready. Not yet.

So he didn't. He gave in, letting himself melt back into her warmth.

Today, the forensics team would begin combing the meadow. He had no doubt they'd find the other missing girls there—and when they did, he'd finally have something concrete to help him track this bastard down.

The profile from HQ had come in the night before: white male, twenty-five to thirty-five. Likely charismatic—charming enough to lure his victims. He'd have a strong need for control, probably reflected in his job. And when they found him, Fox didn't expect to see an ounce of remorse.

Kate squirmed beneath him, and Fox knew she was waking up. Disappointment creased his brow—he had hoped for a little more time with her relaxed under him. He knew that once she was fully awake, her guard would snap into place, and he'd have to work past her walls again.

Raising his head, he watched as she stirred. Her expression was soft, open. She stretched under him like a cat, arching into him, a small, satisfied smile playing at her lips.

That smile sent a jolt through him. In that instant, it hit him—he was in love with her. His heart had known what his mind hadn't been ready to admit. Everything clicked: the need to see her, to speak to her. She was his person.

Funny. His mom had always said he'd know when he met the right one. At the time, he'd dismissed her as sentimental. Now, he could almost see the smug look on her face. She had been right.

With this newfound knowledge came a surge of desperation—a primal need to stake his claim. The possessiveness surprised him, but he accepted it. She belonged to him now, just as he belonged to her. Whether she liked it or not, he wasn't going to let her go.

"Morning," Fox whispered, his smile soft. When her eyes finally fluttered open, she met his gaze. He saw her face flush with a mix of embarrassment and, if he wasn't mistaken, panic.

"Morning," she replied, avoiding his eyes. "What time is it?"

Leaning in, he kissed the tip of her nose. "I'm not sure. I just woke up myself." Reaching over her head, he grabbed his phone. "It's just past six-thirty," he said, tossing the phone aside before slipping his hand back to its warm spot. He waited, watching for Kate's reaction.

Had the situation been different, he would have already slipped her shirt off and started exploring the parts of her that fascinated him most. The urge to have her was becoming more urgent with each passing moment. His only hope was that she would trust him enough to take the next step in their relationship.

"I'm not sure what to do about this," Kate whispered, her voice trembling.

His heart ached at the insecurity in her voice. Wanting to reassure her, he pulled her closer, lifting her face to meet his. He brushed his lips over hers, a silent invitation to trust him. She hesitated at first, and for a moment, he feared she might pull away. But then, he felt her relax. Exultant, he deepened the kiss, silently demanding more than mere acceptance. He wanted to feel her burn.

As the kiss grew more urgent, their legs tangled together. In a frenzy of need, his hands dropped to the button of her pants. But the moment he realized he was justifying it to himself, Fox knew he had to stop. With what little self-discipline he had left, he stilled his hands and rested his forehead against hers, struggling to calm his racing heart. Remembering her words from earlier, he breathed, "Nothing, Kate. You don't need to do anything."

His hands clenched around her hips as he tried to steady himself, but the need to be closer, to feel her, was overwhelming. Sweat beaded on his forehead as he fought the fire inside him.

The sound of his alarm was a welcome distraction. With a heavy sigh, he pushed himself up. "I'm sorry, but I have to go. I need to shower and change before my team gets here." Rising gracefully from the couch, he gathered his things in one arm, brushing the back of his hand against her cheek. "I'll call you later, all right?"

"Yeah, okay," Kate muttered, watching Fox walk out the door. Her eyes lingered on the spot where he had stood just moments before, the echo of his presence still in the air. She remained sprawled across the couch, feeling rooted to the spot, unable to move.

The heat in her face was unmistakable—shame, embarrassment, maybe even frustration. She brought the palm of her hand to her forehead, thumping it lightly, hoping to knock some sense into herself. *How could you be so stupid?*

But what really got to her was that even though she knew he'd be leaving soon and knew that nothing real could come of this, she couldn't shake the feeling that she didn't want him to go. *He's leaving, Kate. He's not staying.* Still, her chest tightened at the thought of him walking out the door for good.

She tried to focus on the harsh reality of her life. She would be across the world in less than two weeks, ending someone's life in a foreign country. She was an assassin—*an assassin.* How could someone like her have a future with anyone, let alone a man like Fox? *They simply had no future together.*

Her mind spun in circles, and she closed her eyes, trying to slow her racing thoughts. Letting her guard down had never been easy. She didn't let anyone in, especially not to the point of falling asleep next to them, of allowing herself to feel vulnerable. The only time she let herself truly rest was in the safety of her home.

Yet, somehow...somehow, Fox had managed to become a part of that. A part of her safe. And she didn't know how that had happened or if she even wanted to know.

Kate threw an arm over her eyes and groaned. It didn't matter that her mind was in turmoil, she had to get up. She had a list of things to do today—practical things, but she couldn't ignore the need for some gossip time with Cara. Out of everyone in this small town, Cara was the one who seemed to know the deepest secrets about everyone.

After seeing Fox's reaction to the pendant, Kate realized he believed the man they were after was local. That meant he was a part of their small town, lurking among them. The thought made her stomach churn. All this time, a monster had been hidden in plain sight, blending in with everyone. It unsettled her to think she might have already met him, spoken to him, maybe even been in the same room as him. How had she never noticed? How had he hidden his true nature so well, especially from her?

If Cara couldn't shed light on it, there would always be Bridgette and April. They were always the first to know what was going on in town. When something happened, whether big or small, they had it covered. But more than that, Bridgette had a keen sense for reading people and understanding their personalities. If anyone could spot the monster hiding behind a mask, it was her.

The irony wasn't lost on Kate. She was hunting a monster hiding in plain sight, yet she herself was a monster of sorts, also blending into the crowd. She knew she'd be ostracized if the town ever learned the truth about her profession. Small-town folks would never understand, only seeing her as a killer. Sometimes, she wondered if Bridgette suspected more than she let on. There were moments when Kate could feel her eyes on her as if searching for the answer to a question that remained unasked.

Shaking her head, Kate pushed the thought aside. There was no time for that now. She wasn't just racing against the clock—she was racing against Fox. If he figured out who was behind the disappearances before she did, there was no way she could eliminate him the way she'd promised Cara. Not that she couldn't find a way, but she couldn't risk being caught or jeopardizing Fox's career. The stakes were too high.

Though she loved Cara and would do anything for her, self-preservation was always the first instinct. She was human, after all.

Fox would be out at the meadow today, and if his hunch was right, he'd probably find the bodies of the other missing girls. That would keep him occupied for a while—likely well into tomorrow. With no risk of him showing up unannounced, Kate could focus on finding this bastard and, hopefully, the little girl he had now.

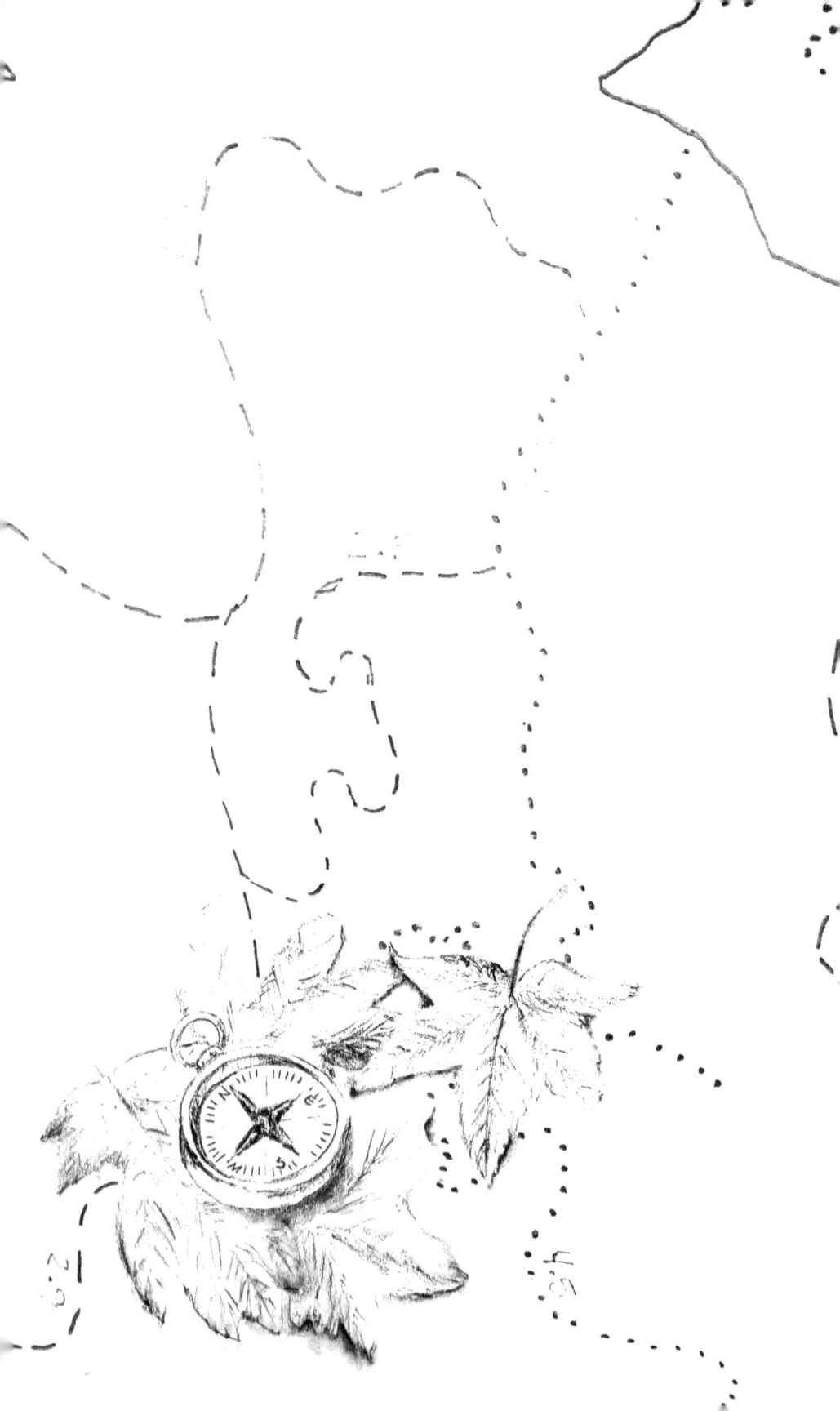

Chapter Twenty-Five

*C*hloe sat on the stained mattress in the middle of the cold, hard floor of the dirty room. She searched for anything that might help her get her leg free. It was freezing, and all she had was a scratchy old blanket full of holes. It didn't help at all. She rubbed her arms and bit her lip, trying not to cry. Momma always said crying didn't fix anything, and if Chloe wanted to get out, she had to do something.

"Stupid," she whispered to herself. Why did she go with him? Just 'cause he said, he'd get her ice cream.

But it wasn't just that. He was...pretty. She'd liked looking at him. Her sister always talked about cute boys, and even though Chloe didn't totally get it, she'd noticed this one. His hair looked soft, like her favorite doll's. She wanted to touch it.

And she did. She pulled it as hard as she could. Then he hit her—so hard her eyes filled with tears, and everything went bright and fuzzy.

It was the first time he'd left her alone since he brought her here. She hoped he never came back, even if he said he would. She hated him now. Even if he was pretty, he was ugly on the inside.

She felt ugly, too. She wiped her eyes, but more tears came. Her chest hurt. She tried to not think about the bad things he did. But they were there, waiting every time she closed her eyes.

What would her momma say when she found out? Would she still love her?

No. Chloe shook her head. She wouldn't tell. She'd keep it a secret. If no one knew, they couldn't see the ugly part inside her.

Sheriff Jacobs sat in his office, staring at his phone, willing it to ring. Shane still hadn't called after checking on Riggs the night before. He'd debated reaching out but decided against it. They were all stretched thin, and he wanted to give Shane a rare moment of peace with his family.

The sound of the front door opening snapped him out of his thoughts. Shane strode into the station, heading straight for his office. Jacobs stood, meeting him halfway.

"Sheriff, sorry I didn't call last night," Shane said without preamble. "I forgot to check on Riggs, so I went over early this morning instead. She didn't answer the door. I tried her home phone, but it rang with no answer. And her SUV's not there either."

Jacobs frowned, concern furrowing his brow. Riggs wasn't the type to flake. In all the years he'd known her, she'd called in sick exactly once—and that had involved a stomach bug and a toilet bowl she couldn't leave for nearly two days.

"Something's wrong," he muttered. Then, louder: "Get back to her house. If you have to break the damn door down, do it. Search the place. Look for her keys, check her car—everything. I want answers now."

He started pacing, glancing toward Riggs's empty desk. A sour feeling twisted in his gut. Sherri's case would have to wait. Anderson and his team were out digging in the woods today anyway. No harm in shifting focus for a few hours.

"I want to know the second you're inside that house," he said sharply. "Mr. FBI will be too busy playing archeologist in the trees. Let's use the time to find Riggs."

He slammed a fist down on her desk.

"Find her, Shane. I don't like this."

"Yes, sir," Shane said, turning for the door. "I'm on it."

"Call Marcos, have him join you."

"What about Johnson?" Shane asked. "Shouldn't he help too?"

"No," Sheriff Jacobs said, voice sharp. "I want to talk to him first. I'll send him your way when I'm done with him."

"Okay, Sheriff. I'll keep you posted."

Jacobs leveled a stern look at him. "Every hour, Shane. I don't want another repeat of last night."

Shane flushed and dipped his head. "Yes, sir. Won't happen again."

Satisfied, Jacobs gave a curt nod. "That'll be all."

"Sir." Shane turned and left without another word.

As the door clicked shut behind him, Jacobs let the silence settle. Shane had confirmed what he already suspected—Riggs wasn't just taking a day off. Something was wrong. The longer he turned it over in his mind, the more certain he became.

If something had happened to Riggs, Shane and Johnson were the last ones to see her.

His gut churned. The hairs on the back of his neck were standing straight up.

Johnson had been the one who said Riggs left early. But no one else had spoken to her since. No texts. No calls. Not even a casual check-in. And now—no SUV, no answer at the house.

Too much silence.

He reached for his phone, thumb hovering for a second before pressing Johnson's number.

It was time to get to the bottom of this.

The FBI team arrived at 7:00 a.m. sharp. Fox led the four agents through the field, showing them where Kate had found the pendant and the general area he wanted them to focus on. Once they tagged the starting point, the team unloaded their gear and began scanning the ground in four-square-foot sections, methodically marking each area after it was cleared.

It didn't take long to find the first set of remains.

Fox felt no satisfaction. His hunch had been right, but this wasn't the kind of moment that ever felt like a win. Finding something was just the beginning. Now came the painstaking process—carefully excavating the body, cataloging every fragment, and sifting through the dirt for anything the killer might have left behind. With any luck, the pendant wasn't the only clue.

"Agent Anderson," one of the agents called, approaching from behind. "We've found another set of remains, sir."

"Where?" Fox asked, already turning.

"About ten feet east of the first site."

Before he could respond, another voice called from across the open field. "Anderson! We've got another one over here."

Three bodies. So far.

Fox exhaled slowly. This was the burial site. He knew it now with certainty. But instead of triumph, a heavy weight settled across his shoulders.

They'd found the lost girls.

The same girls whose families were still clinging to hope—still expecting a phone call, a knock at the door, something other than this.

And once the identifications were confirmed, those calls would have to be made.

That part would fall to him.

Fox rubbed a hand over his jaw and looked out over the field. It was going to be a long day.

Kate pulled into Cara's driveway, lifting the box of donuts she'd picked up fresh from Sue's bakery. It was still early, but she knew Cara would be awake—she'd always been a morning person.

Without knocking, Kate opened the front door and stepped inside. "Cara? Where are you?"

"In the kitchen! Come on back," Cara called, her voice bright and chipper, like always.

Cara's home was its own kind of little paradise—clean, warm, and lived-in. The kind of place that made visitors feel like family. Kate remembered when Cara had first mentioned wanting to paint the walls lavender. She'd thought she was nuts, David would never go for something like that. But when the job was done, Kate had to admit, it worked. The shade leaned more gray than purple, especially with the crisp white trim, and the whole space had a calm, inviting feel.

"I brought donuts," Kate said, setting the box on the counter with a grin.

Cara lifted the lid and peeked inside. "These look amazing. The kids are going to be so excited."

"I figured they'd enjoy a treat."

"They always do, especially when it comes from their favorite Aunt Kate," Cara smirked, then gave her a knowing look. "So...you said you wanted to talk. Let me guess. A certain tall, serious, brooding FBI agent?"

Kate rolled her eyes, laughing. "No, actually. I wanted to talk about the people in town. You always seem to know what's going on around here."

"That's true. What can I say? People like to tell me things," Cara said with a shrug. "Who do you want to talk about?"

"I think the guy who killed Sherri lives here," Kate said, her voice low and hesitant. "Right here in town."

Cara's eyes widened, the color draining from her face. "What?"

"Calm down, Cara," Kate said quickly, her voice firm but gentle. "I need your help, and you've got to stay focused if you're going to be of any use to me."

Cara wrung her hands and took a steadying breath. "Okay. I'll try. Just—tell me what you need."

"I want to know about any weird stories. Anyone who's acted aggressively, done something obscene, or maybe tried to cover something up. Anything off. Does anyone come to mind?"

Cara's brows knit together. "Actually...yeah. A few things, now that you mention it. Do you want me to just start talking? Go down the list?"

"Yes," Kate said, pulling a pen and notepad from her purse. "I want names, ages, how old they were when it happened and how old they are now."

"Okay," Cara said, thinking for a second. "Let's start with Andrew Taylor. You know, the town drunk. He's got more DUIs than anyone else combined. Sue told me his wife finally had enough of him and his lazy ways, packed up and moved in with her mom in Cincinnati. At least, that's what I heard. He's been spiraling ever since. Lost his job, couldn't pay his bills, and the bank threatened to foreclose on the house.

"But even before she left, there were rumors. Supposedly, he got arrested in Columbus for messing around with a minor. They say she was a prostitute, but still, it's gross. The age difference alone makes your skin crawl."

Kate scribbled the name and notes. "How old is he now?"

"I'd say around forty?"

"And when did you hear about the thing in Columbus?"

"Last year."

"Okay," Kate nodded. "Who else stands out?"

Cara didn't miss a beat. "Last year, Kyle was talked to about his inappropriate behavior. I remember how mortified his mother was..."

"What was his inappropriate behavior?" Kate asked, reaching for the box of donuts and selecting one of the maple-glazed ones. She always got an extra one for herself—they were her favorite.

"If I remember right, he was caught peeking in the window of the neighbor girl while she was changing clothes."

Kate sat up, suddenly more alert. "How old was he when this happened?"

"He would've been fourteen or fifteen."

"Oh," Kate sat back again. "He's too young. He must be old enough to drive to the surrounding towns. How old was the girl?"

"Sixteen, I think."

"Definitely not our guy. The girl's too old to fit with his type."

"Justin Flake also comes to mind. I've never liked him. Something about him just rubbed me wrong. He's never been caught, but he's always around when trouble starts. You know the type," Cara said dismissively, waving her hand as if brushing him off.

"I remember this huge bar fight at Randy's—the place out on the edge of town. Three men ended up in the hospital, and only one guy got arrested, but everyone said Justin was there. Some even claimed he started it, but he was never questioned."

"That *is* weird," Kate agreed. "Tell me more about him."

"Let me think... A few years back, there was talk that he had something to do with vandalism at Jenkins' farm. Someone tore up a few rows of crops and ran over their family dog. It was awful. Mrs. Jenkins swore she saw Justin in the truck that did it, but the sheriff wouldn't pursue it. Said her word wasn't enough."

Kate's pen stilled for a second on the page. "The sheriff refused to even look into him?"

"Yep. I always thought that was strange. Even if her ID was flimsy, you'd think they'd at least talk to him."

"Has the sheriff looked the other way for anyone else?"

"He's always had a soft spot for the football players from Windsor Brooke High. Andrew, Justin—even Kyle. They were all promising athletes, stars on the varsity team during their high school years."

"Are there any others that you haven't told me about?"

"Well, his deputy, Cody Johnson, was the quarterback his senior year. He had a few run-ins with trouble, mostly pushing girls too far. One even accused him of raping her after a party. The team had just won a big rivalry game, and they all went out to the woods to celebrate. Some girls joined them, including Sally, who had been dating Bobby—another player. They'd fought a few days earlier and broke up, but when they made up, Cody said she was getting back at Bobby for kissing another girl. When Sally cried rape, the sheriff dismissed it. He said she'd waited too long to report it, and there was no evidence to back up her story. She was only fifteen."

"Are you saying the sheriff covered up a possible rape and then hired him as a deputy—to enforce the law?" Kate's voice rose to a near shout. How corrupt was this town? And all for a stupid game? It was almost too insane to comprehend.

"How sure are you about this, Cara?"

"Pretty sure. I don't have anything concrete. It's all word of mouth."

"Is there anything else strange from Cody Johnson's past?"

"I don't know what happened while he was away at college, but I do know he had a run-in with Charlie Porter after he came back."

"Just before he became a deputy, Charlie confronted Cody about having an affair with his wife. Cody's always been a player—this was just one more example of him crossing a line."

"What happened during the confrontation?"

"Charlie shoved Cody, and Cody punched him. A few guys stepped in and broke it up before it got out of hand. The sheriff was called, talked to them, and sent everyone home. We all figured he let Charlie off the hook for starting it, but now...I wonder if it was Cody he was protecting."

"Was Charlie a football star?"

"No, he played baseball."

"What do you think of Cody Johnson? What have your impressions been?"

"Honestly, I haven't thought much about him. I've never had a reason to cross paths with him. I'm too old to catch his attention, and I don't get in trouble with the law."

"Cara, do you think he could be the one responsible for these girls? Do you think he's charming enough to convince them to go with him?"

Cara hesitated, her expression darkening. "I don't know, Kate... but it's possible."

The door on the far side of the room creaked open. Chloe flinched and scrambled back, pressing herself against the wall.

He clucked his tongue, shifted the bag of food in his hand, and locked the door behind him. Her stomach growled—loud enough for him to hear.

He chuckled as he stepped closer. Filthy, he thought. She looked like she'd been rolling in the dirt. He'd need to bathe her again before he touched her.

"Hi, Chloe," he said gently, his voice dripping with false tenderness. "How are you feeling?"

They were always shy at first, quiet, and scared. But by the third day, they usually understood what he wanted. After a week, the light in them started to fade, and that's when he began to lose interest. Two weeks was the longest he'd ever kept one. Even the brightest little treasures lost their shine eventually.

"Are you hungry?"

She gave a slight nod, not moving from her corner.

He squatted down, holding the paper bag in front of her face, dangling it with two fingers like bait. "I got you a hamburger and French fries. There might even be a toy inside. Want to see?" He flashed one of his dazzling smiles.

She stretched out a tentative hand, eyes locked on his. The second she had the bag, she snatched it and retreated to her corner.

He raised an eyebrow, watching her devour the hamburger in five desperate bites. How long had it been since he fed her? He had to think. Maybe fifteen hours? He grimaced. That was sloppy. He was usually more attentive to his precious little treasures. He'd have to do better.

The quiet ring of his cell phone broke the silence. He scowled, reading the name on the screen. His time with little Chloe would be cut short. He clenched his jaw. Such a pity; she was just starting to break the way he liked.

Chapter Twenty-Six

Johnson was due to arrive any second. Agitated, the sheriff paced his office. When Johnson hadn't come in early, he'd called and told him to be there within twenty minutes.

Shane had already filed his report. He said it didn't look like Riggs had been home in a while. The house showed no signs of anyone who'd spent the day sick. The only thing noticeably off was the trash, it hadn't been taken out for days. Shane said the stench nearly convinced him they'd find a body. Turned out it was just days-old trash.

Unfortunately, there was no sign of her SUV.

Jacobs had debated putting out an APB. In the end, he'd decided to do it. Worst-case scenario, she'd be pissed at being pulled over. He figured it was worth it.

He hadn't heard anything from Anderson yet, but he didn't worry. Right now, Riggs took priority. Something was wrong with his team, and he meant to find out what.

"Sheriff, you wanted to see me?" Johnson stood at the door to his office.

"Yes, come in. Have a seat."

"What's going on, Sheriff? Has the FBI found anything yet?"

"Not sure. I haven't heard from them. Have you heard from Riggs?"

"No, sorry, she hasn't talked to me since she left early."

Jacobs leaned back in his chair, studying Johnson, "You were a great quarterback, you know that? Haven't seen anyone else with the same finesse since—well, maybe Sylvia's boy. But you had some real talent."

Johnson smiled, his posture easing slightly, "Yeah, those were the days. I sure miss the thrill of a good game. You know what I mean, Sheriff?"

"Yeah, I hear ya. What made you decide to become a deputy anyway?"

"I suppose the same reasons as you. I like to help people. The folks in this town know me and respect me. I figured it couldn't get much better than this. Am I right?" His cockiness was fully in place now.

Odd, until now, Jacobs had never noticed how much Johnson was like him. He liked the power, the authority, the respect that came with the badge. It was like looking into a mirror, and he didn't like the reflection staring back.

Comparing himself to Johnson was...unsettling.

He hadn't realized what a cold son of a bitch Johnson was until this moment. The charm, the smooth talk, the laid-back confidence—it was all a mask. And Jacobs, along with everyone else, had bought into it.

Even Agent Anderson had picked up on the tension between Johnson and Riggs. Everyone had. And now Riggs was gone. Her abrupt disappearance had unsettled the whole team, everyone except Johnson.

He was either the most oblivious deputy Jacobs had ever worked with, or...the alternative was far worse.

"Do you have an update on your assignment?" Jacobs asked, rifling through the stacks of paper on his desk until he found the one he was looking for. "What was it again? Cross-checking the local schools' football schedule with the dates of the abductions." He looked up at Johnson, waiting.

"I've been checking in with the families to see if they attended the games," Johnson said, his tone clipped. "I'm still working on the last two." He paused, meeting Jacobs's gaze with a steady, unreadable expression. "I've had to handle it on my own, you'll recall, since Riggs has been MIA."

"Ah, yes. Of course," Jacobs replied, his voice neutral. "Did you learn anything new?"

"Not much. Two of the three families confirmed they attended the football game as a family the same weekend their daughter went missing."

"Sounds like news to me," Jacobs said, leaning back in his chair. "What did Agent Anderson say about the connection between the abductions and the Windsor Brooke football games?"

Shifting in his chair, Johnson began rubbing his hands up and down his thighs as if trying to calm himself. "I didn't tell him yet."

"Why the hell not?" the sheriff snapped.

"Sorry, Sheriff. I figured I'd wait until I'd followed up with the last two families."

"I'm not sure how pleased Agent Anderson will be with that explanation. But he's out at the field where we found Sherri's body, looking for any new evidence."

Johnson's face paled. "Why are they doing that? Did someone find something to suggest there's more out there?"

Sheriff Jacobs arched a brow at the sudden shift in Johnson's demeanor. "Someone found a locket, I believe. Anderson thinks it might have belonged to one of the other victims. He ordered a full search of the area. Weren't you paying attention when he explained that yesterday?"

"I must've missed that part," Johnson muttered. "If there's nothing else, I'll get back to work."

Without waiting for a response, Johnson stood and walked out.

Sheriff Jacobs frowned, watching him pass the front desk and head out the door.

Where the hell was Johnson going?

The town square was busy today, with the park full of families. Kate smiled at the joyful sound of children's laughter. She nodded to a few familiar faces as she walked toward her store. A crisp chill lingered in the air, prompting her to tug her jacket more snugly around herself.

A breeze swept up the leaves from the street, circling them in front of her before letting them fall gently back to the ground. The motion caught her attention, drawing her gaze to the trees lining the square. She hadn't noticed how the leaves had begun to change, now a beautiful melody of yellow, red, and orange.

In their vibrant display, Kate found herself reflecting on how autumn brought change. Maybe her life had entered its own autumn season. Maybe it was time for some changes of her own.

The bell chimed as she opened the door.

Bridgette's head popped up from behind the counter. "Hey, you! What brings you in today?"

"Hi," Kate chirped. "How've things been?"

"Fine, of course. Business has been steady as usual."

"Good, that's always nice to hear." Kate didn't wait long to dive in. "I just left Cara's house. We talked about some of the men in town, and I wanted to get your opinion. You up for a gab session?"

"Absolutely," Bridgette said, rubbing her hands together. "You know I never say no to a good dish."

Kate chuckled. "I knew you wouldn't. Let's go to the back in case anyone comes in."

"Sure thing," Bridgette said, already leading the way.

Kate pulled a chair over to the table they used for tagging merchandise. "Tell me what you know about Andrew Taylor."

"Oh, we're diving straight to the bottom of the barrel, huh?"

"You think he's scum, then?"

"Definitely. He was always a drinker, but after his wife left him? He turned into a total creep. Trying to hook up with a girl young enough to be his daughter—ugh." Bridgette gave a visible shudder.

"How'd you hear about that?" Kate asked, curious whether Bridgette and Cara shared the same source.

"I think that particular bit of juicy goodness came from Sylvia. I don't see her often, but when I do, it's usually when I'm getting my hair done."

Kate fiddled with a paperweight on the table, keeping her eyes shielded. "Have you heard any interesting stories about Deputy Johnson?" she asked, aiming for a casual tone.

Bridgette rolled her eyes with an exaggerated sigh. "Cody is a *tool*. No surprise there. Everyone knows the sheriff loves his football boys. Honestly, short of murder, I think Cody could get away with anything."

Kate raised her eyebrows.

"It all started back in high school," Bridgette went on. "He walked around like the world owed him something. I remember him strutting through town, mouthing off to adults, grabbing snacks off the shelves at the market, and walking out without paying. He barely went to class. The only reason he graduated was that all the teachers gave him a C for showing up once in a while. I don't think he turned in a single homework assignment or passed a test, but he was the star quarterback. Took the team to state his senior year. No one wanted to be the one who benched the golden boy."

Kate frowned. "Why would the teachers agree to pass him if he wasn't even trying?"

"The school didn't do him any favors if you ask me." Bridgette leaned in a little. "I'm friendly with the English teacher, Kathy Winters. She told me the principal pulled her into his office and made it clear—no lower than a C on Cody's report card."

"Did he threaten her job?"

Bridgette shook her head. "He didn't threaten her outright, just said what he expected. But Kathy told me the way he said it made it crystal clear: if she didn't pass him, she wouldn't have a job at Windsor Brooke High."

"That's the most absurd thing I've ever heard." Kate sat back, stunned. "That's full-on corruption...in *high school*. It's ridiculous."

"I know," Bridgette said with a dry laugh. "And it was no surprise when he was later accused of rape. You can't raise a kid to believe he's untouchable and then expect him to play by the rules like the rest of us. Or act like a decent human being. There's a reason he's never left Windsor Brooke. This is the only place where people still treat him like the football hero he *thinks* he is."

Shaking her head in disgust, Kate asked, "Other than high school, has he ever done anything else that made you uneasy? Said anything? Acted in a way that raised red flags?"

Bridgette hesitated before she spoke. "There was this one time..." She began twisting a piece of plastic restlessly in her hands. "I was at the bar over on Stuart Street, meeting a couple of girlfriends for drinks. We had just grabbed a table in the back and sat down to talk when I noticed Cody coming out of the restroom. At first, I didn't think anything of it—I was about to say hi—but as he walked closer, his expression made me pause."

She took a breath, eyes distant. "A few seconds later, Stephanie came out of the same restroom."

"Wait—Stephanie came out after him?"

"Yeah, and she looked rattled. Pale. Like she'd seen something she wasn't ready for... The whole thing was..." Bridgette struggled to find the right word, "...bizarre. Unsettling."

Kate frowned, mulling it over. "You said you were going to speak to Deputy Johnson but stopped when you saw his face. What exactly did you see?"

"There are times when I close my eyes, and I still see it," Bridgette said softly, finally looking up. The fear in her expression caught Kate off guard.

"What? What did you see?" Kate asked, her voice low.

"*Evil*," Bridgette whispered. "A cold emptiness. It was...creepy. Because he was smiling—well, more like smirking—but his eyes..., his eyes were *dead*. Menacing. How does someone look so hollow and still smile like that?" She shivered, hugging herself like she was warding off a chill only she could feel.

"You never talked to Stephanie about it?"

"No," Bridgette said, shaking her head. "Something about the whole situation made me think she wouldn't have welcomed any concern I might've shown."

"What's Stephanie's last name? Does she still live here?"

"Stephanie Garnet. She lives with her parents over on Moore Street."

Kate raised an eyebrow. "She lives with her parents? How old is she?"

"She just turned twenty, I believe. She's in school now, and staying with her parents helps her save money. She wants to move to the city after she graduates."

"Twenty?" Kate asked slowly. "When did you say this happened?"

"That's the thing—it was a couple of years ago. Stephanie must've been seventeen, maybe eighteen. I don't even know why she was at the bar in the first place."

Kate tapped her pen on the table, her expression tightening. "I think it's time someone had a talk with her, don't you?"

They had found all five bodies.

Fox gazed down at the five freshly dug holes, fighting off the feelings of misery that had hung in the air all day. The mood had been somber the moment they discovered the first set of remains. From that point on, the usual banter had vanished, replaced by silence and only the words deemed necessary.

What he saw today had a way of tearing a person down.

Fox had learned the hard way to set his feelings aside—deal with them later. Right now, he had to stay present.

There had always been things about Sherri's case that didn't quite add up. Now, it made sense. The perp had planned to bury her like the others, but something must've gone wrong, something that forced him to leave before finishing his ritual. Knowing they had Sherri's body must have driven him mad. It was likely what pushed him to take Chloe when he did, breaking from his usual cooling-off period between victims.

They still didn't know how long he kept each girl. Sherri had only been missing a few days when they found her, but the fact that she hadn't been buried like the others suggested something had gone wrong—something that forced the perpetrator's hand and made him kill her before he was ready.

That one mistake had led them straight to his personal graveyard.

Now, with the other girls' bodies, they might finally be able to build a clearer picture of who he was—and why he did what he did.

Fox stared at the row of bodies lined up on the dewy earth, chilled by a restless breeze. Each one lay inside a black plastic body bag—bags far too large for their small frames. The corpses were in varying stages of decomposition. But one detail linked them all: long blonde hair, neatly brushed back from their faces, each adorned with a large pink bow clipped into place.

It was just the beginning of a pattern they hoped to uncover.

"Agent Anderson," one of the FBI techs called out, pulling Fox from his thoughts. "Come take a look at this."

Fox stepped over. "What have you got?"

"Under the third set of remains, we found something...unusual." The tech held up an evidence bag. "Not sure what to make of it. What do you think?"

Fox took the bag and held it up to the sunlight. Inside was a single dried white flower.

"A daisy?" he asked.

The tech nodded. "Yeah, I believe so."

"Did any of the other graves have a flower?"

"So far, this is the only one we've found. The remains belonged to one of the last girls buried," the tech said. "I'll double-check the others, make sure it didn't get caught on clothing or something."

"Let me know if you find any more."

"Yes, sir."

Fox studied the flower. What was the significance of a single white daisy? Traditionally, giving someone a flower was a way of expressing human emotion—something their suspect was clearly incapable of feeling, let alone communicating.

Human emotions.

A grim smile tugged at his lips. These days, emotion was all he had left, and none of it helped.

Today had been so hectic that he hadn't had much time to think about Kate. And yet, now that his thoughts had drifted there, he wasn't surprised. Once she entered his mind, it became almost impossible to push her out. She was like a beacon of light pulling him from the shadows, wrapping him in the warmth of her presence.

But she was hiding something. He knew it. It pressed against his thoughts like a pebble in his shoe—small, persistent, impossible to ignore. It festered like a wound he couldn't reach.

Once the case was over, he promised himself he'd spend real time with her. He'd figure it out. Whatever it was.

But for now, he would have to accept the version of the truth she was willing to give him.

Reaching into his coat pocket, Fox pulled out his phone. He hadn't spoken with Kate since leaving her house early that morning, and he suddenly felt the need to hear her voice. He tried not to think about what that meant. After all, he told himself, he'd promised to keep tabs on her. Heaven knows that if he didn't check in, she was bound to get herself into trouble.

The phone rang three times before she picked up.

"Hello," she said, her voice soft and bright.

His heart responded before his brain could catch up. Damn it.

"Hey," he said tightly. "How's your day going?"

"Fine," she said. "I visited with Bridgette and Cara today."

Fox frowned slightly. Something about the way she said it made him pause. Too neat, too quick. He couldn't put his finger on it, but the small warning bell in the back of his head started to chime. Still, he let it go.

"That's good," he said. "Any gossip worth passing along?"

A short silence followed. "Nothing too exciting."

He didn't press. But something in her voice lingered like smoke—thin, cloying, and impossible to ignore.

"How are things on your end?" she asked. "Have you found anything yet?"

"Yeah," Fox said, his voice low. "We found five sets of remains. All appear to be female. Preliminary estimates say the girls were between six and eight years old."

A pause. "I can't believe you found the bodies of those poor girls."

"You should," he said, not unkindly. "You're the one who found the pendant."

"Really? Why is that?" she asked.

"Because for that pendant to be there, at least one other girl had to have been in the clearing. And if she'd been there..." he trailed off, letting the implication hang.

"Then there was a good chance she still was," Kate finished quietly.

"Exactly."

"But if he buries his victims, why didn't he bury Sherri?"

"I think he was planning to," Fox said. "Only we found her body before he got the chance. Something must've gone wrong. Maybe he was interrupted. Either way, it was sloppy. That one mistake led us to all of this."

"I see. Are you almost finished out there?"

"Not even close," he said, glancing toward the excavation team. "We've only just started going through each grave. We'll be here for hours, easy." He hesitated, then added, "Listen...when I'm done here, I want to come over. Will you be home tonight?"

"Yes," she said. "Let me know when you're on your way, and I'll leave the door unlocked for you."

"Okay. I'll see you tonight."

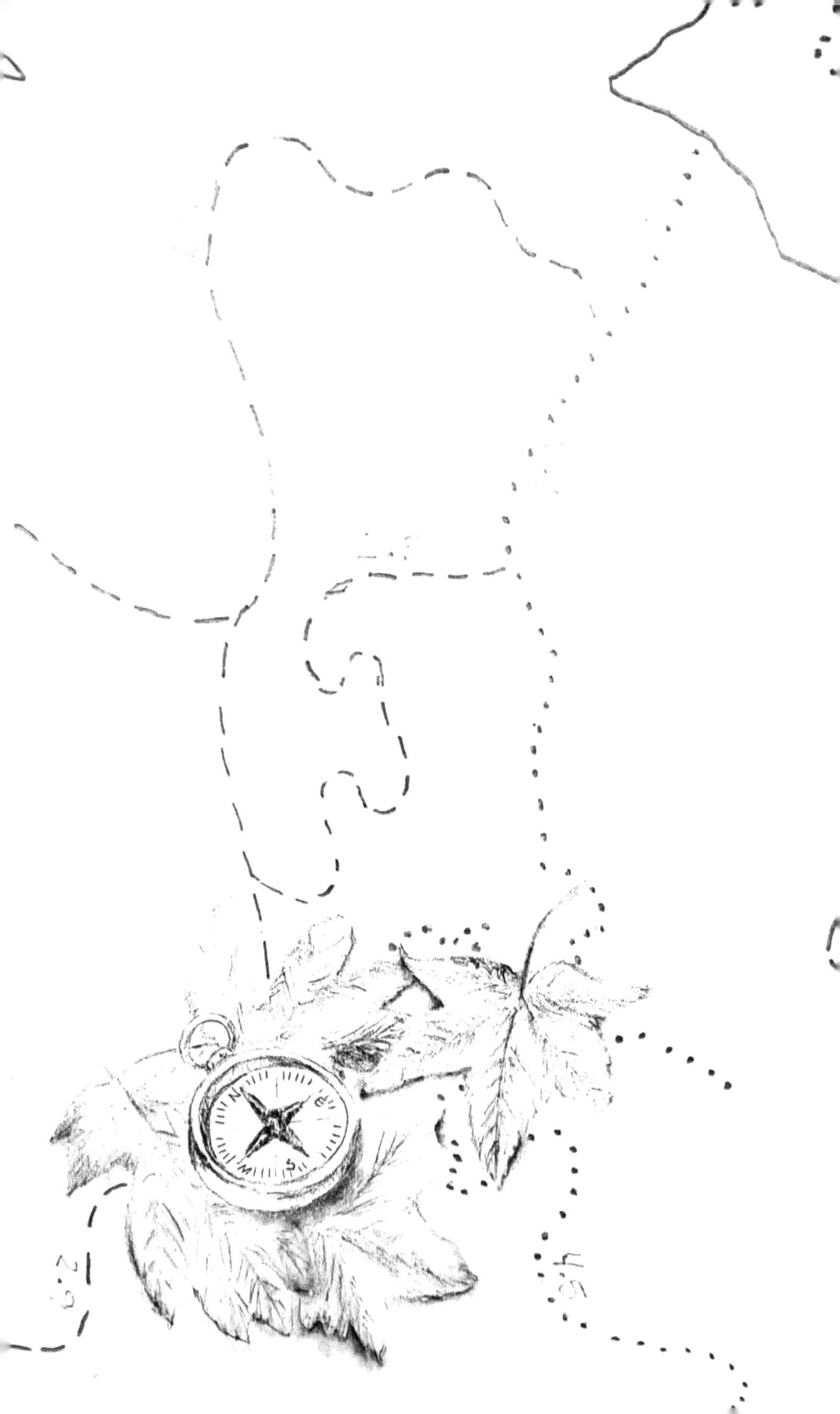

Chapter Twenty-Seven

K ate hung up her phone and looked at the house at the end of Moore Street. It was a beautiful two-story colonial, the kind that could've graced the cover of a home-style magazine. Even the landscaping was pristine—manicured trees, sculpted bushes, not a single weed in sight. It looked like the perfect family home built for love and laughter.

As she walked the cobblestone path to the front door, her mind drifted back to the days before her parents were killed—when she lived in a house not so different from this one. Back then, no one would have guessed what she'd become. People had a way of assuming too much, especially when the surface looked perfect. But assumptions had a habit of knocking you flat. Appearances lied. They always did.

The door swung open at her knock to reveal an older woman in a floral apron, her silver-streaked hair tied neatly in a bun. She looked Kate over before speaking. "Yes?"

"Hi, I was hoping to speak with Stephanie. Is she home?"

"She is. May I ask who you are?"

"Of course." Kate held out her hand. "Kate Millard. I own the little boutique in town."

The woman's face brightened. "Ah, I thought you looked familiar! I *love* your store. There are so many unique pieces. I bought several things you brought back from Venice a few years ago. I do hope you go again soon."

Kate smiled. "Thank you. That means a lot."

"Oh! I'm Becca, Stephanie's mother. Come in, I'll let her know you're here."

Kate stepped inside and immediately noticed a few of her items on display throughout the home. Evidently, Becca was a dedicated customer.

A moment later, footsteps echoed down the stairs. Stephanie appeared, her expression puzzled. "Hi. You needed to speak with me?"

"Hi, Stephanie. I'm Kate." She glanced briefly toward Becca. "I was hoping we could talk about a particular night. Is there somewhere we can sit—privately?"

Taking her cue, Stephanie nodded. "Ah, yes—we can sit out on the patio," she said, leading the way to the back door. "It's this way," she added over her shoulder.

The patio was as beautiful as the rest of the house, with overstuffed chairs arranged around a polished wood coffee table. Kate took the seat closest to the door, her eyes quietly studying Stephanie. She was a striking young woman—tall, at least five-eight, with long blond hair and deep blue eyes. Her lips had a natural pout, the kind Kate suspected made men lose their minds. It wasn't hard to see why someone like Deputy Johnson would have fixated on her. But that didn't make it any less vile.

"I wanted to ask you about your relationship with Deputy Cody Johnson," Kate said, carefully watching for any shift in Stephanie's demeanor.

Stephanie visibly blanched. She sank back into her chair as though trying to physically distance herself from the conversation. Her eyes flicked to Kate's, haunted and glassy.

"I don't want to talk about him," she said, her voice trembling.

"I understand this may be difficult, but it's really important," Kate said gently, leaning forward and tentatively placing a hand over Stephanie's. "I need to know what happened the night you were in the bathroom with Deputy Johnson at the bar a couple of years ago." She held her gaze. "Do you remember which night I'm talking about?"

Stephanie nodded, her eyes falling to her lap. Shame and embarrassment radiated from her posture—shoulders hunched forward as if trying to shield herself from the memory.

"Please, Stephanie," Kate said softly, "I wouldn't ask unless it was absolutely necessary."

"I wasn't eighteen yet," Stephanie began, her voice barely above a whisper. If Kate hadn't been so close, she wouldn't have heard her. "It was March, just a few months before I was supposed to graduate. Deputy Johnson hadn't been a deputy long—still very much the town's football star." A faint smile touched her lips. "I remember my friends and I used to joke about how cute he was, how we wished he'd pull us over."

She glanced at Kate. "You know...silly girl stuff."

Kate nodded silently.

"I was dating Russ at the time—we'd been steady for about two months. I borrowed his car to run an errand one day, and Deputy Johnson pulled me over. I remember laughing to myself, thinking I was the lucky one. I couldn't wait to tell my friends—they'd be so jealous." Her laugh was brittle, hollow. "It's funny how harmless it all felt then."

"I can't believe how foolish I was," Stephanie continued, wiping a tear from her cheek. "I'd been driving on that stretch of highway where there's barely any traffic. I don't remember a single car passing by the whole time he had me pulled over."

She paused, her voice trembling.

"I still remember how casually he walked up to the driver's side window, leaning in like it was nothing. Then he told me to get out of the car. I thought it was strange...but he was the cop, not me. What did I know?" She gave a helpless shrug. "Anyway, I did what he said. I got out of the car. Then he told me to place my hands on the hood... and to spread my legs."

Her voice caught, anguish tightening every word. Kate felt her stomach twist. She knew exactly where this was going, and fury lit inside her, white-hot and blinding. She hated nothing more than men in power preying on the vulnerable.

Reaching for Stephanie's hand, Kate gave it a gentle squeeze. "It's okay. You can do this. Tell me what happened next."

The tears came freely now. Stephanie dabbed at her eyes, her hands trembling.

"He...he patted me down—but it wasn't a pat. He rubbed his hands all over my body," her voice cracked, a sob breaking loose. "He touched me between my legs...he squeezed my breast. I was so scared and embarrassed; I didn't know what to do. I hadn't even let Russ touch me like that yet, and here was this man, someone who was supposed to protect me, touching me...like that."

Kate's throat ached with the urge to say something—anything—to make it right. But there was nothing she could do to erase what had been done.

"I'm so sorry this happened to you," Kate said softly. "You didn't deserve to be treated that way." She reached for the tissue box on the table, pulled a few, and handed them over. "I know this is hard to talk about... but can you tell me what happened next?"

Stephanie held a tissue to her nose and gave a slight nod. After a shaky breath, she began, "After he finished, he told me to turn around. When I did, he grabbed my chin, pinching it hard, and told me no one would believe me if I tried to tell anyone what he'd done. Said I shouldn't waste my time."

Her voice wavered.

"Then he asked if I was planning to go to college in the fall. I told him I was, and that's when he pulled a little bag out of his pocket. He dangled it in front of my face and said it was a shame he found drugs in the car." Stephanie rubbed her arm as if trying to chase away a phantom chill. "He smiled at me. Not a normal smile...it was cold. Evil."

Kate's hands clenched in her lap.

"I told him he couldn't do that—that it would ruin everything my dad had planned for me. And then..." Stephanie swallowed, her voice barely above a whisper. "He told me how I could fix it. Said if I met him at the bar, he'd tell me what he wanted. And once I was done, he'd make the paperwork disappear." She hesitated. "When I reminded him I was too young, that they wouldn't even let me in, he just laughed." Her eyes fell to her lap. "Then he told me to wear a skirt."

Kate had to fight to keep her expression neutral, swallowing the fury that rose in her throat. Stephanie couldn't think the anger was directed at her.

When the girl looked up, her eyes were pleading. "Do I have to tell you the rest? Can we be done now?"

It pained Kate, but she knew what was at stake. Keeping her expression calm and steady, she said gently but firmly, "I'm sorry, Stephanie. I know this is incredibly hard. But I need to know everything."

Stephanie closed her eyes and pressed her fingers to them as if trying to block out the pain, the shame, the humiliation. After a long pause, she gave a small, reluctant nod.

"When I got to the bar, he told me to meet him in the bathroom. I waited a few minutes, and then he came in, locking the door behind him. He said it was time to pay up. That the price would be my panties."

She gave a bitter, twisted smile.

"He laughed when he said it like it was some kind of joke. I felt relieved for a second, thinking that if all he wanted was my underwear, fine. He was just some sick perv with a fetish for girls' panties." She shook her head. "I should've known better. I should've told my mom what happened that day on the side of the road. But I was scared. I thought she wouldn't believe me."

"I'm sorry, Stephanie," Kate said quietly. "I promise—you'll feel lighter once you let someone carry this with you."

"I took them off—my underwear—as discreetly as I could, balled them up, and handed them to him." Stephanie shuddered. Her eyes took on a faraway look before finally looking at Kate again. "He...smelled them." Her voice shook. "Said I smelled as sweet as a peach, and he bet I tasted just as good."

Twisting the tissue in her hands until it nearly tore, Stephanie's gaze dropped to her lap.

"He raped me, Kate," she whispered. "He hurt me. I didn't know it could hurt like that. I didn't know a man could do that to a woman... to a girl."

Tears streamed down her face, her sobs raw and sharp.

"I haven't been with anyone since. He didn't just take my virginity. He took everything—my innocence. My spirit." She wiped her eyes, but the tears kept coming. "Sometimes I see him in town. He walks right past me like I'm invisible like he didn't destroy me. Like I'm nothing."

Her voice dropped, low and trembling but edged with pure fire.

"I hate him. I wish I could kill him. Ruin him the way he ruined me."

The venom in her words was sharp, cutting through the air with stark, searing honesty.

"What happened afterward?"

Stephanie laughed a tortured, broken sound. "Do you mean after he destroyed my life?" Her brows rose in cold inquisition. "Nothing. I went home, showered, and crawled into bed. I didn't leave my room for a week." Stephanie's voice was flat, hollow. "It took that long for the bruises to fade and the bleeding to stop."

Kate's breath caught in her throat.

"When I finally went back to school, I couldn't pretend everything was normal. I stopped hanging out with my friends. I couldn't stand to be touched by anyone, so I broke up with my boyfriend." She gave a broken laugh, bitter and filled with regret. "I still remember Russ's face when I told him. I didn't give him a reason. Just said I didn't want to see him anymore. It hurt almost as much as what Deputy Johnson—" she spat the name like venom—"did to me."

Kate could barely keep the bile down. This was worse than she had feared, worse than she had imagined. Knowing it had happened was one thing; hearing the details and feeling Stephanie's devastation pour into the space between them was something else entirely. How could anyone do that to another person—let alone a child?

"Stephanie," Kate said softly, "you've helped me more than you know." She started to rise but paused. "Before I go, I need to ask you one more thing."

Stephanie nodded, wiping her eyes.

"Did he do anything that made you feel your life was in danger?"

Stephanie was quiet for a long moment. Then she looked up, her eyes hollow.

"Yes," she whispered. "He held me down with one hand around my throat. He would squeeze tighter if I struggled. But then...there was a moment when he just stared at me, and he started to really squeeze. I couldn't breathe. I tried to claw at his hands, but he didn't stop."

Her voice cracked.

"The whole time, he just looked at me. Like he wasn't even human. Like I was nothing to him. I thought he was going to kill me, and for a second..."

She broke.

"I was relieved," she sobbed, her shoulders trembling. "I didn't want to live like that. Not after what he did to me."

Kate stood, unsure of what to do. She needed to leave, but it didn't feel right to just walk away. Awkwardly, she reached out and gave Stephanie's shoulder a gentle pat, clumsy but sincere.

"Stephanie—" The sound of her mother's voice drew both their eyes to the doorway.

Becca held out her arms, tears flowing freely from her eyes, "My sweet baby...."

Stephanie ran to her mother, throwing her arms around her neck. "I'm so sorry, Mom."

"Why are you sorry? You didn't do anything wrong," Becca whispered, stroking her daughter's hair. "All this time, I didn't understand what had happened. I wanted to ask, but you shut yourself away, and I didn't want to push you further."

"I wanted to tell you," Stephanie said, her voice trembling, "but I was so ashamed. I didn't know if you'd believe me."

"Of course, I believe you. I'll always believe you." Becca's voice broke. "You're my daughter. No one comes before you. No one."

Turning to Kate, she extended a hand, her eyes full of gratitude. "Thank you for bringing my daughter back to me. I don't think she would've told anyone if you hadn't come."

Kate took her hand, her voice steady. "I'm sorry this happened to your daughter. But don't worry, he won't hurt anyone else. I'll make sure of that."

She meant every word. And she already had a few ideas about how to make good on her promise.

The office was unusually quiet for this time of day. With all the deputies out on assignment and the sheriff napping in his office, Sylvia was left to field the calls and handle any problems. She preferred it this way—no one interrupting her, no one asking her to fill a coffee cup or make copies. Granted, she was technically a secretary, but those tasks felt demeaning.

This office was her ship, and she was the captain. Sure, the sheriff was the boss, but no one got to him without going through her first. She was the gatekeeper, and she loved sending people away. Sometimes, she'd turn them back even when the sheriff was wide open, just to watch their faces fall. Pathetic.

No one ever questioned her authority here, not like at home.

Resentment festered within her. Her husband had started out charming, attentive, even considerate—until the night she'd left the kitchen a mess after dinner. It had been a long day, and she was tired and just wanted to get off her feet. The dishes would be kept until tomorrow, so what was the big deal?

To him, everything.

He'd gone to get a beer, come back, and without a word, grabbed a fistful of her hair. He dragged her to the kitchen, slammed her against the sink, and told her in a calm, chilling voice, "I think you forgot to do something."

She'd cried through every dish she scrubbed that night. When she finished, she crawled into bed and didn't speak a word.

Things changed after that. She stopped seeking love from him. The only intimacy came when he initiated it, and she never responded; she just turned her face away and waited for it to be over. Eventually, he tired of her silence and found a widow in the next town to satisfy him. They were both fine with that. Their kids were grown. She didn't have to pretend anymore.

No one in town knew the truth. Probably didn't want to. Even her best friends were clueless. And if they ever found out? They'd laugh behind her back. That's what they did.

This was why the sheriff's office mattered. It was hers. Her domain. No one would take that from her.

The phone rang, breaking into her thoughts.

"Windsor Brooke Sheriff's Office. How may I help you?"

"Uh, hi, my name's Buster Gills. I own a little hunter's box on the outskirts of town, and I've got an SUV parked in my driveway. I don't know who it belongs to, but...there's blood on the ground. Thought someone oughta take a look."

"Okay, sir. What's your location? And can you give me the license plate number?"

"I'm just south of Deer Tracks Road. Turn right onto marker fifty-seven, follow that about a mile, then left onto marker forty-three. End of the road, right side."

"And the plate?"

"Right, uh, AJL9945. How long do you think it'll take someone to get out here?"

"I'm not sure yet. Let me run the plates. Hold, please."

"Yeah, sure."

Sylvia typed quickly. The registry popped up. Owner: *Hilary Riggs.* She stared at the screen.

"Uh oh. This is not good."

Picking up the receiver again, she said, "Mr. Gills, someone will be out to your property shortly." She hung up before he could respond, already rushing from behind her desk.

She threw open the sheriff's door with a bang, the wood slamming against the wall.

The sheriff, startled from his nap on the couch, jolted upright, stumbled over his boots, and landed face-first on the floor.

"What the hell, Sylvia? Would it kill you to knock?"

"Sorry, Sheriff. Got a call. I thought you'd want it ASAP."

"What is it?" he asked, rubbing his forehead.

"Some guy named Buster Gills called. Said there's an SUV parked in his driveway. Blood on the ground. I ran the plates..." she hesitated.

"And?"

"It belongs to Riggs."

Jacobs was already out the door.

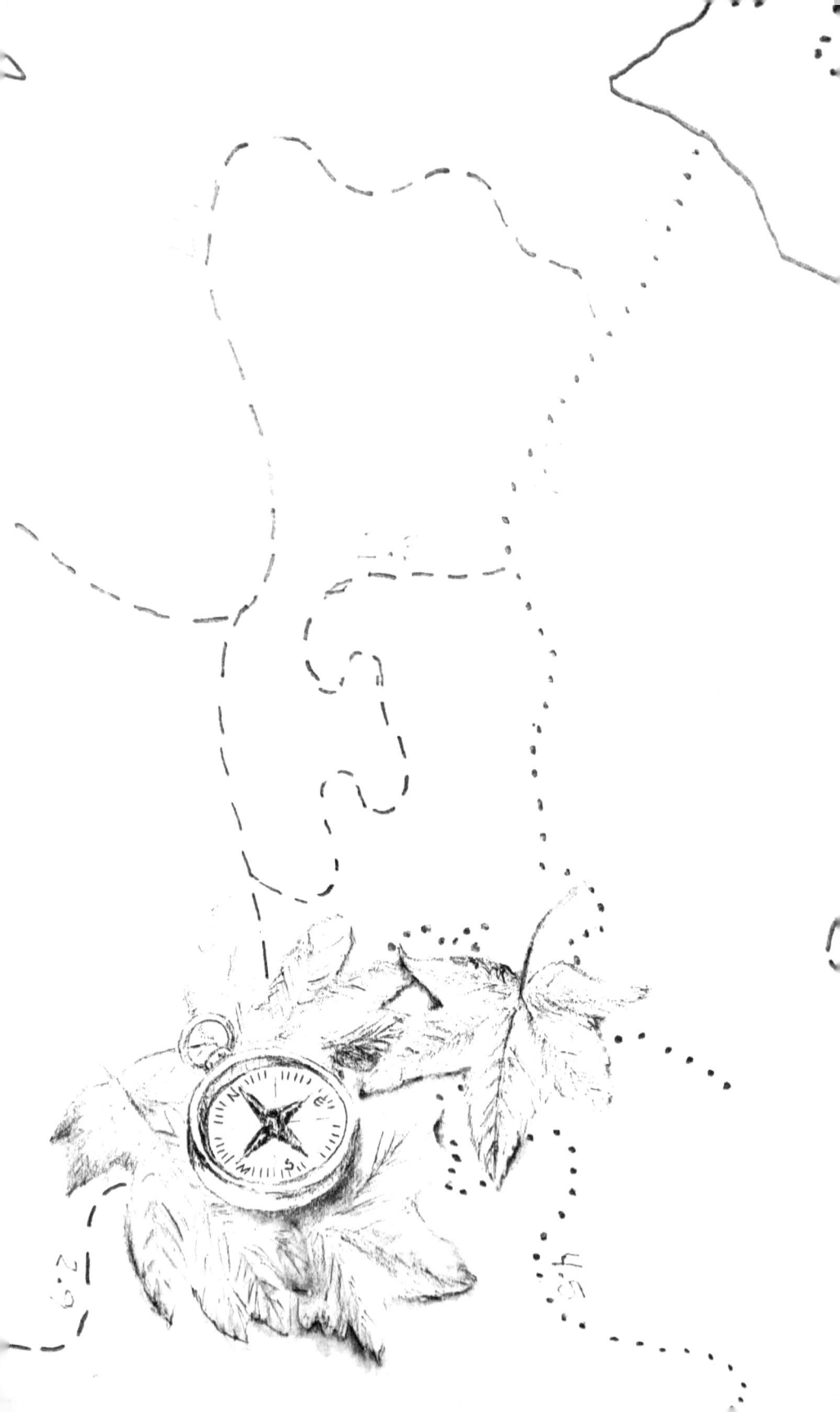

Chapter Twenty-Eight

"Shane, this is Sylvia. Do you copy?"

"I copy."

"We've got a possible sighting of Riggs' SUV. Sheriff wants you to meet him at this location—" she rattled off the directions.

"Got it. We're en route now."

Shane hit the siren and pulled a hard U-turn. He'd had a bad feeling about Riggs ever since she disappeared. He just hoped—*prayed*—they weren't too late.

The dirt road opened into a small clearing on the right side, revealing a tiny cabin nestled against a dense row of oak trees. In front of the tiny home sat Riggs's green SUV.

Shane's heart sank, guilt gnawing at him.

He should have checked on her last night like he was supposed to. If he had, they could have started looking hours ago. All that time lost—because he had been too damn tired.

An older gentleman with a receding hairline and a soft middle ambled over to the driver's side door.

"Deputies, I'm so glad y'all are here. I found the SUV first, then I noticed the blood," he said.

"Blood? What blood?" Shane blurted, feeling the blood drain from his face.

He and Marcos followed the man to a dark, muddy patch near the trees.

Marcos slipped on a latex glove and crouched, touching the ground carefully. When he straightened, bright red liquid glistened on his fingertips. He held his hand out so Shane could see.

A grim understanding passed between them.

"We need to get a sample to the lab right away," Shane said, already turning toward the car to grab their kit from the trunk.

Behind him, he heard Marcos speaking. "Sir, you said you noticed the SUV first, then the blood. When exactly did you arrive?"

Marcos peeled off the glove and pulled out his notepad, ready to take the man's statement.

"I got here this morning. I came in from the back way," the man explained, turning to point. "See over there, through the trees? I didn't notice the car at first. I went in, unloaded my stuff, and opened the windows to air out the place. I saw the car when I went outside to turn on my generator. Thought I should see if anyone was in there, and as I walked around, I saw the blood. I called out and tried to see if anyone would answer. When no one did, I figured I better call y'all."

"Did you walk the tree line at all?" Shane asked.

"No, sir. Just right here, around my house and the car."

"Okay. Thank you for calling us in. If you wouldn't mind waiting inside your house, we'll let you know if we have any more questions."

"All right, I have some other things to do anyway," he said, glancing over his shoulder as he headed back toward the front door.

"Doesn't look good. This amount of blood, the fact that it hasn't completely dried yet..." Marcos shook his head. "If this belongs to Riggs, it isn't going to end well for her. There's no way she would have survived this much blood loss without immediate medical attention."

"I was thinking the same thing," Shane said grimly. "What do you think she was doing here? I thought Johnson said she went home sick. If she were sick, why would she drive nearly thirty miles out of her way to come here?"

"When do you think the sheriff will get here?" Marcos asked.

"I don't know. Best start gathering what evidence we can in the meantime."

"What the hell happened here?" Sheriff Jacobs barked as he strode into the clearing, wasting no time throwing his weight around. He immediately started demanding answers from his deputies.

"We don't know, sir," Shane answered. "We've been over the entire area and haven't found any signs of her body or evidence of a struggle."

"The ground's soaked with blood, Shane. What more evidence of a struggle do you need?" Sheriff Jacobs said with a note of exasperation. "Did you get a sample yet?"

"Yes, sir."

"You canvassed the area?"

"Yes, sir."

"How far out did you go?"

"About a twenty-yard radius."

"I want hounds out here. Call it in. Have them search this entire area," Sheriff Jacobs barked.

"Now, Shane, now."

"Yes, sir. Right away."

Shane bolted toward his squad car, tripping over a root and stumbling hard into the hood.

"Shit, Shane, you all right?" Marcos called out, speaking up for the first time since the sheriff's arrival.

"Yeah, I'm fine. I just tripped over some root, is all."

"Well, get to it then," the sheriff barked. "In the meantime, I want this area locked down. Let's get Mr. Buster a motel room—call Sylvia and have her make arrangements. I also want this area guarded until the hounds get here."

"Yes, sir."

The sheriff stomped to his car, "I'm going back to the office. Let me know when you have something."

Fox watched as the coroners loaded the final remains into the van. It had already been a long day.

Finding the five sets of remains had happened relatively quickly, but processing each burial site was a different story. The killer had been thorough, burying his victims under six feet of soil and covering them with thick layers of leaves. Sifting through all that dirt was taking more time than he had hoped.

Fox loosened his tie. The suit felt suffocating, especially out here.

They had been working the crime scene all day, and now they were beginning to lose daylight. He ran a frustrated hand through his hair.

With the last light bleeding away, he knew he'd have to call it. Dammit, he wasn't ready. He had been hoping for a silver bullet, something that would lead them straight to the killer.

Instead, all they had found were more questions.

Scowling at the setting sun, Fox realized he would need to organize shifts to guard the crime scene overnight.

No way he was going to risk contamination.

Even though the sheriff's department was stretched thin, they'd have to help. It was about time to update the sheriff anyway.

He had just started to dial when Sheriff Jacobs came pushing through the trees.

"Agent Anderson," Sheriff Jacobs called out by way of greeting.

"Sheriff," Fox replied, lowering his phone. "I was just about to call you with an update. What brings you out here?"

"We've got a problem," Jacobs said, his voice grave. "You know how Riggs has been MIA?"

"Yeah."

"We found her SUV abandoned at a small hunter's box not far from here. There was a pool of blood about ten feet from her car—it hadn't completely dried yet." He hesitated, the words heavy. "I think she's dead. And I'm worried the guy who killed Sherri might have gotten to Riggs, too."

"Why do you think the same person is responsible?" Fox asked.

Despite the physical differences between the victims, the chances of two unrelated murders happening this close together in a town this small were almost nonexistent. The sheriff might be onto something.

"This is a quiet town," Jacobs said. "We just don't have problems like this. The odds of two killers showing up at the same time?" He shook his head. "Doesn't make any damn sense to me."

"You have a point," Fox conceded. "Do you know why Riggs was there?"

"Now, see, that's the other problem I'm having." Jacobs rubbed the back of his neck. "If you recall, Johnson's the one who said Riggs went home sick. As far as I can tell, he was the last one to see her alive." He met Fox's eyes. "You don't reckon he's innocent in all this, do you?"

"You know how I felt about Johnson," Fox said carefully. "Things were tense between him and Riggs, I'll give you that. But for him to escalate to murder?" He paused, struggling to make it fit. "And not just his partner — you're saying he might also be behind the six missing girls? I don't know, Sheriff. That seems like a hell of a leap. What evidence do you have?"

Sheriff Jacobs didn't answer right away.

Fox followed his gaze to the five freshly dug holes, frowning at the piles of earth and leaves beside each one. This is where the bastard had buried them—twenty miles from town, twenty miles from the sheriff's office—and no one had known. Fox could feel its weight and sympathize with the pained expression on Jacob's face.

"Sheriff?" The sound of his name brought him back.

"Sorry," Jacobs said, clearing his throat. "I don't have any evidence. Just suspicions. For one thing, Johnson was the last person to see Riggs alive. He's the one who said she left sick. And when I reminded him, you were out here, looking for evidence..." Jacobs shook his head grimly. "He damn near turned white as a sheet."

"We're wrapping up here for the day. Why don't you call Johnson in? Have him sit down and talk with you and me."

"Okay. I think you should handle the questioning. I'm out of my depth with all this," he admitted.

Fox was surprised to hear the sheriff admit any kind of weakness. He'd made it clear he wasn't thrilled about the FBI being involved.

"All right. Let me finish up here, and I'll meet you back at the office," Fox said, glancing at his watch. "Give me about an hour. Six o'clock?"

The sheriff nodded and started the trek back to his car, the weight of the world heavy on his shoulders. He looked like a man about to crumble.

"Where the hell is he?" Sheriff Jacobs barked at Sylvia.

"I'm not sure. I called Johnson and told him you needed to speak with him, just like you said. He told me he'd be here by six-thirty."

"Well, it's six-forty-five now. You sure he understood he was supposed to come today?"

"Yes, sir. I made sure."

Fox walked over to Sylvia's desk.

"Why don't you give him another call? Maybe he lost track of time."

"I'm giving him fifteen more minutes," the sheriff snarled. "If he doesn't walk through that door, I'm hunting him down myself."

Fox rubbed the back of his neck. He was tired. Bone tired. He'd been pacing alongside the sheriff for the last half hour, and the day had been ghoulish. He was ready to call it.

The unexpected turn with Deputy Johnson had thrown a wrench into his plans for the evening, which included seeing Kate.

Damn, when had this need to see her become such a driving force in his life? Her absence had left him with a knot of unease in his stomach. Knowing Kate, she could've gotten herself into all kinds of trouble.

This obsession was interfering with his work. He caught himself drifting; earlier at the crime scene, one of the techs had to call his name twice before he snapped back to the task at hand.

Watching the sheriff pace the cramped office, Fox couldn't help but feel the same restless frustration.

The case was moving forward but too slowly. The pressure weighed on all of them, and now, with Riggs missing and presumed dead, the stakes were higher than ever.

And on top of all that, he was falling for Kate Millard.

Prickly, complicated Kate—who had more layers than an onion, and every damn one of them was just as hard to peel away.

What was he supposed to do about this whole mess with her anyway?

Something told him she wouldn't be interested in relocating to his cramped townhouse.

Why would she? She had all this land, her store, and her life was here.

He didn't see her walking away from any of it.

The real question was, *is she worth it?*

Without hesitation, his heart screamed: *Yes.*

"Anderson, let's go find Johnson."

The sheriff's voice cut through his thoughts, yanking him back to the task at hand—just in time.

He knew his time here was limited, but he wasn't ready to dig too deep into where his heart was heading.

Falling into step beside the sheriff's long stride, he asked, "Sure. Where do you want to look first?"

"His favorite bar," Jacobs muttered. "If he isn't at work, he's usually there."

"And if he isn't?"

"Then we'll check his house. He's somewhere around here—and we're going to find him."

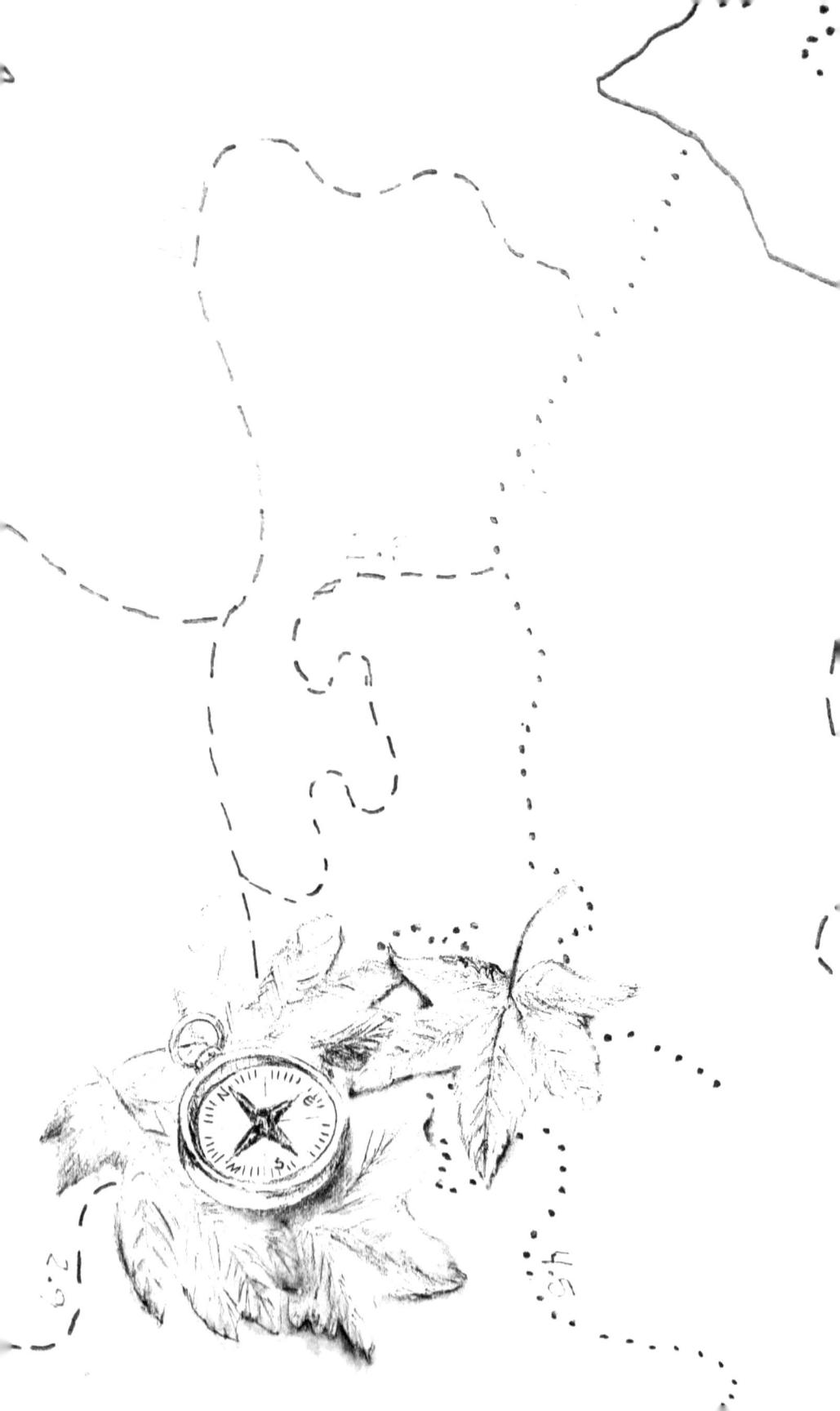

Chapter Twenty-Nine

The sound of her heart pounding drummed in her ears as she ran the well-worn trail that only she used. It had been days since her last run, and she needed it after listening to Stephanie's terrible story.

She loved the crisp bite of fall air on her skin as she picked up speed. With her blood pumping, her mind began to clear. How could the sheriff employ someone as abhorrent as Deputy Johnson? He couldn't have known. She refused to believe he would ignore the mistreatment one of his deputies inflicted on others.

Rage flared in her chest. She pushed herself harder, trying to outrun the words swirling through her mind. At least now Stephanie's mom knew what had happened. Hopefully, with counseling and a little closure, Stephanie could heal.

Skipping over rocks, vaulting off fallen trees, and rolling smoothly before springing back to her feet, Kate pushed herself harder. She liked to mix up her runs, sometimes giving her body a brutal beating in the process. Routine dulled reflexes. She refused to let hers slip. Brutal runs like this kept her instincts sharp.

As she settled into the rhythm of her pace, thoughts of the case slipped into her mind. It was clear now: Deputy Johnson was a slimeball of the lowest order. She had no doubt he'd been abusing his position for years, but had he killed Sherri?

It could fit. Stephanie was blonde, blue-eyed, petite, and young-looking. If Kate hadn't known her real age, she would have guessed she was still a teenager. Stephanie's assault had happened six months before the first girl's disappearance. The timeline fits.

The real question was whether Johnson had been willing to take that risk. Taking someone so close to home was dangerous—running into the victim's family was a daily possibility. But maybe the temptation had been too strong. Maybe, for him, it had been worth it.

The other complication was Fox. Up to this point, she had only shared a limited amount of information with him, but now she found herself torn. He knew how to track killers—something she had no experience with. If she'd told him what she had discovered about Deputy Johnson, he might be able to confirm her suspicions. On the other hand, he might take what she shared and run with it, removing her option to eliminate Johnson herself. It boiled down to how much she cared about finding the right guy. When she made her move, Johnson would have to die whether he was guilty or not. Unless he confessed and told her where to find his latest victim, she would never know for sure, but did it even matter in the end? She had no doubt he would continue to prey on young girls, and that was something she could stop. On the other hand, if she killed him too soon, the missing girl might never be found.

This only left her with one option: torture.

Kate didn't particularly care for it. Some in her profession found a morbid pleasure in the act, but not her. She knew exactly what it cost.

Her mind flashed to Bangladesh, four years ago. The last time she'd watched a man break.

She'd been sent to retrieve a target, paired, to her dismay, with a partner she didn't trust. Stuart. She hadn't seen him since the start of the AOD project, since training at the Ranch. He'd been a degenerative jerk even then. She should've known something was wrong the moment they assigned her a partner.

When they found the target, Stuart hadn't extracted him as she'd expected. Instead, he dragged him into a hidden shack, already outfitted with tools designed to break men open like fruit.

Kate had stood by and watched, her face a careful mask, knowing that to flinch would be fatal.

Three endless days of screams.

When it was over, she was the one who had to drag the broken man to the extraction point, only for him to die en route.

She had sworn then: never again. Never another partner. Never another lie. And certainly, never another moment of mercy for monsters.

Fox couldn't be an exception. No matter how much she liked him, she had to do this alone.

Johnson lived on the far side of town, tucked into one of the smaller neighborhoods.

It took Kate almost an hour to find his house and another fifteen minutes to park where she wouldn't be noticed.

Luck was on her side, an alley ran behind the two rows of homes, and Johnson's backyard had a gated entrance.

The back door gave way with a slight push. For a law enforcement officer, he was embarrassingly careless with security.

Kate rolled her eyes. Small-town folks, always thinking the people they knew wouldn't hurt them.

A quick sweep of the house confirmed he wasn't home.

Choosing a chair facing the front door, Kate settled in to wait for her prey.

"Shit."

The sheriff wanted to talk to him again. Johnson slammed his phone down on the bar.

He'd been hiding out in his favorite hole, hoping all this would blow over. Now, he wasn't so sure.

He was planning to move her car in a couple of days, but it didn't matter anymore. They'd already found it.

Of all the rotten luck. Who would've guessed Buster would come back to his hunting spot two weeks early? What the hell?

He needed a plan. Fast.

First, he'd go home and pack.

He had enough cash stashed to live sweetly in Samoa. If he moved fast, he could cross the border and catch a flight before anyone realized he was gone.

All he had to do was get home and grab the essentials. Everything else could be replaced.

The porch light was out, not unusual, although he could've sworn he left it on that morning.

Fumbling with the door, he cursed under his breath. The dark, the booze, and his frayed nerves made even simple things harder.

Finally, the door gave way, and he stumbled inside, slamming it shut behind him.

He headed straight for the bedroom.

He threw a bag on the bed and ripped drawers open, stuffing clothes and cash with no rhyme or reason.

There'd be time to sort it later. Right now, he just had to move.

"Going somewhere?"

Cold fear shot up his spine at the sound of the husky whisper.

Turning slowly, he was stunned to see Kate Millard standing in his doorway.

He forced a nervous laugh. "What are you doing here? You scared me shitless," he said, wiping sweat from his brow.

"Did I?" she asked, quirking an eyebrow. Her expression was playful, but her voice was flat—dead. It sent a tingling sensation racing over his skin.

"You okay?" he said, trying to sound casual. "You're...you're acting kinda strange."

Fumbling for something to do, he shoved more clothes into his duffle bag.

Kate moved deeper into the room and quietly shut the door behind her.

"Cody, we need to talk. It's okay, I call you Cody, isn't it?"

"I don't have time for this," he said, zipping the bag closed with a loud, nervous yank. "I was just leaving—"

Kate just smiled at him—a serene, almost pitying smile—and locked the door.

"Look, I don't know what you think you're doing, but I have—" His words cut off with a grunt as the room spun and the floor rushed up to meet him.

Johnson woke to find his hands tied to a chair with his own neckties.

He flexed his fingers, testing the knots, then pulled harder.

For a split second, part of him tried to twist the scene into one of his usual fantasies. But reality—pain, fear, humiliation—was setting in fast.

He shook his head, trying to clear the fog, but reality slammed into him.

"What the hell do you think you're doing?" he bellowed. The veins in his neck bulged as he strained against the ties, but they held firm.

Kate didn't flinch.

"We're going to play a little game," she said coolly. "I'll ask you a question. You give me an answer. If I like your answer, nothing happens. If I don't—"

She knelt and unrolled a long black tool kit across the floor. Slowly, she pulled out a set of pliers.

"—I suggest you don't tempt me."

Panic laced Johnson's voice. "You can't be serious. I'm a Sheriff's Deputy! You can't do this to me!"

An icy smile played on her lips, sending a fresh jolt of fear through him. She dragged a finger over the knot at his wrists, slow and deliberate.

"It seems I can. Now, shall we get started?" she said, her voice smooth as silk, terrifying in its calmness.

He watched, helpless, as Kate dragged a chair between his legs and sat down, twirling a pair of pliers in her hand like it was some kind of game. His skin crawled when she ran the cold metal up the inside of his thigh. He couldn't stop the tremor that shot through his leg.

"Cody, tell me what happened with Stephanie," she said, the pliers tracing slow, lazy paths against his skin.

"Stephanie? I don't know anyone named Stephanie," he stammered.

She clucked her tongue. "Tsk, tsk, Cody. Wrong answer."

Before he could brace himself, the pliers clamped down high on his inner thigh. Blinding pain exploded through him. He opened his mouth to scream, but she shoved a towel over his face, muffling the sound.

"Cody," she said, her voice almost gentle, "I chose not to go higher. But next time, if I don't like your answer, I will."

"Wait, wait," he sobbed, "I don't know who you're talking about. Tell me more, maybe I just don't know her name. Or maybe I forgot. Give me something. I want to answer, I swear." He blinked through the tears streaking down his face, heart hammering against his ribs.

Kate stared at him, her eyes cold and flat. He couldn't tell what she was thinking, but it sure as hell didn't look good.

"Stephanie," she said, her voice cutting like a knife. "The girl you raped in the bathroom at Al's Bar. Ring any bells?"

Before he could react, she jabbed him sharply with the pliers, making him yelp.

"W-wait a minute!" he blurted, struggling against the ties that held him. "I didn't rape her! She wanted it! When I opened the bathroom door, she was standing there with her panties dangling from her fingers, asking if I was hot for her. What was I supposed to do? Leave her standing there for the next guy? I did her a favor! No one else would've shown her as good a time as me!"

He waited, breathing hard, watching her for any sign she believed him. But she didn't say a word, just looked at him with that same dead-eyed stare. His stomach twisted into a hard, cold knot.

Finally, she spoke.

"All right, Cody. I know you've been busy lately. Why don't you tell me what you've gotten yourself into?"

Johnson blanched. How the hell did she know? Had the sheriff told her? The old bastard always had a soft spot for her, still clinging to the good old days.

Now he was tied to a chair with this crazy bitch holding his balls hostage, and he was scared shitless about what she might do if he didn't give her what she wanted.

"Look, it's no big deal, I swear," he said quickly. "She wanted to go to the house. I just took her there. Who knows what happened once she got there? I mean, I left, and she was still there. Maybe a bear came along or something."

Kate gave him a look that could have burned a hole through him. "Are you suggesting a bear killed her?"

"I'm telling you, I don't know if she's dead or not, but if she is, I'm sure a bear got her," Johnson insisted, nodding his head.

Kate leaned back in her chair, arms crossed. She wasn't saying anything, just staring at him. He could almost see the gears turning in her head, weighing whether to believe him or to break his legs.

"Where exactly did you leave her?" she asked at last, voice low and dangerous.

"At Buster Gill's place," he blurted.

"Why did you leave her there?"

"I already told you. She wanted to go there!"

"Okay," she said slowly. "So why did she want to go there?"

He licked his lips nervously. "She thought the other girls might be there."

Kate's expression remained blank. "She has a name. I want you to use it when you tell me why she thought the girls might be there."

He hesitated for a moment until Kate twitched the pliers near the junction of his thighs. He flinched and stammered, "Riggs thought the hunting box was a good remote location to keep the girls without being disturbed. That's why she wanted to go there. Happy now? Will you let me go?"

"Tell me about Chloe," she said.

"What about her?"

"Where is she?"

"I don't know," Johnson snapped. "How the hell should I know that?"

"Now, you've been doing so well," Kate said, inching the pliers a little higher. "You don't want to get me angry, do you?"

His breath hissed between his teeth. "Listen, you stupid bitch, I don't know anything about the missing girl!"

She didn't even react. Methodically, she opened the pliers wide enough to grab a chunk of skin and squeezed. Johnson's eyes rolled back, the pain hot and sudden.

"Shhh," she whispered in his ear. "It's not nice to call names." She patted his cheek like he was a little boy, then asked again, voice syrupy sweet, "What did you do with Chloe?"

Tears streamed down his cheeks. "I didn't do anything with her. I don't know what you're talking about," he sobbed.

Kate sighed—a soft, disappointed sound that made him whimper.

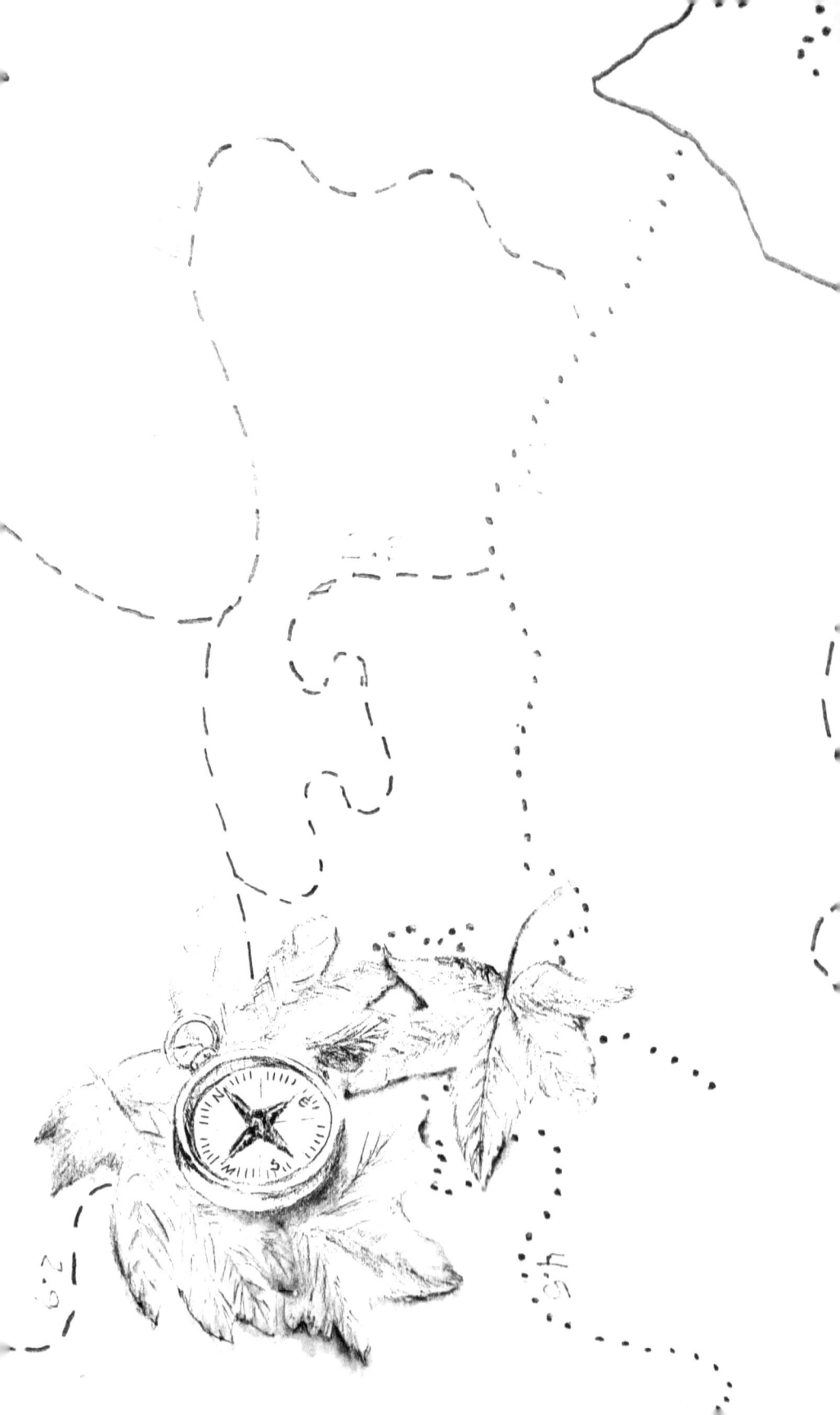

Chapter Thirty

The local bar was set up like most small-town dives. A long counter lined with battered stools ran the room's full length, except for a gap at the far end where a door led to the kitchen. Eight scattered tables filled the rest of the floor, with a few cracked leather booths crammed into the corners. The lighting was dim, the air stale with the musky scent of sweat, fried food, and old beer.

Fox had never been a fan of bars. His job sometimes dragged him into places like this, but he never went by choice. There were a thousand other things he'd rather be doing than sitting in a poorly lit, crowded room that smelled worse than a locker room after a losing game.

A man with silver hair and a long, unkempt beard stood behind the bar, drying glasses with a stained towel. He waved them over.

"What can I get you, gentlemen?"

"Hi, Joe," the sheriff said easily. "We're looking for Cody. Have you seen him today?"

Joe sauntered down the bar with an effortless smile half-hidden behind his thick beard. "Sure did. Came in around one or so. Hung out a couple of hours before heading out."

"What time did he leave?" the sheriff asked, keeping his tone light.

"Oh, I don't know, around five, I suppose. No later than five-thirty."

"What was his mood? Did he seem upset or distracted while he was here?" the sheriff asked.

"No—well, until he got the phone call. Then he seemed to get real agitated. I asked him if it had been bad news. He didn't answer, though; he just stood up, dropped a couple of bills on the counter, and left. Without so much as a backward glance. I even tried to call him back, seeing as he overpaid, but he didn't care." Joe shook his head, still looking perplexed.

"Thanks, Joe. Let me know if he comes in again tonight."

"Sure thing." Joe paused, eyeing them curiously. "Is there a reason you're looking for him? What, he ain't answering his phone?"

The sheriff laughed the question off, "No, nothing like that. You know how these young kids are—always on their phones, losing track of time."

"Sure do. Just the other day, I had some young kids in here drinking together. Don't think they said a word to each other the whole time—just sat there staring at their phones. Damn shame, if you ask me. Kids don't know how to talk anymore."

"I hear that." Jacobs signaled Fox toward the door. "You call if you see him," he added over his shoulder.

"You bet," Joe said.

"Where to now?" Fox asked as they walked to his car.

Wasting no time, Jacobs hustled into his seat. "Johnson's house," he said, "Something ain't right here. I can feel it."

Fox had to agree. He couldn't think of any reason Johnson would miss coming in to speak with the sheriff unless he had something to hide.

"We need to get to his house. Now." The sheriff's mouth set into a grim line.

It was freezing. The walls were ugly and bare. Chloe was tired of looking at them. She was tired of a lot of things. She missed her mom. She wanted to go home.

The bad man hadn't been back for a long time, and she was starting to worry. What if he forgot about her? What if she was going to be stuck in this room forever?

The doorknob rattled. She froze. He was back. He hadn't forgotten her after all.

Fear twisted in her stomach. She hated being alone—but she was even more afraid of him, of what he would do.

He would come in and sit beside her, rub a hand over her hair, and call her pretty.

And then it would be her turn.

Nothing was ever free.

She had learned that quickly. Every nice thing he did would cost her later.

She didn't want to pay anymore.

"Hello, Chloe. How are you doing?" His voice was always so nice, so fake.

"Okay," she answered, forcing the word out. She knew better than to say she missed her momma.

"Good. That's a good girl." He patted the spot next to him. "Why don't you come sit with me?"

The fear was paralyzing.

She didn't want to sit next to him.

She didn't want to touch him.

Her eyes burned.

No, no—she told herself—she couldn't cry. If she cried, he would get mean.

"I missed you," his smile was derisive, "Did you miss me?"

The tears came anyway. She couldn't stop them.

She hated him.

Johnson lived on a quiet street. The lamps cast a warm glow on the empty sidewalks. Everyone was home, eating dinner and settling in for the night.

"Let's go see if anyone is home," the sheriff said.

The house was as silent as a tomb. No lights. No sounds.

The sheriff pounded on the door, calling Johnson's name.

Nothing.

Fox started down the porch steps, "I'm going to take a look around back."

"Yeah, okay. I'll knock again."

The back of the house was just as dead as the front.

Fox peered through the windows as he made his way along the siding. None were open. Nothing looked out of place.

Until he reached the master bedroom.

He froze, then turned and sprinted back toward the sheriff.

"Sheriff! We need to break down the door!"

The sheriff frowned, his gaze flicking past Fox. "Why, what did you see?"

"Johnson—in the bedroom. It doesn't look good."

The sheriff gave Fox the go-ahead, and with one swift kick, the doorjamb shattered. The door slammed against the wall as they rushed inside.

Fox's gut twisted the second he saw the scene in the back room. Johnson sat slumped in a chair, a gun dangling from his hand, blood pooling under his head.

Across from him, Sheriff Jacobs stared for a long beat, his face hard, before he turned away. His shoulders sagged, the fight draining out of him.

Fox swallowed against the grim knot in his throat. "I know this isn't how you wanted it to go," he said quietly. "But we have to call this in. If Johnson was tied to Chloe, we need to tear through everything he left behind. He was our only real lead."

"I'll go call it in," Jacobs muttered, his voice ragged.

"Are you going to be able to handle this?" Fox asked, watching the sheriff closely.

Jacobs' head snapped up, his eyes narrowing. "What exactly are you implying?"

"I'm not implying anything," Fox said, keeping his voice level. "I know you were close with Johnson. Losing a team member...it's rough. But if you can't stay objective, I need you out of the way. Your call."

"Damn right, it's my call," the sheriff barked. His face was flushed with anger. "Now, why don't you make yourself useful and start searching his room? Maybe there's something that'll tell us what the hell is going on."

Fox nodded and turned away, biting back a comment. No sense escalating it now.

It didn't take long before the house was swarming with people. Johnson's body was gone, hauled off toward autopsy, the gun bagged and tagged. Everything pointed to suicide—a coward's way out. He probably knew they were onto him. No cop in his right mind wanted to end up in prison. Fox knew firsthand that once you crossed that line, the badge didn't mean shit inside.

He dug through Johnson's closet, dresser, and nightstands—finding nothing but hardcore porn and garbage. Nothing that told them where Chloe was. Nothing that proved Johnson had killed Deputy Riggs either. Hours later, they had nothing concrete. Just circumstantial evidence that painted a picture of a man who was a predator, a liar, and now a corpse.

The sheriff was ready to call it. Ready to close the case and write Chloe off as dead. Fox understood the logic and even respected the instincts that came with years on the job, but it didn't sit right with him.

If Johnson had killed her, why wasn't there a shred of proof?

Fox stared at the empty room, feeling the cold press of doubt in his gut.

He wasn't ready to give up yet, not on Chloe.

"Agent Anderson," Deputy Shane called, holding something up. He'd been combing the scene alongside Fox, and Fox could tell the kid was itching, feeling like they were still missing something.

"What do you make of this?" Shane asked.

Fox crossed the room. "Looks like a passport, Shane. What's your point?"

"Uh, sorry, sir. It's not the passport itself—it's where I found it."

Fox narrowed his eyes. "Where?"

"Under the bed," Shane said, pointing. "Lying open, face down. About a foot under."

Fox dropped into a crouch, lifting the blanket hanging low. An odd thing to just leave lying around.

"Probably got kicked under there," Shane added.

"Maybe," Fox muttered. "Bag it. We'll run it with the other evidence."

"You got it."

They'd torn through every inch of the place by now—closets, drawers, attic, garage—nothing but trash and dead ends. Fox watched as the techs dusted the last clean surface, the sheriff standing off to the side, looking hollowed out. His eyes were dark under the brim of his hat, and the fatigue in his stance was obvious.

"Sheriff Jacobs," Fox said, stepping over. "I think we've learned all we can tonight. Don't you agree?"

Jacobs exhaled slowly as if the breath hurt. His shoulders sagged under the weight of it all. "Yeah," he said.

"Let's call it," Fox said. "Come back at it fresh tomorrow."

"I don't know what more there is to see," Sheriff Jacobs said, his voice rough with frustration. "Deputy Johnson was our killer. He murdered those girls and Riggs when she got too close. Seems pretty damn clear to me, Agent Anderson."

Fox kept his voice even. "I think we need to wait for the autopsy before we decide anything. Things don't look great for Johnson, sure—but we need hard evidence before closing this."

The sheriff slammed his fist down on the dresser, rattling a lamp. "I'm ready for this to be over," he growled. "Before any more of my town gets torn apart."

"I get it, Sheriff," Fox said. "But if we're wrong—and the real killer's still out there—what then? Are you ready to tell more parents their daughters are missing because we rushed it?" He watched Jacobs stiffen. Good. The sheriff's pride was the key. One more push.

"Of course," Fox added casually, "there's always next year's election to think about. Voters might not be too forgiving if we let a murderer walk."

The sheriff's eyes narrowed into slits. His voice was low and dangerous. "All right, you win. We'll wait for the autopsy." He jabbed a finger an inch from Fox's face. "But we're making a decision by the end of the week. You read me?"

"That's fair," Fox said, masking his satisfaction. "How about we meet at your office tomorrow morning at nine?"

"Fine," Jacobs barked. He turned to his deputies. "Clean it up. We're done for tonight."

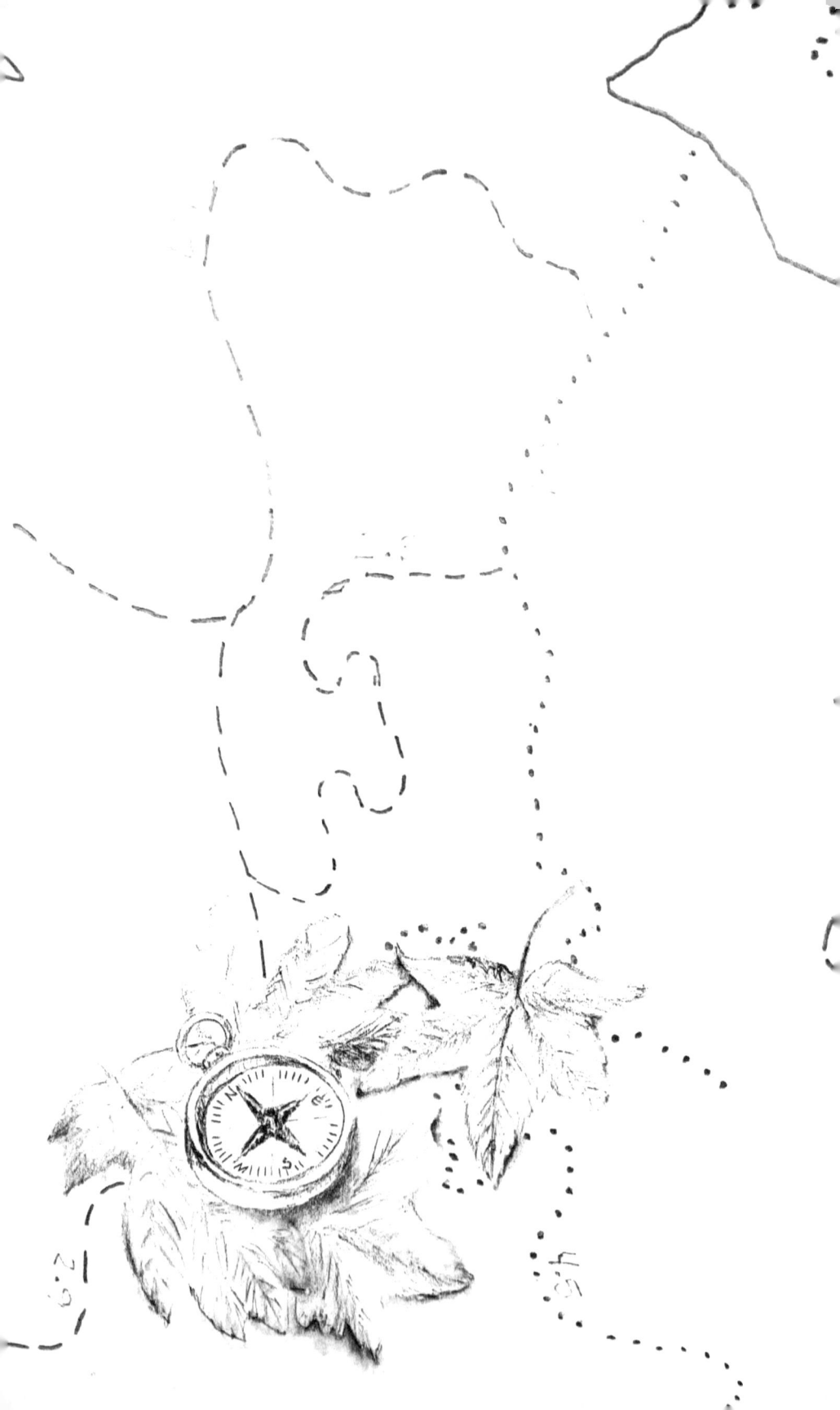

Chapter Thirty-One

The night was a sanctuary in the woods for creatures that preferred to hunt in the darkness. As the last light faded, other senses sharpened, and the sounds and smells of the forest magnified. The soft melody of insects during daylight turned deafening in the deep shadows of twilight. A heavy musk of pine and oak blanketed the air, masking every other scent with its raw, earthy power.

Kate was always most comfortable in the evening hours. Her foot kept the porch swing swaying as she surveyed the woods around her. She caught the shifting of leaves, glimpsing the silhouette of a small critter scrambling up a thick oak across from her porch. She wasn't alarmed. She had always felt a kinship with the animals that scuffled through the brush, rummaging for food under the cover of darkness. Like her, they weren't welcome in polite society.

There was no place for the likes of them, Kate acknowledged wryly.

Tonight, even the animals seemed to sense her solemn mood. The forest held its breath. Overhead, the only light came from a thin sliver of moon, blurred by heavy clouds she hadn't noticed gathering. They pressed down on the night, making the air thick and hard to breathe.

Kate shifted on the swing, uneasy. The darkness that usually comforted her tonight felt like a warning.

Cody hadn't confessed.

Sure, he had cried and pleaded with her to let him go. Not that that was a surprise. They always begged once they realized they were going to die.

Kate had pushed as hard as she could to get him to admit to taking Chloe. He wouldn't even acknowledge raping Stephanie. In the end, she simply ran out of time.

The killing was the easy part.

Staging the scene only took a few minutes, and the cleanup was always the worst. Fortunately, blood was essential to sell a suicide, and pliers were great for hurting someone without leaving a mess.

His body would be found soon enough. She was confident enough in her work to know they wouldn't trace it back to her.

Still, none of it solved her real problem. She still didn't know where Chloe was.

Bright lights shattered the darkness, weaving through the trees in the distance. Someone was coming up her road.

Scowling at the intrusion, Kate wasn't in the mood to entertain anyone. She had already given up on seeing Fox tonight, a fact that left a bitter sting she refused to acknowledge.

It was late.

A glance at her watch told her it was fast approaching midnight. She arched a brow. Kate couldn't imagine anyone showing up at her home, especially at this hour.

When the car broke free of the dense forest wall, recognition sank in.

The familiar headlights told her who was rude enough to show up, and the flutter in her stomach told her she didn't really mind.

"What are you doing here?" Kate asked, trying for sullenness. She didn't want him to know how pleased she was.

"It's been a hell of a day," he said, climbing the steps. "I needed to see you."

Fox grabbed her hands and pulled her gently off the swing. He brushed her lips with a soft, tentative kiss, then slid his arms around her waist, pulling her closer. He nuzzled into the curve of her neck.

Kate sighed.

"Fox, it's late. What are you doing here?" she tried to hold herself back, but the fight was already slipping out of her. No matter how hard she pushed, he always pulled her in.

He kissed her neck, slow and coaxing, nipping lightly at her collarbone. She felt him smile when he caught the shiver that ran through her.

"I missed you," he murmured against her skin. "Did you miss me?"

Without thinking, Kate tilted her head to give him more room—and cursed herself for it.

"I can't go there with you," she said hoarsely. "I know you want me to, but I can't." She pulled away, turning toward the house.

Fox caught her arm and spun her back to him. "Kate," his voice was a sweet, dangerous caress, "we're going to talk."

"No." She shook her head, pulling free.

She couldn't do this.

Nothing good could come from it. He didn't know who she was—what she was capable of. And when he found out, he would leave, just like everyone else. The thought alone almost crippled her.

He made her heart race simply by being there. Her skin burned wherever he touched her. She shivered as he brushed his thumb over the sensitive skin on the inside of her wrist.

She was coming apart. Exposed. Vulnerable.

"Fox," she whispered, pleading, "I can't."

The hard set of his jaw made Kate's stomach twist. She could see the heat burning in his eyes and feel the strength in his grip when he caught her chin in his big hand, holding her still. His kiss was sudden and searing, stealing the breath from her lungs—and just as abruptly, it was over, leaving her stunned and reeling.

Fox dipped low before she could find her balance and scooped her into his arms.

"Put me down," she demanded, crossing her arms in stubborn defiance. But part of her wanted to stay right there, held, wanted, safe, and that part scared her more than anything.

He chuckled, the low rumble of it vibrating against her side. Shifting her weight easily, he kicked the door open and carried her inside like it was nothing. She stiffened, but he didn't even hesitate, marching straight through the living room and up the stairs to her bedroom.

Panic prickled under her skin.

"What do you think you're doing?" Kate snapped, her voice pitching higher than she meant.

"What we are doing," he said through clenched teeth, "is setting some new ground rules for our relationship. Because, like it or not, we *are* in a relationship, and it's about damn time we started acting like it."

He dropped her on the bed first, then yanked at the buttons of his shirt, talking over her startled protest.

"For starters," he continued, "I'm staying here. Tonight. And every night until this case is over."

"Oh no, I don't think so," Kate said, scooting backward on the bed. Her spine hit the headboard with a little thump, but she didn't stop. "I told you no sex. I mean it. I am *not* changing my mind just because I like kissing you."

A slow, broad smile spread across his face. "So you *do* like kissing me," he said, pleased.

She rolled her eyes so hard it hurt. "Leave it to a man to only hear what he wants to hear," she muttered, crossing her arms tightly across her chest.

"You are not sleeping here," she added, but even she could hear how weak it sounded.

Tossing his shirt and tie onto the dresser, Fox started unfastening his pants, letting them slide down his legs without ceremony.

Kate felt her stomach twist. Was he serious?

He gave her a hard, no-arguments look. "I'm sleeping here. I already checked out of my motel. My suitcase is in the car. Before bed, I need a shower. I need to wash today off me."

Before she could guess his intent, he stripped off the last of his clothes.

Kate let out a strangled noise and slapped a hand over her eyes. "*Holy shit!* Fox, this is way, *way* inappropriate!" she shrieked.

Mortified by how childish that sounded, she dropped her hand onto her lap and sat there, stiff as a board, her face burning from her scalp to her chest.

She stared fixedly at the ceiling, then the wall, then the dresser. Anywhere but at him.

It didn't help.

Even with her gaze averted, her imagination painted vivid pictures. Broad shoulders. Lean, hard muscles. Tanned skin. She could *feel* his heat from across the room.

What scared her most was that, despite everything, she wanted to look.

From the corner of her eye, she caught him standing there—casual, sure of himself—except for the faintest tell: his fingers flexed at his sides, betraying a hint of nervousness.

"You've never seen a naked man before, have you?" he asked, his voice rough, almost gentle.

Kate gritted her teeth, refusing to answer. She didn't trust herself to speak without making things worse.

"I don't think that's any of your business," she snapped, her eyes still refusing to meet his.

"Well, you see, that's where you're wrong," Fox said, easing down beside her on the bed. "This is part of the new boundaries we'll be setting."

"I'm not getting naked with you, Fox!" Kate yelled, her voice rising with frustration. "And I'm not saying it again." She wanted to leave, to escape. And yet...she didn't want to, not really.

Fox lifted a hand to the loose strands of her hair and wound them around his finger, rubbing the silky strands before letting them fall back into place. "I didn't ask you to take your clothes off, did I?" he asked, his voice soft.

"No." Kate huffed, her arms crossed, leaning away from him. "Not yet, at least."

"That's right," he said, his voice low, full of confidence, "Not yet. You will, though. Eventually, but I won't force you. Believe it or not, I wanted to see how much experience you've had with men, and my gut told me you wouldn't be open to talking about it. I couldn't think of another way to get an honest answer from you. Looks like I'll be a lot of your firsts."

He rubbed his knuckle down her cheek, his eyes softening with an intensity that made her heart skip. "Don't worry, though, because I plan on being your last, too."

Kate stiffened, the words hitting harder than she expected. Her pulse quickened. Her mind raced. Could she go there with him? Could she let him in that much?

Before she could respond, Fox kissed her nose softly and stood, heading to the bathroom.

A few seconds later, she heard the shower kick on. Then, Fox's head popped around the doorframe. "Would you mind grabbing my bag from the car? I was so happy to see you, I forgot it." His voice was playful, almost sheepish, and Kate found herself staring after him, fighting the rush of conflicting feelings his words left behind.

Before realizing what she was doing, she had the front door open and walked out to his car. What was happening to her life? His words made her head spin, and a part of her wanted to believe him. But could she? Could he really stay with her? The ache in her chest said she wanted it more than anything, but the fear of him leaving when he found out who she was...was a constant shadow.

She dropped the bag next to the bathroom door, her hands trembling slightly as she tried to shake off the tension. When she turned to leave the room, his voice stopped her in her tracks.

"Kate, wait on the bed for me. I will be out in a minute."

Kate toyed with the idea of leaving the room, her fingers tracing the edge of the bed. She knew he would follow her, and she wasn't ready for the argument. She dropped her gaze to the floor, the weight of the moment pressing down on her.

It didn't take long for Fox to finish his shower. He emerged in a t-shirt and basketball shorts, looking completely at ease, like someone who belonged.

"You waited," he said with a smile. Then, a twinkle entered his eyes. "I thought I'd have to hunt you down. You've been skittish with me."

She didn't care for his teasing tone, especially the word "hunt." It was something she did for a living, and being the target of a predator was never a good feeling. She refused to think of Fox in those terms, though. "I figured it would be best to get this over with."

"Not sure I like our conversation being called something you have to get over with, but I'll take it."

He sat beside her, trapping her between the headboard and his body. "Kate, I need you to understand something," he said, pausing to take a deep breath before blurting out, "I love you. More than I thought was possible in this short time." He kissed the tips of her fingers.

Kate felt the slight tremble in his hand, and it surprised her. His eyes, stormy gray, held hers, and for a moment, everything seemed to stand still. He loved her. She wanted to say it back, wanted to tell him how much she loved him too. But the words caught in her throat.

Then doubt crept in. She had been loved before, but they were long gone. She shook her head, her voice tight. "You can't love me. I don't know why you think you do, but you can't. It isn't possible."

"Why isn't it possible?" he asked, his voice low and soothing. His fingers tilted her chin up, and before she could stop him, his mouth brushed lightly over hers—a whisper of a kiss that made her heart lurch painfully in her chest.

Kate stiffened, overwhelmed by the tenderness she didn't know how to handle. She caught the frown pulling at his mouth a second before he spoke again.

"You have to have noticed," he said, his voice gaining a harder edge. "We're like two magnets being pulled together. There was nothing I could've done to stop this. We're meant to be together. The sooner you accept it, the smoother things will be."

Meant to be. The words slammed into her, too big, too dangerous to believe.

"Wow," Kate muttered dryly, forcing herself to sound unimpressed even as her heart raced. "How romantic."

He ignored the jab, pushing forward like he hadn't even heard her. "Not only am I sleeping here from now on, but we're going out to dinner—in town—where everyone can see us. I won't be your little secret. We'll start there. Once you're comfortable, we'll add a few more things."

Kate stared at him, her pulse hammering. Her walls were crumbling fast, and he didn't even realize it.

"I'm beat. I'm going to bed," he said as if it were the most natural thing in the world. "Are you ready, or do you want to stay up a bit longer?"

"I'm ready," she mumbled, feeling oddly numb as she climbed into her queen-size bed — a bed that, for the first time, she worried might not be big enough. Well, if it wasn't, that was his problem. She had bought a bed that suited her, not one she ever expected to share.

Fox slid in beside her and pulled her into his arms without hesitation. She felt the warm press of his mouth against the back of her neck, a soft kiss that made her heart twist. Within moments, his breathing evened out, deep and steady, like he had no doubt he belonged there.

Kate lay still for a long minute, staring into the dark. Her body melted into his even as her mind warned her not to. But she couldn't help it. He fit against her so easily, so naturally, and it scared her more than she wanted to admit.

Entering the Sheriff's Office the next morning felt like stepping into the middle of a lightning storm. The air crackled with tension, leaving Fox's skin tingling. Sheriff Jacobs and his two remaining deputies were practically tripping over each other, hustling around with evidence bags and field notes. No one seemed interested in organizing the chaos.

Fox lifted two fingers to his lips and let out an ear-piercing whistle. All three men froze and turned to him.

"What the hell, Anderson?" Sheriff Jacobs stormed over, wagging a finger in his face. "I don't have time for any bullshit this morning. You hear me?"

It was almost fascinating to see the once-laidback sheriff snap orders like a drill sergeant. The right pressure could bring out the fighter in a man.

"Sorry. No disrespect intended," Fox said, hands raised. "Just thought you might want a little help making heads or tails out of what happened yesterday."

"We sure would," Deputy Shane said quickly, looking relieved.

Fox motioned toward the center table. "All right. Let's sit down. What do we have so far?"

Shane pulled out a chair and sat. "We know Johnson killed Riggs—and it looks like he killed himself once he realized we were onto him."

"Has anyone questioned the neighbors?" Fox asked.

"I did," Marcos said, flipping his notes. "One heard something like crying around six."

"Interesting," Fox drummed his fingers on the table. Something about Johnson's suicide didn't sit right. Johnson had seemed to be conceited and self-serving. The last type to kill himself. He would've pegged him as a runner, not someone who took the easy way out.

"When do you expect to have the autopsy results, Sheriff?" Fox asked.

Sheriff Jacobs looked up, scratching the back of his neck. "I'm not sure. It seemed pretty clear-cut to me, so I didn't push for a rush on it," he admitted, sounding sheepish. Given everything that had happened, he probably should have.

Fox bit down hard on the curses that rushed to his tongue. "Sheriff, I get that it looked straightforward, but we're potentially talking about a man connected to the five bodies my team dug up yesterday—and the disappearance of Chloe Hooper. Don't you think pushing for a priority autopsy might be...prudent?"

"Yeah, sure. I'll get right on that," Jacobs said, his tone making it clear Fox would probably have to call in some favors to make it happen.

Fox let it go for now. "Did anyone find anything linking Johnson to the girls?"

The room was silent. One by one, the deputies shook their heads, grim-faced. The seriousness of it wasn't lost on any of them.

"Shane, Marcos," Fox said, "head back to Johnson's house. Tear it apart if you have to. We need to find something—anything—if we're going to find Chloe."

The two deputies stood. "Sure thing," Shane said. They grabbed their gear and were gone in under two minutes.

Fox turned back to Jacobs. "I'm heading out to the burial site to meet my team," he said flatly. "I'll leave you to your own devices."

He didn't bother hiding his frustration. If the sheriff wasn't going to follow his advice, fine—he was on his own. They didn't have time for this kind of bullshit.

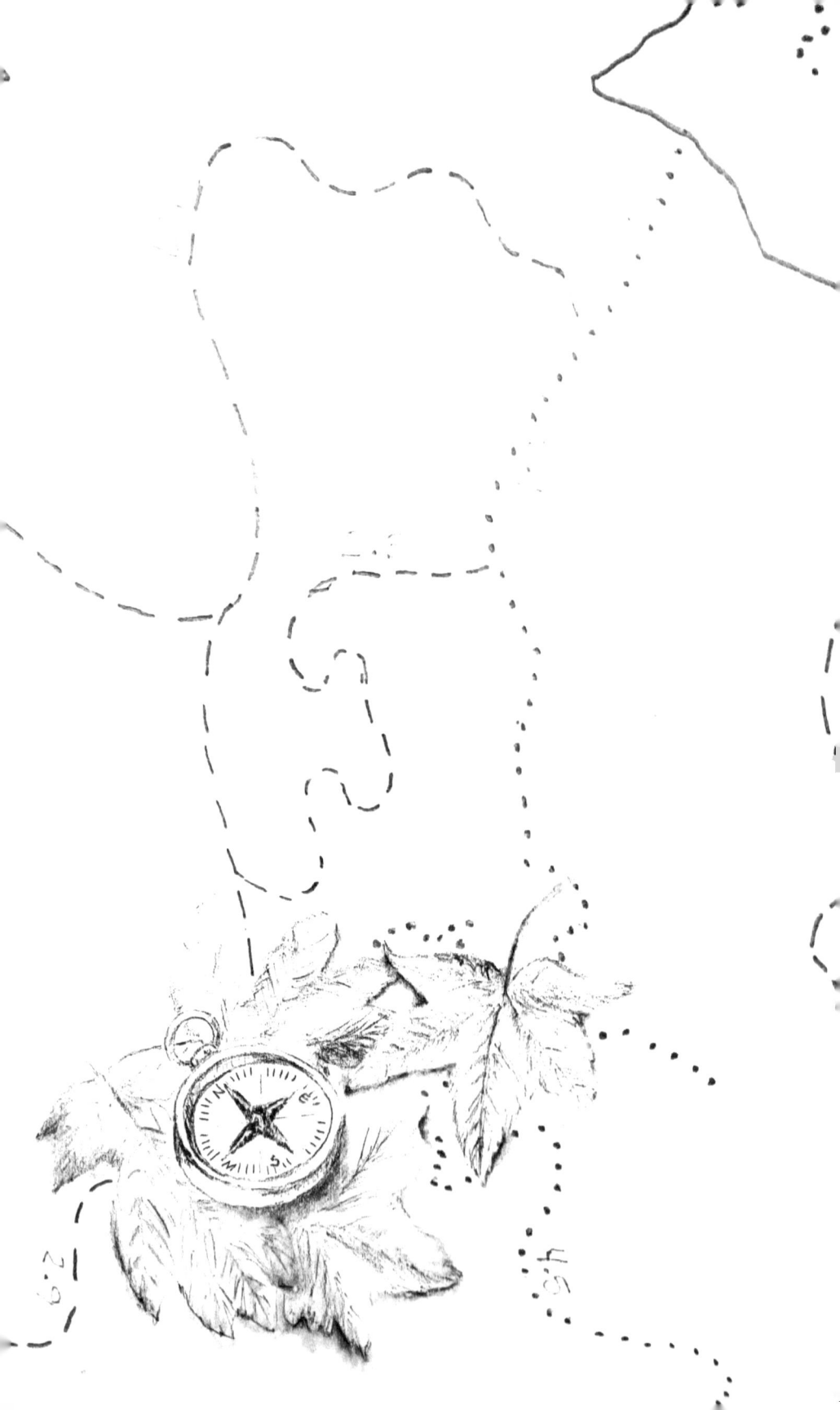

Chapter Thirty-Two

"Bridgette?" Kate called the second she stepped inside.

"Ya, girl," came the reply from somewhere in the back.

Kate found her cross-legged on the floor, parts of some half-assembled furniture scattered around her. A crooked metal rod caught Kate's eye; she couldn't even guess what it was supposed to be.

"I need some perspective. You up for it?" Kate asked.

Bridgette flashed her a bright smile. "You bet!" she said, grabbing another random piece from the pile. "What's on your mind?"

Kate hesitated. Sharing too much was always dangerous. She needed advice, not trouble later.

"I thought Cody Johnson might have been the one taking and killing the girls," Kate said carefully. "But it looks like it wasn't him. He was a piece of shit who abused his position...but he didn't kill Sherri."

Bridgette nodded, still working. "I wondered if that's where you were headed," she said, not looking up.

"Well, it was a wrong turn for me. Now, I'm not sure where to go from here. He was my one strong lead."

Feeling boxed in, Kate started pacing the store, picking up random items and fiddling with them as she walked.

"How about you walk through what you've learned so far and see if anything jumps out?" Bridgette suggested.

"Yeah, that's a good idea." Kate dragged a chair from the back and plopped it in front of Bridgette.

"Okay, let's start with the family I visited. I learned from Emma's parents that she had snuck out to meet a friend. According to the friend, they didn't tell anyone they were meeting. Davey, the friend's brother, and one of his buddies overheard them making plans. Davey didn't seem suspicious. Honestly, he was more interested in flirting with me than talking about his sister."

"What about the buddy?" Bridgette asked.

"Not sure. I didn't get his name. Davey said he's away at school."

"Okay. What else?"

Kate hesitated, debating how much to share. Finally, she admitted, "I've felt him watching me."

Bridgette paused mid-assembly, lifting her head to stare at Kate. "What do you mean you've *felt him watching* you?"

"The first time was when I went to where they found Sherri's body. I could feel him watching me—all the hairs on the back of my neck stood up. I just *knew*." Kate shivered at the memory. "Then once, when I was helping you with the window display. And again...at my house."

"What?" Bridgette squeaked, her voice jumping in alarm. "At your house? Are you saying he knows where you live?"

"Yes, but don't worry, I upgraded my security."

"Well, there's *something*," Bridgette said, her voice thick with sarcasm.

Kate smiled faintly and pressed on. "Anyway, the day I felt him watching me in town, I took a good look around the square. I made a point to verify where everyone was when the last girl disappeared. I turned up nothing, but figured he must be a local for him to watch me that often without raising suspicion. That's why I was questioning you yesterday."

"Sounds reasonable," Bridgette said, frowning thoughtfully.

"I thought so, too. Only now...I'm stuck. I don't have proof it was Johnson, and I don't know how to find Chloe."

Kate hated the helplessness clawing at her.

"Maybe you should focus on finding Chloe," Bridgette suggested gently. "What would you need to figure out where she is?"

"Good question. I have no idea," Kate admitted. She thought for a second, then mumbled, "I guess I could ask Fox for advice."

Instantly, she winced. She probably should've kept that to herself. Bridgette was like a dog with a bone; once she grabbed onto something, she never let it go.

"Fox? Who's Fox?" Bridgette asked, brows lifted. "I'm assuming this is a person and not a literal woodland creature? Because if you're talking to animals like some fairy tale princess, I might have to worry."

"He's just an FBI agent, I know," Kate said quickly, waving a hand like it was nothing as the front door chimed.

Both women turned to look, and Kate's stomach dropped.

"Oh shit," she hissed, shooting up out of her chair before Bridgette could react.

"What?" Bridgette demanded, craning her neck to see.

"Fox," Kate whispered, panicked.

Before she could move, Fox was in front of her, kissing her square on the mouth.

To his credit, there wasn't much heat behind it. But still, it was their *first* kiss in public, and Kate felt her face catch fire. Her body tensed, caught between instinct and panic.

Fox nuzzled her ear and whispered, "Had a few minutes. Thought I'd take a look at your shop."

His hands squeezed her hips, his smile lazy. "Good thing, too—I was just thinking about how much I wanted to kiss you."

Bridgette cleared her throat loudly. "And who is this, Kate?"

Resigned, Kate stepped back and made the introductions. "Bridgette, this is Fox Anderson. Fox, Bridgette, my store manager."

"I see," Bridgette said, offering her hand with a raised brow. "Fox, is it?"

Fox shook her hand easily. "Nice to meet you. Great shop you have here." Then, directing the question to Bridgette, he added, "Are you responsible for the displays?"

"Yep. I handle all the displays and placing the merchandise Kate brings back from her travels," Bridgette said, nudging Kate playfully.

Fox turned to Kate, lifting a brow. "All your travels? Where exactly have you been?"

Kate shifted, avoiding his gaze. "Oh, here and there. Nothing too remarkable."

Bridgette snorted. "Pfft. She's been to Paris, Rome, Brussels, Berlin—all over the place."

Fox's eyes locked onto Kate's, a silent promise that this conversation wasn't over.

"You don't say," he murmured. "You're full of surprises."

Kate shrugged, feeling cornered. "We can talk about it later. Since you're here, maybe you can help us?"

His mouth quirked with amusement. "What do you need help with?"

"I want to try to find Chloe—the missing girl," Kate clarified. "Only, I don't know how. What should I even be looking for?"

Fox leaned against the counter, thoughtful. "It's hard to find someone without narrowing the search area," he said. "But if you assume he wanted to stay relatively close to where he left the other victims, you could start within a twenty-mile radius of the burial site and work outward."

Kate frowned. "So you think if he's keeping her alive somewhere, it would be within twenty miles?"

"Potentially, yes."

Fox stepped closer, taking her hands gently. His voice dropped, firm but kind. "But don't get your hopes up too high. It could still turn out to be a wild goose chase."

Before Kate could answer, the door chimed.

"Hi, Tuck!" Bridgette called out from her corner. "What brings you in today?"

"Just looking for a gift for my mother. It's her birthday, you know." Tuck said jovially, though his eyes flicked curiously to Kate and Fox.

"I didn't know it was your mother's birthday. Will you tell her happy birthday for me?" Bridgette followed Tuck's gaze, "Tuck, you remember Kate, and this is Fox Andersen."

"Yeah, I think I met you in the sheriff's office the other day," Tuck said.

"Oh, I think you're right," Fox replied amicably. He glanced at Tuck. "Sylvia is your mother, right?"

"Yep. She always loves filling me in on the latest happenings in Windsor Brooke." Tuck grinned, impish and knowing. "Things have been unusually busy lately."

"Yes, I would imagine she would have more to tell you soon," Fox replied, looking at his watch. "Kate, I've got to go. Call me later?" he said, arching his brow. "I want to know where you end up heading."

Kate's back stiffened. She wasn't used to having anyone expect updates from her, and she wasn't sure she liked it. It felt like Fox was claiming a little more ground than he had a right to. Frowning slightly, she answered warily, "All right."

Smiling, Fox leaned in and kissed her pouting lips—a quick, warm kiss he couldn't resist repeating.

"Thank you," he murmured against her mouth. Then, pulling back, he nodded to Bridgette and Tuck. "Nice meeting you both."

And with that, he was gone.

He didn't come last night.

He always came at night. Always brought her something to eat, let her walk around the room a little before chaining her back to the bed. But this time...nothing.

Chloe hugged her knees to her chest and rocked herself. Tears streaked down her cheeks. She thought she had no more left, but they still came.

Her stomach hurt. She was hungry. She was scared.

What if he wasn't coming back?

What if he left her here—alone—forever?

She pushed herself up and stretched the chain as far as it would go. Reaching, straining, trying to brush her fingers against the door handle. It was no use. She even tried lying on her belly and wriggling closer, but she still came up short.

All she got for her trouble was a bleeding ankle where the cuff rubbed her skin raw.

She had tried before to get the cuff off—yanking, twisting—but when she bled, he got so mad.

He spanked her, just like Daddy used to when she was bad.

And he said, in a voice so scary it made her sick inside, that if she ever tried to escape again, he'd hurt her momma. Chloe believed him. She never messed with the chain again.

Sometimes, when she was really sad, she sang to herself the song her momma used to sing at bedtime:

"When you wish to see, make a wish and see.

When you miss me, remember to make a wish for me.

Wishes are for you and me,

Something we can share

Just for you and me to show how we care."

"I'm sorry, Momma," Chloe whispered. Saying it out loud made her feel a little less alone.

When they opened the door, the smell hit him like a wall—old blood and bodily fluid, all rotting in the air. It was worse than it had been yesterday, and the house being closed all night only made it worse. Shane couldn't stop the gag reflex that took over as the rancid odor smacked him in the face.

Marcos held his breath, turning his face away as he walked in, clearly struggling with the stench.

"We need to get every window in the place opened up," Marcos muttered, already heading for the living room windows.

Shane hurried into the kitchen, flinging open the back door and a window, hoping the cross breeze would help clear the air faster. "Damn, it smells like hell in here," he muttered, trying to breathe through his mouth. That was a mistake. The foul taste that hit his tongue made him gag again. "Shit, don't breathe through your mouth either. You'll be tasting it."

Marcos was already rummaging through the kitchen drawers, dumping everything onto the floor. "Let's just get this over with so we can get out of here," he grumbled.

Shane didn't argue. He didn't expect to find much, but they had to try. Part of him still couldn't believe Johnson had killed Sherri. The guy had been a jackass, sure—said some messed-up things about women—but Shane had never pegged him as a predator.

"I'm not seeing anything. How 'bout you?" Shane asked, tossing a stack of unopened mail onto the counter as he walked over to check on Marcos. The smell was slowly dissipating, but it still felt wrong, knowing Johnson had ended it all here yesterday.

"Nope. Got nothing." Marcos spun around the room. "Did you check the bedroom?"

Shane fiddled with some of the junk Johnson had cluttering the bookcase. A lot of it looked like decor—stuff his wife would've liked. He wondered if Johnson had picked it all out himself or if some woman had been involved. His phone rang, cutting through the heavy silence.

"This is Shane."

"Hi, Deputy Shane? This is John, Davey's employer. I just wanted to let you know that he showed up to work again. If you need to talk to him, his next shift is tomorrow."

It took Shane a second to remember who Davey was. "Right," he said, nodding as if the guy could see him. His mind was already spinning; things had changed since they found Johnson dead. Johnson had been their primary suspect, but now things were up in the air. Shane wasn't sure if he'd still need to talk to Davey, but the more he thought about it, the more he figured they might as well take care of any loose ends. "Thanks for the call. What time is his shift tomorrow?"

"He works the mid-shift, so he should be here by two."

"Yeah, okay, I'll see you tomorrow. Thanks again for calling." Shane ended the call and turned to Marcos, who watched him closely.

"Well? Who was it?" Marcos asked, clearly eager for some info.

"You remember that Davey kid?" Shane replied. "The one whose sister was supposed to sneak out with one of our victims?"

"Sure. What about him?"

Shane pocketed his phone, the conversation still fresh in his mind. "His boss just called. Looks like he's shown up again. Davey's supposed to work tomorrow at two." He glanced at Marcos. "You up for a drive?"

Marcos raised an eyebrow. "You think it's necessary? Johnson's the prime suspect, after all. What difference does it make talking to some kid's brother?"

Shane leaned against the counter, considering it for a moment. "I thought the same thing initially, but I figured we should be sure. What if we're wrong? What if Johnson didn't do it? We need to cross off every possibility." He let out a breath, shifting his weight. "Besides, after the way we got our asses handed to us last time, I want to make sure we cover all our bases."

Marcos grunted, clearly not thrilled but processing it. Shane could see the moment Marcos realized he was right. The last thing either of them wanted was a mistake hanging over them. "Yeah, okay. I guess it makes sense."

Shane nodded and turned back toward the hallway. There was still work to do, and the sooner they finished, the sooner he could get away from this awful smell.

Kate laid a topographical map on her kitchen table, smoothing the edges. She placed a paperweight in each corner to keep it flat. The map showed the land details of the forest area surrounding the location of the girls' remains. With a pin over the crime scene, she used a marker and string to measure a twenty-mile radius, drawing a circle around it. It was a rudimentary method, but it allowed her to visually see the terrain she needed to cover. Her heart sank as her mind pictured the uneven and remote areas outlined before her. There was no hope for her to cover this kind of ground. The enormity of the job settled heavily on her.

Kate shoved away from the table, pacing the small confines of her kitchen as she contemplated the problem at hand. What she needed was a bird's-eye view. Her gaze dropped to her phone. Perhaps some aerial footage of the area in question could be helpful.

"Hey, it's Kate. I need any images you have for a twenty-mile radius from these coordinates." Listening for a moment, "Okay, send it to my email when you can." Hanging up, Kate tapped her pen against the map.

Satisfied she should have what she needed by tomorrow, Kate sank into her chair, leaning her head back to rest against the wooden frame, and stared at the ceiling. She felt restless and had nothing to do but wait for an email. She needed to be moving, making things happen. Her foot tapped impatiently against the floor as her agitation grew. Then she jackknifed off the chair in horror. Her next job was a little over a week away, and she had forgotten all about it. She'd been so consumed with everything else that she'd forgotten to look at the file.

Her file cabinet stood in the corner of her office. Kate preferred to keep things simple, never hiding her files in secret places. Instead, she kept them filed alphabetically in her cabinet, locking the drawers for security. Thumbing through it, she found the one she was looking for and pulled it out, laying the pages on the table covering the map.

Grimly, she realized she needed to finalize her travel plans for the Morocco job. She had let herself become consumed by this case...by Fox. If she didn't get her life back on track soon, she might not have one to go back to. Checking the time, she could go to the gym in Omaha, get some laps in, and be home before Fox was finished for the day. She got up and grabbed her gym bag. After all, if she was going to make changes, she needed to start now.

A petite woman in her early fifties with a cute pixie cut sat behind the reception desk at the private gym where Kate had a membership. The receptionist was all smiles unless you weren't supposed to be there. Then, she could turn nasty. No unwanted guests ever got in. This was one of the reasons Kate had chosen this particular gym.

"Hi Kate, it's been a while. What brings you in?"

"I'm going to use the pool. Anyone else in there?"

"Not today. Middays are usually slow for us; everyone's got that nine-to-five schedule."

Perfect. Kate would be able to push herself harder if she were alone. Not that anyone ever paid her any attention. She just liked to be cautious. After all, there was no telling who anyone really was. Wasn't she the perfect example of that?

The locker rooms were large, with rows of spacious individual dressing areas. Each space had four separate lockers, and Kate had yet to meet the other three owners of the lockers in her designated area. All the lockers were assigned to gym members, but their schedules never seemed to overlap.

The lockers held top-of-the-line locks that were tough to break into. Kate knew this well, having spent a good amount of time testing their resilience. She'd wanted a secure place to leave an extra go-bag in case she ever needed to leave in a hurry, and she wasn't willing to risk someone breaking in and taking it. Once, she'd tried every feasible way to open one of the lockers next to hers—without success—she'd been relieved to know her possessions were safe.

Kate wasn't much for cloak and dagger. Simplicity made more sense to her. Her go-bag contained a change of clothes, basic hygiene items, and a key to a safety deposit box she'd opened three years ago. In her line of work, anonymity was key. But Kate had found that hiding in plain sight worked better for her. Instead of wasting time creating aliases, she used her real name when she traveled and bought items for her store. No one ever questioned her motives. If anyone wondered what she was up to, she appeared to be nothing more than someone who enjoyed traveling.

Even with her simple strategy, there was always a chance her identity would be discovered. As a precaution, she had developed one alternative identity. The passport, ID, money, and weapons were securely stored in her safety deposit box, and a second set was hidden in the wall safe at home. Though she didn't anticipate needing them, it was a comfort knowing they were there.

Kate made a clean dive into the pool, letting her body absorb the water's movement. Her strokes were smooth and strong, breaking the surface and propelling her forward. Swimming was therapeutic for her, and the rhythmic motion helped to clear her mind.

After a few warm-up laps, she found her rhythm, and her thoughts drifted back to the case. She still felt uneasy, sensing something was off. It was like trying to see through a smoke screen—the facts were distorted, the truth obscured by false leads and misdirection."

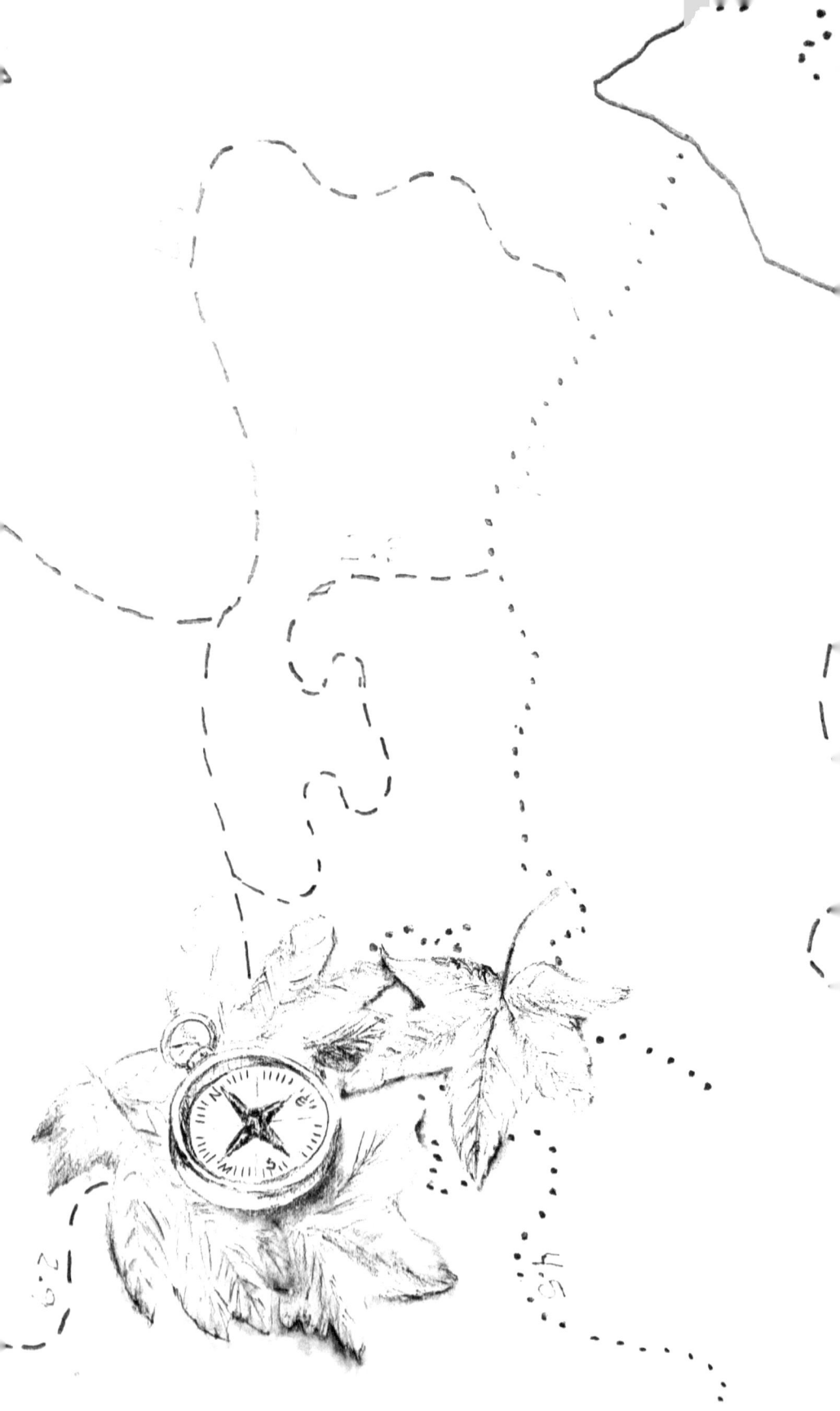

Chapter Thirty-Three

T he day had been long. Dirt and sweat covered every inch of him, but they finally finished processing the burial sites. Unfortunately, there hadn't been any additional evidence to help point towards a suspect. Despite Sheriff Jacob's insistence, he wasn't convinced Johnson was responsible. What they needed was Johnson's autopsy report.

He felt like he was chasing his tail in this case. The Sheriff's Department was losing people right and left. One deputy was dead, and another was missing and presumed dead, too. Sheriff Jacobs had lost control of his team, dragging the entire investigation down. With his department splintering, the sheriff's attention was divided. Fox knew they were at a crucial point in this case, and if they didn't find Chloe soon, they never would.

Fox had been spending so much time at the Sheriff's Office that it was starting to feel familiar. Even Sylvia's sour expression had evolved into a steady constant.

"Hi, Sylvia. I hear you have a birthday coming up. Any special plans?" Fox asked, making himself comfortable on the edge of her desk.

Sylvia gave him a blank look. "Who told you my birthday was coming up?"

"I ran into your boy over at Kate Millard's shop," Fox said, chuckling. "He said he was looking for something for your birthday. I hope I didn't just spoil the surprise."

Sylvia's mouth curled into a brittle smile. "I wouldn't worry about it. I won't say a word to him," she assured him, returning to her computer screen.

"Good." Fox tapped a finger against her desk. "Is the sheriff in his office?"

"Yes, go on in."

Fox felt his greeting falter the moment he saw Sheriff Jacobs. The cocky, self-assured man he'd first met now sat slouched in his chair, looking deflated—defeated even. When Fox first arrived, Jacobs was confident and sure of his place in both the department and the town. Now, he cradled his head in one hand, absently doodling on his desk pad, not even looking up when Fox entered.

Finally finding his voice, Fox said, "Sheriff, I thought we should go over everything again and see if we might have missed anything."

Jacobs threw his pen down and looked up at him. "Sure," he said, rising slowly from his chair, just as the phone rang. Pausing, he answered, "Sheriff Jacobs."

"Sheriff, this is Morgan from the county morgue. I wanted to let you know that we found DNA on one of the remains. We've sent the samples out, and we should be able to confirm the killer's identity once you have someone in custody."

"Thank you, Morgan. Would you mind sending in a sample from Deputy Johnson as well?"

"Sure. What are you looking for?"

"I want to see if it matches the DNA you found."

There was a pause on the other end before Morgan said, "I see. I'll take care of it right away."

Calmly, Jacobs hung up the phone. "They were able to find DNA on one of the bodies you recovered. Hopefully, we'll have a match with Johnson and can put this whole mess behind us."

Fox stared at him. "And what about the missing girl?"

"We've already discussed this. She's probably dead. We're not going to find her. Why waste more time? Johnson did it. He killed himself. Why are you still questioning it?"

Fox realized the sheriff was going to be of no help. The case was over for Jacobs, and without his support, there wasn't much more Fox could do.

"Have Shane and Marcos finished searching Johnson's house?" he asked, keeping his voice even.

"They haven't made it back yet, if that's what you mean." Jacobs moved toward the door, a clear dismissal. "Why don't you just call it a day? I'll have the boys call you in the morning with what they found."

Fox didn't miss the hint. Giving the sheriff a grim look, he turned and said over his shoulder, "Sure. Have them call me tomorrow."

Grabbing his coat, he stalked out of the office, the door slamming shut behind him.

Fox drove up the winding dirt road, weaving his way through the forest. The last light of day filtered through the trees, casting a soft, mystical glow. It had been a long day, and he was ready to relax.

He smiled to himself. Kate's house was beginning to feel like home.

He wondered if she'd have dinner waiting for him, but the thought faded as soon as the house came into view. Her car was missing, and the lights were off.

He shrugged off the flicker of disappointment. This was better. It gave him a chance to prepare the house for her, to show her what life with him could feel like. If only he could get her to lower her guard.

Turned out that asking for a key after announcing he was moving in had been a smart move. Sitting outside on that porch swing had lost its charm real fast. He'd expected a fight, some kind of negotiation, but Kate kept surprising him. She'd handed over her spare with only a mild protest—reluctantly, sure, but she had.

Which, in Fox's mind, had been a small yet significant victory.

As for tonight, he was determined to win Kate over with a slow and deliberate assault on her senses.

He lit the three candles on the front entrance table, then the two on the kitchen counter. Moving through her cabinets, he searched for dinner options. He was surprised by how well-stocked her pantry was, especially with ingredients he didn't recognize.

He pulled out a box labeled *Falafel Mix* and stared at it.

"What the hell is a falafel?" he muttered.

The box described it as some kind of Mediterranean dish. Not tonight. He tucked it back in place and settled on something simpler: pasta and marinara sauce.

Smooth jazz drifted through the air while he cooked, stealing glances at the security monitor by the fridge.

He tossed the pasta with the sauce and added a few finishing touches to the table.

The monitor buzzed. A car had passed the first checkpoint on the property.

Right on time.

Kate lumbered to her front door, her steps heavy. On the other side waited reality—a truth she wasn't ready to face. Fox had proclaimed his love, but it hadn't been tested. Not really. She'd tortured and killed someone he was investigating, and Fox might eventually learn it was her. Fox loved who she was now, but would he still want her if he knew the truth?

Her hand hovered over the doorknob when something shifted in the air. A presence. Cold, familiar, wrong. Sherri's killer was here. Watching her. It hadn't been Johnson, after all.

The sun had sunk below the treeline, casting long shadows that bled into the forest. The moon had begun its slow ascent, washing the landscape in a faint, romantic glow. But beneath the trees, the dusk was swallowed by darkness.

A gnawing frustration tugged at the fraying edges of her patience. Where was he? Her eyes swept the treeline, straining for movement. He was out there—she could feel it. Watching her. Kate hated that he could see her when she couldn't see him. A tremor of unease raced down her spine, heavy with the weight of impending doom.

Kate didn't hear him approach—she only felt a hand settle on her shoulder, and she reacted. Instinct took over. She swept her foot behind her, knocking him off balance. A thrill surged through her at the satisfying thud of flesh hitting the ground, followed by a grunt of pain.

She spun, fist already drawn back. Her knuckles connected solidly with flesh, then a hard muscle beneath it.

Only then did she see the familiar profile of the man she loved. Fox was doubled over, gasping for air as he clutched the spot she'd struck.

Her face paled visibly with concern as she reached a tentative hand out to him.

"Oh no, Fox, I'm so sorry," Kate stammered as he straightened, brushing dirt from his clothes.

Fox groaned. "What the hell, Kate?"

"I swear I didn't mean to hurt you—I thought you were someone else."

"Really?" He rubbed his stomach with a wince. "May I ask who you were expecting and why they deserved such a *warm* greeting?" he jeered.

Kate's mind scrambled. She gave him a wary look, taking a small step back. This was the moment she'd hoped to avoid altogether.

"This is probably something I should've mentioned earlier," she said, hesitating.

Fox folded his arms. "Yeah? Do tell." The derision in his voice made her want to drop him again.

"When I went out to the site where Sherri's body was found—and I discovered the pendant—I also felt someone watching me," she said, her tone clipped, unapologetic.

Fox's eyes narrowed. "What do you mean, *felt*? Did you see anyone?"

She shook her head. "No. But I could sense him like a predator stalking prey. And it wasn't just that once. I felt it again, back in town."

"Exactly how many times have you felt someone watching you?" Fox snapped, each syllable laced with irritation.

"Including just now? Four times."

"You mean you felt him just now," Fox whirled around, scanning the trees.

"Don't bother. I think he's gone now. I had just felt his eyes on me when you touched my shoulder. That's why I attacked you. My basic instinct took over." She said, substituting "basic" for "killer." He didn't need any more surprises today.

Not relaxing his guard, Fox continued to stare out into the trees, "When was the other time?"

"Here, a few days ago. It's why I installed cameras." Fox glanced back at her hopefully, "Sorry, no dice—he's managed to avoid every camera so far."

Fox scanned the area again, and the worry on his face faded. She could almost see him shift gears, frustration giving way to something else—something that looked a lot like determination.

He grabbed her hand and pulled her toward the door. She noticed a subtle blush rising on his cheekbones as he looked back at her. "I made dinner," he said, with a note of hesitancy. "Why don't you get comfortable, and I will pour us a drink."

A smile touched Kate's lips. "Are you trying to woo me with your domestic side?" She asked him, giving him an unabashed wink.

Wrapping his arms around her waist, he pulled her close. Nuzzling her neck, he placed a soft kiss behind her ear. "You know," he whispered, "a few inches south, and you could have made a eunuch out of me."

She elbowed him in the stomach. "It's rude to bring that up. I already told you I was sorry. Besides, it's not my fault you have terrible reflexes," she said, laughing at his pained expression.

"I'll only be a minute," she said over her shoulder, taking the stairs at a measured pace. Things were already more complicated than she'd anticipated, and she didn't know how to slow them down. Fox seemed determined to embed himself into every part of her life.

Standing in front of her bedroom mirror, Kate studied her reflection. The woman staring back looked younger, the cynicism that usually pulled at her mouth softened by a rare smile. No doubt, another direct result of Fox.

But it didn't change the truth. The worry still clung to her, heavy and unrelenting.

Life was chaos.

She craved something solid. Something certain. She wanted stability.

She wanted Fox.

The realization stopped her cold. She sank onto the edge of the bed, stunned by the weight of it. Admitting it—really admitting it—meant everything could change. Could he ever accept her if he knew the truth? Not just what she'd done, but what she *was*?

What if he walked away?

It didn't matter whether she was ready. The clock had run out.

Grabbing the first outfit within reach, she dressed quickly and headed back downstairs. It was time they talked. Whatever happened next... she'd have to face it.

Fox glanced at his watch, then up the stairs. *What was taking her so long?* How long did it take to change clothes? He sat at the table, staring at his plate but not really seeing it.

Why did they keep having this dance?

He still couldn't believe she hadn't told him someone had been watching her. Not that he was fully convinced there *was* someone, but still, she should have told him.

Later. First, they were going to have a nice meal. He'd cooked, after all, and damned if one of her evasive half-confessions was going to ruin the romantic night he'd planned. Tomorrow was soon enough to get to the bottom of who the hell was stalking her.

He heard her coming down the stairs like the devil was on her heels. A smile tugged at his lips. Maybe she was just as eager as he was to see where this night would take them.

She walked into the kitchen wearing a soft blue lounge set. The top hung off one shoulder, casual and quietly sexy.

"I began to think I was going to have to come looking for you," he said with a grin.

"Sorry, you know how women are. Selecting a change of clothes is always a major decision." She paused, sniffing the air. "Something smells good."

"I'm glad you think so." Fox pulled out a chair for her and dimmed the lights, letting the candles cast their golden glow over the room. As he served the pasta, he sat close—closer than necessary.

Tonight, he planned to be in her space every chance he got. To brush against her, touch her, make her familiar with him in every way he could. The kind of intimacy that settled deep under the skin.

Music played softly in the background—the kind that made you want to dance. And later, after dinner, that's exactly what he planned to do: pull her into his arms and hold her close while their bodies swayed together.

"Mmm, Fox, this marinara sauce is amazing. I can't believe you made this."

Grinning, he said, "It's my mother's recipe. One of the rules in her house was that we each had to cook dinner one night a week. We all started when we were twelve and kept at it until we moved out. My night was Wednesday. I got lucky—my sister had Fridays and complained every weekend about missing out on dates because she had to stay home and cook. I think my mom did it on purpose. My sister always had guys following her around, and this was her way of keeping tabs."

"I love your mother already. What else can you cook?"

"Just about anything. We ate pretty healthy, so I got good with vegetables. But I can grill a mean steak. We didn't have meat too often, but whenever my mom went out of town, my dad would bring home these massive cuts to throw on the grill. It was our guilty pleasure." Fox smiled at the memory. "What about you? Any kitchen skills?"

Fox leaned back in his chair, watching Kate swirl pasta on her fork. He found himself smiling again—he did that a lot around her.

"I usually just follow a recipe for whatever looks good to me," she said casually. "I don't repeat meals often. Most of the time, I just grab something from town. Cooking for one doesn't seem worth the effort, you know?"

Fox nodded. "Yeah, I don't cook much for myself either. Only when I'm craving something from my childhood."

There was a pause, one of those quiet moments where he felt the door crack open between them. He took a breath and leaned into it.

"Your turn," he said gently. "Tell me a favorite memory from your childhood."

He didn't miss the way she stiffened. Maybe it was too much to ask. He knew her family had been taken from her—violently, and dredging up anything from that part of her life might cut deeper than he intended. Still, he wanted to know her. The *real* her. Not just the version she let him see in the daylight.

She looked down at her plate, silent for so long he thought she wasn't going to answer.

But then she spoke.

"We used to have family dinners on Sundays," she said, her voice quieter now. "No matter what, we'd sit at the table together. My dad would tell stories about his childhood, and we'd hang on every word, laughing, teasing. After dinner, we'd play games for hours. Board games, card games—whatever we felt like."

She cleared her throat, blinking fast. "I think I miss that the most. The games. The way it felt to just...be a family."

Fox's chest ached at the raw honesty in her voice. She was letting him inside, and he didn't take that gift lightly.

"Tell me one of the stories he used to tell you," Fox said, drawn in by the softness in her expression.

Kate tilted her head. "Oh, I don't know... He and his brother used to get into all kinds of trouble. One time, they snuck onto this old man's farm to go cow-tipping—apparently, it was a favorite pastime."

She gave him a playful glance. "I never saw the appeal, personally. Anyway, the farmer got wise and adopted this mean dog from the pound. So one night, while my dad and his brother were out causing mischief, the dog came tearing out of the house and chased them across the field. My dad barely made it over the fence, but not before the dog took a nice bite out of his pants."

The smile playing at the corner of her mouth faltered. Her expression darkened with the memory. The light in her eyes dimmed, and Fox watched her shoulders stiffen as the weight of the memory sank in. Her breath hitched.

He was out of his chair before he even thought about it, pulling her into his arms. She didn't resist. He murmured quiet reassurances, rubbing his hand in slow, steady circles along her back until she softened against him.

Guiding her gently, he began to sway with the music, easing her into the rhythm.

Even if the memory brought pain, the fact that she'd shared it with him meant something—meant *everything*. And now, in this quiet moment, he wanted to offer her comfort the only way he knew how: by holding her close and letting her feel how much he cared without saying a word.

Slowly, he guided her into the living room, their bodies still swaying in rhythm. He could feel the tension bleeding from her, the way she leaned more into him, letting him hold the weight of her pain.

He loved the feel of her—warm, real, close. He ached for her. A wry smile curled his lips.

One day, she'd understand the full measure of his restraint—and maybe even sympathize. But for now, he'd take whatever she was willing to give. Because even a little of her was worth the world to him.

The music wrapped around them, their bodies swaying in rhythm as his hands traced the curve of her back. Slowly, deliberately, he slid his fingers into her hair, tilting her face toward his.

He hovered there, brushing his lips against hers—just a whisper of a kiss, teasing, asking, waiting.

"Kate," he whispered into her mouth, adjusting her slightly so he could deepen the kiss. His heart was already pounding. It happened every time—every single time he kissed her. He kept thinking he'd eventually get used to it and be able to enjoy the closeness without losing himself. So far, that hadn't happened, maybe in fifty years or so.

Without breaking rhythm, he danced her backward toward the couch and eased her down, settling between her legs. A groan rumbled from his chest, this was exactly where he wanted to be. When she wrapped her legs around him, holding him to her, something clicked into place. It wasn't just desire anymore. It was acceptance. She was letting him in.

He moved his hands from the cushion, then slid his hands under her shirt, the heat of her skin hitting him like a jolt. He'd dreamed about this—touching her, exploring her—but the reality made his head spin. Her softness under his hands, the way her body arched into his touch, the tension in her breath—it all lit a fire inside him.

Fox pulled back just enough to see her face. What he saw there—unguarded, beautiful, vulnerable—hit him harder than anything else tonight. But then her expression shifted. Something flickered in her eyes, and she flinched, pulling back slightly.

Fox froze, his hands going still on her skin. "Kate?" he said softly, worry piercing through the haze. "What is it?"

Fox caught her wrists gently but firmly, guiding them above her head and holding her still as he kissed her again, slower this time, deeper. He didn't let her go until he felt her soften beneath him until her fight bled into something quieter.

"I don't know what's going through your head," he said, his voice low, rough with emotion, "but let me be clear, I'm not going anywhere."

His heart pounded, frustration tightening his jaw. This was her pattern. She gave him everything in one breath, then tried to pull it all back the next. The second vulnerability crept in; she threw up her walls, trying to shut him out and push him away.

Not this time.

Her eyes flashed, the passion giving way to fire. She tried to pull her arms free, but he held on, not to overpower her, but to ground her. To stop her from fleeing again.

"Easy," he said, softening his grip just a little. "Let's talk about this before we spiral. Because clearly, we need to have that conversation about us again. What will it take for you to realize I am not going anywhere? I want you. Do you understand that?"

Her lips trembled. "And what about tomorrow?" she asked, voice tight. "Or next month? Will you still want me when you know who I am? What I am?"

Fox stilled.

What I am.

The words landed hard. What the hell did she mean by that? What was she carrying that made her look at herself that way?

His chest ached. Still, he met her gaze without flinching.

"I don't care what secrets you're holding," he said. "I love you, Kate. That's not changing. Do you hear me? I love you—and I'm not going anywhere."

He released her hands and pushed off the couch, breathing to steady himself. Then, calm and patient, he held out a hand.

"Come on," he said. "I'm going to clean up dinner. You can help if you want."

He turned toward the kitchen, leaving the choice to her.

Chapter Thirty-Four

*T*he sky was as gray and heavy as his mood.

He had been watching her house for most of the day, and she still wasn't home. Where the hell was she, anyway? It wasn't like he had all the time in the world to sit around waiting. Sweet Chloe was waiting for the new playmate he had promised her.

Before he left, he had glanced back to find Chloe curled into a ball, facing the wall. He couldn't hear her crying, but he saw her shoulders shaking. Poor little innocent, he thought with a snicker. Well, maybe not so innocent anymore.

He was surprised to realize he was already bored with her. Usually, it took a couple of weeks before he tired of his little treasures, but Chloe wasn't enough. His mind kept drifting back to Kate.

There was something different about her.

He didn't know how, but he knew she would be special. They had a connection he had never experienced before.

The stupid bitch hadn't even noticed him when he passed her by.

When the time came, he'd be able to walk right up and take her. She wouldn't even see it coming.

Even the Sheriff's Department was too busy chasing their own asses to notice him. Idiots. They actually believed Deputy Cody Johnson had been *smart enough to abduct and kill Sherri. Johnson was a sick bastard, sure — but he liked them rough, not young.*

He heard the low rumble of a car approaching and felt his pulse quicken.

Finally, she was coming home.

Finally, it would be time.

His excitement surged through him, wild and dangerous. He forced himself to calm down.

He couldn't afford to mess this up.

He was seething. What was Mr. FBI doing in her house? He was ruining everything. He watched Kate pull up next to the other car in her driveway. His eyes followed her as she walked up the front steps of her porch. Then he watched breathlessly as she stopped and slowly turned to stare into the woods. She felt him. A primal excitement boiled inside him, through him. All he had to do was be near her, and she could feel him. They belonged together. She just didn't know it yet.

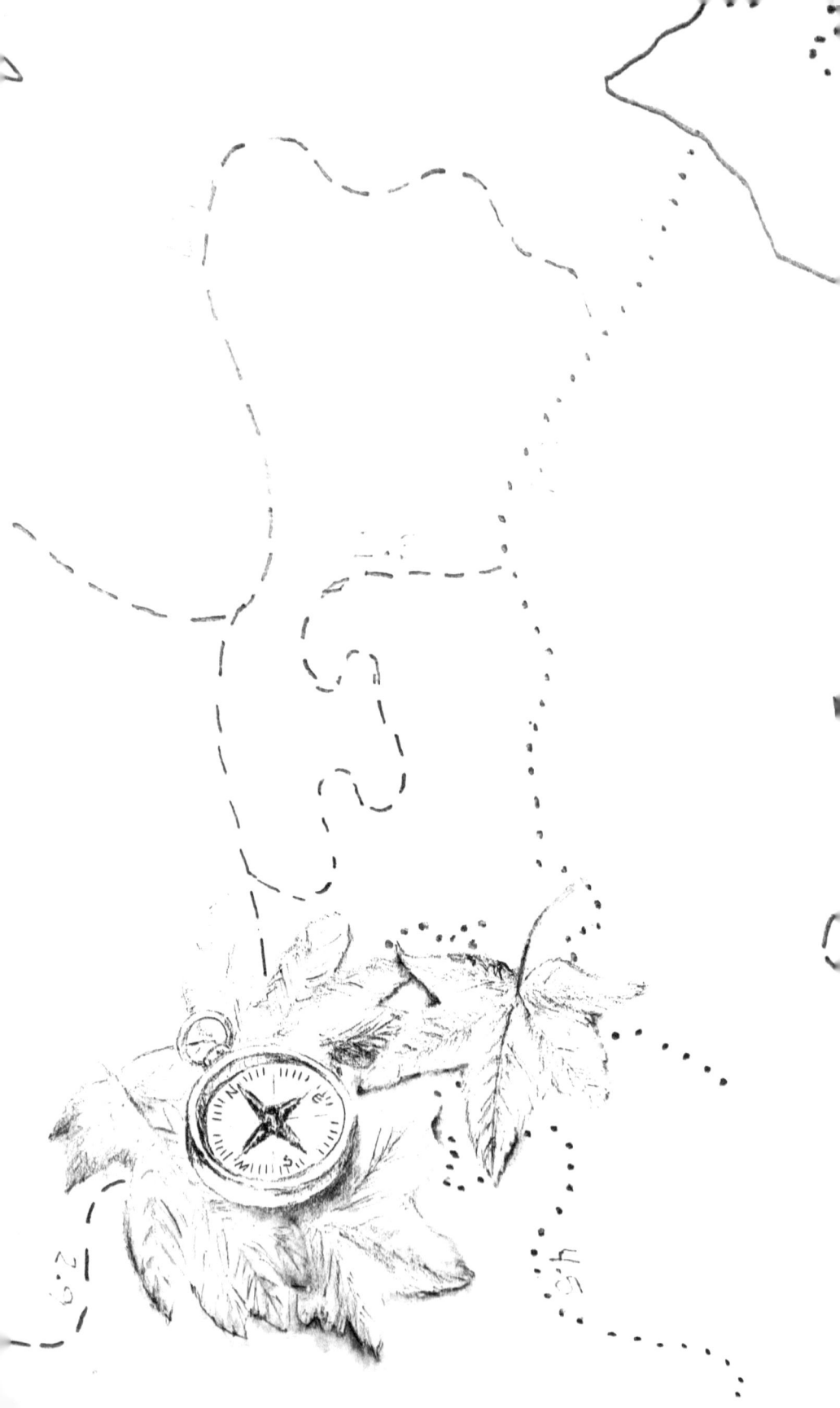

Chapter Thrity-Five

T he shrill ring of his phone jarred Fox out of a dead sleep. Eyes still closed, he reached blindly toward the nightstand, muttering a curse as he fumbled for the device. Without checking the caller ID, he answered with a groggy, "Hello?"

"Agent Anderson, I hear you've closed your case."

Fox blinked, instantly more alert. Of all the people he expected, Director Roberts wasn't one of them. He glanced at the clock—7:00 a.m. Rubbing the sleep from his eyes, he sat up straighter. "Not exactly, sir. We haven't located the last missing girl, and I still have serious doubts about Deputy Johnson's guilt."

"Yes, I've heard all about your doubts," Roberts said coolly. "Sheriff Jacobs says the case is closed, and frankly, based on the reports I've read, I'm inclined to agree."

Fox's jaw tensed. "With respect, sir—"

"No buts, Anderson. I want you back here by tomorrow. There's a case out in Oregon I want your eyes on."

Fox's gaze drifted to Kate, who had stirred beside him, now sitting up and watching him with guarded eyes. He didn't like the look on her face—wary like she was already bracing for the distance.

Still holding her gaze, he said into the phone, calm but firm, "Understood, sir. But I'd like to request some time off before reassignment. If you recall, I went straight from my last case into this one without a break."

There was a long pause before Director Roberts spoke again. "Very well. I expect you to report in next Monday. Do you understand?"

"Yes, sir. Thank you, sir."

"I mean it, Anderson. This case is over. Pack up and move on. I don't want to hear from the sheriff that you're hassling him."

Fox's hand tightened around the phone. "Understood, sir."

He ended the call and tossed the phone onto the bed with more force than necessary.

"What was that all about?" Kate asked, though she already knew. Roberts hadn't exactly been quiet.

"Case is closed," Fox said. "Time to pack up and head home."

Kate nodded slowly. A flicker of desolation flashed in her eyes.

"When?" she asked, her voice low.

Her brow furrowed. "But he said—"

"He did. And I told him I'm taking some time off. In case you missed that part." He gave her a pointed look.

Kate slid out of bed without responding. "Someone's testy this morning."

Fox grabbed a pillow and chucked it at her. She ducked it easily, then shot him a glare.

"What the hell was that for?"

"Because you keep poking at something you know is already raw," he snapped. "Why do you do that?"

Kate squared off with him, chin high. "Because no matter what you say, you'll leave. I want you to admit it."

"I've already told you—I'm not leaving." His voice was low but intense. "What's it going to take for you to believe me?"

"How can you say you're staying when your job is in Virginia? What are you going to do, quit?"

"No, I'm not quitting." He threw off the covers and stood, crossing the room. "But I want you to admit we're in a relationship so we can decide what *we*—" he emphasized the word "—are going to do next."

He was nose to nose with her now, his jaw tight, heart pounding.

Kate's chin shot up. "Who says I want a relationship with you? Maybe you're just being presumptuous, assuming this is anything more than a fling over a couple of weekends." Her words hit harder than the punch she'd landed on him last night—straight to the heart, no warning.

Fox stood perfectly still, hands planted loosely on his hips. His pulse thundered in his ears. Part of him wanted to shake her, to make her see what they had. But he forced himself to stay calm, to hold the line.

"I'd say you're lying." His voice was low, steady. "You're trying to push me away. But you can't make light of what we have. I know it means as much to you as it does to me."

"It means exactly what I said—a good time. Nothing more." Her tone was brittle, and her face was pale. "Why can't you admit it would be impossible for us to be anything else?"

He ran a hand through his hair and turned away, pacing once before spinning back toward her. "Fine. Let's break it down." His voice was steel. "Do you want me?"

"Yes!" she snapped, then quieter, almost ashamed, "You know I do."

The tightness in his chest loosened slightly. He took a breath. "Okay. Good. Now tell me—do you love me?"

She froze.

He watched the color drain from her face. She shook her head and started to turn away, but he reached for her—his hand firm yet careful as it cupped her chin. Gently, he tilted her face back toward him, eyes locked on hers.

"Kate," he said quietly, "look at me. I'm going to ask again. Do you love me?"

Her eyes filled. Her voice trembled.

"I can't, Fox."

His breath caught.

"I know what you want from me...but I can't give it. That part of me died with my family." A tear slipped down her cheek. "I want to, I swear I want to—but I just...can't."

His expression softened as he slid his hand from her chin to her arm, guiding her into him. "I know what I'm asking, Kate," he murmured. "But I need you to believe me. You *can* trust me with all of it. With your heart."

She didn't answer.

To soothe the tension in her shoulders, Fox gently ran his thumb along the curve of her neck, brushing a kiss to her brow, then another to her closed eyelids. Her tears met his lips—warm, salty, and breaking his heart. He hadn't meant to push her this far. But he needed the truth. He needed *her*.

His mouth found hers, the kiss soft and unhurried. Not to stir heat, but to anchor her. To remind her she was safe.

"Kate," he whispered between kisses, "tell me what you're feeling."

She clutched at his shirt, fingers curled into the fabric like it was the only thing holding her together.

"Kate," he said again, lips brushing hers, "I need to hear it."

"I..." Her breath hitched, her voice trembling. "I feel—"

"What?" he coaxed, kissing the corner of her mouth, her jaw, her throat. "Tell me."

She shuddered. "Just kiss me, Fox. Please."

He pulled back just enough to look at her. His voice was low but steady, "I could kiss you forever, Kate—but not until you tell me."

A long pause. Then, barely a whisper:

"I love you."

With those words, something in him broke loose—his careful control shattered, giving way to a rush of pure, aching need. Lifting her effortlessly, he wrapped her legs around his waist and pressed her back against the wall. Then he kissed her—just like she asked—deeply, completely, like he'd waited forever for this moment.

He didn't rush. He took his time, savoring every inch of her mouth, every breath she gave him. She *loved* him. The thought echoed through him like a victory drum. He could've taken on the world in that instant.

"Kate." His voice was thick with emotion as he cupped her face in his hands. "I need you to hear me, trust me. I love you. You love me. That means we're in this together. I'm not going anywhere."

She nodded, breathless. "Okay."

Slowly, he let her legs slip from his waist, easing her back to the floor. He studied her face for a long beat, then gently lifted her chin.

"Oh—and one more thing. Why the hell didn't you tell me someone's been following you?"

Sheriff Jacobs ended the call with Anderson's boss and leaned back in his chair, satisfied. With the director's support, he could finally close the case—officially and cleanly—without worrying about Anderson digging around where he didn't belong. Once the paperwork was finalized, he'd head out to the Crawford place. They deserved answers about what happened to their little girl. It was time to lay Sherri to rest.

Johnson had left the place in chaos. The bastard had wrecked more than the station, he'd nearly wrecked Jacobs' career. Good thing he'd offed himself. Saved the county the cost of a trial and saved Jacobs the trouble of spinning the truth in court.

An open file sat on his desk. Riggs. No local family—just a sister listed in Montana. He hadn't made the call yet. He was waiting for the lab results. Judging by the blood left behind, there was no way in hell she'd survive. Once forensics confirmed it, he'd notify the next of kin.

Jacobs shut the file and dropped it on the stack of folders teetering at the edge of his desk. Another name to bury. Another loose end to tie up.

Fox stepped into the empty squad room. It looked the same as yesterday, untouched. As if the chaos of the last few days hadn't happened at all.

"Morning, Sylvia," he said. "Where is everybody?"

"Shane and Marcos went to follow up on a lead they had from before. They should be back in a few hours. Sheriff's in his office."

Fox nodded and drifted toward the bulletin boards still set up in the middle of the room. He stared at the photos. Read the notes. Let every conversation he'd had with Johnson replay in his mind.

There had been signs, small ones. The way Johnson's face darkened when Riggs put him in his place. For a flicker of a second, he'd looked like he could kill her. And maybe he had. Fox had tried to warn Jacobs that something was off, but the sheriff had written him off as paranoid. He wondered if Jacobs regretted that now.

Still...the profile didn't sit right.

Whoever they were looking for should have been more involved, obsessed even. Drawn to the victims' photos, eager to monitor the case closely. Johnson had been involved, sure. But he'd never once lingered over the photos. Never visited the burial site. There hadn't been that telltale pride or twisted pleasure the profile predicted.

And intelligence. That was another red flag. Johnson wasn't dumb, but he wasn't clever either. He cruised on his charm, not his brain.

Profiles weren't gospel, but they were tools. And right now, the profile doesn't support Johnson, it excludes him.

Fox ran a hand through his hair. He'd been ordered to shut it down, call it solved, and go home with a pat on the back.

But his gut said otherwise.

Shane sat across from Marcos in the center booth of a small neighborhood café. The cushions were worn, the table scarred with years of use—"Chris" had even carved his name into the corner beneath the salt shaker. Shane scanned the menu, his stomach already growling.

"Everything on here looks good," he said without looking up. "What are you getting?"

"Hungry man platter," Marcos replied, tossing his menu aside and taking a sip of coffee. "Not bad."

"I think I'll go with the pancakes," Shane said, glancing out the window. "Think he'll show?"

"Unless someone tipped him off, I don't see why not."

Shane frowned, tearing a straw wrapper into pieces. "I just want this over with. It still doesn't sit right—Johnson. I mean, yeah, he was a dick, but this? Killing Riggs? Kidnapping those girls?"

Marcos shrugged. "We collect facts. Anderson figures out the rest. Let's just make sure we get what we need from Davey."

Shane pulled out his notepad. "Right. First—his friend's name."

"And what weekend he stayed over."

"Got it." Shane scribbled quickly. "Think he stayed more than once?"

"Could be. We'll ask and feel it out."

Their waitress arrived, sliding plates onto the table and refilling their drinks before being pulled away by another table.

"I'm glad we got here early," Shane said, scooping up a forkful of eggs. "Just hope he doesn't show up—"

Marcos cut him off with a nod toward the window. "Too late."

Shane turned and saw Davey approaching, hands in his hoodie pockets, strolling down the sidewalk like it was any other day.

"Damn it," Shane muttered, jamming one last bite into his mouth. He dropped a couple of bills on the table and slid from the booth. Marcos followed.

As they stepped outside, Shane muttered, "Let's hope he's more helpful than he looks."

Kate had watched Fox's car disappear up the dirt road to the highway. It had taken nearly an hour to convince him to leave her behind. When she told him he had nothing to worry about, reminding him she was more than capable of taking care of herself, he'd given her a strange look but finally relented and drove off to speak with the sheriff alone.

The air was crisp and clean. She always felt a surge of exhilaration running through the woods. No one was around to hear her footfalls or question where she went, just her and the trail. The soft thud of her steps was muffled by damp earth, and the wind whispered through the trees in an eerie tune.

Alone, her thoughts drifted—inevitably—to Fox. She worried about what he might ask of her. What came next. She couldn't see how it was possible despite how much she longed for a happy ending with him. Some part of her still felt broken. Some part of her still didn't believe she deserved it.

As she rounded a curve, the forest changed. A stillness settled over the trees, unnatural and sudden. The hairs on the back of her neck lifted. She felt it—danger—before she saw a thing. Adrenaline surged. Instinct kicked in.

She was still too far from the house. Too far from safety.

Her eyes scanned the trees, wild and searching, hoping to spot the threat before it was too late. Her heart pounded in her chest. She'd never been afraid in these woods before, never had a reason to be until now.

Close calls weren't new to her line of work. They came with the job. Usually, they only sharpened her edge and gave her a rush. But this was different. She didn't know who she was up against or how to defend herself from something she couldn't see.

She pushed harder, legs moving faster, her pulse thudding in her ears. Then she saw it: the roof of her house through the trees. Relief slammed into her.

Almost there. Just five more minutes, and she'd be out of the woods. Then there'd be nothing between her and safety.

The blow came out of nowhere.

White sparks burst behind her eyes. Pain exploded in her skull. The only thing that kept her on her feet was the conditioning she'd drilled into herself over the years. Dropping to her knees, she rolled to the right, hands cradling her head, trying to contain the shockwave rattling through her brain.

But the attacker was fast. He seized a fistful of her hair and yanked her backward, jerking her neck at an unnatural angle. Panic flared—she couldn't twist, couldn't strike. Her legs flailed, but her kicks met only air.

Then came the sound that chilled her more than the blow: a low, cold chuckle.

"Now, Miss Kate," a man's voice whispered in her ear, "I promised Chloe a playmate. We don't want to disappoint her, do we?"

She thrashed, trying to break free, but it was no use.

The second blow was worse. It silenced everything. As her consciousness slipped, she felt something wet and vile drag across her cheek.

"Yuck...that's disgusting," she whimpered.

The world spun sideways. Her mouth moved, but no sound came. Then...nothing.

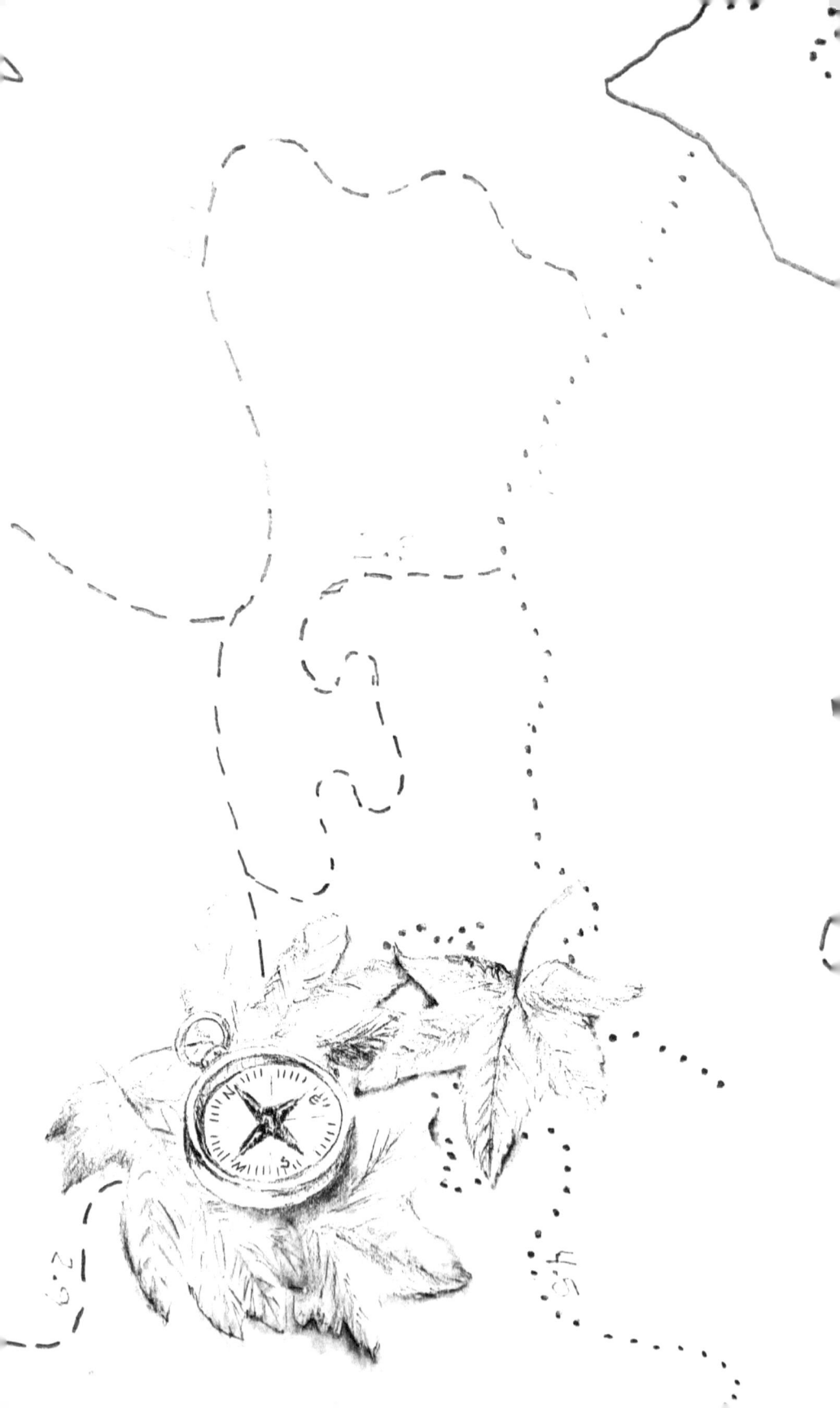

Chapter Thirty-Six

"Wake up, please wake up," a small voice cried.

The fog in Kate's mind lifted slowly. As clarity returned in small degrees, she first noticed the pungent smell of mildew, thick and suffocating in the air. Then came the rough, uneven texture of the mattress beneath her.

When she finally managed to open her eyes, a pair of wide blue ones stared down at her.

Kate shook her head, trying to clear the lingering haze. She eased herself up onto her elbows and took quick stock of her condition. Her head throbbed violently, and a painful lump pulsed behind her ear—but nothing seemed broken.

Kate turned her gaze to Chloe and took in the full extent of her condition. The girl was bruised and filthy, her clothes hanging off her in tattered rags. Each purple mark on her skin stoked the fire of Kate's rage. But the final insult—the one that twisted her gut—was the heavy chain snaking across the bed, locked around the girl's ankle. He had chained her like an animal.

Chloe whimpered, and Kate immediately reached out, wrapping an arm around her.

"Oh, sweetheart. I'm so sorry," she whispered. "Are you hurt anywhere?"

Rubbing her eyes, Chloe looked up at her and nodded. "He hurts me here," she whispered, pointing to the place he had violated her.

Kate's stomach twisted, but she forced herself to stay calm. Losing control wouldn't help either of them now.

"Okay," she said softly, brushing a strand of hair from Chloe's face. "Don't worry. He won't hurt you again. Do you know when he's coming back?"

Chloe shook her head. "No. He came in and dropped you here. Then he put a chain on you like he did to me." She pointed to the chain clamped around Kate's ankle. "He said he'd be back in a little bit." A tear rolled down her cheek. "I'm scared. I don't want him to come back. I want to go home." Her voice cracked as she sobbed.

"I know, sweetheart." Kate wrapped her arms around her gently. "Let me see if I can find a way out of here."

She looked around the room. There wasn't much to work with. No windows. Just a single metal door—thick and solid. The walls were made of rough stone, stacked and mortared, offering no weakness to exploit. A small table and chair stood in the far corner, out of reach of the bed. On the floor beside the mattress sat a half-full jug of water.

Kate stood and stretched the chain as far as it would go—only halfway across the room. The lock around her ankle was simple, something she could easily pick if she had the right tool. A paperclip, a scrap of metal, *anything*. But the room was spotless. No trash, no loose screws, no luck.

Frustration gnawed at her.

She had searched every inch—run her hands along the cold stone walls, lifted the mattress, checked under the bed. Nothing. The bastard kept the place too clean.

She clenched her jaw. The only comfort she had was knowing that if he got within reach, she'd kill him. No hesitation.

Kate shook her head. She *should* have seen him coming. If she hadn't been so damn distracted, so wrapped up in her emotions, he never would've gotten the drop on her. *Some professional,* she thought bitterly.

Chloe had curled up beside her, refusing to let go. Kate had only convinced her to loosen her grip by promising to hold her hand once she was done searching. So now they sat side by side, Chloe's small fingers nestled in hers—no closer to escape than when he first dumped her here.

As Kate brushed a strand of hair from Chloe's face, her fingers grazed something hard, and she froze. Releasing Chloe's hand, she gently parted the girl's hair.

A hairpin.

Yes. She nearly gasped. Carefully, she slipped it free from the tangled mess and immediately turned to her ankle. It took only seconds—*click*—the lock popped open. She moved to Chloe's next, and after a few tense moments, it gave way, too.

Relief rushed through her like a wave. She pulled Chloe to her feet. "Can you walk?" she asked.

Chloe nodded.

Kate eased to the door and tugged on the handle. No surprise, it didn't budge. From the feel of it, it was likely bolted from the outside.

"Shit," she muttered, frustration prickling at her skin. So close. She kicked the chair, the dull thud echoing off the stone walls. *Now what?* Her eyes drifted to Chloe, who watched her with silent, fearful hope. Kate *had* to get her out.

Then came the sound, heavy and slow footsteps vibrating through the floor and up the bare walls. Chloe bolted to the far corner, curling into herself, head buried in her knees, rocking.

But Kate didn't flinch.

Her eyes narrowed. Her pulse steadied. *Good,* she thought. Let him come. Let him walk in, thinking she was still chained to the wall.

A grim smile crept across her face. *Let's see how good he is now.*

The building was old and neglected. Cracked linoleum covered the floor, with chunks missing in several places. The walls were a lifeless shade of gray. Two small picture frames hung crookedly over a sad little seating area. Between the wicker chairs sat a table that looked like it had been dragged out of a biblical excavation.

Behind the cluttered reception desk—piled high with papers, old magazines, and candy wrappers—sat a large blonde woman in a creaking roller chair. She seemed far more invested in the video playing on her tablet than the two men standing in front of her.

Shane cleared his throat. "Ma'am? We'd like to speak with Davey Hollis."

Without looking up, she hit the call button on her desk phone and barked, "Davey, front desk."

Then, she disconnected and ignored them completely.

Shane glanced at Marcos and raised a brow. Marcos just shrugged.

They didn't have to wait long. Davey pushed through the door moments later—then froze when he saw them.

"Hi, Deputies. What brings you here?" Davey asked, his voice hesitant.

"We've got a few more questions," Shane said, pulling out his notepad and flipping to a marked page. "Took us a hell of a time tracking you down."

"Yeah, sorry about that," Davey mumbled, blushing. "I guess you heard my dad kicked me out."

"We heard," Shane said, uninterested in lingering on the topic. He got straight to the point. "Davey, we forgot to ask—what's the name of the friend who overheard the girls talking to you?"

Davey blinked. "Oh. Why does that matter?"

"We'd like to talk to him," Shane said evenly. "See if he has anything to add."

Davey squirmed, glancing from Shane to Marcos, then back again. "He asked me not to tell anyone about him. I don't want him finding out I talked to you."

Shane exchanged a look with Marcos, then turned back. "Why would he want to stay a secret?"

"He just...likes his privacy, is all," Davey replied, defensive now. "Besides, I don't see him anymore."

"Privacy's not an option anymore. I still need his name."

A flicker of fear crossed Davey's face. Subtle but there. Shane caught it.

"Are you afraid of him, Davey?"

Davey stiffened, trying to recover. "No. Of course not. He's my friend. He just has a temper, and I'd rather not be on the receiving end, is all."

"I get it," Shane said quietly. "You don't want to let your buddy down. But we'll get his name either way. You might as well make it easy on yourself."

Davey's shoulders sagged. "Okay," he muttered. "I'll tell you."

He sighed, then added, "His name is Tuck. Tuck Williams."

Fox knocked firmly on the sheriff's door.

"Enter," came the curt response.

"Sheriff, you got a minute?" Fox asked, stepping inside.

The sheriff looked up, tossed a folder aside, and gestured to a chair. "Sure, have a seat. What's on your mind?"

Fox didn't sit right away. "I'm sure you know my boss is pulling me off the case now. He considers it closed and wants my report by tomorrow."

The sheriff nodded, his tone flat. "Yes, he called me this morning. Can't tell you how much we've appreciated your help."

Fox didn't return the sentiment. "That's all well and good, but what I need to know is what you're going to do about Chloe?"

The sheriff leaned back, his expression hardening. "As far as I'm concerned, that's a case for her town to solve. We solved ours. I don't think it's necessary to dedicate more resources to it, especially with two officers down." His voice held a hint of finality.

Fox's jaw tightened. "What about Shane and Marcos? Don't you think you should at least wait until they get back before making a decision?"

The sheriff waved him off dismissively. "There's no point. They're not going to find anything. There's nothing to find."

Fox's fists clenched, but his cell phone rang just as he was about to push back. He exhaled sharply and answered, his voice colder. "Agent Anderson."

"Anderson, it's Shane."

"Hey, Shane, the sheriff and I were just talking about you. Did you find anything?"

"I don't know if it's pertinent, but...it's weird."

Fox arched a brow. "What's weird?"

"Davey's friend—the one who overheard the girls' plans. His name is Tuck Williams."

Fox's forehead creased. "Why does that name sound familiar?"

"Here's the kicker," Shane said. "Tuck Williams is Sylvia's son."

A cold weight dropped in Fox's gut.

"Wait a minute," he said slowly, his mind racing. "Are you telling me the kid I've seen in the office—around town—is the same boy who overheard the girls talking about sneaking out?" He pinched the bridge of his nose. "Shit."

"Exactly. What do you want us to do?"

"Come back. I'll handle the sheriff."

Fox ended the call and planted his hands on the edge of the desk.

"We've got a problem."

Jacobs looked up, frowning. "What kind of problem?"

"The boy who overheard the girls' plans? It was Tuck Williams—Sylvia's son."

The sheriff went pale. He glanced instinctively toward the secret window, though the canvas cover blocked his view.

"You don't think Tuck had anything to do with this, do you?"

"I'm not sure. But first, I want to know everything Sylvia has had access to—and what she knows about these cases." Fox stood, but his eyes caught something: a light on the sheriff's desk phone, flickering off just a second after being on.

"Sheriff, why would a light be on your desk phone?"

A look of confusion crossed Jacobs' face as he glanced down. "It's on when a line is in use. Why?"

"Would it be on if someone else in the office was using their phone—even if you weren't?"

Jacobs shook his head. "No, it's only on when this unit's in use. Again, why?"

Fox was at the door in two long strides. He threw it open. "Because, Sheriff, that light's been on every time I've been in your office. Except now—when I just watched it turn off."

He smacked his palm against the doorframe. Damn it. Sylvia's desk was empty.

"Sheriff, it looks like Sylvia has been listening in on your conversations. Whether she did it out of nosiness or to protect her son, we're going to find out. I suggest you try calling her."

The sheriff picked up the phone, frowning. "No answer."

"Then let's go knock on her door. I want to know where her son is." Fox was already heading for the exit. "It's time we talked with him."

The Williams's home was like every other house on the street—interchangeable, save for the numbers posted by each door. The lawns stretched seamlessly from one to the next, property lines all but invisible. Whether by competition or silent agreement, every blade of grass was trimmed to the same height, with not a weed in sight. The path to the front door was spotless, with not a leaf or twig in view.

Sheriff Jacobs reached the door first and knocked firmly on the frame. They heard movement inside—shuffling footsteps—before the door opened, and Sylvia appeared. Her face was pale and drawn tight, her smile brittle as she looked from the sheriff to Anderson and back again.

"Hello, Sheriff. What brings you here?" she asked pleasantly, her voice strained and hovering just this side of hysteria.

Jacobs tipped his hat. "Sylvia, we were surprised to see you'd left the office so suddenly. Everything all right?" His tone was calm, almost casual.

"Oh, yes. Everything's fine. I just remembered I needed to come home, that's all." Her smile didn't reach her eyes.

Fox stepped forward, mirroring the sheriff's relaxed posture. "We had a few questions we were hoping to ask. Is now a good time?"

Sylvia hesitated in the doorway for a beat too long, then finally stepped aside. "We can talk in here," she said, gesturing toward the sitting room just off the entryway.

"Thank you, Sylvia. We appreciate you inviting us in." Sheriff Jacobs gently touched her arm as he stepped past her.

"What questions did you have for me?" she asked, smoothing her hands over her blouse.

Fox glanced around the room, his eyes lingering on what was clearly a shrine to her son. Trophies, framed photos, and awards lined the mantel and filled the built-in shelves on either side of the fireplace.

"I've heard your son was an excellent football player," he said, nodding toward a large photo of Tuck in uniform.

Sylvia's posture eased. "Oh yes, he's amazing. He earned a full-ride scholarship to the state college, first one from our school to ever do that for football."

"Impressive. I heard he's got a good arm. Is he a lefty?"

She hesitated. "Yes, but he can throw with either hand. Almost equally well. He usually saves the left for championship games. He says it keeps defenses guessing."

Fox smiled. "Bet he liked traveling with the team. Did he make many friends from other schools?"

"A few. I know he was close with Davey. And there were the older Davis boys—they played for one of the rival schools. When they played them, Tuck would usually stay the night before coming home." Her smile softened. "He's a good boy. Not like those others. He'd never..." Her voice broke off, and she blinked rapidly. "He wouldn't hurt anyone."

"I'm sure he is," Fox said evenly. Then, with a pause: "Where is he now? We'd love to clear up a couple of things with him."

"Oh, he's at school. He won't be home again for a couple of weeks."

"I see," Fox said, glancing at Sheriff Jacobs. "When was the last time he was in town?"

"A few days ago, at least."

"Can we get his number? I'm sure we can handle our questions with a phone call."

Relief flickered across her face. "Yes, absolutely. Let me write it down for you."

She grabbed a sticky note, scribbled a number, and handed it to Fox. "Please...just don't do anything to jeopardize his scholarship."

Fox schooled his expression. The fact that she was more worried about a football scholarship than a connection to half a dozen murder victims told him plenty—but he didn't let it show. He smiled as he folded the note. "Of course."

Outside, as the door clicked shut behind them, Sheriff Jacobs asked, "What do you think?"

Fox glanced over his shoulder. "I'll get this number traced. Then I'll give him a call—see if he answers."

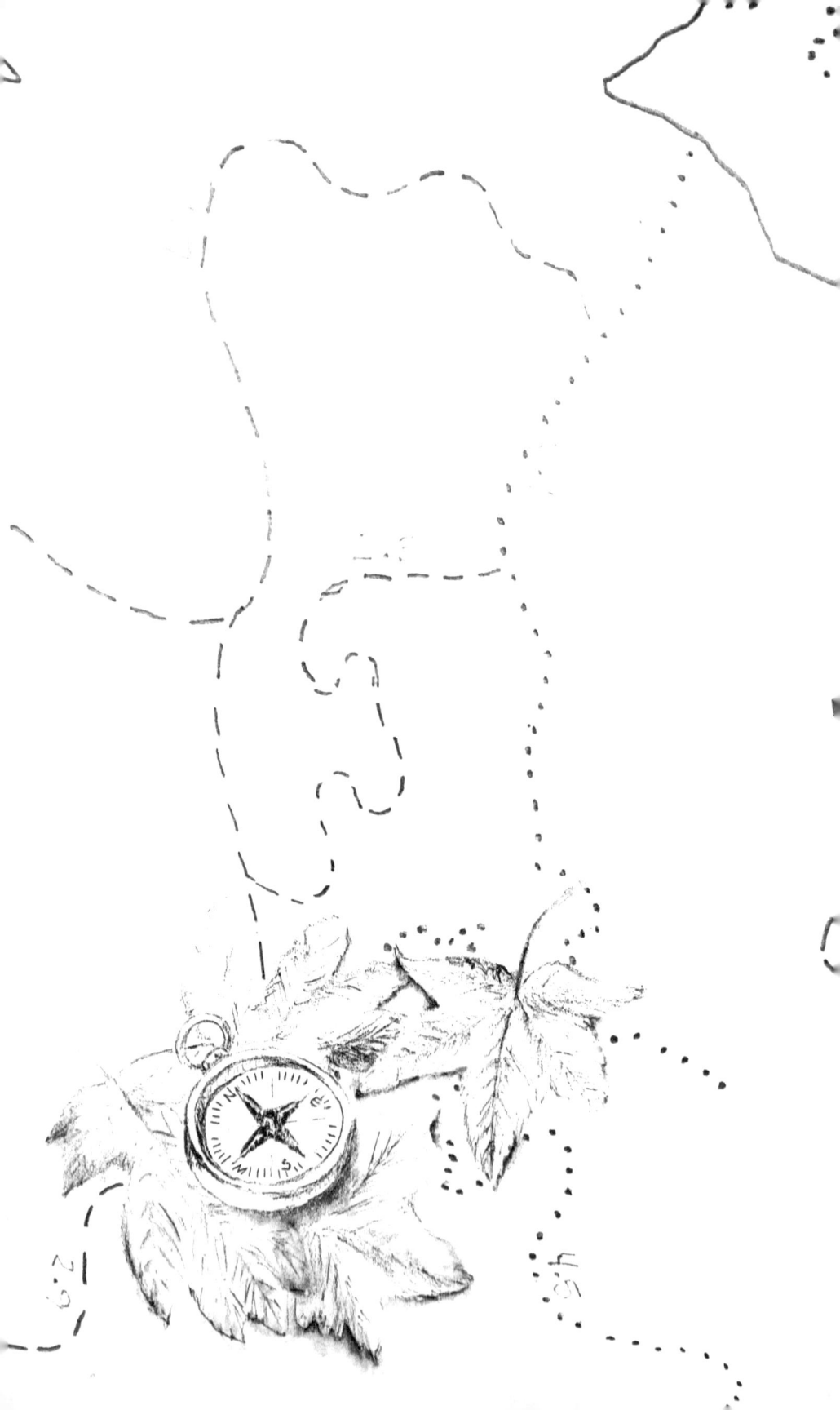

Chapter Thirty-Seven

"Hello, this is Tuck."

The male voice was confident, sure of himself—too sure. It set Fox's teeth on edge. He nodded to the sheriff and put the call on the speaker.

"Hi, Tuck, this is Sheriff Jacobs. I was hoping you could come by the office. We'd like to talk with you about your mother."

"My mother? Why? Has something happened?"

His concern sounded genuine—surprisingly so, considering they suspected him of murdering six girls.

"Don't worry, she's fine. We just had a little incident in the office. Would you be able to come in?"

A pause. Then, "I'm at school. It'll take me a few hours to get there."

"That's no problem," the sheriff said smoothly. "Take your time. Like I said, it's nothing urgent."

"I'll head your way now, then."

"Sounds good, son. We'll see you soon."

The call disconnected. Fox didn't waste a second. He switched lines. "Did you get that?"

"Yeah, we pinged the phone," came Heller's voice through the speaker. "He's about thirty miles from your location. I'm sending the coordinates now. Oh—and that other thing you asked about? I dug it up."

Fox frowned at the dash, sifting through the mental files. Then it hit him like a bolt. "You did? Is it something I need to see?"

"You could say that."

Fox's pulse ticked up. "Hold on to it. I'll let you know where to send it."

"Copy that."

Fox ended the call and glanced at Jacobs. His voice was low, tight. "He lied. Said he was at school. He's not even close."

Jacobs exhaled, rubbing a hand down his face. "Okay...so what do you want to do about it? You know, we don't have anything solid on him yet. This could all still be a coincidence."

"Maybe. But I'll feel a hell of a lot better once we know for sure. Wouldn't you?"

Jacobs nodded. "Yeah. Let's go pick him up."

Fox made another call as they got into the car, frowning at the unanswered ring. "Hey Kate, it's me again. Where the hell are you? Call me as soon as you get this."

That was the third message he'd left her today. It wasn't like her not to answer.

Jacobs cast him a sidelong glance. "You and Kate...is that serious?"

Fox raised an eyebrow. "Not that it's your business, but yeah. We're serious."

He noticed the sheriff pale slightly. Fox frowned. "There a reason you care?"

Jacobs looked away, muttering, "No. It's nothing."

Fox leaned back in his seat. "If it's not too personal...why have you never married? A guy like you, I bet the town considers you quite a catch."

"It's no secret. I didn't want to get tied down. I like my freedom."

"I get it," Fox said. "I've had the same thoughts. It's hard to keep a family together in our line of work. Most who try end up divorced."

The sheriff's gaze cut sharper than expected. "Do you still feel that way?"

Fox hesitated. "I'm not sure what I feel about marriage and divorce anymore. I guess time will tell."

They turned off the highway onto a nearly hidden road. If Fox hadn't been watching, they might've missed it altogether.

A cattle corral and rusted gate marked the entrance. Low-hanging branches clawed overhead, and thick brush squeezed tight against the one-lane dirt road. Jacobs pulled in as far as the cruiser would go and waited for Shane and Marcos to arrive.

Kate felt the lock give and nearly cried out in relief. It had taken longer than she'd hoped—her head still pounded—but at least they were getting out.

"Chloe, sweetheart, come on. Let's get out of here," she said, reaching out her hand.

Timidly, Chloe approached her, each step more unsteady than the last. Concern pulled at Kate's brow. "Are you sure you're not hurt?"

Chloe nodded. "I'm just tired and cold. I want to go home. That's all. I just want to go home."

Her little fingers were like icicles—cold and bony. Kate tried to picture what Chloe had looked like before she was taken. Her hair was dull and tangled, hanging in matted strands down her back. A few pieces had fallen forward to cover her eyes. Her shirt was torn and caked in dirt and filth, the original color impossible to guess. Her pants were ripped at the knee and thigh.

The circles beneath her eyes were dark and sunken. She looked...used up.

Kate kneeled and gently brushed Chloe's hair aside. "I promise I'll get you home, okay?"

Chloe threw her arms around her neck, clutching tight.

"Everything's going to be okay," Kate whispered — but then she felt Chloe's small body tense.

"What is it, Chloe? Are you alright?"

Then Kate felt it—*eyes* on her.

A voice slid out from the shadows.

"What have you two been up to while I was gone?"

Kate turned—and stared into a face she had known for years.

Tuck.

Only now, his eyes were wrong. Cold. Empty. Until now, she hadn't realized a person could fake the sparkle in their eyes. His smile, once charming and disarming, was twisted into something cruel. The truth hit her like a punch—he'd been hiding who he really was this whole time. A killer.

"Tuck," she said slowly, rising to her feet. "I admit...I'm surprised. I never even thought of you as a suspect."

He leaned against the doorjamb, arms casually crossed over his chest. His head tilted slightly as he studied her, his expression unreadable.

"Really? Why not?"

"Because you're a child. What are you, eighteen? Nineteen?"

He sneered, something dark curling at the edges of his mouth. "I can assure you, I've been at this longer than you think."

His tone shifted, almost reflective.

"My first was when I was fourteen. My family went on vacation to California—one of the few we ever took. My parents rented a beach house for the week, and since I was 'old enough to fend for myself,' they hardly noticed me."

He smiled, distant and pleased with the memory.

"I still remember the first time I saw her. Little Sophia. Blonde hair, big blue eyes...she looked like an angel. So innocent. So pure. All I had to do was promise her some ice cream. She followed me without hesitation."

His voice dropped, quiet and intimate.

"My parents were out for the day. I had the house to myself. Only a couple of hours...but they were perfect. When I was done, I dumped her body in the ocean and watched the tide carry her away."

"No one even suspected. She wore a gold necklace with a little heart pendant," he said softly, almost fondly. "It was the only piece of her I could keep. I knew it wasn't enough. She was mine, and I wanted all of her."

Kate's stomach twisted.

"So I started planning the next one as soon as we got home. I have two other places where I keep my treasures. Mr. FBI was stupid enough to think he'd found everything." He sneered. "Those were just the recent ones."

Kate swallowed hard. "How many more are there, Tuck?"

He ignored her.

"I like to make a circle of them. My first two were circles of four. The last one...was going to be my biggest." He let out a theatrical sigh, disappointed.

Eight. Her mind raced. There were eight more. Families who didn't even know.

If she killed him now, those families would never get closure. Maybe she could stall—get him to tell her where the bodies were first.

"Where did you bury the other girls?"

Tuck's smile widened. "Now, Kate, why would I tell you that? Those little treasures are for me. Not even you get to know. Even though..." he leaned forward slightly, "you'll join them when I'm finished with you."

He straightened and began to move toward her. Slow. Deliberate. A predator.

Kate tensed.

She hadn't realized how big he was. She'd only ever seen him as a boy. But he stood six inches taller, easy and had at least fifty pounds on her.

She couldn't let him get close. If he landed another blow to her head, it would be over.

She'd have to move first—and strike hard.

"Tuck, there's something you need to understand. I'm not what you think. If you want to get out of here alive, you need to walk away now."

His laugh was cruel, mocking.

Kate ignored it. She flicked her hand in a subtle gesture, signaling Chloe to stay in the corner. This asshole was already a dead man walking. He just didn't know it yet.

"You think you can kill me?" he taunted, disbelief, twisting his face into a sneer.

Kate shifted her stance, lifting her chin and letting her expression fall blank. Calm. Unreadable.

"I know I will. It's just a matter of when."

"Then let's make it now. Show me what you've got."

He stepped into striking distance and she didn't hesitate.

Her fist shot out, catching him hard in the face as she kicked his kneecap with her opposite foot. He collapsed with a grunt, swearing as he hit the ground. But she gave him no time to recover. She jabbed her fingers into his throat, making him gag and clutch his neck.

That's when his eyes changed. He realized she was trained.

He blocked her next blow and retaliated, his fist slamming into her ribs. Pain lit up her side—possibly cracked—but she shoved it aside. There'd be time for pain later.

She drove her knee into the inside of his thigh. He grunted but caught her on the recoil with a vicious backhand that split her lip. The force knocked her off balance.

He didn't stop. With a snarl, he kicked her hard in the stomach, sending her flying. Her body hit the wall with a sickening thud.

Breathing hard, Tuck pushed himself off the floor, wiping blood from the corner of his eye.

"You bitch!" he roared, his face twisted with fury, lip curled into a snarl.

In the corner, Chloe curled tighter into a ball, trying to disappear.

Kate hauled herself upright, swaying slightly. The sound of Chloe's whimpers clawed at her focus. She hated hand-to-hand combat. Without a weapon, he had the advantage. Even with all her training, he was stronger—faster at this moment, too. Every attempt she made to land a killing blow, he deflected.

Her muscles trembled from exhaustion. Her strength was fading her vision swimming. Blood slid down her chin, and she wiped it away with her shoulder. The last hit had rattled her—her skull still rang from the impact, dizziness creeping in.

For a terrifying moment, she faltered.

What if I can't beat him?

Almost an hour later, they arrived at the coordinates the FBI had provided—but there was nothing. No house, no road, no visible structure—just trees and silence.

Fox turned in a slow circle, scanning the area for anything out of place. It didn't make sense.

The sheriff huffed, clearly unimpressed. "Well, Anderson, what do you want to do?"

Fox bit back a retort. "The ping had a one-mile radius. We're close. We just haven't found it yet." He pointed toward a denser patch of woods to the southwest. "Sheriff, you and Marcos head east. Shane and I will go north. Walk for fifteen minutes, then double back."

With a grumble, Jacobs turned. "All right, Marcos, let's get this over with." He started wading through the brush and fallen limbs.

Shane hesitated, glancing into the trees. "You really think it could've been Tuck all along?" Just then, he tripped over a root and reached out, catching himself on a nearby tree.

"Shit, Shane—you good?" Fox asked, offering a hand.

Flushing pink, Shane nodded. "Yeah. Wasn't watching where I stepped."

Fox grunted, his foot rolling on a rock. "Easy to do out here," he muttered. "I'm not sure about Tuck. I don't know much about the kid. What can you tell me?"

They moved deeper into the forest, both more cautious now.

"He's your typical all-American kid from a small town. Pretty popular in school—star quarterback and all. I've seen him play. The kid's got a hell of an arm. Throws everyone off when he switches from left to right without missing a beat. It's really something."

"What about girlfriends? Did he have any?"

Shane was quiet for a moment. The only sound was the crunch of leaves and twigs beneath their feet as they walked.

"You know, I don't remember him ever having a steady girlfriend. I think he'd go out with girls from his class, but nothing serious. Do you think that matters?"

"Right now, I'm not sure what matters or doesn't. We just need to gather as much as possible and see which pieces fit the puzzle. Did you ever have to pick him up for anything? Any trouble when he was younger?"

"No, nothing," Shane said, then paused. "Well...there was the incident with the squirrel."

Fox glanced over. "Oh? What incident?"

"It was nothing, really—just a few boys messing around. They tied a firecracker to a squirrel's tail. Poor thing died from fright. If I remember correctly, it was Cara's boy, Tuck, and another kid I can't place right now."

Fox frowned. "Do you know whose idea it was? The firecracker?"

Shane let out a quiet chuckle. "If you believe the way Cara tells it, it was Tuck's idea. I don't know for sure. I always thought it was strange—Tuck hanging out with those two. He's at least five years older than them."

Fox suddenly froze, crouching low. He raised a hand, signaling Shane to do the same. "You hear that?" he whispered.

Shane crouched beside him, eyes scanning the woods. "No... what do you hear?"

They huddled behind a fallen tree, still as stone, listening to the forest's sounds. Then Fox heard it again—a faint, low, and strained groan. He scanned the area, trying to locate the source.

A tortured scream suddenly tore through the woods. The anguish in the sound ripped through him, unmistakable and raw.

Fox shot to his feet and broke into a sprint. Shane thundered behind him, both of them charging toward the sound. They bolted up a moss-covered hill, their boots slipping slightly on the slick grass. But when Fox reached the top, he came to a sudden halt, teetering on the edge of a sharp, nearly vertical drop.

The slope looked unnatural as if someone had carved a slice out of the earth.

Peering over the edge, Fox spotted it: an entrance tucked into the hillside.

He signaled for Shane to stay quiet and pointed down. They carefully descended the steep slope, their movements slow and deliberate. The dirt shifted beneath them, but they kept their footing. At the bottom, half-concealed by brush and rock, stood a heavy metal door with a small rectangular opening near the top.

Fox pressed his back to the rock wall, drawing his weapon. He could feel the loose earth sliding under his boots. Shane gave a sharp nod, then nudged the door open with his foot.

Through the dim light, Fox saw a narrow hallway encased in concrete. At the far end, a staircase led down. The faint whimper they had heard above grew louder as they neared the stairs. Someone was definitely down there.

A single light fixture hung halfway down the stairwell, casting a warm glow into the tunnel below. Fox nodded to Shane and took the lead. They moved quietly, keeping their steps light as they descended.

"I want to go home," came the cry of a little girl.

Fox stiffened. She wasn't alone.

At the bottom, a door stood slightly ajar, bright light spilling through the narrow opening. Fox eased it open with his left hand, weapon ready in his right. As the gap widened, he raised the gun—and froze, his mouth falling open.

Fox barked, "What the hell are you doing here?"

Kate's head jerked up when she saw him, and she started limping toward him—but Fox didn't move. He stood still, watching her with a storm gathering behind his eyes.

Blood streaked her chin and cheek. Her lip was split, her shirt torn, and a fist-sized hole gaped in her pants, a dark bruise already blooming around it. Every step she took looked painful.

A cold fury slid through him, sharp and biting, while betrayal settled like acid on his tongue. This was why you didn't get close. Why you didn't let people in. A bitter reminder of why it was better not to let emotions rule you.

Behind her, Tuck lay sprawled on the floor, making a wet, choking sound. His eyes were wide and vacant, fixed on the ceiling. Off to the side, Chloe was huddled in the corner, sobbing. She flinched every time Shane tried to approach her.

Fox's gaze snapped back to Kate. She was still struggling toward him, too damn slow for his liking. He closed the distance in three long strides and caught her in his arms, locking her against his chest. One hand threaded into her hair as he held her, his jaw clenched tight.

She was here. She was alive.

His eyes scanned her injuries again. The bruises. The limp. He knew she'd been through hell. And yet, he couldn't stop the words before they spilled out.

Over her shoulder, his eyes returned to Tuck, and the ice in his veins began to thaw. Anger surged up like lava, hot and uncontrollable, shaking through him.

His voice came out low and cold as steel. "Would you care to explain to me what the hell you're doing here with this piece of shit?"

Fox saw the shift in Kate the moment his words hit her. Her expression changed—confusion, then disbelief, and finally, the familiar spark of anger. She took a step back from him like he'd slapped her.

"Excuse me? Are you mad at me?" she asked, her voice sharp with shock.

He clenched his jaw. *Mad?* That didn't even begin to cover it. "No, I'm not mad. Madness is a controllable emotion. What I am is furious."

He didn't shout. He didn't have to. The fury burned hot and clean in his veins, and every word was laced with it. But watching the way she recoiled from him made something crack under the surface.

"If I didn't need answers from you," he continued, "I would drag you home so fast your head would spin. But right now, I need to know what you're doing here. How did you find this place? And what the hell did you do to him?"

She stared at him like he'd betrayed her—*him*, not the boy lying gurgling on the ground. Fox opened his mouth to explain, to soften—something—but Kate cut him off.

"You think I *wanted* to be here?" Her voice shook, but not with fear. With fury.

She pointed to Tuck. "That asshole knocked me out and dragged me here. He *abducted* me."

Fox's stomach dropped.

"I freed myself. I fought him. I survived. Don't worry, I didn't kill him, though I was close. I think I paralyzed him. It should make your interrogation easier."

She stepped back, folding her arms like a wall slamming shut. "You're welcome."

Before he could respond, she turned from him, limping toward Chloe and reaching out. The little girl scrambled into her grasp without hesitation.

Kate didn't spare him a glance. "We'll be outside. If you need us."

Fox watched Kate and Chloe limp out the door, a storm of conflicting emotions churning inside him. Then he turned to Tuck.

He squatted beside him, studying the boy's pale, sweat-slicked face. Tuck's eyes flicked toward him, wide and watery with fear.

"I'm so glad you're here," Tuck said, his voice trembling. "I was out walking in the woods when I heard someone screaming. I came down here to help, and that crazy bitch attacked me. I think she broke my back. I can't move—my arms, my legs—they're not working. You've got to arrest her. Don't let her get away with this."

Fox raised an eyebrow slowly, letting the silence hang before glancing up at Shane with a look that said *Are you hearing this bullshit?*

"Don't worry," Fox said evenly, turning back to Tuck. "We'll get this all straightened out."

He rose and dusted off his hands like the conversation bored him. "I'll make a call; get someone down here to check you out."

He looked at Shane. "Why don't you keep our friend company while I look into things?"

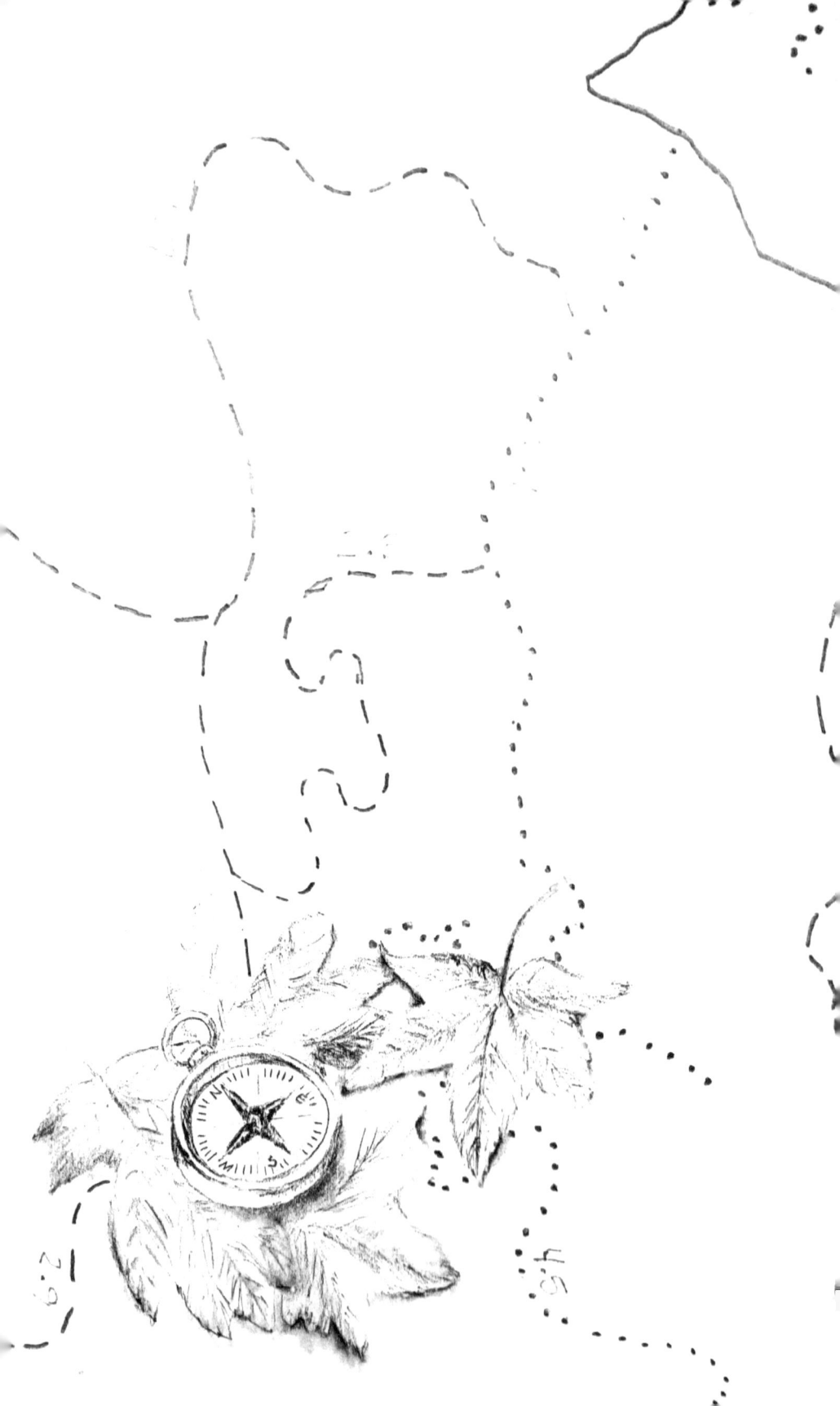

Chapter Thirty-Eight

An hour later, the woods pulsed with sirens and flashing lights. Agents from multiple government branches had swarmed the area, along with deputies from the town where Chloe had been taken. Her parents had been notified, and she was whisked to the hospital. She'd need medical care before she could go home.

Tuck had to be hauled out of the hole he'd made his lair. It took four men to carry him up the slope, and they'd only dropped him once. No one paid much attention to the stream of lies he kept spewing. Once the hospital cleared him, they'd have a proper heart-to-heart.

Fox wasn't sorry to admit he'd privately wished Kate had finished the job. But once he learned there were more victims out there, he understood why she'd stopped short of killing him. They still needed answers—and now, at least, Tuck would never be able to hurt anyone again.

Kate had also been taken by ambulance. Despite her protests, Fox overruled her and made sure she was loaded up and sent off without delay. He wished he could have gone with her, but as the lead on the case, he had to stay behind to oversee the scene, process evidence, and finish what they'd started.

Now that his temper had cooled, he knew he'd overreacted.

The image of her—battered, bloodied, sitting in the middle of that room with the perp on the floor—had short-circuited his ability to think. All he'd seen was her betrayal. Rage had clouded everything: that she'd come here alone, that she hadn't told him about a lead, that she'd taken matters into her own hands.

Worse, he hadn't even considered that she might have been abducted. When she first explained what had happened, it sounded so farfetched that his instincts were to assume she was lying again.

It wasn't until he spoke with Chloe that he realized how wrong he'd been.

Unfortunately, he'd figured it out too late. Kate had already been taken to the hospital, and during the entire time the EMTs examined her, she hadn't looked at him once. He watched her from across the chaos of flashing lights and shouting voices, silently willing her to lift her eyes. But she never did. She kept her head bowed, shoulders hunched in what looked like defeat.

If he could've, he would've kicked his own ass for being such a jerk.

He still remembered how she'd smiled when she first saw him—relief and love shining in her eyes. That expression had gutted him. Now, all he could hope was that he hadn't destroyed the fragile thing they'd been building. He needed to get to her before she had too much time to think about what an ass he'd been.

Even though the doctor hadn't been thrilled about releasing her, Kate convinced him. After the initial exam, she had no intention of staying in the hospital a moment longer. Once he realized it was in his best interest to discharge her before she lost her temper, he handed over a list of instructions and sent her on her way.

Now, she sat on the porch swing in front of her house, gently rocking back and forth, waiting for Cara.

She spotted the glow of headlights cresting the hill just before Cara's car barreled into the driveway, gravel spraying behind it. The door flew open, and Cara launched herself out, arms waving.

"I came as fast as I could!" she cried, bounding up the porch steps.

She dropped onto the swing beside Kate, panting as she caught her breath. "Okay. Tell me everything."

Kate stared out into the night. "It was Tuck. Sylvia's boy." Her voice was quiet, measured. "He snuck up on me, knocked me out, and took me to where he was keeping the little girl, the one who was taken a few days ago."

"I know the whole town's talking about it." Grabbing Kate's hand, Cara clasped it tightly between hers. "Why didn't you kill him, Kate? I was so surprised to hear he was in the hospital. I thought you were going to take care of him."

"I couldn't, Cara. I'm sorry." Kate's voice was quiet, steady. "He told me there were more girls—more families who still don't know what happened to their daughters. I couldn't kill him without knowing where the other bodies were. You understand, don't you?"

"But what if he gets out?" Panic rose in Cara's voice, trembling at the edge of hysteria. "What if he comes back here?"

Kate gave her hand a firm squeeze. "Don't worry. I paralyzed him. He won't be able to do anything but move his mouth for the rest of his life. There's no way he's coming back."

Relief flooded Cara's face. "I knew you wouldn't let me down. I just knew it."

Her face brightening, Cara launched into a breathless update, filling Kate in on everything the town was buzzing about, leaving out not even the tiniest detail.

Only half listening to her friend, Kate wished Cara would leave. She was grateful her friend's mind was at ease, but right now, she was the one who needed comfort. She didn't want to talk to anyone but didn't want to be alone, either. The clash of feelings left her restless and flustered. She wasn't comfortable in her own skin anymore.

Cara seemed to sense her distress and fell quiet, studying her face. "What's wrong, Kate? Aren't you glad it's all over?"

"Sure," Kate said, offering a smile she didn't feel. "I just need to get ready to head out of town."

"You're leaving again so soon?"

Kate shrugged. "When duty calls."

Cara tilted her head. "What about the FBI guy? I thought there might be something there," she said, wagging her brows.

"There's nothing to tell. The job's wrapping up. He'll be home in less than a week," Kate replied, fighting the sudden sting behind her eyes.

"Kate, I know you better than anyone. I can tell something's wrong. Just tell me what it is."

Brushing away a tear, Kate said softly, "If I want Fox in my life...then I have to tell him who I really am."

"So?"

"Cara," Kate said, exasperated, "I'm a killer. Do you think that conversation is going to go over well?"

"I think you'd be surprised how much a man is willing to accept when he's met the woman he loves."

Kate rolled her eyes. "I think you're just a hopeless romantic."

Cara gave her a long, knowing look. "Don't let this opportunity slip through your fingers, Kate. You'll never forgive yourself if you do."

Both women turned at the sound of a vehicle approaching.

"Looks like someone's coming for a visit," Cara said, grabbing her purse and shooting Kate a wink as she headed for her car. "I need to get home anyway. Call me if you need me."

Cara had just left when Fox pulled up. Not wanting him to think she'd been waiting for him, Kate got up from the porch swing and walked into the house, leaving the door open behind her.

"Kate, wait up a second," he called from behind. "We need to talk."

She ignored him, heading straight up the stairs. She wasn't ready—not yet. Still, knowing he was in her home eased something in her that nothing else had all day.

"Kate," he said again, his voice following her up the steps. "Just let me explain."

The sound of the door clicking shut behind her felt surprisingly satisfying. She couldn't help the small smile that tugged at her lips. Oh yes, things were finally beginning to look up.

Until the door slammed open behind her.

She jumped, spinning toward it. Fox stood in the doorway, one hand braced against the frame, eyes burning with frustration.

"Maybe you didn't hear me," he ground out. "We. Need. To. Talk."

The sharp edge in his voice sparked something stubborn in her. The thrill of another one of their heated exchanges began to pull her out of the darkness. She planted her hands on her hips.

"And what if I'm not in the mood to talk?"

He stalked into the room, trying to intimidate her with his sheer presence. He leaned in close, so close she could feel the heat of him.

"Too bad."

They stood nose to nose. His warmth and scent—faintly musky and familiar—seeped into her skin, calming her in a way nothing else had all day. The weight of everything hit her at once, and her fight faded.

"I'm tired," she said softly. "It's been a terrible day, Fox. I just want to go to bed."

His expression softened immediately. He brushed a strand of hair behind her ear, then cupped her cheek.

"I'm sorry, Kate. You're right. Go to bed. We'll talk in the morning."

Kate stared out the window of her hotel room overlooking the bay. Everything was set for tonight. Her gear was stashed by the dock; all she had to do now was wait.

Her phone chimed again.

She didn't need to look to know who it was. Since the morning she'd snuck out, Fox had called and texted her every fifteen minutes. At first, his messages sounded worried—soft, pleading. But it hadn't taken long for that concern to boil over into rage. After the first blistering voicemail, she stopped checking her phone altogether. He'd give up eventually. He was due back at the Bureau in a few days. Once he was immersed in work again, he'd move on.

Walking away had been harder than she'd imagined. But she knew, truly knew, that he could never be okay with who she really was. Not long after she made up her mind, her contact had sent word that her target would be in play sooner than expected. The timing couldn't have been more perfect. Her bag was already packed. All she had to do was slip out before Fox noticed she was gone.

What she hadn't planned for was the pain.

Her head insisted it had all been a fantasy, something fleeting. But the ache in her chest said otherwise. She kept praying for numbness, but every time her phone lit up with his name, it cracked her open all over again.

Eventually, the numbness would come. It always did.

For now, she sat alone with her memories—and waited.

It felt good to be home—at least, that's what Kate told herself as she pulled into the driveway. According to Cara, things had settled down in town. They still hadn't gotten any information out of Tuck; from what she'd heard, he refused to speak to anyone.

Fox had left the day after she'd run. Cara hadn't seen him herself, but word around town was that no one dared approach him—he was about as friendly as a grizzly bear. The thought made her chest ache with guilt. She had hurt him, and she knew it. Still, she told herself it was for the best.

She unlocked the door and stepped inside.

The silence was brutal.

His absence lingered in every corner of the house. Her gaze fell to the couch they had shared, and she wondered if it still smelled like him. Her chest tightened. Squeezing her eyes shut, she tried to block out the rush of grief.

Her hand gripped the banister as she forced herself to climb the stairs, each step a battle against the ache inside her. She let her bag fall to the floor in her bedroom and wandered blindly into the bathroom. Maybe a long, hot shower would help.

Maybe it would wash away some of the emptiness, too.

The hot water beat against her skin in a steady, therapeutic rhythm. With one hand braced against the shower wall, Kate rested her forehead against her arm. Bittersweet memories flashed through her mind like a cruel slideshow of everything she had lost.

She had thought she'd cried herself dry back in Morocco—clearly, she'd been wrong. A ragged sob tore from her chest, and she let it come, her pain echoing off the tile.

When she finally turned off the water, she wrapped a towel around her emotionally battered body. Pressing her face into another, she released a shaky breath—then froze.

A voice, low and familiar, cut through the silence.

"It's about time you came home."

Her heart lurched. She reached out to steady herself against the sink.

Turning toward him, she whispered, "Fox...what are you doing here?"

Her eyes drank him in. It had only been a few days, but it felt like years to her aching heart.

"We still need to have our talk," he drawled, "or have you forgotten?"

The anger simmering beneath his words was palpable, but she didn't flinch. She welcomed it. Missed it. Missed *him*—his passion, his fire.

"No," she said softly. "I haven't forgotten you wanted to talk. I just thought...after the way I left, you wouldn't want to anymore."

Fox stalked toward her in a slow, deliberate stride, backing her up against the bathroom counter.

"So, you admit what you did was a pretty shitty thing?"

"Yes." Her heart pounded so hard she thought it might beat out of her chest. "I'm sorry. I was planning on leaving for a job—I just had to go sooner than I'd expected."

She knew it sounded weak, but seeing him again had emptied her mind of every thought but one: *He's here.*

Before she could react, he had her in his arms.

Kate became painfully aware that the only thing between them was her towel. Her face flushed with heat.

"Fox, if you give me a minute, I'll get dressed, and then we can have that talk you've been asking for," she said, her voice unsteady.

A smug smile curved his lips. "Oh, I don't know. I think you might be more receptive to me this way."

"Fox," she warned, though a smile tugged at her lips, "I mean it. Give me a minute. Please."

He leaned in, his expression softening. "If you insist. But before I go..."

His lips brushed hers in a slow, tantalizing kiss full of promise. Kate sighed into his mouth, her body melting against his. She had missed this. Missed *him* more than she thought possible.

He nuzzled her ear, his breath warm against her skin.

"I know who you are."

Thank you for reading!

We hoped you enjoyed *The Darkness Within* by Lanie Windsor.

If you enjoyed *The Darkness Within* and would like to get updates on new releases and exclusive content sign up now to join Alane Middleton's mailing list. Be the first to hear about ARC reader opportunities and special promotions!

Sign up now!

https://www.alanemiddleton.com/

Also By

Alane Middleton

Dunton Legacy Series
Storm Rising
Tempest
Aftershock
Vortex
Firestorm

Home For The Holidays Series
Frosted Christmas
Snowflake Kisses
Seasoned Wishes

AOD Series
Those Who Can
Hidden Truths
The Darkness Within
Killer Instincts Coming Soon